"WHAT'S THE MATTER?" SHE LOOKED UP AT HIM QUIZZICALLY.

Hoarsely, he said: "There's only one way to tell you." He enfolded her in his arms. He pressed his mouth down on her parted lips.

At first she hung limp in his grasp. Then, with rising passion, she responded to the hot blood coursing fiercely through her veins. Her arms were fast about his neck, drawing him urgently against her.

"Darling, love," he murmured. His mouth devoured her ears, her eyes, the racing pulse in the side of her throat.

She opened the buttons of his shirt and nuzzled his bare chest with her nose and mouth. "I want you so much," she said breathlessly.

SCARLET KISSES

STEPHANIE BLAKE

PLAYBOY PAPERBACKS

SCARLET KISSES

Published simultaneously in the United States and Canada by Playboy Paperbacks, New York, New York. Printed in the United States of America. Library of Congress Catalog Card Number: 81-80079. First edition.

ISBN: 0-872-16847-6

First printing July 1981.

BOOK ONE

CHAPTER ONE

They stood naked on the garden terrace of the penthouse apartment, looking out across New York Harbor all aglitter with myriad lights limning the hulls, masts, and spars of the 225 Tall Ships from thirty nations gathered here to celebrate the Bicentennial.

"It looks like a fairy-tale fleet straight out of the *Arabian Nights*," Gilberta observed.

"It literally takes one's breath away," Jules said, in a deep voice laced with a distinctive New England twang.

"Makes me proud to be an American," she added with fervor. "So many said we could never recover from the chaos of the past thirteen years—assassinations, race riots, the youth rebellion, recession, Watergate—but this Bicentennial celebration is just the medicine the country needed to restore its pride, self-esteem, and faith in itself. Our people are a family again—love for one another and love for the good old U.S.A."

He laughed softly and placed a hand on the small of her back, then moved it down over the lush contours of her buttocks. "You sound like a politician. Like your good husband Harmon, as a matter of fact. Practicing for your speech tomorrow down at city hall, I suppose?"

"Yes, but it's not political lip service; it comes straight from the heart." She reached behind her and grasped his fondling hand. "Only you're distracting me."

"Do you want me to stop?"

"Not on your life." She faced him and put her arms around his neck, pressing her soft belly against his male hardness. "Patriotism always makes me feel sexy. . . . Let's go inside, Julie. I want to be made love to—right now."

"Only too happy to oblige. Just give me a minute. I've got a phone call that can't be postponed. It's about that land deal I'm trying to close. Your brother Terry promised to enlist the help of his good friend the senator from Idaho."

Jules Marston, jokingly referred to as the "potato king" by his friends and business associates, was the principal stockholder in Marston, Limited, a produce conglomerate that controlled production of more than half the vegetables canned and frozen in the United States. A lean, muscular, dark-haired man with rugged good looks, he appeared much younger than his forty-five years.

Gilberta sighed. "Terry has his fingers in more political pies than a toad has warts. He's still a young man. Why does he have to push so hard? If only he'd stop meddling in other people's affairs—like this land deal of yours—and pay more attention to his senatorial campaign, he might stand a chance of giving Harmon's boy Prescott a run for his money in November."

"You sound like you're rooting *against* Harmon, Gilly. With him backing Prescott, it'll be no contest."

"Not so, Julie. Harmon may be governor, but he's getting too complacent, and his puppet, Prescott, isn't exactly an earthshaker. Besides, I don't like the idea of a De Beers getting his ears pinned back in a fight. It's no sin to lose; it's *how* one loses."

Jules laughed. "Don't you fret about Terrence De Beers Finch, my girl. He's a very popular fellow in Jimmy's camp. Thick as thieves with Jordan and Powell."

"But not as popular as you are, Julie," she said with sly malice. "All you farm boys, you really stick together, don't you."

"Listen—don't put Jimmy down. And don't underestimate him, either. Those good old Southern boys, they like to convey the impression that they're all hayseeds. Their opponents think the fight is going to be a breeze, and next thing they know they're flat on their backs."

Gilberta squinted against the glare of the bedroom lights as they parted the draperies covering the sliding glass doors that opened onto the terrace. "Lucky this building is higher than any of the others around it, or our neighbors would be getting some real X-rated shows when we're in town," she said. She walked to the king-sized bed, which was badly disheveled from their recent amorous tumblings.

"I'll use the phone in the den," he told her.

"Don't want me eavesdropping?" She smiled.

"Frankly, I don't." He was suddenly grim.

Gilberta's eyebrows lifted. "Ex-CIA men are like leopards; they never change their spots. All right, darling, you toddle into the den and perpetrate your latest intrigue. Maybe I'll phone Harmon on this line."

She sat down on the bed and watched him leave the

room, admiring his broad shoulders and narrow waist, the way the muscles in his buttocks flexed when he strutted. A "strutting cock"—that was the perfect description of Julie, she thought, and laughed lewdly. She stood up to get a cigarette, watching herself in the mirror as she approached the vanity.

Like her lover, Gilberta De Beers Finch Killington looked younger than her thirty-five years. A strict regimen of tennis, swimming, and golf had preserved the figure. She was not a sexy woman in the literal sense of the word—that is, her breasts and hips were small—but men found her slim, shapely body and sensual features infinitely appealing. Most striking, in the cameo-perfect face, were her enormous violet eyes—a startling contrast to her short, jet-black hair. Those eyes had, in the words of the ballad from *Gigi,* sent hordes of lovesick males "crashing through the ceiling."

Filled with a deep sense of satisfaction, Gilberta went back and lay down on the bed to smoke her cigarette. *Truly my cup runneth over,* she mused, and closed her eyes the better to reflect on her blessings.

Gilberta De Beers Finch was born in 1941 with the proverbial silver spoon in her mouth. She was heiress to a fortune founded on the rich deposits of carbonate-ore-bearing lead and silver mined by her great-great-grandfather Lars De Beers in the mid-1870s in a shanty town called Silver City, Colorado. By the time the De Beers Mining and Development Corporation finally passed into Gilberta's capable hands, the family empire had expanded into the diverse fields of cattle raising, railroads, oil, and uranium.

No poor little rich girl she. In the interest of fairness, she often thought objectively, she might have been born homely—cross-eyed and bow-legged—but no; from birth, Gilberta was blessed with exquisite fairness of form and face. In her late teens and early adulthood, she had joined the ranks of the jet set, hopping back and forth between London, Paris, Rome, Monaco, Acapulco, and the Bahamas, and had engaged in so many torrid love affairs that she lost count. But then, abruptly, to the shock and disbelief of her peers, she dropped out of the social whirl to marry an obscure attorney from Denver—Harmon Killington, a widower with a thirteen-year-old daughter.

"What in the devil ever got into you to do it, Gilly?" her father, Terrence Finch, demanded when she announced her engagement.

Her eyes flashing mischievously, she replied, "Why, because of a wager, of course."

"A wager? What sort of wager?"

"I bet cousin Diana that I could pick any man at random, no matter how unpersonable, unassuming, and dull, and make him into someone famous and exciting —you know, *Pygmalion* in reverse. Think of me as a female Professor Higgins."

"That's absurd!" her mother shrilled. "Terrence—do something at once!"

Father and daughter both laughed.

"Such as what?" he asked. "You know as well as I do that when Gilly makes up her mind about something, it would take a hydrogen bomb to blast her off her set position. You are serious about this thing, aren't you?"

"Indubitably."

"But Harmon Killington . . . I mean, he's a decent enough chap—fair lawyer, they say, but not exceptional. His forte seems to be playing toastmaster. I've heard he's a highly entertaining speaker."

"He has a positive talent for it, and that's the thing of it," Gilberta said. "I heard him speak at a meeting of the League of Women Voters, and I thought, if he was campaigning for public office, every woman in the room would cast her vote for him. Harmon Killington is a born pitchman, which is just another way of saying he was born to the political life. And with little Gilly as his helpmate, he can't miss."

"So *that's* what's behind it. You aim to become a politician's wife."

"Not a mere politician; the big time. They say money is power. Not the way I see it. Being at the helm of the ship of state—now, *that's* power. I'd give it a go myself if the time was ripe, but I don't think this country is ready yet for a woman president. So I'll take the next-best thing. Just look at Lady Bird Johnson. She's the brain behind their business empire, and I'll lay odds that she's currently the power behind the throne."

Her father shook his head and laughed. To his wife he said, "Linda, such modest ambitions our daughter has. . . . Gilly, I hate to say it, but the chances of a second-rate Denver lawyer like Harmon Killington ever gaining the presidency are about equal to a snowball's chances in hell."

Gilberta grinned and patted his cheek. "Daddy, that is precisely what they said about a second-rate haberdasher from Independence, Missouri, name of Harry Truman."

Gilberta De Beers Finch became Mrs. Gilberta De Beers Killington in 1966. It was traditional in the dynasty for all the descendants of Lars De Beers to retain his surname.

With the De Beers wealth and influence behind him (Gilberta hired speechwriters and a general staff worthy of any team enlisted by any of the Kennedys), Harmon was elected to a seat in the state senate. In 1972, the same machine that had put him there won him the governorship of Colorado, running on a strong platform of civil rights, withdrawal of American troops from Vietnam, social reform, higher minimum wages, and equal rights for women. "Let us not forget," he reminded his constituency, "that it was our noble state that first granted women the right to vote!"

On their first night in the governor's mansion, Gilberta and Harmon made passionate love in the big canopied four-poster bed.

"Bet you never figured you'd be screwing the governor of Colorado one day," he quipped.

Gilberta gave him a whack on the behind. "Naughty boy; you should have your mouth washed out with soap." Then, slyly: "Fact is, I mostly figured on screwing the *president* one day."

And I'm still figuring on it, she said to herself, stirring from her reverie. She put out her cigarette, got off the bed, and padded barefoot to the door. "Hey, Julie!" she called down the hall. "Haul your ass back in here and do your manly duty. You've been on the damn phone for a half-hour!"

"Keep your pants on, lover. If you can't wait, start without me."

"Fuck you! Now *you* can wait!"

In exasperation, she went into the bathroom and stepped into the glass-stall shower. She manipulated the faucets until she achieved a soothing tepid spray, then set the shower head to needle sharp. She took the full force of it, breasts thrust out, shoulders back, and thighs spread wide, shivering with visceral pleasure. Bathing was definitely a sensual experience for Gilberta. She soaped her breasts, enjoying the sight of her turgid nipples, now crimson with rising desire; slippery fingers kneading the flesh of her flat belly and pert buttocks, unable to resist the urge to dally in her cleft. *Start without me,* he'd said.

She was rinsing off when he came into the bathroom and opened the shower door:

"Room for one more, ma'am?"

"Up yours!"

"No, it's the other way around . . . or else it soon will be."

"Beg for it. Say 'Pretty please with sugar on it.' "

"Anything you desire, baby." He kneeled down and put his arms around her hips, pressing his lips against her stomach.

She shivered and thrust her pelvis hard against his face. "Oh, Jesus! That drives me crazy."

His mouth moved down through her pubic hair, and his tongue probed skillfully.

Gilberta moaned and threw her head back, holding fast to the supports in the tile walls to keep from sliding to the floor; her legs were all jelly. "Julie, quick, or I can't hold it back any longer. I want you inside me."

Marston stood up and lathered his jutting erection. Then, with a finesse attained through constant practice, he slipped between her thighs and slid his turgid member back and forth until his glans found the way. He thrust upward with vigor, and Gilberta's whole body convulsed with the ecstasy of being one and two all at once, mind, body, and soul. She climaxed before he had completed his third stroke, and it went on and on until she cried out one last time, quivered, and went limp in his arms. He gathered her fiercely close until he had spent his own orgasm; then he turned off the faucets, lifted her in his arms, and carried her back into the bedroom.

"You're like a rag doll—no bones," he said, smiling.

"I *feel* boneless."

He laid her down on the bed and stretched out beside her. "Want a cigarette?"

"Not yet; I'm still too bushed to hold it."

"You can share mine." He lit up, took a drag, and held it to her lips.

Gilberta inhaled. She began to come out of the swoon. "How did your phone call go?"

He shrugged. "We'll work it out."

"Who's *we?*"

He smiled. "Haven't you heard? Curiosity killed the kitten"—he reached over and tweaked her nose—"kitten."

"I don't believe it had anything to do with the Idaho land deal. You never get so intense over a lousy land deal. You've got more acreage than Carter has peanuts."

"I'm *not* intense."

"You most certainly are. And not even making love has loosened you up."

"Hey, did you phone Harmon?" he said, abruptly changing the subject.

"Okay, I'll let up. . . . No, I changed my mind. He probably went to sleep early. Tomorrow's going to be really hectic for him. The Bicentennial is bigger in Colorado than in any other state. After all, it's our *Centennial.* Harmon's promised to appear at at least a dozen different celebration parties."

"Speaking of which, have you finished your speech?"

"Last night."

"Want to give me a sample?"

"You'll get the whole treatment tomorrow. You *are* coming, aren't you?"

"Wouldn't miss it. . . . By the way, Anita will probably tell you I called you this morning at the Essex House."

"You *called* there?"

"I was expecting you earlier, and when you didn't show, I got worried. But don't get excited. I told her I just wanted to wish you success with your speech, and that if you had time, would you give me a call. What was she doing there, anyway? I thought you told me she was flying in tonight."

"She and Jeanette wanted to do some shopping, so they came in last night. They expected me to show up at the hotel sometime this morning."

"Jesus, Gilly, where are you going to say you've been?"

"At the cabin, polishing my speech."

"You think Anita will buy that? She's a pretty clever girl."

"She'll buy it; she's also my best friend."

Anita Thatcher and Gilberta De Beers Finch had been roommates at Colorado State University. Close friends all through college, they had maintained the friendship after graduation. The Thatchers did not move in the same social circle as the Finches and the De Beerses—Anita's father owned a small plumbing business in Leadville—but Gilberta's family treated Anita like a second daughter. And when Linda De Beers Finch and her husband, Terrence, appointed their heirs as officers of the De Beers Mining and Development Corporation—Terrence, Jr., as president, and Gilberta as executive vice-president—Gilberta hired Anita as her personal secretary and companion.

Terrence, Jr., from the start, was temperamentally unsuited for his position. From his college days, his consuming interest had been in politics. Like Harmon, his brother-in-law, he was a natural, and in less than two years after his resignation from the corporation, he had won a seat in the state legislature.

"I've always wondered why Anita's never married," Jules commented. "She's a very attractive woman—somewhat thick through the thighs and hips, but eminently sexy."

"As far back as college, she vowed she'd never get

married and have kids. Saw a lot of strife at home. She was one of ten kids, and her father, a drunk, used to beat them and their mother."

"Shame."

"Don't get the wrong idea, though. Anita's no hothouse flower. She enjoys the same sexual adventures I, a married woman, enjoy." She stroked his flaccid penis.

"Is that your way of saying you think she's having an affair with Harmon?"

Gilberta pursed her lips. "It's not impossible"—her brow furrowed in thought—"but no, I don't think so; Anita is too loyal to me. Not that I'd give a fig. No, delete that. I most certainly *would* give a damn; a scandal could ruin Harmon's political career, or at least taint it. Look at Ted Kennedy; he'll never live down Chappaquiddick. In any case, if Anita *was* having an affair with Harmon, she'd tell me sooner or later. A long time ago we took a vow to always level with each other, no matter what the cost."

"Hmmm . . ."

"What's *that* supposed to mean?" She propped herself up on one elbow and stared at him.

His eyes were evasive. "Nothing very profound. You know the old joke: 'What are the three biggest lies in the world?' Answer: 'The check is in the mail; I promise I won't come in your mouth, honey; Would I lie to my best friend, old buddy?' "

"Very funny." Her voice was frigid.

He smiled, showing perfect white teeth, and put his arms around her, wrestling her down on the bed. "Enough idle chatter. Let's screw."

"No, Julie; no more sex for tonight."

"You've got to be kidding. . . . What did you say your name was? You may *look* like Gilly Killington, but you sure don't *act* like her."

It was true, she had to admit. She could count on only one hand the number of times she'd become turned off by sex, and even then she couldn't figure it, it was so contrary to her nature. She switched off the bed lamp and lay back, staring at the ceiling, listening to the drone of distant traffic.

Jules lit another cigarette. "Gilly . . . does Anita know about us?"

She hesitated. "I don't think so."

"You don't *think* so!" His voice was heavy with sarcasm. "You mean you didn't *level* with your best friend? What about that schoolgirl vow sealed with blood?"

"I don't bare my soul to anyone, not even Anita. It's nobody's business who I sleep with. Now, if you had been her guy first, then I most certainly would have given it to her straight, no cheap deception. Do you understand?"

"I think so."

"Incidentally, while we're on the subject of 'deception' . . . Do you believe the management of this place buys our act, that you and I are a stodgy married couple?"

"Why shouldn't they? I signed a two-year lease for the most expensive apartment in the joint. Gave them a stack of legit references."

"Under the name Milos Alansky."

"Yeah, my man Friday. You talk about friendship. That man is closer to me than my two brothers. He'd cut out his own tongue rather than bad-mouth me."

"So you've said."

"It's true. . . . Besides, whenever we stay here we're loaded down with luggage. This is no screw-and-run act. We've got a maid who comes in three times a week. Face it, Gilly, we're a very domestic couple. The super knows that my business makes us shuttle back and forth from one coast to the other. I slip him a C-note every time we leave so he'll keep an eye on the place. So relax and go to sleep."

Sleep, though, did not come easy to Gilberta and it troubled her. Sleep and sex were as natural a part of her existence as eating and breathing and yet, in the past hour, she had reneged on both. It was an ominous omen.

CHAPTER TWO

When she finally did fall asleep, Gilberta slept like the dead, and when she awoke, at eight the next morning, it was with a sense of apprehensive displacement. She bolted upright.

"What the hell?" she mumbled, and looked at the place beside her, which still bore the imprint of Jules's body. Where was he?

She got out of bed, threw on a robe—a deep-cowled flow of maroon velour that emphasized the flawless figure beneath—combed her hair with her fingers, and then went out onto the terrace, squinting against the blazing sunlight.

Jules was standing at the far end with binoculars fixed to his eyes. He was wearing the tiger-striped Jockey shorts she had given him as a joke on his last birthday.

She went up in back of him and kissed him on the right shoulder blade. "Good morning, darling."

He turned around and lowered the binoculars. "Hi there, love. You were really sacked out when I got up.

I figured it was best to let you sleep, considering the rough day you have ahead of you."

"Thanks." She kissed him lightly on the lips. "Sorry if I was testy last night."

He dismissed it with a laugh. "As I said, we behave like an old married couple. 'Sorry, darling, but I have a beastly headache.' "

She slapped him playfully on the cheek. "That's a low blow. I'm never like that. So one out of three times I wasn't in the mood. You still batted six sixty-six. That's strictly big-league percentage."

"Who's complaining? Say, you've got to see this spectacular show in the harbor."

They leaned against the wall and gazed out across the harbor at the unparalleled panorama of nautical pageantry. The Tall Ships were preparing to move up the Hudson River, in a regal procession resurrected from a bygone century.

"Look at those windjammers!" he exclaimed. "What was Masefield's line?"

" 'All I ask is a tall ship and a star to steer her by.' "

He handed her the glasses. "See the one with the Maltese crosses on the mainsail? That's the Portuguese bark *Sagres Two.*"

Majestically the Tall Ships paraded up the Hudson toward the George Washington Bridge. In the background, draped from the Verrazano-Narrows Bridge, was the largest national flag ever lofted, a one-and-one-half-ton Stars and Stripes that was bigger than a football field.

Jules Marston, an avid boatsman, was able to identify each one of the 225 ships without hesitation. "See that four-masted Chilean barkentine, the *Esmeralda?* After President Allende was deposed, she was used as a political prison and torture chamber by the military junta."

Gilberta grimaced. "It doesn't seem proper to me that such a ship should have been invited to participate in a celebration that symbolizes human liberty."

"You're not alone in that opinion. But, after all, a ship is an inanimate object and not responsible for what her masters do. And she is a true beauty."

"I'm famished. How about you? Would you like me to fix us some breakfast?"

"Later. I don't want to miss any of this fabulous show. . . . There's another beauty, the Italian frigate *Americo Vespucci.* And look at that square-rigger, Columbia's *Gloria.*"

Gilberta stifled a yawn; she did not share her lover's boyish enthusiasm for ships and the sea. "You enjoy yourself, darling. I'm going to take a quick shower and then whip us up a soufflé."

In the shower, she found herself thinking back to the day, nearly a year ago, she'd first met Jules Marston, at a governors' conference in Colorado Springs. He'd been a staunch supporter of her husband's bid for the governorship, and had backed him all the way, earning Harmon's deep gratitude and friendship.

That night, there was a fancy-dress ball, and the magnetism that flowed between Gilly and her husband's handsome friend was a palpable force. They danced without a word passing between them. There was no need for words; the eyes said it all. At the end of the evening, they agreed to meet at his hotel room the very next day. It was the beginning of a whirlwind romance that had not diminished in intensity to this day. It couldn't lead anywhere, but then she didn't want it to—not as long as Harmon had a chance of getting his foot in the White House door. No, this arrangement—rendezvousing in Alansky's apartment whenever business called her and Julie to New York—suited her fine. . . .

Gilberta turned the cold water on full and gasped as it punished her warm body. When she stepped out of the shower, her flesh was festooned with goose-bumps. She toweled herself briskly, went back into the bedroom, and climbed into a pair of black silk lounging pajamas, not bothering to put on underwear. They'd be coming off again in any case before noon, she was confident. She slipped her feet into black satin slippers and headed for the kitchen to turn on the oven in preparation for the soufflé. Then, whistling "America the Beautiful," she went to join Julie on the terrace.

The hymn held a special significance for Gilberta: It was from the summit of Pike's Peak, named after a relative of her great-grandfather's, that Katharine Lee Bates, a teacher at Colorado College, had been inspired to write it.

"Julie," she called, as she opened the sliding doors. She didn't see him. "Where are——" Suddenly, out of the corner of her eye, she noticed a bare foot protruding from behind a thick shrub at the far side of the terrace.

"Julie!" she shrieked, and ran to the shrub, heart hammering in her chest, her breath burning in her throat.

She stopped at the back side of the triangular patch of soil and gaped in horror. Jules Marston was lying prone on the concrete deck in an ever-widening pool of blood. The back of his head had been crushed like an eggshell. There was no doubt in Gilberta's mind that he was dead.

With tears streaming down her face and one hand clapped to her mouth, she dashed back into the apartment and into the bathroom. Just in time. She stood spraddle-legged and hunched over like a football center, heaving into the toilet bowl. When she could bring up nothing more, she washed her face in cold water, dabbed witch hazel on her swollen eyelids, and shakily made her way to the living room, where she poured herself a finger of scotch and downed it. It made her queasy, but she poured another. She had to *think*.

Despite her initial shock over Jules's death—*murder,* she thought grimly—Gilly was not surprised. His enemies were legion—the inevitable consequence of years of ruthless commerce during which he had destroyed countless business rivals and incurred the hatred and envy of even those who worked for him. And there were the women he had loved and left. Harmon had mentioned Marston's amorous exploits to her once, when she'd asked why he wasn't married: "He's having too much fun." Not to be discounted, either, were the ten years he had served as a secret agent of the CIA. When he drank too heavily, his morbid preoccupations were targeted on the agency. He'd once told her: "I know too much, baby. It's just like belonging to the Mafia; it's a lifetime job. Nobody quits the agency. The only difference is, when you die, you get buried with full military honors and an American flag."

She reached for the bottle of scotch. And then it hit her; she must call the police! Glass in hand, she went to the phone, lifted the receiver, put it back. Her mind was racing. Gilberta De Beers Killington was a consummate pragmatist, and with a pragmatist's reasoning, she realized it would be sheer insanity to alert the NYPD. She would first of all have to explain her presence in the apartment, and in a day or two, news of her affair with her husband's primary backer would be in every big newspaper in the country. Then too, the police might not believe her story, and accuse *her* of murdering Julie. No . . . her lover was dead—killed in cold blood—but she, Gilberta, was very much alive. And she intended to stay that way!

Give or take a few hours, it would be a day before

the corpse was discovered; the housekeeper would be coming in tomorrow morning. Twenty-four hours to remove all her clothes and personal possessions from the apartment. Expensive wearing apparel could easily be traced.

The building superintendent and the rental agent would testify that the penthouse had been leased by a Mr. and Mrs. Milos Alansky, and the authorities would be seeking the absent wife, but only until they learned that the dead man was not Milos Alansky but tycoon and entrepreneur Jules Marston, who was a bachelor. At that point, of course, they would be anxious to learn the identity of the imaginary Mrs. Alansky, obviously Jules Marston's mistress. But that didn't worry Gilberta. If Julie's faith in his friend's loyalty was to be counted on—and she believed it was—Milos would never give her away.

She dressed in a one-piece set of green denim coveralls and matching floppy hat and put on dark glasses. Then she packed the two suitcases she kept at the apartment and carried them out to the elevator. Luck was on her side: she made it all the way down to the basement parking lot without encountering any of the other tenants.

When they had first moved in, seven months earlier, Jules had purchased a second-hand Dodge panel truck.

"We need some kind of transportation while we're in town," he'd said, "something that won't attract attention being parked down here for long periods of time unattended. Like cats, all panel trucks are black in the dark. They're not visible the way a Caddy or a Lincoln is."

She thanked him for his foresight as she carried the suitcases inside, closed the door, and commenced to unpack them. When all of the clothing was neatly folded on the floor in one corner, she carried the suitcases back to the elevator and took it up to the penthouse. There she repacked them and made another trip down to the truck. Once more and the task would be complete.

On her third ride down, two women boarded the elevator at the fifth floor, and Gilberta's breath caught, but they scarcely noticed her, so engrossed were they in their gossiping.

This time she left the suitcases in the truck and went back to the apartment for one last reconnoiter. She carefully checked all the rooms and the terrace for any telltale evidence that she'd been here; emptied the ashtrays, cleaned up the kitchen, rinsed out her scotch glass. In the bedroom, she went through Jules's wallet to ensure that it contained nothing that would incriminate her: a picture, a card, a phone number. There was nothing; Jules was too shrewd to run such a risk. Fingerprints did not concern her particularly; there were too many sets in this apartment, including those of Alansky's own lady friends.

Satisfied that she had taken every precaution, she left the apartment, took her final trip down to the basement garage, and climbed into the truck.

Twenty minutes later she pulled into a parking garage just off First Avenue near the Midtown Tunnel, informed the attendant she'd be leaving it for at least twenty-four hours, then went out on the street and hailed a cab.

It was a little after noon when she entered her sixth-floor suite at the Essex House on Central Park South. She picked up the phone and dialed the room in which Anita Thatcher and her stepdaughter, Jeanette Killington, were staying:

"Jen . . . this is Gilly."

"My God! Where have you been? Anita and I have been tearing our hair out. You have to be at city hall at two o'clock. The limo will be here at one-thirty."

"No sweat, honey. I drove up to the cabin yesterday to work on the final draft of my speech. I can't concentrate on anything serious here in New York, especially now when the whole city is so hyped up over the Bicentennial. Anyway, I think it's pretty good now. Did you and Anita get some shopping done?"

"A little. Do you want to speak with her?"

"No. I'll be down just as soon as I'm dressed."

There was a strained silence before Jeanette said testily, "You might have had the consideration to let me know where you were going. I've been worried sick and so has Dad. He phoned at least six times yesterday trying to reach you."

"I'm sorry; it was thoughtless of me. Forgive me."

"Well, okay, you'd better shake your arse, Gilly. I'll see you later."

Gilberta took off the coveralls and lay down on the bed in her bra and briefs. She lit a cigarette and reflected on the frantic series of events since her discovery of Jules's body. Her evacuation of the apartment was a considerable tour de force in itself. Dame Fortune had been on her side or she never would have managed those trips between the apartment and the garage without being recognized by someone—a neighbor, the superintendent, one of the maintenance crew. Tomorrow she would check out the truck and drive up to the cabin, where she would transfer all her clothes to her bedroom there.

The big problem was the truck itself. She thought of leaving it at the cabin and chartering a flight from the airport nearby, but vetoed that idea. She could not risk keeping such a bulky piece of evidence in her possession. And evidence it certainly was. On his application for parking space at the Towers, Jules had been required to list the van's license number. Doubtless the police, when they discovered Jules's corpse and commenced their investigation, would learn of the missing van and send out an all-points bulletin. The truck had to be disposed of with dispatch. But how? Sell it to a used-car dealer? No, that would never work; to do that she'd have to sign over the registration, and that would be sheer suicide. Of course, she might get rid of the plates and . . .

You're making things too complicated and involved, my girl, she soliloquized. There was an old axiom handed down through the generations of De Beerses: When confronted by a formidable problem, always seek out the simplest solution. With that in view, she came up very handily with the perfect answer. There was no need to drive up to the cabin at all. Early tomorrow morning she would claim the truck and drive it to Riverside Heights, park it on a side street, and hop a subway back to the hotel. It was almost 100 percent certain that within twelve hours the truck would be stolen and its contents distributed among the family and friends of the perpetrators!

At 1:15 Gilberta knocked on the door of the room that Jeanette and Anita were sharing. Anita opened it. Her smile was stiff.

"Gilly . . . you damn near scared the life out of us! We were sure you had been done in by muggers. If you had phoned just ten minutes later, you would have been a statistic in the missing-persons files."

The two women embraced and touched cheeks, and Gilberta followed Anita into the sitting room.

"I know it was thoughtless," she said. "Truthfully I'm sorry. It's just that I've been so preoccupied with getting my speech the way I want it that I've blocked out everything else."

Anita lifted an eyebrow. "That doesn't sound like the unflappable, superconfident Gilberta Killington *I* know."

Gilberta sighed. "I, too, have feet of clay. . . . Darling, that dress is very chic." Anita was wearing a lemon-yellow sport dress with a ribbed top and flat-knitted skirt.

"Thanks, Gilly. And you look positively charming. That gown is just the thing for the occasion."

Gilberta smiled. "I want to be the personification of the pioneer spirit that founded the Centennial State." She had chosen to wear a simple prairie-plaid gown with high yoke collar and deep hemline flounce.

"Do you want a drink?"

"Yes, please. Make it a light scotch and soda." Gilberta sat down on the divan and lit a cigarette.

Anita called to her from the kitchen: "By the way, Jules called here for you yesterday. Asked if you'd give him a ring when you got in."

"Did he leave a number?" Gilberta asked casually.

"On the pad by the phone. He's staying at Milos Alansky's."

Just as Anita returned, carrying two drinks, Gilberta dialed Milos's number. She waited for ten rings before she shrugged and hung up. "He must have gone out. I'll try him after the ceremony."

"Want to audition your speech for me?" Anita said, handing Gilberta her scotch.

"Not really. Practice, contrary to tradition, does not make perfect in all cases, especially public speaking. When you chew your cud too much, the address loses spontaneity."

Suddenly the door to the bedroom opened and

Jeanette appeared. "Well, the prodigal mother has returned."

"She never left. How are you, Jen?"

"Bored. I'll be glad when we board the jet back to Colorado."

Stepmother and stepdaughter measured each other warily. Theirs was an adversary relationship, though by tacit consent they strove to keep their hostility submerged in the company of other people, especially in the presence of the governor.

Jeanette Killington was a pretty, dark girl whose features were somewhat too sharp. Her good body was diminished by legs that were thin and shapeless from the knees down. Nature had compensated her, though, with a magnificent bosom. For the occasion, she wore an elegant black velvet jacket over a ruffled-jabot shirt and coordinating wool herringbone slacks.

"That's a stunning outfit," Gilberta offered sincerely. "Did you buy it here in New York?"

"Yes, in a little boutique on Fifth Avenue." Some of the belligerence in her voice dissipated. Jeanette was childishly grateful for flattery, even more so when it came from Gilberta, who was a bellwether of style among Denver's high-society women. "Did you phone Dad?"

"Right after I spoke to you," Gilberta lied. "He had already gone. Poor dear . . . he'll probably be a basket case tonight after all those appearances. Well, luckily, he has to do it only once every hundred years," she said, laughing.

"Speaking of which," Anita said, looking at her watch, "the limo should be waiting right now. Let's move it, team."

Gilberta finished her drink, tamped out her cigarette,

and got to her feet. "You know . . . I'm really nervous."

"Just opening-night jitters," Anita threw back over her shoulder. "You'll knock 'em dead, as always."

Opening-night jitters . . . Anita should only know what had evoked her present state of mind!

CHAPTER THREE

From the speakers' platform, Gilberta swept her eyes around the sea of faces in the sizable audience as cameras whirred and strobe lights flashed continuously. She scanned her notes on the lectern for the last time and made a minor adjustment in one of the network microphones.

She half turned to acknowledge the other speakers, seated at the back of the podium: "To Mayor Beame and to the members of the mayor's staff, who have treated me with such kindness, cordiality, and generosity, I wish to express my deepest appreciation." Then she addressed the audience: "And to all of you in this distinguished assembly, I wish to say . . . *I love New York.*"

When the applause had subsided, she continued: "Today marks one of the proudest and most glorious events in the history of this, the greatest nation in all the world—the signing of the Declaration of Independence. At this time, I would like to quote from the second paragraph of that historic and most remarkable document, for Thomas Jefferson expresses what I am feeling at this moment far better than I can: 'We hold these truths to be self-evident, that all men are created equal, that they are endowed by their Creator with certain unalienable Rights, that among these are Life, Liberty and the pursuit of Happiness.' My fellow Americans, that is what we are celebrating today, both here and all across the land—two hundred years of freedom of a form that no other nation has ever attained.

"We who are assembled here share a common inheritance, a common bond unlike that of any other people on earth. Our forebears were the refugees who crossed vast oceans from the four corners of the world to make a new life in this raw land of opportunity. My own great-great-grandfather Lars De Beers was among those 'huddled masses yearning to breathe free.' He was a shoemaker by trade, but he had a dream, and boundless energy and spirit to make that dream come true. Like other settlers who, in the wake of the great gold rush, took up the slogan 'Pike's Peak or Bust,' he brought his family to the Colorado territory.

"Unhappily, for some of those pioneers, it was a total 'bust.' But there were others, many of them, like Lars De Beers, who persevered. . . ."

Suddenly Gilberta's vision blurred, and the faces of the spectators on the steps of city hall merged into one —that of the face of the man whose courage and foresight had always been an inspiration to her: Lars De Beers. So real did he seem to her right now, she felt she could reach across the barrier of time and touch him. . . .

Lars De Beers, his wife Mina, their six-year-old son Nils, and their infant daughter Karen arrived in Denver in a covered wagon weighted down with supplies and mining equipment on July 4, 1858. They made camp in the hills beyond Denver, in a tent-and-shanty village that had sprung up almost overnight where two miners had struck it rich two months earlier. Two months later the camp was abandoned, and its inhabitants went scurrying off to another site rumored to be rich in the precious metal. Like desert nomads, the diggers and panners wandered all over the territory, literally, searching for the pot of gold at the end of the rainbow.

After a backbreaking summer that netted him nothing, Lars moved his family back to Denver and opened a small shoemaking and shoe-repair store. In no time he was swamped with work, and Mina and little Nils had to assist him at his cobbler's bench.

"For this we had to come halfway round the world," his wife grumbled one night as they lay in the big feather bed in their two-room flat above the shop.

"Patience, woman; you must be patient. Rome wasn't built in a day. One day I will make a big strike."

"When it's Christmas in July." She turned over and slapped at his hand working its way slyly underneath her nightgown. "Stop that, Lars! I'm exhausted from being on my feet all day and taking care of the baby as well. Besides, in our circumstances we cannot afford to have another child. If you put me in the family way again, I won't be able to help you in the shop."

Lars sighed and turned away from her. "*Ja,* you are right." It had been over a year since he had enjoyed a woman's body. Tomorrow he would ask his friend Tony the barber about the five whores who had set up a tent of ill repute on a hillside overlooking the diggings. In the meantime, to relieve his sexual tension so he could get to sleep, he masturbated into his handkerchief.

The next summer, Lars invested the nest egg they had from the small business in supplies, loaded the family into the wagon, and set out for California Gulch, on the Arkansas River, where a prospector named Simon had made a big strike early in the spring.

The miners already there were pleased to see Lars and his wagonload of supplies. Within one hour he had sold all of the food, shovels, picks, pans, and other paraphernalia to them, except for what was required to nourish his own dependents and sustain his prospecting exertions.

To show their gratitude, the prospectors helped Lars erect a log cabin for his family.

"What you should do is to buy a bigger wagon next time you go back to Denver and haul in enough supplies to open a store," one of them suggested.

A roar of approval went up from the others, and right then and there, they built an extension onto the main cabin.

There was gold in California Gulch. A prospector working the claim on one side of Lars panned $70,000 worth that summer. The man on the other side of Lars's claim took out more than $100,000. Lars cleared barely $900!

"I guess I wasn't cut out to be a gold miner," he lamented that night to his wife.

"God intended you to be a good shoemaker."

"And a shop owner." He told her about his plans for opening a store in the flourishing community.

Next winter it was back to Denver, where he bought a big Concord coach; and leaving Mina and the children in Denver, he trekked straight back to California Gulch with two tons of food and supplies.

That winter Lars earned over $10,000 as a combination shopkeeper and shoemaker. Next summer when he went back to Denver to claim his family, he told Mina jubilantly:

"This is a much easier way to get my gold dust."

"*Ja.* And now maybe we can afford another baby," she said, with a twinkle in her eyes.

Lars beamed at her, and this time when he slid his hand up the inner side of her thigh, she did not reject him.

When the De Beerses returned to the gulch, Mina was astonished to observe how the mining community had expanded. Almost all of the tents had been replaced by cabins, and the demand for supplies was so large that Lars had to return to Denver three times that summer to replenish his stock.

It was the first winter they spent together as a family at the camp. The word "camp" was no longer an apt description of the community; it was a city. One morning a group of the most influential miners arrived at the De Beers store and informed Lars that he had been appointed postmaster.

"A stage is gonna begin running mail into Karenville come spring," their spokesman said.

"Karenville?" Lars was baffled.

"Sure; since you're the big tradesman in these parts, we figgered this town should be named after your daughter Karen. If her beauty wears off on her namesake, we should be the showcase of the territory within five years."

During the ensuing fifteen years, Karenville flourished, and so did Lars De Beers. Business so expanded, he moved his family into a new white-frame home overlooking the town, and the old cabin was converted to another shop. By 1870, Lars employed three clerks and a bookkeeper.

And Karen grew and blossomed along with the town named after her. At the age of fourteen she had a figure that bordered on the voluptuous—bosomy, slim-waisted, and full-hipped, all of which were emphasized by the peasant dirndl costumes she liked to wear.

"You look like a Dutch china doll," her father would say proudly.

It was true. Her head was as perfect as an apple, and her silky blonde hair, worn short and cut square across her forehead, fit it like a golden cap. Her ivory skin was flawless; her eyes, sky blue.

"When Karen walks into the classroom, it's as though a dazzling ray of sunshine streamed through the window lighting everything up," her teacher once told Mina. "Even the other students seem to brighten up."

One of her classmates who warmed even more than the others to Karen's appearance was a lad named Robert Parker. At sixteen, Robert was the tallest boy in the form and the oldest. He had blond curly hair, perpetually unruly, slate-gray eyes, and craggy features that lent him an aspect of uncommon strength and character. Karen's heart melted the first time she set eyes on him, two years earlier. Yet, in all that time, she continued to treat him with aloofness and a hint of disdain. Her best friends, Rose Crory and Jennie Snead, were aghast.

"Every girl in Karenville is wearing her heart on her sleeve for Bob Parker," Rose exclaimed. "Even a smile from Bobby Boy makes my day worth living."

" 'Bobby Boy'—*ugh!* You are too infantile."

Jennie closed her eyes and clasped her hands together. "I would do anything for that boy, *anything.*"

Rose and Jennie giggled while Karen pretended to be too disgusted for words.

One day she walked into her father's store, and Karen could not believe her eyes. Standing behind the counter was Robert Parker, wearing a white apron. She gaped at him, speechless.

"Can I help you, miss?" he asked with a wooden face.

"What are you doing here?" she said foolishly.

"I work here."

"You? You work here?"

"That's right. Your father hired me to help out on weekends and to deliver important mail. Now, what can I do for you?"

"I came to ask my father for money for a new dress I saw in the dry-goods store."

"You could try Fisher's saloon. He's down there talking to two men who are looking for a grubstake."

(Lars De Beers may have given up active prospecting, but the dream was still in his heart. He indulged his incurable yearning to search for a golden fleece vicariously by staking needy prospectors to food and supplies so that they could go on digging and sluicing and panning. In return, they would cut him in for a share of their claim.

"Such a waste of money," Mina had chided him. "You've grubstaked a dozen losers."

But Lars had only hugged her and said jovially, "Number thirteen might be my lucky number.")

"I wouldn't think of setting foot in a saloon, thank you. I'll wait until he gets home tonight," Karen said crisply.

She was on her way out the door when he called to her: "Karen."

She stopped but did not look back. "Yes?"

"Why don't you like me?"

She turned and her eyes met his. "Who said I didn't like you?"

"Nobody has to say it. The way you treat me, as if I didn't exist."

She shrugged her shoulders. "It's just your imagination. I think you're a very nice boy . . . and quite smart in school."

"Prove you don't hate me, then."

"Don't be silly. How can I prove such a thing?"

"By going to the Fourth of July picnic at Oro with me next week. There'll be fireworks, a big barbecue, and after dark a barn dance. What about it?"

She hesitated. "I had planned to go with my family."

"Maybe your father would let me ride along in your wagon?"

"I'll ask him about it."

His face lit up radiantly. "Wonderful! Then, you *will* go with me?"

She restrained a smile. "No; *you'll* be going with *me.*"

Bob laughed. "Any way you want it, Karen. The point is, you'll be *my* date."

"Besides being very nice and very smart, you are very pushy."

Suddenly the two of them were laughing uproariously.

Gasping and holding her sides, Karen said, "I've got to leave now. I'm meeting my mother at the dairy."

"See you in school on Monday," he called after her.

That night at the supper table, Karen casually introduced the subject of Robert Parker. "I thought it would be all right if he came to the picnic with us."

Her brother snickered. "So, the haughty princess of Karenville has finally decided to act human for a change. That poor kid has been mooning over you for over a year, and you've gone on looking straight through him as if he wasn't there."

Nils De Beers at twenty was the image of his father—long, lean, and muscular, with merry blue eyes—only his hair was thicker and not graying.

"Stop teasing your sister," Mina said sternly. "It's time she had a young man."

Karen turned crimson. *"Moth-er!* He is *not* my young man!"

"Then, why are you blushing?" Nils asked. "Listen, Bob Parker is the best catch in town"—he cleared his throat self-importantly—"except for me, of course."

Lars and Mina laughed, but Karen frowned and stuck out her tongue. "You're a conceited oaf, and I don't see what Mary Wentworth sees in you, anyway."

"She worships the ground I walk on."

"You're taking Mary to the picnic with us?" Mina inquired.

"No, we're going with Billy Cox and Celia Towns in a carriage."

"Now look who's stuck-up," Karen said.

He grinned. "You and your beau can come with us if you like. You can neck in the back and we'll promise not to peek."

Karen balled up her napkin and threw it across the table at him. Nils ducked, and it flew past him and knocked a glass figurine off the sideboard behind him. The ornament shattered on the wood floor.

"My favorite Hummel!" Mina cried, and clapped her hands to her cheeks. "What a bad child you are!"

"I am not a child! Anyway, it was Nils's fault. If he hadn't ducked, nothing would have happened!"

Nils and his father stifled their laughter in their napkins as Mina fumed. "Karen! You will go to your room at once and stay there until I make up my mind how to punish you."

"I know how to punish her," Nils said, winking at his father. "Don't let her go to the picnic."

Karen balled her hands into fists and glowered at him. "You shut up and mind your own business, you . . . you . . . you . . ." Her eyes brimming with tears, she fled from the room.

Upstairs, she shut her door, threw herself down on the bed, and buried her face in her pillow to muffle the sobs that now came unchecked. If she was not allowed to go to the picnic with Bob, she would kill herself! All this time, so many months, she had worshiped him, but her pride had kept her from showing her true feelings. Let Rose and Jennie and all the other silly girls she knew wear their hearts on their sleeves; that was not Karen's style. She was highly sensitive and her feelings ran deep. She thought of herself as an "intensely passionate woman."

There was a gentle rapping on her door. She sat up and wiped her eyes, glad that it was dark in the room.

"Who is it?"

"Mama."

Her throat constricted with sheer terror. "Come in," she said faintly.

Mina opened the door and stood on the threshold. She was carrying a candlestick. "Karen . . . I wanted to tell you not to fret about the picnic. Of course you're going. Nils was only teasing."

Karen swallowed hard. "Thank you, Mama. . . . And, Mama . . ."

"Yes, child?"

"I'm sorry I was rude before. And I'm sorry I broke the Hummel; I'll pay for it out of my allowance."

Mina smiled. "That won't be necessary now that you have admitted that you did wrong and regret what you did. I think you have learned a lesson and it will not happen again."

"No, it won't. . . . Oh, Mama, I love you!"

Mina walked over to the bed and sat down on the edge. She placed the candle on the night table, and mother and daughter embraced silently.

Karen lay awake for a long time that night. Over and over she kept repeating to herself, "Robert Parker . . . Bob Parker . . . Mrs. Robert De Beers Parker." A warm flush suffused her body, focalizing in her breasts and her pubic region—a tantalizing sensation that caused her heart to beat faster and her breathing to quicken. Unable to curb a powerful urge, she slid her hand down across her belly and lifted her nightgown up over her hips. She gasped as her fingers brushed the hot inner sides of her thighs.

In school, the older girls whispered and giggled when they talked about it: "Every time Gladys sees Teddy Burns, she rushes into the john and plays with herself!" It was a thing nice girls did not do, or even contemplate.

"I guess I'm just not a nice girl," Karen murmured. It was too irresistible. She shut her eyes and thought about Bob—Bob lying naked beside her in the big bed, his strong yet gentle hands caressing her, his fingers titillating the lubricious cleft. Karen arched her back and ground her buttocks rhythmically against the mattress. And then it happened.

The rockets' red glare, the bombs bursting in air . . .

Just the way the sky would be lit up on the night of the Fourth of July picnic.

In their own bedroom, Lars and Mina were just completing a shared intimacy of a similar nature. Afterward, as they lay close in the dark, Lars sighed:

"How strange we humans are. Here I have been making love to you and enjoying it thoroughly. Yet the idea of my daughter having sex with a man is repugnant to me. I can't let my mind even consider it."

Mina laughed. "One day you'll have to face up to it, Lars. Even now she is a woman physically."

"Yes, I know. Now I'm not sure it was a good idea to say the boy could come to the picnic with us."

CHAPTER FOUR

The following Wednesday, two grizzled prospectors in high boots, heavy trousers, and red shirts tied up two mules in front of the De Beers store. Their packs and saddlebags were empty. The taller of the two had red hair and a bushy red beard. They entered the building, boot cleats clomping on the floorboards.

Mina eyed them with distaste. She could spot them a mile away: impoverished diggers looking for a handout.

The redhead tipped his crumpled hat. "Afternoon, ma'am. I'm looking for a Mr. Lars De Beers."

"He's not here." Rudely she ducked beneath the counter and commenced to rearrange sundries on the bottom shelf.

The men were on their way out when Lars came out of the back storeroom. "Did I hear my name?"

"Mr. De Beers?" The redhead introduced himself: "I'm Jim Swensen and my pard here is Wally Franks. We've been going over old discarded claims far up the river and finding enough overlooked gold to eke out a living."

Mina sniffed. "Don't appear that way to me."

"What happened is, we ran into a stretch where some grimy black sludge was clogging our sluices. Right put us out of business."

Lars nodded sympathetically. "That's the reason a lot of prospectors abandoned their claims up there."

"Driving us near crazy. Wonder what the stuff is."

"Why don't you send a sample up to the assay office and find out?"

"Ain't worth the trouble to find out. All I know is, it makes it impossible to wash gold out of the river. We got another location staked out where there ain't none of that gook, but we need a grubstake."

Lars grinned and gestured toward the shelves. "Help yourselves, boys. Always like to lend a helping hand."

Their faces lit up. "Gee whiz, thanks, Mr. De Beers. Word gets around about you, that you're a good Samaritan."

"That you're a fool," Mina said in Dutch.

When the two prospectors had filled their saddlebags and packs, Lars tallied it up. "Comes to sixty dollars."

"Don't you worry, Mr. De Beers, you'll get it, every cent. Jim Swensen never welched on a debt in his life. And by the way, you're our silent partner. Do you have a pen and a piece of paper?"

Mina grudgingly fetched it for him, and Swensen scrawled a simple, roughly worded agreement stating that Lars De Beers was a full partner in the claim Jim Swensen had staked in California Gulch.

"Good luck, boys," Lars said as they left. He followed them out to the mules and whispered, "Come by the back door and I'll throw in a couple jugs of whiskey on the house. Gets cold in them hills at night."

Swensen cackled and put a hand on Lars's arm. "You're one helluva feller, Mr. De Beers. God bless you."

Lars observed that there was one small saddlebag they had left empty. He queried them about it.

"Oh, that," answered Franks. "That one got all dirtied up with that black goo Jim was telling you about. We're gonna throw it away."

"Mind if I see it?" Lars said.

Swensen laughed. "Don't get it on your clean shirt and trousers."

Lars opened the bag, scooped out a small amount of the mulch, and tested it with his fingers; then he sniffed it.

"It ain't dung, if that's what you're thinking," Swensen said.

"No, and it's not mere mud, either. . . . You know, I do believe I'll send a sample to the assay office to satisfy my curiosity."

"Like you said, Mr. De Beers, be our guest."

When they'd gone, Lars transferred the mulch to a brown paper bag, took it down to the stage depot, and asked the clerk to send it to the assay office in Denver.

And promptly forgot about it until a week later, when one of the stagecoach drivers came into the store to deliver the mail and handed Lars a letter from the top of the pouch.

"Feller said it was very important, rush."

"Thanks, Bob." Lars opened the letter and scanned the report, mouthing the high points: "Carbonates of lead . . . silver . . . high grade . . . assay out at nine hundred dollars a ton . . . *my God!* I don't believe it!" He ran into the office, where Bob Parker was taking inventory.

"Bob, I've got to leave. Emergency. Will you watch the store until Mina comes down from the house?"

"Sure, Mr. De Beers. Nothing serious, I hope."

"Serious? Damn right it's serious! Nothing more serious ever happened to me in my life! Not bad serious; good serious." He left the store and ran up the hill to the house.

Bubbling over with excitement, he told Mina and Karen what had happened. "This could change our whole lives."

Mina was unenthusiastic. "You'll see, it was a mistake, or else those two hooligans you grubstaked are trying to dupe you."

"You have no faith in anyone, Mina."

"That's why I'm never disappointed."

Quickly Lars changed into denim riding pants and a heavy wool shirt and packed a saddlebag with a change of socks and underwear and cans of tinned food and hard biscuits.

Downstairs he kissed Mina and Karen. "I should be back by tomorrow. Next day at the latest."

Lars went out to the barn and saddled up his horse. "We're going to be rich, Barney," he spoke to the animal. "And then you'll have a bigger barn and lots of company."

Minutes later he was heading up California Gulch toward the site where Swensen and Franks had staked their claim. He rode into their camp on the banks of the Arkansas River at sundown.

The two prospectors were repairing their sluice. They looked up in astonishment as Lars dismounted, his face wreathed in a smile.

Swensen straightened up from his chore. "Mr. De Beers, what in blazes are you doing here?"

When he told them about the assay, they were flabbergasted.

"You sure it's for real?" Franks asked suspiciously. "No mistake by the assayer?"

"You sound like my wife," Lars said. "Now, put that sluice aside and break out the picks and shovels. What you boys dug up was surface chaff. The real ore is deep down. . . . Too dark to start now. First thing in the morning."

They sat around the campfire eating beans and bacon, washed down with scalding coffee laced with the whiskey Lars had donated to their stake. Too excited to sleep, they lay in their bedrolls making plans for the future.

"I aim to go to Paris, France, and spend two weeks in one of them French cathouses," Franks declared.

"A noble ambition, but not for one of my age," Lars said jovially. "I think I'll stay right here in Colorado. This land has been good to me. Now I want to do something in return for the land."

"Like what?" Swensen asked.

"Work for statehood for Colorado, for one thing; civic improvements; strengthening and building our legal system and our law-enforcement agencies."

Just before dawn they fell asleep out of sheer exhaustion. The sun woke them at seven o'clock. Without taking time to eat breakfast, they started digging. The deeper they dug, the more abundant was the lead-carbonate ore.

Finally Lars shoved his spade into a mound of earth. "No sense going any farther, boys. We're sitting on a gold mine, no doubt about it."

"You mean a silver mine," Swensen said, with a broad grin.

The three of them leaped around in a circle like Indians on the warpath, hooting and howling and pummeling one another affectionately.

"You boys sit tight out here until I can get a lawyer and make sure our claim is legal and properly filed, and then I'll get a mining engineer to come out and get the operation going."

Lars mounted his horse and rode back to Karenville at full gallop.

In the few days before the Fourth of July, much was accomplished in consolidating the project. Lars hired a lawyer to represent the organization's interests and consulted a mining engineer. The three partners named their claim the Little Karen Mine, and Lars suggested to the mayor and his city officials that it would be more appropriate now if the town was renamed Silver City.

Lars was exuberant as they set out for the big Fourth of July picnic at the Oro fairgrounds. So was Karen, but for a different reason. Sitting beside her was Bob Parker, looking red in the face and uncomfortable in his first store-bought suit; he kept running his finger around the inside of his high, suffocating collar. She'd been delighted by his reaction when she came down the stairs after spending two hours dressing and preening for the occasion. It was the first time her mother permitted her to wear rouge and face powder.

"You look *gorgeous,*" he'd said, his eyes wide with awe.

She was a living dream in a summer gown Mina had sewed on for weeks: a porcelain-blue-chintz print of wild flowers, birds, and butterflies, trimmed with grosgrain ribbon round the elbow-length flounced sleeves and just above the hemline flounce of the softly shirred bouffant skirt.

"And you look very handsome," she said, feeling the blood rush up into her neck and head like the red liquid in a thermometer on a hot summer day.

Now they were sitting on the makeshift seat that her father had rigged up in the back of the open wagon. She was alarmingly aware of his knee touching hers, fearful that he might feel the scorching heat of her body through the layers of their clothing. She was also blushingly aware of the growing lump pushing up on the right side of his trousers, which he strove desperately to conceal with the skirt of his jacket.

Karen had become acquainted with the physical differences between male and female at a very early age. For a long time after their arrival in Colorado, the De Beers family had lived out of a wagon or in a one-room cabin. Such enforced intimacy with a father and a brother had accustomed Karen to the sight of partially clad or nude male bodies. But that didn't count. Sex was something quite different—an exciting, alluring, mysterious attraction between men and women not of the same tribe; the eternal topic of conversation among teenage girls when they congregated in cliques in the schoolyard during recess or behind the barn on sultry Sunday afternoons. She had listened to innumerable stories related by older, bolder girls about what men and women did together in the privacy of their bedrooms.

At first mention of sexual intercourse, she had protested indignantly, "Not *my* mother and father!" It was unthinkable that her gentle, shy father would do *that* to her poor mother!

The other girls had hooted at her. "How do you think you and your brother got here?"

After that, Karen had been sensitive to the subtle nuances of behavior between husband and wife: an affectionate touch on an arm or a leg or a pat on the buttocks. At night she would lie still in the darkness, ears straining to pick up the conversation in her parents' room on the other side of the thin partition. She heard enough to verify what her schoolmates had claimed about men and women; that and the rhythmic creaking of the springs in Lars and Mina's big four-poster bed. No, sleep was not the only thing people went to bed for.

Repugnant as the sexual act had appeared to her once, now, at fifteen, she regarded it with eager anticipation. Oh, to share the wonderful sensation she'd discovered alone last night with a boy like Bob Parker! Just thinking about it made her loins ache; it felt as though there was a pocket of warm jelly simmering in the pit of her tummy.

"How are you kids doing back there?" her father called back to them.

"Enjoying the scenery, sir," Bob said in a strained voice, holding fast to the bottom of his jacket and not daring to look at the innocent angel beside him.

By the time they reached the fairgrounds, boy and girl were in a state of tension that could be relieved only by vigorous physical action.

Even before the wagon stopped, Bob vaulted over the tailgate: "Race you to the pond!"

Karen leaped to her feet and gathered up her skirts, preparing to emulate his reckless departure, but a sharp reprimand from Mina stopped her:

"Karen, I let you wear a young woman's dress and put on rouge and powder, and I expect you to behave like a young lady, not like a tomboy in dirty denims!"

"Yes, Mama." Karen stood demurely at the back of the wagon until her father lowered the tailgate and offered her his hand. Then, trying to control her rising excitement, she said, "I'm going down to the pond now. That's where all the kids are."

"All right, but come back in time for lunch, and make sure that Bob comes with you," Mina said. "I have enough food for an army."

"I will; don't worry."

At a ladylike pace, Karen wended her way among the picnic tables, the horseshoe players, the beer drinkers, savoring the atmosphere of celebration, goodwill, and excitement that pervaded everything and everyone. The ladies, decked out in the special finery they usually reserved for Easter Sunday, gossiped gaily, while the men, most of whom had hastily discarded coats and ties, gathered in clusters apart from the women, talking loudly and exchanging off-color jokes. A gawky lad with buck teeth tossed a string of tiny Chinese firecrackers at Karen's feet. She laughed and skipped nimbly to one side as they exploded in a chain of crackling bursts, skidding this way and that like a thing alive.

As she approached the pond, Rose Crory and Jennie Snead joined her, and, arms intertwined, the three of them skipped off to the pond. At the water's edge, they joined a group of girls who were cheering for an athletic event being staged by two teams of boys in rowboats. Each boat held three boys—two seated on the center seats, one standing in the prow, armed with a makeshift jousting staff composed of a broomstick with thick padding on the business end. While the rowers maneuvered the boats, jockeying for position, the combatants jabbed and feinted with their staffs.

There was frenzied applause as one of the boys evaded a hard thrust and jabbed his foe deftly on the leg that bore most of his weight, upsetting him into the pond fully clothed.

Karen looked around for Bob and saw him with a group out on the end of the rickety pier. He removed his jacket and tie and folded them neatly on the dry boards, then rolled up his sleeves.

"Look—Bob is going to give it a try!" someone shouted.

"Bobby Boy is gonna get knocked on his arse," the school bully snarled.

"Says who?" Bob called.

"Says me." George Dawson removed his jacket and his shirt so that the girls could ogle his bulging muscles, the result of having labored in his father's blacksmith shop since the age of nine. A surly lad with tightly curled red hair and a pug nose, he could whip any boy in Silver City—and a good many grown men, to boot—in boxing and wrestling.

Huge fists clenched, he walked the length of the pier and confronted Bob. Dawson was a full head taller and fifty-odd pounds heavier. "What do you say, Parker?" he snarled. "Got the guts to take me on?"

Bob met his malevolent glare unflinchingly. "Any time you're ready, Dawson." He signaled for the rowboats to come alongside the pier.

The lad who had won the previous joust leaped up onto the landing and handed his staff to Bob. "Good luck."

The loser's staff was retrieved from the pond and given to Dawson. He jumped down into the prow of one boat. "Come on, Parker, don't stall."

Not deigning to reply, Bob hopped lightly into the other boat. The two boys stood hipshot with their staffs held at the ready as the two boats were rowed out into deeper water. They took up positions about twenty feet apart, nose to nose.

"Time!" an unofficial referee on the beach shouted, and the contest began.

The oarsmen bent to their chore, and the adversary boats closed.

"Not too close," Bob warned his crew. "We mustn't let him take advantage of his brute strength."

Skillfully, the two oarsmen eluded the oncoming foe. As the boats slid past each other, Dawson flailed wildly with his staff. The padded broomstick was a foot short of Bob's head.

"None of that, Dawson!" the referee shouted, and the spectators booed their disapproval, too. "You're not supposed to knock his head off. It's a game."

"Up yours!" Dawson cried. "Come on over here, Parker. I thought you wanted to fight, not run away."

"Bring her almost alongside and swing the prow

sharp to port," Bob directed, "then back hard to starboard."

The maneuver was executed with precision, and just when Dawson thought he had a clear shot at his opponent's head, Bob was whisked out of reach. A moment later, as Dawson was struggling to regain his balance, the other boat swung back, and Bob jammed his staff squarely into the bully's stomach. Dawson grunted and gasped as the air was forced out of his lungs. He doubled half over and almost dropped his weapon. Then, as he leaned over the gunwale, grasping at the wet, slippery stick, Bob delivered the *coup de grâce*—a tap on the back of the head, just hard enough to topple him headfirst into the water. Dawson came up spitting and fuming.

"You lousy sonovabitch!" he cursed at Bob. "You don't play fair!"

Bob laughed, and all the boys and girls on the pier and the beach joined in.

"That's the funniest line of the day," Karen said. She rushed out onto the pier to welcome the conquering hero ashore.

Bob accorded her a deep, flourishing bow and said in a solemn voice, "I dedicate this victory to the ravishing Lady Karen De Beers."

"Aye! Bravo!" Cheers went up from the gallery.

When Bob had put on his tie and jacket, the group moved back to the picnic grounds. It was nearly time for lunch, which was to be preceded by a welcoming address delivered by the mayor of Oro.

At the De Beers picnic table, under a stately Douglas fir, Mina was laying out platters and utensils on a snowy-white tablecloth. She looked up as the youngsters approached.

"Let me help, Mother," Karen offered.

"I can manage, dear. You and Bob can fetch a pail of water from the spring."

Bob picked up the empty pail, and he and Karen walked slowly down a path that led into a small ravine where pure ice-cold water bubbled up out of a subterranean spring.

"That was wonderful how you paid that bully his dues," she said, feeling herself blush. It was practically an admission that she cared for him.

"I think *you're* wonderful, Karen," he said awkwardly.

Now they were both blushing as they felt their way gingerly and self-consciously into the unfamiliar territory of romance. He took her hand shyly, and Karen thought her legs would give way and she would collapse on the ground, a lovesick mass of jelly. Ever so gently she returned the pressure he was applying on her fingers. She had never felt so feminine in her life as she did at that moment with her slim, soft hand swallowed up by his big, callused one.

They reached the spring, and Bob dipped the bucket into the crystal-clear water. They started away from the spring when, suddenly, he placed the bucket on the ground and faced Karen.

She looked up at him quizzically. "What's the matter?"

His face was flaming and he kept taking deep breaths.

"Bob, are you sick?"

"Sick? . . . In a way."

"What is it?"

His throat was so dry he could hardly answer her. Hoarsely he said, "I don't care what happens; I've got to do it."

"Do what?"

He placed trembling hands on her shoulders and looked deep into her eyes. "Karen, I . . . I . . . Hell, there's only one way to tell you!" Clumsily he enfolded her in his arms and pressed his mouth down on her parted lips.

At first she hung limp in his grasp; she felt she was floating on a fleecy cloud high up in the rarefied air of heaven. Then, with her rising passion, she responded to the hot blood coursing fiercely through her veins. She was acutely aware of her body, every square inch of it, every nerve ending. Of his body as well: the quick rise and fall of his chest against her flattened breasts; the flex of his biceps against her rib cage; the heat of his loins scorching her belly and thighs; most of all, the powerful thrust of his manhood measuring itself against the length of her from *mons Veneris* to navel.

Her arms were fast about his neck, drawing him urgently against her. She opened her mouth to his probing tongue and ground her pelvis against him. It required all her willpower not to cry out in sheer ecstasy. *Ecstasy, euphoria, rapture*—words one encountered in spelling bees. The closest Karen had come to experiencing such heady emotions had been at the height of her lonely passion the night before. Until this moment.

The kiss ended, and Karen took a step back. They held hands and looked at each other in blissful silence. In an intuitive gesture, she brought up his right hand and touched it to her breast. He caressed the soft, resilient mound with tender reverence.

Tears welled up in her eyes. Swallowing the lump in her throat, she spoke softly: "I love you, Robert Parker."

His eyes were misty, too. "And I love you, Karen De Beers."

"We'd best get back to the picnic or they'll be sending out a search party."

He nodded and lifted the bucket and they started back up the path, their fingers loosely entwined.

Nils and his girl were sitting at the table when Karen and Bob returned.

"What kept you two?" Mina demanded. "So long to fetch a bucket of water?"

Nils grinned. "Bet they were spooning."

Their crimson faces gave them away, and everyone hooted with laughter.

Karen scooped a handful of water out of the bucket and flung it in her brother's face. "Not everyone is like you and Mary."

Mary Wentworth tried to look prim. "What a terrible thing to say, Karen."

"Is it? It's all over town how you and Nils acted on the hayride last month."

Mary put her palms to her flaming cheeks and her mouth formed a shocked oval. "Karen De Beers! You ought to have your mouth washed out with soap."

"All right, that's enough, all of you," Mina said. "No more teasing. It's time to eat."

Enormous quantities of fried chicken, baked ham, potato salad, and roast corn were consumed, notably by Nils and Bob.

"I don't know where you young fellows get your appetites," Mina observed. "Lars, I don't recall your having such an appetite at their age."

Lars chuckled. "You don't? I remember your father threatening to charge me board if I continued to eat over at your house."

"That's how it is with us young bucks," Nils said airily. "These hot-blooded young wenches sap all our energy, and we have to replenish it constantly."

Mina was outraged. "Nils De Beers! If my brother had spoken to our mother like that, she *would* have washed out his mouth."

Lunch over, the women cleared the table while the men strolled over to where the horseshoe contests were under way again. Nils and Bob played the first game. Then Lars took on Bob, the winner, and trounced him thoroughly. The lad didn't seem to mind.

"I've had enough for now," he said. "You two play. I promised to go for a walk with Karen."

Nils clapped him on the shoulder. "You sound henpecked and you're not even going steady yet."

Father and son laughed as Bob went hurrying back to the eating area. Mina was sitting with her back to the fir tree, knitting. Mary and Karen were seated at the table, on which Mary was laying out playing cards in three rows of fourteen cards each.

"What are you doing?" Bob inquired.

"Mary's telling my fortune."

Bob sat down and observed.

"Ahhh . . . your destiny in the phase of the full moon is dominated by the heart. Yes, affairs of the heart will figure predominantly in your future for the next month."

"Oh, Mary, don't copy Nils."

"I'm serious. I see a tall, handsome man in your life. Yes, he's got blondish hair and"—she cut her eyes mischievously at Bob—"and light-blue eyes . . . No, maybe they're gray; I can't be sure."

Bob's collar was getting tight again. He dared not look at Karen.

Mary went on. "Oh, yes, this is going to ripen into a very serious relationship, possibly even lead to marriage."

Bob stood up. "I think I'll go for a walk. See you all later."

He was almost to the pond when Karen caught up with him. "Why didn't you wait for me?" she chided.

"I didn't think you'd want to leave before your fortune was done."

"Oh, *that!* Mary and Nils are two of a kind, always teasing. You don't think I took her seriously, do you?"

He stopped and faced her. "No? She was right about the man in your life. I have gray eyes and blond hair, and I consider our relationship extremely serious. As soon as I finish school and get a job, I'm going to ask you to marry me."

"At our ages?" She was incredulous.

"Why not? My mother was fifteen when she married my father, and he was just two years older."

"Come to think of it, my parents were married in their teens," she admitted.

They fell silent as they walked around the pond and up the hill, their clasped hands swinging to and fro, their spirits soaring like the birds overhead. Suddenly the oddest-looking creature Karen had ever seen scooted across their path. It had the tail of a raccoon, the body of a squirrel, the front feet of a cat, and the head of a fox.

"Ugh! What was *that?"*

Bob laughed. "You've never seen a ring-tailed cat before? Looks like God got a bit confused when He put them together."

On the summit was a grassy mesa that fell away to the west in a sheer drop of a thousand feet. They walked to the edge and gazed out across the majestic grandeur of Çolorado, the same view that had inspired Katharine Lee Bates to compose "America the Beautiful." To the east, north, and south loomed the rugged crags of the Rocky Mountains, etched sharply against the cloudless sky, the "three-mile-high wall" that separated the eastern and western halves of the state. To the east, the prairie land stretched off to near infinity, broken up like a checkerboard by squares of green and gold where the farmers had conquered the sage and tumbleweed.

On distant slopes, the aspen trees in full bloom lay like a great glowing blanket across the countryside, while flourishing in the shade of their golden boughs were clusters of columbine that matched the intense azure of the sky. Dominating the panorama was the splendid spike of Pike's Peak—not the tallest mountain in Colorado but, standing alone in the flatland, certainly the most outstanding.

"It's so breathtakingly beautiful that I get a lump in my throat," Karen said, and massaged the front of her neck.

Bob slipped an arm about her slim waist. "Breathtakingly beautiful is what *you* are, Karen."

She smiled and leaned close against him. "I never think of myself as beautiful. There are scads of girls far better-looking than I am."

"Not in my eyes. As far as I'm concerned, there are no other girls in the world except you."

She turned within the curve of his arm and, closing her eyes, pressing her body against his, tilted her head back, waiting for his kiss.

Their lips met chastely at first. Then, gradually, the tempo of the foreplay quickened.

"Darling, love." His mouth devoured her ears, her eyes, the racing pulse in the side of her throat.

"My one and only sweetheart," she murmured, her hands caressing his hair, the back of his neck. She opened the buttons of his shirt and nuzzled his bare chest with her nose and mouth, and once again she felt the urgent thrust of his inflamed manhood against her quivering belly. She was intensely aroused herself. "I want to do it," she said breathlessly.

"Do it?" He couldn't believe he had heard right.

"You know, silly—make love."

Bob was shocked; frightened. "Oh, Karen, we

couldn't. I mean, I couldn't do that to you. I respect you too much."

"Don't behave so childishly. I'm a grown woman and you're a grown man. I want you so badly, I think I'll go out of my mind if you don't do it to me right now. And don't tell me you don't want to." She reached between them and grabbed his erection through his trousers.

Bob gasped and recoiled as if he had been seared by a branding iron.

"Now, let's get on with it." She turned her back to him. "Unbutton me."

Bob's jaw sagged. "What are you going to do?"

"What do you *think* I'm going to do?" she said in exasperation. "I'm taking off my dress so it won't get wrinkled. How would it appear if we went back to the picnic with me looking like one of the rumpled whores on the hill?"

His fingers were shaking so badly that he barely managed to unbutton the back of her gown, and when Karen gripped the hemline and drew it carefully over her head, he could only stand transfixed at the sight of her in her petticoat and corselet. The corselet lifted her breasts and bunched them together in a most provocative fashion.

"Stop gawking at me and take off your clothes. You'd think you had never seen a girl undress before."

He shook his head. "I never have."

"That makes us even. I've never seen a naked boy before, either," she said, obviously not placing her brother and father in the same category with Bob. She removed her shirtwaist, corselet, and petticoat. She was nude now but for a pair of lace-trimmed pink bloomers. Squaring her shoulders, she walked over to Bob and unbuttoned the front of his trousers. "Am I going to have to undress you like a little boy?" she asked impatiently.

With her assistance, he managed to remove his shoes, socks, trousers, and shirt.

"Take off your drawers," she instructed, and she slipped her bloomers down to her ankles and stepped out of them.

They stood immobile and silent now, both as naked as the day they were born, Adam and Eve in the Garden of Eden. Desire consumed Karen as she ran her eyes over Bob's lean, hard body. He desired her as intensely; that was plain to be seen. She clasped his rigid member and stroked it lovingly. With a deep sigh, he pulled her down gently in the soft, thick, sweet grass.

"Soft as a bridal bower," she whispered.

They kissed and nuzzled and fondled each other like two young innocent animals. His hands and mouth caressed every part of her body.

"I can't believe you've never been with a girl before," she said.

"Karen!" He was hurt.

"I mean, you're so good at it. You know just what to do to make me feel glorious."

He laughed. "That's a lift to my ego, thanks. But I can say the same of you. You know all the right things to do to please me. . . . Oh, Lord!" he gasped, as her gentle hand cupped his hard testicles.

"I guess it just comes naturally to people who love each other," she said. "Oh, Bob . . . *now!*" She lay back in the grass and urged him between her eager, inviting thighs.

"I can't do it, darling," he complained as he met the solid resistance of her virginal membrane.

"You've *got* to do it, Bob," she insisted. "We can't stop now. Push as hard as you can. I mean it!" She gritted her teeth, locked her heels at the small of his back, and pulled him into her as hard as she could. There was an instant of sharp pain, as if a knife had been drawn up through the middle of her. Small price to pay for the surging, raging pleasure that immediately followed it, totally obliterating the discomfort.

His rhythm matched hers in perfect harmony, his powerful spasms keeping pace with her vigorous contractions. Their joy seemed to endure forever, and as the blissful sensation began to subside, Karen strove desperately to prolong it.

"Oh, darn!" she lamented. "Why did it have to end?"

He held her close and stroked her flank. "My beloved, it will never end for us. For the years to come, you and I will be making love time after time, and it will always be as wonderful as this first time."

"I know." She looked up at him adoringly. "Do you know, I feel as though we're married, Bob."

He smiled and patted her cheek. "We *are,* my darling, in the only way that counts. After today, we truly belong to each other through all eternity."

They kissed tenderly while their bodies once more commenced the passionate orchestration of love.

CHAPTER FIVE

In the month after the Fourth of July, the Little Karen Mine was producing $25,000 a week. Anticipating the future plans of Bob Parker and his daughter, Lars De Beers made a decision.

Late on a Saturday afternoon he called Bob into his office and closed the door. "Sit down, my boy, and have a cigar." He pushed the humidor across the desk.

"No, thank you, sir."

A gleam shone in the older man's eyes. "Man's old enough to get married, he's old enough to smoke."

"Married?" Bob's voice cracked.

"That's right. You're seventeen, right?"

"Yes, sir."

"Same age I was when I got married." A pregnant pause. "And my Mina was exactly Karen's age, maybe a few months older."

Bob was speechless; his knuckles were white where they were locked to the arm of the chair.

"Bob"—Lars sucked on his cigar—"since the Fourth of July, you and Karen have been seeing each other every night." He got up and walked around the desk, then sat hipshot on one corner of it, looking down at the lad. "Don't think I don't know what goes on in the sun porch between you two after Mina and I go to bed. I was young myself, you know."

Bob sat there rigidly, staring straight ahead, his face crimson.

"Young hot-blooded boy and girl . . . well, it's only doing what comes naturally. Point is, when it gets to that stage between two young people, it's time to make such hanky-panky legal, if you get my meaning."

Bob gulped and found his voice. "I . . . I . . . I think so. Sir, if you think Karen and I are seeing too much of each other, then I'll——"

"I didn't say you were seeing too much of each other. I said it's time you two tied the knot."

Bob swallowed hard. "But, sir, I'm still going to school."

"Quit school and get a job."

"Fellow without education, what kind of job could he get?"

"A damned good one. You'll work for me."

"I *am* working for you, but I don't make enough to——"

"A better job, full time. I'm turning the store over to you, the whole kit and kaboodle. Post office, too. You and my little girl will be very comfortable. Even build you a house next to ours."

Bob shook his head in bewilderment. "This is all so sudden, sir. I can't quite comprehend it."

"Sure, my boy, I understand." Lars patted him on the shoulder. "You take some time, think about it, talk it over with Karen. I'll go up and see what's happening at the mine. I'll be back tomorrow morning."

He took his hat from the pole rack and left the office,

leaving a stunned and apprehensive Bob Parker alone. Very much alone.

On the first of September, Lars De Beers bought out Swensen and Franks for $100,000.

"You must be crazy, Lars," Swensen said to him as they signed the agreement. "Way we see it, this claim is already starting to peter out."

Lars shrugged. "Always was a gambling man. Good luck wherever you go, boys."

They shook hands all around, and Franks confided, "Jim and me are heading for Florence. Heard a feller struck oil over there. We're gonna stake ourselves a few claims."

Meanwhile, the romance between Bob and Karen had cooled perceptibly since her father's "ultimatum," as Bob preferred to think of it, the month before.

"Ultimatum! That's ridiculous," Karen said to him during a serious discussion they were having in the hayloft one balmy afternoon after making love. "My father doesn't issue ultimatums."

"Your father is a lot different since he's making all that money on the silver mine. He's getting, I don't know, bossy and filled with a sense of his own importance."

She, too, had observed changes in her father's character over the summer. So had her mother. Just a week ago, Karen had heard a heated argument going on in their bedroom:

"It's all over town about you and that actress the week you spent in Denver."

"Damned lies, all of it! People slander me because they're jealous. So, I asked a pretty young lady to join me at my table for a glass of champagne. What of it? Nothing happened between us."

"You expect me to believe that?"

"I don't give a damn what you believe, Mina. I speak the truth!"

"Ha! You haven't laid a hand on me the past month. Knowing you so well, Lars, that can only mean one thing: you're getting it from another woman."

"Instead of pointing the finger at me, you'd do best to pay attention to what your daughter and Bob Parker are up to. It's been a *month* since I made him that proposition."

Karen had been surprised but not displeased when Bob first told her of it.

"Yes, your father was a much nicer man before he became the Silver King," Bob was saying. "That's what they call him around town. Did you know he turned down an offer of one million dollars for the Little Karen Mine from a big eastern syndicate?"

"I don't believe it."

"It's true. I heard him telling Jake Tabor, his lawyer."

"Let's leave my father out of it, Bob. The subject I want to talk about is us. I get the feeling that you're losing interest in me. The past few times we've made love, you seemed to be forcing yourself. Today I had to play with you for five minutes before you could get it up."

He turned crimson. "For God's sake, Karen, it's different for a man than it is for a woman! You can do it any time. A man can't, especially when he's got a lot of problems on his mind."

"And what problems do *you* have?" she asked coldly. "My father offered you the store and the postmaster's job. Other couples I know get along on less."

"Couples," he said listlessly.

She was furious. "Yes, *couples*—like us. We *are* a couple, aren't we?"

He bent his head into his hands. "Karen, I love you,

truly I do. But the truth is, I'm not ready to get married yet."

"Your ardor cooled off very fast, didn't it? Back on the Fourth of July, you couldn't *wait* to get married. You wanted me so bad, you were salivating. I guess the old saying is right: 'If you're getting all the milk you want, why buy a cow?' "

"Jesus! That's a hell of a way to put it! Look, I talked it over with my dad. He said if I wanted to be owned by the company store, go ahead and get married. I don't want to be owned by your father."

"That's pure rot and you know it. You're just looking for an excuse not to marry me."

He got up on his knees and took her hands in his. "That isn't true. I *do* want to marry you . . . someday."

"Someday." She laughed disdainfully.

"Yes, when I finish college and become an engineer. Miss Holland at school says I have a natural bent for mathematics, that I should study engineering."

Karen hated him at that moment. "Finish college? That's years away. I'll be an old maid by the time you're an engineer."

He stood up. "Karen, this isn't getting us anywhere. I think I'd better be going. I've got to study for a test."

"Bob, please don't leave me on this note." Tears were streaming down her face. "I'm sorry if I sound bitchy lately, but there's a reason."

Without answering, he walked to the edge of the loft and prepared to descend the ladder.

Something exploded in Karen's brain. Face contorted with rage, her voice rising to a banshee wail, she sprang to her feet and charged after him, her hands held high in the air. "You bastard!" she screamed. "You don't realize what you've done to me! Right now I'm carrying your child!"

Bob's face registered total shock. Reacting instinctively, he threw up his hands to protect himself as she came at him, arms flailing wildly. The abrupt motion cast him off balance and he went toppling off the loft, somersaulting backward once before he landed flush on a pitchfork that a hand had carelessly jammed into the soft loam that covered the barn floor. He cried out once, an inhuman, tormented sound that was earsplitting.

Karen covered her ears with her hands and closed her eyes, but the scream went on and on, echoing through the corridors of her mind until she thought she must go insane. Merciful blackness engulfed her, a great dark wave that carried her into oblivion.

Bob Parker was discovered by Mina when she went out to the barn to look for her daughter. It was a sight she would never forget until her dying day. At first glance in the dim barn, he appeared to be alive: lying on his back in a pile of loose hay, his sightless eyes staring fixedly at Mina, his lips drawn back over his teeth in a death's-head grin. Then she saw the blood seeping out from under him, and the pitchfork—broken off at the hasp by the impact of his fall—with the tines protruding from back to front clear through his neck and left shoulder. Mina ran screaming from the barn.

Karen was not seen again for more than thirty-six hours. It was as though she had vanished from the face of the earth. Posses were formed to scour the countryside around Silver City in all directions. A day and a half later, they found her huddled in a small cave twelve miles from town. She did not speak, nor did she respond in any way to the questions posed by her rescuers. She was taken back home in a wagon.

Lars, Mina, and Nils wept openly when they saw her. Karen evidenced no more response to the love and concern lavished on her by her family than she had accorded the posse members. The town doctor was summoned, and he was as impotent as everyone else in breaking through the barrier she had erected between her inner self and the outer world.

"She appears to be in a state of deep shock, no doubt brought on by seeing her friend fall out of the loft and onto that cursed pitchfork."

"Whoever left it there should be strung up," Nils growled.

Dr. Hoffman shrugged. "Only thing we can do is put her to bed and wait for her to snap out of it."

"But you do think she'll be all right?" Mina asked worriedly.

"Right as rain," the doctor replied confidently. "Medical journal is full of cases just like Karen's. The shock will wear off in time."

His prediction was accurate, though incomplete. Karen slept for twenty-four hours without interruption, and when she awoke, she appeared to be completely normal. Humming to herself, she got out of bed, put on a robe and slippers, and went downstairs. She walked gaily into the kitchen, where her mother, father, and brother were having a midafternoon snack. "What time is it?" She looked at the wall clock and blinked in disbelief. "Three o'clock! It's impossible! I couldn't have slept all this time. Why didn't someone wake me?"

Mina, tears streaming down her face, rushed to her and embraced her. "My child, my dear little Karen, you've come back to us!"

Karen recoiled. "Come back? Whatever are you talking about, Mama?" She looked over her weeping mother's shoulder at her father and brother. "Papa? Nils? Why are you looking at me that way? Won't somebody please tell me what this is all about?"

Lars got up and went to them. Gently he led mother and daughter back to the table. "Sit down and have some coffee and cake."

"Yes, I'm famished," Karen said. "This is all very mysterious and aggravating. Now, somebody say something."

Nils assumed the responsibility: "Karen . . . it's Bob Parker."

She frowned. "Bob? What about Bob? Has he been looking for me today?"

Lars and Nils exchanged grim looks, and Mina cried even harder.

Alarm registered on Karen's face. "Has anything happened to Bob? Has he been hurt?"

Nils's eyes brimmed with tears. "Karen, honey . . . Bob . . . Bob is dead."

Her face went ashen. "Bob dead? I don't believe it. What's wrong with all of you? I don't think you're real. This is a bad dream. Bob is *not* dead." At first barely above a whisper, her voice rose higher and higher to a pitch of hysteria.

Nils went to her and put an arm around her shoulders. "Calm down, Karen, and listen to me. This is not a pretty story, but it must be told. . . ."

All the while Nils spoke, Karen sat immobile, her eyes vacant.

"Doc says you had a spell of amnesia—the mind's way of blocking out things too awful to confront—but you're going to be all right," he finished lamely.

A small smile worked its way across her face then, but it didn't reach those vacant eyes. The three of them looked at her uneasily.

"Karen, what are you thinking?" Mina asked anxiously.

Still smiling, she looked at her mother and replied matter-of-factly, "I haven't lost Bob, not really." She placed her hands over her stomach. "I'm carrying his baby, so I know that he would never leave me. I know what he's done. He's gone to Denver to buy an engagement ring and a wedding band for me. We're going to be married next week. Aren't you all surprised?"

They stared at her, speechless, as if they were contemplating an alien being from a distant planet.

Karen perpetuated the delusion that Bob Parker was alive and well and would shortly be coming back to join her and their unborn baby. She pretended to family and friends that her "husband"—she even took to wearing a wedding band—was traveling on business, and quoted passages from his imaginary letters. The townspeople treated her with compassionate deference. After all, she was the daughter of Silver City's "first family."

Lars De Beers had acquired the reputation of a financial wizard. Six months after he bought out Swensen and Franks, he sold his interest in the Little Karen Mine to the eastern syndicate for $1 million. The new owners renamed it the Karen Consolidated and issued public stock. Lars invested the entire million in the new venture, and when, shortly thereafter, the share value skyrocketed from $7 to $35, his net worth was $5 million.

Acquiring wealth and power had become an obsession with Lars De Beers. Mina guessed it was a means to sublimate his deep grief over Karen's affliction. He formed the De Beers Mining and Development Corporation, which invested in gold and silver mines in Colorado, Texas, Utah, Arizona, and New Mexico; then branched out into cattle ranching, oil drilling, and railroad building within the territory. He appointed himself chairman of the expanding board of directors, and his son Nils corporation president.

On a mesa atop a hill in the shadow of Pike's Peak, he created a vast estate surrounded by a ten-foot stone wall, encompassing some 400 acres dominated by a medieval castle that had been transported from France stone block by stone block and reconstituted in Colorado by an army of 1,000 laborers. It rose majestically amid a setting of rolling green lawns, exotic shrubs and trees, and dazzling flower gardens. Equally sumptuous was the period furniture within the castle—Louis XV, Louis XVI, Directoire, and Empire. When one of his decorators complained that it was too much a pastiche, Lars told him:

"I want to touch all the bases; that way I can't go wrong."

Lars spent huge sums of money lobbying in Washington, D.C., for Colorado statehood and in developing advancements in the territory that would make that end seem palatable to Congress.

One of the major obstacles that delayed settlement of Colorado was the Rocky Mountains—the "two-mile-high spite fence," as it was known. To overcome this barrier, Lars De Beers and a committee of other prominent Coloradans conceived of pushing the Denver and Rio Grande Railroad, of which Lars was a major stockholder, through Royal Gorge and over the Continental Divide at Marshall Pass.

Meanwhile the territory had been connected with the transcontinental railroad in Cheyenne, Wyoming. With the increasing prosperity of the cattle business and the overthrow of the monopolistic cattle barons, which made it possible for settlers and homesteaders to close off the vast rangeland with fences, the prospect of statehood became increasingly viable.

Finally, on August 1, 1876, Colorado became the thirty-eighth state to be admitted to the Union. It was a gala occasion for the proud Coloradans, and from this point on, they would have double cause for celebration on Independence Day. Theirs was *the* Centennial State!

August 1, 1876, was a day of even greater celebration for the De Beers family. On that illustrious morning, at exactly 6:45 A.M., Karen gave birth to a baby girl.

She named the child Tara De Beers Parker.

CHAPTER SIX

Gilberta concluded her speech:

"All across this promised land, Americans of every color, creed, and ethnic background are celebrating this glorious Bicentennial Fourth of July. But it is more than a landmark day we are all honoring. We are paying tribute not only to the spirit of the Declaration of Independence but also to the spirit of those courageous, indomitable pioneers who, in the year 1806, literally pushed the boundaries of the United States from sea to shining sea.

"I now invite you to join myself and the other guest speakers on this platform in the first stanza of 'America the Beautiful.' "

Gilberta felt a lump rise in her throat as the crowd clasped hands and lifted their voices, singing not just the first stanza but all three. When the trailing echoes of the hymn had at last dissipated down the canyons of Broadway, Park Row, and Chambers Street, Gilberta, Anita, and Jeanette made their way to a room in the city hall where a group of selected luminaries had been invited to attend a small, intimate reception given by the mayor.

As she stood by a window overlooking city-hall park, Gilberta was joined by a state senator, an assistant district attorney, and a movie producer in town for the shooting of his latest film.

In reply to a query from the senator, Gilberta said, "No, the fact that we've leased a floor in the World Trade Center does not imply that we are transferring our major operation to New York. Denver always has been and will continue to be the home office of the De Beers Mining and Development Corporation. As you are aware, we have offices in London, Paris, and Milan, as well as junior branch offices in ten cities in the United States."

She fielded another question from the young D.A. "Is it true, Mrs. Killington, that Governor Killington is going to campaign strongly for Jimmy Carter?"

"Governor Killington has always been a confirmed Democrat, and, yes he will support Governor Carter in his bid for the presidency."

"In your opinion, does a Southerner stand a chance of becoming president of the United States?"

Gilberta flicked the ashes of her cigarette into a potted plant. "I think that *any* competent person, if his platform has strong appeal for the American people and they believe him to be sincere in his vow to carry out his campaign promises, can be elected president."

"Even a Jew?" the Jewish producer put in slyly.

Her violet eyes impaled him. "There was a time, you recall, when it was an impossibility for a *Catholic* to become president. Then came John F. Kennedy. Yes, indeed, I am confident that before this century is over, there will be a Jew in the Oval Office . . . maybe even a black."

The producer looked at the other two men with a

supercilious smile. "Do you gentlemen agree with Mrs. Killington?"

The senator, who, it was rumored, was a closet anti-Semite, was unflappable. Without hesitation he answered, "I agree one hundred percent. As everyone knows, I'm a great admirer of Senator Javits. If he was younger, I think he'd stand an excellent chance of being nominated."

The producer's smile expanded. "Like hell you do!"

The discussion was interrupted by the appearance of one of the mayor's aides: "Excuse me, Mrs. Killington, I wonder if you would accompany me. There are two gentlemen waiting in the study. They say it is extremely urgent that they speak with you."

Gilberta frowned. "Who are they?"

The aide squirmed uncomfortably and avoided her gaze. "I believe they are policemen, Mrs. Killington."

"Policemen!" Gilberta, Anita, and Jeanette exclaimed in unison.

Gilberta's heart skipped a beat. Could they have discovered Jules so soon? No; it was impossible! Still, she felt the cold sweat beading up on her brow. "Okay," she said, forcing a smile, "I admit it: This morning I jaywalked across Fifth Avenue. So, they finally caught up with me." She threw up her hands. "I'll go quietly. Lead on, sir. . . . Excuse me, folks; I won't be long, I hope."

She followed the aide out of the reception room and down a corridor.

"Seriously," she said, "don't you have any idea what they want?"

"No, I don't, ma'am. They were not very communicative. . . . Well, here we are." He opened a door and stood aside to let her precede him into the room.

Two men, smoking by a window, looked up when Gilberta entered. The taller of the two was quite good-looking, she noted: dark, thick, wavy hair, brown eyes, strong features, good physique underneath the seersucker suit. He came toward her:

"Mrs. Killington . . . I'm Captain George Laurentis, New York City Police Department, homicide division." He showed her his credentials.

Homicide! So, she'd miscalculated when she thought Jules's body wouldn't be discovered till Monday morning, when the maid came in. "What can I do for you, Captain?" she said.

"Do you know a Mr. Jules Marston, Mrs. Killington?"

This is it, Gilly. The chips are down, and you had better play your hand like a riverboat gambler.

Wide-eyed, hand to her throat, she stared at him. "Just a moment. Did you say homicide division?"

He nodded; waited patiently. "Shall I repeat the question, Mrs. Killington?"

"Jules Marston? Of course I know him. He's a dear friend of ours—my husband's and mine. Why? What's happened? Has he been in an accident?"

"What makes you think he's been in an accident?" He hadn't taken his eyes from her face.

Gilberta was aware that the second policeman, a squat fellow in a too-tight suit, with close-cropped red hair and watery blue eyes, had moved to her left side. She made no effort to hide her very real concern—concern not for Julie's neck now but for her own! "He promised he would make an effort to attend the Bicentennial ceremonies here at city hall, since he told my husband he had some business in New York this weekend, but I haven't seen him." Then, with the dramatic flair of Joan Crawford, she did a horrified double take. "Homicide . . . Oh, no! He's not——"

"I'm afraid so. Mr. Marston is dead, but it wasn't an accident."

"How, then?" Gilberta asked in a choked voice.

Laurentis exchanged looks with his partner.

"It appears he committed suicide."

Her reaction then had the ring of perfect pitch, but not for the reason the police might think. "Suicide?" Her knees buckled, and she would have slumped to the floor had Captain Laurentis not stepped forward to support her.

"I think you had better sit down, Mrs. Killington."

He led her over to a rose-colored loveseat against one wall and let her down gently. All the time, Gilberta kept shaking her head and mumbling, "Suicide . . . suicide . . . Jules? No, it's impossible . . . impossible . . ."

It was the absolute truth. Moreover, the theory was fantastically absurd! A dead man with the back of his head bashed in! Either the police were idiots, or else they were playing a deadly cat-and-mouse game with her.

Laurentis's eyes narrowed. "You say that with great conviction, Mrs. Killington."

"*Total* conviction. Jules would never commit suicide."

"Yet the facts appear irrefutable."

"What facts? Just how did he die?"

"It would appear that he leaped to his death from the penthouse of the Tyson Towers apartment complex."

"Milos Alansky's apartment," she said with deliberateness.

"Yes. You knew he was staying there?"

"He usually did when he came to New York. My personal secretary, Anita Thatcher, informed me that he had called me yesterday at the Essex House from Milos's apartment and asked that I return his call if I had time. I did, this afternoon, when I got back to the city, but there was no answer."

"Got back?"

"You see, I spent Saturday up at our summer home upstate, near Oneonta, working on the final draft of my speech, the one I delivered here today."

"Why didn't Mr. Marston phone you there?"

"We—my husband and I—didn't install a phone in the cabin. It's a place we retreat to when we want to be alone, individually or together, where we can cut ourselves off from the outside world and relax completely." She did not tell him that Anita had had no inkling where she'd disappeared to for an entire day. With luck, that detail would be obscured by more weighty testimony.

"What else did Mr. Marston say to Mrs. Thatcher when he phoned the Essex House?"

"It's *Miss* Thatcher, and I suggest you ask her. She's here at the mayor's reception."

"Yes, I'll do just that." He nodded at his partner. "This is Lieutenant Cavelli, Mrs. Killington. . . . Bill, will you ask Miss Thatcher to join us, please?"

"Captain, have you notified Mr. Alansky?"

"Yes; we reached him at his West Coast residence, Palm Springs. He's flying in tonight. He verified that Jules Marston was staying at his New York apartment. Apparently he used the place as much as Alansky did."

"Yes, I know. Milos and Jules both traveled constantly. They were business associates, you know."

"So Mr. Alansky informed us." He produced a pack of cigarettes and offered one to her.

"Thank you." She put the cigarette in her mouth and bent to the Zippo lighter he extended. "This is all like some horrible nightmare. . . . You say Jules *jumped* from the penthouse?"

"Over the terrace wall, wearing nothing but a pair of Jockey shorts."

Gilberta inhaled deeply. "I still don't believe it. No; he must have been pushed."

She had come dangerously close to saying "thrown over," and that would have been the kiss of death. Suddenly the stark significance of what must have happened in the apartment after her departure struck her like a thunderbolt. Whoever murdered Jules had obviously been lurking somewhere in the apartment all the while she was packing and carrying luggage down to the truck, waiting for the moment he could dispose of the body. Why he'd spared *her* life, Gilberta had no idea.

"Why are you so positive he didn't commit suicide?"

"If you knew Jules, you would be, too. Ask Anita Thatcher; she'll tell you the same thing. He was such a vital person, so in love with life. I mean, he was *the* man who had everything."

At that instant, Cavelli returned with Anita. She was a ghastly white, and her eyes were glazed over from shock.

"I told her about Marston," the lieutenant said.

Anita rushed to Gilberta and threw her arms around her. "Oh, Gilly, isn't it *horrible?*"

"There is no word to describe it, Anita; it's unthinkable."

"Miss Thatcher, according to Mrs. Killington, you spoke to Mr. Marston yesterday on the phone."

"Yes, in the morning."

"Did he say why he wanted to speak to Mrs. Killington?"

"He wanted to wish Gilberta luck with her speech. When I told him I was expecting her any moment, he left a number and asked that she call him if she had time."

Gilberta held her breath, wondering whether the subject of the summer home near Oneonta would be pursued any further.

"When you spoke to Mr. Marston, how would you evaluate his state of mind?" Laurentis continued.

"Do you mean did he sound depressed? Quite the contrary. I've never heard Jules in better spirits. He was not a man given to moods, anger, self-indulgence. It's inconceivable that he would commit suicide."

Laurentis looked to Cavelli. "The ladies almost have me convinced. How about you, Bill?"

Cavelli shrugged. "It's beginning to make a lot of sense, the possibility that he was pushed."

"Unfortunately, there's no evidence to support that theory. The apartment was locked; no signs of forced entry. That would indicate that Marston knew his alleged killer, that he admitted him to the apartment and had no inkling that the man—or woman—had murder on the mind."

"It would be too much for a woman to accomplish," Cavelli reasoned. "Marston was a big man and in good physical condition, I'd say."

"He's right," Gilberta affirmed. "Jules was a powerfully built man—slender, but all of him steel cord."

"Still, if she caught him off guard . . . Well, first we've got to establish that someone *did* murder him."

"What about fingerprints, Captain?" Anita inquired.

Gilberta's heart skipped a beat.

"A lot of them, Miss Thatcher, and mostly blurred. It's not quite the way they portray it on television. A good set of prints is extremely hard to come by."

Casually, Gilberta offered, "And in this case fingerprints are meaningless. Scores of people have visited at Milos Alansky's apartment, men and women. Both Milos and Jules did a lot of entertaining when they were in New York. You'd most likely find Anita's fingerprints somewhere in the apartment; mine, too."

He nodded. "Yes, we don't expect to establish anything conclusive by fingerprints." He lit another cigarette. "Well, Bill, I don't see any reason to detain Mrs. Killington and Miss Thatcher any longer, do you? Thank you both for your cooperation, ladies. . . . Incidentally, how long will you be staying in New York?"

"We have reservations for a nine o'clock flight tomorrow morning. Will it be all right to leave then?" Gilberta said.

"Certainly. If we need any further testimony from either of you, we'll get in touch. And if anything comes to mind that you think may be significant, please let me know." He removed a card from his wallet and handed it to her. "We'll be off now and let you go back to the party."

"I don't feel very much like celebrating anything at the moment," she said. "I think we'll excuse ourselves and go back to the hotel."

He nodded and glanced at Cavelli. "Let's go."

When they got back to the reception hall, Gilberta approached one of the mayor's aides and explained why she, Anita, and Jeanette would have to cut short their visit: "The unexpected death of a very dear friend." No need to present the grisly truth.

Jeanette, who was very cozy in a corner with a handsome French diplomat, was incensed when Anita told her they would have to leave. "But why? I'm having such a good time!"

"We'll tell you when we get outside. Gilly is making our apologies to the mayor. She'll meet us in the vestibule."

Jeanette was still complaining when Gilberta joined her and Anita. "Now, what's all this about? A tempest in a teapot, no doubt."

"Hardly, dear." Gilberta took a deep breath. "Jules Marston is dead."

"Oh, my *God! How?"*

"The police aren't sure. They think he either committed suicide or . . ."

"Or what?" Jeanette demanded.

"Or . . . was murdered."

To Gilberta's complete surprise, Jeanette covered her face with her hands and began to cry. Gilberta had believed, up until this moment, that her stepdaughter disliked and resented Jules; she was certain Jeanette suspected that she and Jules were having an affair.

"Darling, we *all* feel terrible about it." She put a comforting arm around the girl's shoulders.

Jeanette tensed at her touch and pulled herself together quickly. She wiped her eyes and said in a controlled voice, "I'm sorry for acting the gushy baby, but it's such a shock. I mean, I always thought of him as being . . . oh, I don't know . . ."

"Immortal. . . . Yes, Jules had that aura of immortality about him. That's what makes it so impossible to believe. But believe it we must."

"I feel so . . . drained, exhausted," Anita said as they headed for the elevator.

"A nap will do us all good," Gilberta replied. "Then we'll go out for a late supper. I'll call your room around seven."

But there could be no sleep for Gilberta—not just yet. . . .

Back in her suite at the Essex House, Gilberta hurriedly changed into gray slacks and a white silk shirt and donned a pair of aviator sunglasses that covered almost half her face. The premature discovery of Jules's body required that she revise her timetable. Sometime —possibly even at this very moment—the superintendent was going to discover that the truck was missing from its basement parking slot, and he would inform the police. The make, model, year, and license-plate number were on record in the rental agent's office. Captain Laurentis would issue an all-points bulletin, and in a matter of hours the truck would be located. It was imperative that she get rid of it immediately. Pausing only long enough to grab her purse, she rushed out of the suite.

She had no trouble getting a cab; the streets of the city were relatively deserted.

"Everybody's down by the waterfront watching the Tall Ships," the cabbie told her.

He dropped her at the public garage where she had left the truck earlier in the day. Gilberta rummaged in her purse for the ticket, took a deep breath, and purposefully walked up to the attendants' booth. Smothering a yawn with the back of her hand and leaning on the counter nonchalantly, the picture of boredom, she laid the ticket on the counter, along with a twenty-dollar bill. Inside, her heart was racing as adrenaline pumped through her veins. She picked up her change with trembling fingers.

For all she knew, the police had already located the truck and had the garage staked out, waiting for the owner to claim it. She gritted her teeth as the nose of the truck appeared around a bend in the ramp, half expecting to see Captain Laurentis and Lieutenant Cavelli sitting in the front seat. When it braked to a stop and the attendant hopped out of the driver's seat, she was so relieved she handed him a five-dollar bill.

"Hey, *thanks,* lady."

Brushing past him, she climbed into the van, shoved it into gear, jammed her foot down on the accelerator, and sped out of the garage. She was limp as a piece of wet spaghetti and perspiring heavily, a physical condition atypical of Gilberta.

She drove across town on Forty-second Street and then uptown on Riverside Drive, past Columbia University. Finally she turned into a side street seeking a vulnerable place to ditch the truck.

Ah, here we go, she said to herself when she came to a block where a gang of youths were throwing a baseball back and forth. Halfway, she pulled over to the curb, into an illegal parking zone, and climbed out of the truck, leaving the key in the ignition. Then she went around to the back and slipped a key into the lock that secured the van door, and hurried back down the block in the direction of Riverside Drive. Five minutes later, she was in a cab on her way back to the Essex House.

Safe in the suite at last, she poured herself a stiff scotch and drank it and another while waiting for the tub to fill. Just ten hours ago, she had been on the terrace atop the Towers with Jules Marston, gazing out at the Tall Ships in the harbor. Ten hours—it seemed like an eternity. This terrible day would never end.

The jangle of the phone startled her. Certain it must be Anita, she picked it up and said confidently, "Hello, dear."

There was silence at the caller's end.

"Hello . . . hello . . ." she repeated impatiently. "Are you there, Anita?"

"I'm afraid not," a masculine voice replied. "This is Captain Laurentis, Mrs. Killington. I'm sorry to bother you so soon after the ordeal we put you through this afternoon, but after Lieutenant Cavelli and I went back to the precinct, I realized that we had overlooked something very important when we questioned you and Miss Thatcher. . . . I'd be extremely grateful if you could spare me a little more of your time. It shouldn't take more than five or ten minutes. Would you care to come down to the lobby and join me in a drink or a cup of coffee?"

Gilberta hesitated. "Well . . . I was just about to take a bath."

"That's all right," he assured her. "Take all the time you want. I'll read a magazine."

She bit her underlip thoughtfully, then made up her mind. "Captain, I really don't feel like getting dressed again. . . . Look, why don't you come up here? I have scotch, if that's satisfactory."

"More than satisfactory. I could use a drink after the day I've put in. Say, a half-hour? Then you don't have to rush your bath."

She gave him the room number, continuing to hold the receiver to her ear though he'd already hung up. Everything had gone off without a hitch—the trips to the basement garage of the Towers, her speech, the dumping of the truck.

Or had it?

CHAPTER SEVEN

When Laurentis arrived punctually a half-hour later, Gilberta greeted him at the door, wearing over her black silk panties and camisole a balloon-sleeved negligee of pale-peach silk organza trimmed with dotted-Swiss lace.

"Well, hello again," she said. "Please come in."

Laurentis had marvelous teeth and a boyish smile that belied his somber profession. "I truly apologize for bothering you at this hour, but it *is* important, and I know you're leaving in the morning."

"That's perfectly all right, Captain." She led him to the sofa, handed him a scotch and soda, and then sat down in the wing chair opposite him. "Cheers." She lifted her glass.

"Prosit." He took a long swallow and put his glass down on the coffee table to light a cigarette.

Gilberta drew her legs up underneath her and gazed at him thoughtfully. "Now, what is this important matter you neglected to bring up when we spoke this afternoon?"

He shook his head and looked sheepish. "You're going to think I'm one dumb cop when I tell you."

Sure, she thought. *Dumb like a fox!* "I doubt that."

"I forgot to ask you whether Jules Marston had any enemies—I mean, the sort who might wish him dead."

Gilberta threw back her head and laughed. "You have *got* to be kidding, Captain."

His eyebrows lifted. "What's so funny?"

"I'm sorry; it really isn't funny at all. But a man like Jules Marston, a man who clawed his way to the top of the heap over the bodies of his competitors, a ruthless man who commanded so much power and money—he was bound to have enemies. You might just as well ask if the Kennedys have enemies."

"I understand. . . . Well, could you name a few off the top of the list?"

"I could, but I think you'd do better to ask Milos Alansky about Jules's enemies. As Jules's strong right hand, he's in a much better position to know what went on behind the scenes, in both Jules's professional life and personal life."

"I'll do that," he said, and made a move to get up.

"No, don't leave. Finish your drink."

"You must have plans."

"Only a late supper with my stepdaughter and my secretary."

"Yes, your stepdaughter. . . . Have you notified Governor Killington regarding Mr. Marston's death?"

Gilberta sighed and looked unhappy. "No . . . I've been postponing that chore. I don't want to ruin my husband's gala Bicentennial day. I'll inform him later tonight. . . . You see, as I mentioned to you earlier, he and Jules were very dear personal friends."

"So you said."

There was an uncomfortable gap in the conversation. Laurentis stared into his glass, swirling the amber liquid around the melting ice cube.

"Captain Laurentis"—Gilberta broke the silence—

"if you'll forgive me for saying so, you don't strike me as being the type of man who would make police work a career."

He grinned. "Why do you say that?"

"Oh, I don't know. . . . Somehow I see you in a tweed jacket with leather elbow patches, sitting behind a professor's desk in an Ivy League college."

"That's pretty fair detective work, Mrs. Killington. I actually came close to taking that route. I majored in criminal law at Harvard. Then, in my junior year, there was a Rhodes scholarship. It was in England that I became interested in criminal psychology, so I switched my major. When I returned to the States, I was offered a position on the Harvard faculty, and after some deliberation, I decided not to accept it. . . . You see, I came to realize that the only way to truly get inside the criminal mind is at the grass-roots level. That's why I joined the force."

Gilberta's eyes were wide. "I'm astonished . . . and immensely impressed."

"Don't be. There are more and more college graduates, who feel as I do, who are joining the department every year." He stood up reluctantly. "Now, I really do have to go. Got to check in at the precinct."

Gilberta stood up and saw him to the door. "I wish I could have been of some help," she said.

"You were. Thanks for seeing me." He had taken no more than three steps along the hotel corridor when she called to him:

"Captain . . ."

He turned and looked at her leaning against the door, with her cheek resting against the edge.

"You really didn't have to come all the way up here to ask me that question."

"I know that," he said candidly. "I wanted to see you again."

She smiled coquettishly. "Did you, now?"

"You're a very beautiful woman, Mrs. Killington. Don't misunderstand me; I'm not coming on to you. I feel about you the way I feel in the presence of a work of art. You give immense satisfaction and enjoyment to those who look at you."

"That's very sweet, Captain, although I'm disappointed that I do not stimulate a more . . . emotional response in you as well."

"Oh, but you do," he said quickly. "Unhappily, you are a married woman."

"Yes, I am. . . . What about you?"

"Divorced. Cecile abhorred being married to a 'pig,' as she liked to refer to me."

"That's too bad. She must have been a stupid woman to let a man like you get away."

Something flashed across his face, an expression she could not fathom. "Thank you for bolstering a faltering ego."

"Wait just a minute, Captain; I'll be right back."

Leaving the door ajar, she went back into the bedroom and took a business card from her desk. She brought it back and handed it to Laurentis.

"I'll be back in New York next Thursday for a couple of days on business. This is my number at the office. Why don't you call me, say Friday, before noon, and we can have lunch. I'll be anxious to hear what progress you've made on Jules's case. Neither the governor nor I will be able to rest until his murderer is caught and punished."

"I understand. . . . You can depend on it. I'll phone you next Friday, Mrs. Killington."

She smiled. "Let's make it 'Gilly'; that's what my friends call me."

"I'd like to be your friend . . . Gilly." He locked eyes with her. "Well, then, *auf wiedersehen.*"

" 'Till we meet again,' " she translated. "That's so much nicer than 'good-by.' *Auf wiedersehen* . . . George."

She closed the door and leaned back against it, aware that her heart was beating unnaturally fast. There was no denying it—she had felt it earlier this afternoon: there was definitely a powerful chemistry at work between her and Captain Laurentis!

She went into the bedroom and phoned Anita from the bedside extension.

"I just woke up," Anita said in a slurred voice. "Jeanette is in the shower."

"Don't rush. When you're both ready, come down here. I'll make a reservation for dinner. Any preferences?"

"How about Sardi's? I could use a little pick-me-up."

"Fine with me. See you later."

It hadn't occurred to her to mention the captain's visit to Anita. If she were to tell her the reason he gave, Anita would only jump to the wrong conclusions. *Strike that; the* right *conclusions.*

She was laying out her clothes for the evening when the phone rang. It was Harmon, and he was distraught:

"Gilly . . . I've been trying to reach you since Saturday morning! And now I just heard the news on the radio, about Jules. You knew, of course?"

"Yes, since early this afternoon. I'm sorry you couldn't reach me yesterday, darling, but I was frantic over my speech and at the last moment decided to go up to the cabin, where I wouldn't be distracted. I was hoping you wouldn't learn about Jules's death until after your day was over."

"You should have let me know, anyway."

"What would have been the point? He's dead, and nothing anyone can do will bring him back."

"Do the police have any idea what *really* happened?"

"You don't buy the suicide theory any more than Anita and I do?"

"Of course not. Jules would never kill himself."

"That's what we've been telling the police, and I think they're becoming convinced that we're right."

"The police have questioned you, then?"

"Yes; both of us. And next they'll be questioning Milos. He's flying in from Palm Springs tonight or tomorrow. Poor Milos; he's probably a wreck. I really wish I could see him. If anyone could shed light on this whole horrible affair, *he* could."

What she couldn't tell Harmon was that she was anxious to see Milos before the police did!

"Why don't you stay over another day, then?"

"I don't think Jeanette will like the idea. She's turned off by New York."

"Then, let her come back tomorrow. . . . Listen, Gilly, I saw you on the six o'clock news. You were terrific." A sly edge to his voice: "You'll make a great First Lady one day."

"Flattery will get you everywhere. . . . Look, dear, I've got to take Anita and Jeanette out to supper. I'll stay over one more day, and I'll phone you after I talk to Milos."

"Good girl. Enjoy your supper and give Jen a big kiss for me."

"Will do. Good-by, Governor."

He chuckled. "Sleep tight. Love you, sweetie."

"Me too."

Supper at Sardi's was not the festive affair Anita had envisioned. Jules Marston's death dominated their conversation, and when Gilberta repeatedly suggested that they change the subject, talk ceased altogether. All three of them listlessly picked at their food, and they left the restaurant without ordering dessert or coffee.

"I napped for two hours and I'm still bushed," Jeanette said.

Anita nodded. "What we all need is a full night's sleep."

Once back at the hotel, they didn't even have a nightcap but went directly to their rooms. Gilberta found a message slipped under the door, asking her to phone Milos Alansky at the Plaza Hotel.

She dialed the number after she'd poured herself a brandy. His voice, when he answered, sounded strained:

"Is that you, Gilly?"

"Yes, Milos. Are you . . . are you all right?"

"Not too bad, under the circumstances." He hesitated. "Actually, I feel like hell. Can you have a drink with me? I think it's important that we talk . . . before I speak with the police tomorrow, a Captain Laurentis."

"Yes; I met the good captain. Of course we can talk. I'll meet you in the bar downstairs. Ten minutes?"

"I'll be there."

Bracing herself, she left the room and took the elevator down to the lobby.

The bar was not crowded, and she had no trouble finding an empty booth way off in the corner. She ordered a brandy and lit a cigarette. Milos arrived before the drink was served. He stood in the doorway, squinting around the dimly lit room through thick lenses with heavy black frames. Gilberta smiled and waved.

"I know how difficult this must be for you, Gilly," he said, pecking her on the cheek and sliding next to her in the booth.

"For you, too."

"A calamity."

The waiter served Gilberta, and Milos ordered Grand Marnier on the rocks.

"Now, tell me about it from the beginning, from the instant you and Jules met at the apartment."

"Well . . . I got there around noon on Saturday. Jules was already there. That day and night were uneventful. We never left the penthouse. . . ."

She recounted in minute detail all that had transpired, ending with the traumatic moment when she walked out onto the terrace and discovered Jules's body.

Milos's brow furrowed. "That phone call he made —you said he appeared to be disturbed afterward."

"Yes; he was unusually tense. Even after we made love, he seemed preoccupied, far away."

Milos didn't blink an eye at her candor. "Hmmm . . . You're *sure* it wasn't your brother he was calling?"

"Positive. I made a little joke about eavesdropping, and he looked . . . I don't know, grim. Said he didn't want me to. Now, if it was Terry he was calling, and about that land deal in Idaho, he wouldn't have *cared* if I'd listened in. Which, of course, I had no intention of doing."

Milos took a cigar out of his breast pocket and rolled it around in his lips to moisten the end. "Do you realize, Gilly, that whoever murdered Jules—and I'm sure it *was* murder—was with you all the while before you left the penthouse?"

She hugged her arms across her chest and shuddered. "All too vividly. I keep wondering why he didn't kill me, too."

"It would ruin his plan, as I see it."

"What plan?"

"To make it appear that Jules committed suicide. And it looks as though he accomplished his purpose. I doubt the police can prove that his head was bashed in before he was hurled off the terrace."

"Not unless I tell them."

Alarm showed in his black eyes, magnified by the thick lenses. "Gilly, don't make bad jokes. There's nothing to be gained by incriminating yourself. And it would without doubt ruin your husband's political career."

She sighed. "You're right, of course. It wouldn't be fair to Harmon."

"Believe me, Jules would want you to remain anonymous. He detested martyrs."

She smiled. "Yes, I know."

"Dead is dead, he used to say. The only thing you can do for the dead is bury them. . . . Gilly, I can't tell you how much I admire the cool-headed manner in which you acted in the aftermath of Jules's death. Clearing out all evidence of your presence in the apartment—that was smart, took guts. . . . You're certain you thought of everything?"

"If the police had found anything to connect me with Julie, I'd be in custody by now."

"I suppose so." He frowned and rolled the cigar around from one side of his mouth to the other. "One thing bothers me: the van. It was risky, abandoning it that way."

She shook her head. "Not at all. I'd stake my life on it, that van was stripped five minutes after I left it."

"I hope you're right."

"What do you intend to tell Captain Laurentis tomorrow?"

"Exactly what Jules and I determined I'd say in the event of any emergency: that I leased the apartment and Jules had an open invitation to use it whenever he was in New York, which was often. If you hadn't removed your possessions, I would claim that they belong to a friend of mine, who, being the wife of a state-supreme-court judge, must remain anonymous."

Gilberta covered his hand with hers. "Dear, loyal Milos . . . Do you know what Jules said shortly before he died? He said that you were closer to him than either of his brothers."

Milos's eyes misted over. "I felt the same way about Jules. I'm going to miss him."

"Yes. . . . Life will never be quite the same again without him."

He let out a long, shuddering sigh. "But, as he said, dead is dead. We will bury him and get on with life."

"I assume you'll be taking care of the funeral arrangements," she said softly.

He nodded. "Were you planning to go home tomorrow?"

"Well, yes, unless . . . Will the funeral be tomorrow, do you think?"

"Probably Tuesday. Do you suppose you could postpone your flight?"

"I don't know, Milos; Harmon's expecting me. I could be back in New York Tuesday morning." Seeing his crestfallen look, she added, "Well, I'll think about it."

His face brightened somewhat, then grew serious again. "I don't know if Jules ever had occasion to mention this to you, but he appointed me executor of his will."

"I'm not at all surprised," she said, squeezing his hand.

"*This* may surprise you. He made handsome bequests both to Harmon and to your stepdaughter, Jeanette."

Gilberta was astonished. "Are you serious?"

"Absolutely. A million dollars apiece."

"A million—— But why, Milos? They don't need

the money, for one thing. More to the point, while Harmon and Julie were good friends, they weren't *that* close."

"There was a side to Jules that he never revealed to anyone. Not even you," he added gently. When she looked at him questioningly, he went on: "Jules was a man with very high standards, values, a man of conscience. If you were his friend, he . . . his sense of obligation . . ."

He was floundering badly, and Gilberta rescued him with her candor:

"What you are trying to tell me is that he felt he owed my husband a debt because of me."

Milos could not meet her level gaze. "That's part of it, certainly. But also he was aware of your high ambitions for Harmon, and thought he'd have an excellent political future but for one handicap: your wealth."

"That's preposterous!"

"Not really. He wouldn't be the first to believe that without financial independence, a politician is vulnerable to temptation from those who try to barter favors for monetary recompense. He wanted Harmon to be above such temptation."

Gilberta was still skeptical. "Yes . . . I can see his point, but I know Harmon, and he's not the kind of man to stoop to a bribe, or to any other form of deceit, for that matter. In any event, it doesn't explain why Julie included Jeanette in his will." She snorted. "I assure you, she has no intention of running for office."

Jules had always said that Milos Alansky was the most honest man he had ever met. If Gilberta had any reason to doubt his evaluation, Milos dispelled the doubt once and for all. Looking her straight in the eye, he replied:

"Two years ago, Jules had an affair with Jeanette.

He broke it off when he met you. As I said, Jules was a man of conscience."

Gilberta clasped her hands against the sides of her head to arrest the sensation that it was about to shatter into a million pieces. "Jules and *Jeanette?* It's too incredible."

She didn't want to believe it, but she did: remembrance of things past; conflicts between her and her stepdaughter ever since she had taken Jules as a lover. While her relationship with Jeanette in the ten years she'd been married to Harmon had never been affectionate, they had always treated each other with mutual respect, and strove to preserve an illusion of family harmony. But lately Jeanette had become moody, surly, and outright rude on occasion. Now it all made sense. That the girl suspected Gilberta and Jules of being lovers was confirmed now in Gilly's mind. But that her resentment was over her father's being cuckolded was only half the story; first and foremost, Jeanette hated Gilberta for taking Jules away from her.

She downed her drink and asked Milos to order her another. "I may require a dozen more, if you've got any more surprises up your sleeve."

"I'm sorry, Gilly. Jules used to say there was only one way to serve up whiskey or bad news—straight."

"He was right, and so were you to tell me." Her eyes narrowed. "But why *did* you tell me, Milos? I mean, I'm not family—Jules owed me nothing—and you certainly are under no obligation to me."

"Obligation, no; but there's no doubt that you're in a compromising position, and I think you deserve to know anything that might have a bearing on Jules's murder."

"You don't think that *Jeanette* had anything to do with it?"

"Quite frankly, I don't know, but I'll keep you advised of everything I find out."

"Find out?"

"I've engaged a private investigation team to work on the case."

"The police may not like that."

He shrugged. "If this Captain Laurentis is realistic, he'll welcome having a back-up team working in conjunction with his department. God knows those boys are understaffed and overworked." He toyed with a pack of matches. "Speaking of which, Gilly, I think it would be advisable for you to have some sort of protection, just till this mess is resolved."

"Milos, that's the most absurd thing I've ever heard! Look, the murderer had his golden chance right after he killed Jules to do me in as well. It proves beyond a shadow of a doubt that he has no designs on *my* life."

"Not then. *Now* is a different story. Look, Gilly, my guess is that he didn't expect to find anyone but Jules in the apartment, and when he realized you were there, he had to do some quick thinking. As I said before, obviously his plan was to make Jules's death appear a suicide, so he couldn't kill you, too. He could only hope that when you discovered the body, you'd panic and beat it out of there as fast as you could. Of course, he was taking a big gamble: you might have called the police. But you didn't; you played right into his hands. He waited all the time you were clearing out your things, and as soon as he saw you leave for good, he threw Jules's body off the terrace."

"And you think he'll come after me now?"

"Well . . . you *are* the only one—you and the murderer, that is—who knows that Jules *didn't* commit suicide." He removed his glasses and rubbed his eyes. "But maybe . . ."

"Maybe?" she prompted him.

"He doesn't *have* to kill you. An anonymous phone call to the police, informing them that Mrs. Harmon Killington was in Milos Alansky's apartment on the morning of July Fourth. . . . They'd be bound to put two and two together and realize that you, Gilly, were Jules's mistress—the fictitious Mrs. Alansky—and they might even take it a step further, assume that *you* killed him and——"

"My God, Milos! That's insane!"

"Is it? There are more things in heaven and earth, Gilly, than are dreamt of in your philosophy, to plagiarize the Bard. You've got to face it: you're in very real jeopardy."

"But you're assuming the killer knows my name."

"If he doesn't already, he will by tomorrow. After the speech you gave today, your face will be in all the newspapers, on TV . . . I'll bet the public already saw you on the six o'clock news."

"If you're trying to frighten me, Milos——"

"I *am*—so that you'll keep your guard up. Remember: as we say in tennis, it's match point and the advantage is his. Chances are he already knows who you are, but you have no idea of *his* identity." He glanced at his watch. "Say, it's late. We both better get to bed. Shall I see you up to your room?"

"No . . . thank you, Milos. I feel perfectly safe here."

He walked her to the elevator. "I wish you'd take what I said seriously—about protection."

"I won't hear of it. I'll be damned if I'm going to let this turn me into a raving paranoid." She kissed his cheek. "Good night, Milos, and thank you for everything. We'll talk tomorrow."

She was punch-drunk from emotional and physical fatigue. Back in the suite, she quickly undressed, leaving all her clothes in a disarrayed heap on the floor, and, without even washing up or brushing her teeth, staggered into bed and collapsed.

Total exhaustion had carried her past the threshold of sleep. She lay on her back, staring at the ceiling, her body rigid as a board. Gradually a carousel appeared in her mind's eye, racing dizzily, like her thoughts, the plastic horses circling, moving up and down in piston rhythm, sightless eyes bulging, their faces set in demoniac leers. She shut her eyes. The faces were still there, but human now. She recognized Julie, Harmon, Anita, Jeanette, Laurentis, and, closer to the axis, faces out of the past: her mother Linda's; her great-grandmother Tara's . . .

Tara—the bastard.

The faces disappeared, and Gilberta sank into a deep, tormented dream. . . .

CHAPTER EIGHT

Tara De Beers Parker was not fair like her mother and grandmother. She inherited the bloodline of her paternal grandmother, who was part Cheyenne Indian. At the age of twelve, she towered over Karen and Mina.

"You and Colorado were born on the same day," Lars told her, "and you are growing as fast as the Centennial State."

A slender, willowy girl with a dark complexion and striking violet eyes. High cheekbones and an aquiline nose along with straight black hair that fell to her buttocks were testimony of her partial Indian heritage. A heritage of which Tara was deeply proud.

She fell in love with horses the first time she set eyes on one, and she could ride before she could walk. On her twelfth birthday, Lars presented her with a palomino stallion the color of pale honey. She would never ride another horse again so long as "Rascal" lived.

The two were inseparable, and summer or winter, Tara would make distant rides into the mountains or across the amber plains. She and Rascal were a common sight to the prospectors, explorers, and travelers who traversed the region around Silver City. A part of the wilderness, they seemed: horse and rider silhouetted against the blue sky on a high ridge, often in the company of friendly Arapaho or Shoshone Indians.

Tara was more at home in the woods and mountains than she was on the opulent De Beers estate; more comfortable in a man's woolen work shirt and durable denim trousers and boots than she was in a feminine frock and patent-leather dress shoes.

"It's time you outgrew being a tomboy," Mina said to her one evening shortly before they were to have dinner. "You are a young lady now and you must behave like one. Boys like feminine girls."

Tara paraded up and down the sitting room in mock imitation of a "feminine" girl, fluttering her eyelashes and wiggling her hips. "Here I am, all you big, strong, manly boys," she said in a piping voice, "little Miss Femininity herself. Ain't I purty in my ruffled dress? Want to see my sissy drawers?"

"Tara!" Mina exclaimed in shock. "Don't you *ever* use such language in front of the opposite sex."

"You mean drawers?" the girl asked innocently.

Grandfather and Uncle Nils were trying vainly to stifle their laughter.

"Never mind, tell your mother supper will be ready soon."

Overnight wealth had not spoiled Mina De Beers. She flatly refused to hire a cook despite her husband's protestations. Although his perseverance compelled her to accept a housemaid and a butler.

When Tara returned from upstairs, Lars inquired: "What is your mama doing?"

Tara was as stoic as an Indian. "She is writing a letter to—"

No need to complete the statement. She was writing

to her beloved "husband." In Denver or in New York or in Washington, D.C. She even wrote letters abroad.

In all other respects Karen De Beers Parker appeared to be a perfectly normal, healthy woman.

At school, Tara had the reputation of being a loner. Though courteous and responsive when addressed by teachers, she was aloof and withdrawn from her schoolmates. She had no close girl friends among her peers. As for her relationship with the boys, they were wary of the tall, hard-muscled girl with the proud carriage and the intimidating violet eyes.

Behind the schoolhouse, there was a rectangular outhouse partitioned in half for boys and girls. One day during the lunch hour there was a class picnic at a nearby pond. Tara finished her sandwich quickly and walked back to the school. She went down the winding path that led through a pine grove to the outhouse. She locked the door of the girls' room, unfastened her belt, and unbuttoned the front of her denim trousers. She was just pulling down her white cotton drawers when her eye was distracted by a curiosity on the wooden wall to her right. She'd seen the knothole any number of times, only this time there was something odd about it. It took her a moment's observation to detect what was different: the knot was missing!

Blushing furiously, Tara yanked up her pants and buckled her belt. She threw open the door and went outside. Purposefully, she flung open the door of the boys' room and was instantly transfixed by shame and embarrassment.

Kneeling on the floor at eye level with the hole in the wall was a boy named Eddie Smythe. His trousers were tangled about his knees, and the fingers of one hand were encircling his hard, upright penis.

Tara could only stand there, mouth agape, staring at what she then regarded as grotesque. At thirteen, she was acquainted with the physical differences between male and female, as well as with the "facts of life," as her grandmother Mina delicately referred to sexuality. But she had only a vague concept of the mechanics of sex. Now, suddenly, it struck her that this phenomenon she was observing was what made coupling between men and women possible.

Her voice quavered with indignation as she stomped a foot and braced her hands on her hips. "Eddie Smythe, you dirty little snot-nosed peeping Tom! Pull up your pants and hide that filthy thing!"

Red and mortified, the boy leaped to his feet and drew up his pants. With trembling fingers he buttoned his fly and buckled his belt. Trying to restore his dignity, he complained, "What do you mean, busting in on me like this? I wasn't doing anything."

"I know perfectly well what you were doing. Come on out of there."

Tara was a full head taller than Eddie and physically more formidable. As he brushed past her on his way out, she gave him a resounding clout on the side of the head that sent him sprawling. Yowling like a tomcat with a can tied to its tail, he scrambled up on all fours and fled back down the path, with Tara right on his heels. She caught up to him and slammed a heavy boot against his buttocks. Again he went sprawling.

"You leave me alone, you bitch!" he cried, and tried to get up. Another well-placed kick sent him headlong once more.

Deciding he had had enough, Tara stalked off with her nose in the air.

For days afterward, Tara could not shake off the memory of that electrifying scene in the outhouse: Eddie kneeling there rubbing his . . . "thing," was all she knew to call it. One day he would put that *thing* inside a girl and plant the seed that would make a baby.

Tara was faithful to her vow throughout her teens and into her early twenties, though not for lack of suitors, most of whom were from the ranks of Denver's growing social aristocracy, heirs to industrial and agricultural fortunes made by their pioneer grandfathers. While at finishing school in Denver, she did make certain concessions to convention and the social graces, attending teas and dances, where she exchanged idle banter with the other girls and waltzed with the young men. But, as summer vacation approached, she was like a caged wild animal straining to be set free. She couldn't wait to fling off her frock, her silk undergarments, her stockings and garters and narrow, uncomfortable shoes; couldn't wait to don her tomboy trousers, shirt, and boots and ride off into the hills on Rascal.

If she lacked ambition for mathematics, literature, and other classic subjects taught at the school, Tara applied herself zealously to learning the internal affairs of the De Beers Mining and Development Corporation, whose main offices were contained in a five-story building in the heart of Silver City.

At seventy, Lars De Beers had relegated himself to the role of figurehead chief of the firm, leaving major decisions in the hands of his son, Nils, now forty-six, with a family of his own. After her second year at school, Tara sacrificed her glorious vacations spent exploring the wonders of nature in the hills of home in order that she might work full time for the corporation. She took to business the way the proverbial duck takes to water.

"She's absolutely amazing," Nils told his father. "At first the other office workers, notably the men, resented her employment, but within one month she won their respect and friendship. Every department head is vying for her services"—he laughed—"but they're out of luck. I'm the boss, and I want Tara for my executive assistant. That way, too, she'll learn the inside track on corporate planning."

The old man looked grave. "You mean she's not going to finish school first?"

"She rejects it unequivocally, says it's a waste of time, and I'm inclined to agree with her. De Beers—*that's* where her future lies. . . . There is another consideration, and I wouldn't bring it up to anyone but you, Father. I had a physical examination last week, and Dr. Lewis warned me to take things easier than I have been. It's my heart. Now, don't look so horrified. I'm not going to give up the ghost for a long time, but better to be safe than sorry. What I mean is, it will be a while yet before either my little Karl or Tess can step into my shoes; and Karen is out of the question, naturally, which leaves Tara. With her natural ability and driving ambition, she'll be my strong right-hand man—I should say *woman*—within a year."

Thanksgiving was almost the gala occasion that Christmas was for the De Beers family.

"We have more than most to be thankful for," Lars, the clan patriarch, declared as they drank a pre-dinner toast. "We came to this wonderful country as outcasts, just as did the Pilgrims, and here we are gathered together today, surrounded by so much abundance and happiness."

They drank in reverent silence and took their places at the long table: Lars and Mina at either end; Karen, Tara, and Nils's son, Karl, on one side; Nils and his wife, Marjorie, and their daughter, Tess, on the other.

The upper-class women of Denver being no less sophisticated than their sisters in New York or Paris, Mina, Karen, and Marjorie sported the high fashion of the era: bell skirts worn over boned corsets that gave them wasp waists, and lacy, ruffled, high-necked blouses with leg-o'-mutton sleeves. Only Tara refused to submit to the tyranny of the corset. She was wearing an ankle-length woolen gingham dress—small black squares against a scarlet background—that had pearl buttons running from throat to waist and a deep hemline flounce.

Conversation was animated throughout the meal—a veritable feast, consisting of poached salmon; pea soup laced with ham and bacon; roast turkey; candied yams and a variety of green vegetables; imported French wine and apple cider. As it always did at family gatherings, the topic of conversation eventually centered on Tara's single state.

"If you don't grab a man before it's too late, you're going to be left on the shelf," Nils teased.

"There's not a man in Colorado good enough for my little Tara," Lars said staunchly.

"Little girl?" Karen threw up her hands. "She's twenty-two years old, or soon will be. So many nice young men have courted her, but she puts them all off."

"Oh, *Mother,*" Tara said irritably. "One day I may decide to marry; but right now all of my time is occupied with my career."

"Career!" Mina was shocked. "I don't know what the younger generation is coming to. Imagine, Lars, a refined, genteel young woman speaking about a *career?*"

"You make it sound obscene, Grandma. In your day, the only career open to a female was walking the streets. That's changed, and it's going to continue to change. I consider myself the intellectual equal of any man, and I intend to receive equal recompense for my contributions to the world of commerce and industry."

"Wait till your father hears about this," Karen warned her. "I must insist that he write you and give you his views on the subject."

There was an uneasy silence, and the festive atmosphere was considerably diminished. Karen's statement served to remind the others that there was one blemish on their spirit of thanksgiving.

White-faced, Tara pushed back her chair and stood up. "Will you all please excuse me? I must have some exercise to work off this mammoth feast. I think I shall burst if I even look at another morsel of food."

"You mustn't leave now, darling," Mina implored. "I made your favorite—custard pie."

Tara stooped to kiss her grandmother on the top of the head. "Later, Grandma, after I digest what I've stuffed into myself. I feel like the turkey."

"Where are you going?" Lars inquired.

"I'll change and take Rascal out for his daily constitutional. He hasn't been getting enough exercise since I went to work for the firm. I'll see you all later." She waved and left the dining room.

It was bitter cold this Thanksgiving day, with a biting wind blowing in from the northwest. Tara was dressed in long woolen underwear, heavy work pants, a flannel shirt, two sweaters, and a thick knee-length mackinaw lined with lamb's wool. On her head was a heavy woolen scarf, tied babushka style. Still, when the wind gusted, it cut right through to her bones, and even Rascal's sides shivered against her thighs. It should have served as a warning; but even as a sudden shower of snow pellets stung her face like blowing sand on the summer desert, Tara urged Rascal forward: "Let's go up the North Fork, feller."

Obedient to the tug on the reins, the horse started up a trail through a winding ravine that made a gradual ascent into the foothills of the Rocky Mountains.

The snow was falling harder now and the wind rising sharply, but, owing to a thick umbrella of aspen boughs over the ravine, Tara was oblivious to the ominous shift in weather. Near the summit of the high hill, they broke out into the open, and the full fury of the storm attacked them.

For a moment Tara couldn't breathe as the snow was driven into her eyes and mouth. Dropping the reins and using her hands in front of her face as a barrier, she screamed above the banshee wail of the wind, "Come on, boy, we'd better go back! Looks like a blizzard sneaked up on us!"

Rascal, spooked momentarily by the sudden onslaught, whinnied and nervously made several full turns.

"Steady, boy! Steady." She bent low over his neck and caressed him with her hands in an endeavor to calm him down. When he finally quieted down, she grasped the reins and slapped him gently on his side. "Here we go."

Rascal went back into the woods, and the welcome refuge of the trees heartened Tara. "Once we reach the river, we'll be fine," she mused. "Just follow it back to town."

A little farther along, however, she was dealt a rude shock. Without warning, the trail narrowed and soon ended altogether at a barrier of solid brush and trees. Her heart began to beat faster as she looked in vain for an opening. Too much of a woodswoman to panic, she nevertheless appreciated the very serious danger she was now confronting. In desperation, she turned the horse around and started back up the hill to the ridge. Once again the snow and wind assaulted them as they emerged into the open.

"What we have to do, Rascal, is keep moving to the left, try the next trail down. Sooner or later we have to find the right one."

Without a fixed point of reference, man, with his limited senses, is as helpless in the middle of the desert or in a blinding snowstorm as he would be cast away in outer space. It was no different for Tara. On the third excursion downhill, they reached another impasse. No, not "another"; the *same,* she realized with a sinking heart. There, still fresh in the protected snow beneath the leafy canopy, were the hoofprints of a horse—Rascal's!

"That does it, old feller. We're good and lost. Only thing we can do now is wait it out."

She dismounted, and holding Rascal by the bridle, she led him back up the trail until she reached a spot, about twenty yards into the woods, that offered maximum protection against the snow and wind. It was a small clearing rimmed by three large tree boles that were flanked by clusters of stunted fir trees, a natural lean-to. She removed the saddle blanket and saddle, along with the two saddlebags, and placed them on the ground. Then she unfolded the blanket and spread it the length of Rascal's back.

"That'll keep you warm some."

One of the saddlebags contained oats; the other dried beef, hard biscuits, coffee, a jug of water, and matches in a waterproof pouch. She withdrew the matches, set the bag of oats before Rascal, and went about gathering fuel for a fire. In minutes she had all she needed. The forest floor, littered with the duff of centuries, provided a bounty of dried twigs, pine needles, and larger branches, all of it bone dry because of the sub-freezing temperature. Wind was the only deterrent. It required four of the precious matches before she was able to ignite the pile of litter within her sanctuary. When it was a healthy blaze, she piled on a few of the larger branches, and in no time she had a roaring inferno warming her near-frozen fingers and toes and lighting up the area all around her. After his meal, Rascal came over and turned his rump to the flames.

Tara gave him an affectionate slap on the flank. "Who says horses are dumb? Hell, I know plenty of people who are too dumb to come in out of the rain." She nibbled on the cold meat and biscuits, washing the food down with coffee she brewed in a small saucepan over the fire. "All the comforts of home, eh, Rascal?"

Minutes later, her eyelids growing heavy, she removed a thin spare blanket from the saddlebag, wrapped it around her, and settled back against the stout tree bole. The frenzied wind tearing through the crown of the forest was a demoniac symphony that lulled her into deep sleep.

CHAPTER NINE

She awoke with a start in near-total darkness. The dying embers of the fire glared at her like devil's eyes. The snow filtering down through the branches had covered her legs, and, from the sound of it, the storm was raging more fiercely than ever.

Tara stood up, shook out the blanket, and brushed off her clothing. Gathering more branches and duff, she stoked the ebbing fire, and within minutes it was blazing brightly once again. She brushed the snow off Rascal and gave him some more oats. Breaking out her own supplies, she brewed another saucepan of coffee and finished off the jerky and biscuits.

"It's got to break soon," she said aloud; but there was a nagging doubt inside her. Colorado blizzards had been known to go on for days, even weeks. She shook her head to clear it of such pessimistic speculation. *Think positive, my girl.*

For a long while she sat cross-legged in front of the fire, wrapped in the blanket, hypnotized by the changing patterns of the flames. And then, suddenly, above the din of the storm, she thought she detected another, different sound. Abruptly she sat bolt upright, ears straining. Again she heard it—a sound as of twigs snapping underfoot. Someone—some*thing*—was coming up the trail! A mountain lion, was her first thought; no human creature would be prowling around in a blizzard. With a chill that had nothing to do with the cold, she realized she'd ridden out of the estate without her rifle! Quickly she unsheathed her hunting knife from its belt holster and picked up a heavy branch that had shed its foliage, prepared to defend Rascal and herself to the death.

Whatever it was was crashing through the underbrush that separated them from the main trail. Tara took a deep breath and crouched, ready to do battle.

"Hello in there! Who are you?" a husky male voice called out.

Her heart, literally, leaped for joy. Tara, too, leaped —high in the air. "Hello yourself!" she sang out. "Come on in and enjoy the fire!"

He appeared from the darkness beyond the ring of firelight: a tall man bundled up for a storm such as this, his face all but indistinguishable because of the mask of snow and ice that adhered to his cheeks and eyebrows. His eyes peered out at her as from within a white cocoon. "You must be Tara De Beers," he said.

"How on earth do you know?"

He laughed. "Hell, woman, we've been searching for you for hours! Must be fifty men spread out all around here. Your family is worried sick." He held out a mittened hand. "By the way, I'm Samuel Pike."

"Glad to meet you." She shook his hand vigorously. "Am I *ever* glad to see you. What do we do now?"

"Sure as shooting, we can't take you home till this lets up some, which may be awhile. What we'll do is strike out for the travelers' shack a ways down the east side of the mountain."

"I thought I explored every trail down this damned mountain," she said.

He grinned. "You just *thought* you did. One tends to lose all sense of direction under conditions like this —unless, of course, you're as familiar with this area as I am."

"Are you a mountaineer, then, Mr. Pike?"

"Government topographer. We're mapping out the entire state of Colorado."

"Pike . . . Any relation to Zebulon Pike?"

"My great-grandpappy."

Tara smiled. "I am duly honored."

"Thanks. But the two of us will be duly frozen if we don't find that cabin. The storm is getting worse every hour. Come along; my horse is waiting up trail."

Tara took Rascal's bridle and followed Pike out of the woods and onto the trail. His horse, a sturdy, short-legged animal with large hooves, whinnied and pawed the snow at his master's approach.

"Randy's not as pretty as your mount," Sam said, "but he's better adapted to snow and ice. Climb aboard and we'll get you two to shelter."

Atop the ridge, the snow was falling like a white waterfall. It was all Tara could do to see the broad rump of Pike's horse. If she fell more than three feet behind, Randy would vanish in the white sea.

"Not so fast!" she yelled. "You'll lose me!"

It seemed like an eternity to her, the arduous trek across the mountaintop and down an eastern trail, before Pike at last reined in the horse and stopped.

"Where are we?" she asked, peering into the white shroud that enveloped them.

"Right there in front of you is the shack. Get off and see for yourself."

Dismounting, she tentatively took a few steps in the

direction he was indicating and ran directly into a wall of the small building. "I'll be damned."

"You go on inside and light the oil lamp and some candles while I attend to the horses. There's a shelter behind the cabin just big enough to house them."

She groped her way along the wall until her hand detected a doorjamb. She found the latch and pushed the door inward. Now Stygian darkness enveloped her, but she welcomed the contrast from outdoors. She shut the door, took a match from the pouch, and struck it on the rough wall. A balloon of light exploded, revealing the dim interior of the cabin.

She estimated it was about ten-by-ten feet. The appointments were spare: a double-decker bunk bed against one wall, and a small table flanked by two straight-backed chairs. There was a fireplace that dominated the wall opposite the bed, with firewood stacked nearly to the ceiling on each side of it.

Tara lit the kerosene lamp on the table, and the room emerged in vivid relief. She was in the act of laying a fire when Pike came in, stamping and shaking the snow off.

"The horses are fine. I brushed them off and covered them with blankets. . . . Here, let me give you a hand with that." He kneeled down beside her on the hearth and finished stacking the logs over dry kindling, then put a match to it and stood up. "Soon as it gets going, we can take off these heavy clothes. It'll be warm as toast in here within ten minutes."

It was even sooner than that. Tara backed away from the intense heat radiating off the firebricks and removed her mackinaw and scarf, shaking out her long black hair.

Pike, following suit, looked at her admiringly. "I've heard that Tara De Beers is the most beautiful girl in all of Colorado. Now I see it's true."

"Thank you"—her deep violet eyes were serious—"but my name is Tara De Beers *Parker.*"

"To be sure," he said, reddening. It was no secret that the girl was illegitimate; but his blunder was inexcusable. "You could be an Indian maiden," he said. "A goddess."

"You are given to hyperbole, Mr. Pike," she said with amusement. "However, I *am* part Indian."

She regarded him boldly. Sam Pike was lean as jerky, slim-hipped, with a hard, flat belly, broad shoulders, and a face as craggy and weatherbeaten as the peak named after his ancestor. His ice-blue eyes made Tara feel that he could see right through her, into her inner self. It was disconcerting. Gooseflesh rose on her arms, and her breathing quickened. She found this man more exciting than any she had ever met.

"Mr. Pike, would you like me to brew us a pot of coffee?" She'd noticed that on the mantel above the fireplace was an assortment of pots and pans, tin plates and cups, and cans of various sizes.

"Let me do it, Miss Parker; I know where everything is. Would you like me to cook us up some hunters' stew?"

"Would I? I'm positively famished! But where——"

"There's some frozen venison out back in the shed, and those cans up there"—he pointed to the mantel—"they've got dried vegetables and meat. Yes, indeedy, we'll have ourselves a hardy stew."

"You, Mr. Pike, are a true lifesaver, and that is *not* hyperbole. I most certainly would have perished out there if you hadn't come along when you did. By the way, how did you find me?"

"Spotted the glare from your fire from the summit, a reddish cast through the snow. You learn to sharpen your senses when you spend all your waking time in the forest, become more like a mountain beast. . . . Say, I'd appreciate it if you'd call me Sam."

Tara smiled. "I'd like that . . . Sam. And please call me Tara."

"Pretty name, that. Goes with the rest of you."

To her chagrin, Tara felt herself blushing. She walked over to the mantel and took down two of the larger cans. "Let's get busy on that stew, eh, Sam?"

The stew was a great success, even if the vegetables were a bit stringy and the dried rabbit and sausage were tough.

"It tastes better than anything I've ever eaten," Tara declared.

He grinned and stuffed a forkful of potato and green beans into his mouth. "To a castaway, a drink of water is nectar of the gods. Back home you'd turn up your nose at fare like this."

"No, I wouldn't; I'm not like that." She studied his strong features in the flickering light of the lamp. "Tell me about yourself, Sam. How did you become a topographer?"

"Guess it runs in the blood. Old Zebulon Pike, he was the first white man to explore this territory for the government right after the Louisiana Purchase. I love the wide open spaces."

She judged him to be about thirty years old. Casually, so as not to appear inquisitive, she said, "It must be hard for your family, having you away so much."

"Both my parents are dead. I have a brother in Alabama and a sister in Delaware."

"And your wife?"

He stopped eating and looked at her uncertainly. "I'm not married. Never had the time. Anyway, no woman wants to marry a man who moves around as much as I do. No roots. Soon as this storm breaks, my crew will be traveling north to Fort Collins."

They ate in silence for a while before Sam asked Tara, "Who's the lucky man who owns you?"

She put down her knife and fork and her eyes flashed dangerously. *"Owns* me—is that what you said?"

"No offense," he hastily assured her.

"Well, the offense is there nevertheless. What do I look like, a head of livestock?"

"Now, Tara——"

"No, you listen to me, Sam Pike! I am a woman, but I am also a human being just like you and your equal in every respect. Do I make myself clear?"

"Perfectly clear. . . . I'd like to make amends."

"In what way?"

His smile melted her heart. "I am volunteering to wash the dishes."

Tara laughed. "That's generous of you, Sam, but the way I see it, we'll *both* wash the dishes. When I marry, that is how it will be in our household: fifty-fifty, share alike."

"You're engaged, then?"

"No. As you said before, I never had the time . . . or the inclination."

"It's hard to believe that a beautiful young woman like you could have avoided a romantic liaison for so long. I'll bet the young bucks were beating a path to your door since you were knee high."

He had a talent for making her blush. "Actually, all my life I've scared off boys, and men. I seem to intimidate the average male."

He took out a Mexican cheroot. "Mind if I smoke?"

"Of course not. Do you have one to spare?"

He blinked in astonishment. "Do you smoke?"

"Started at fifteen. The ranch hands taught me how to roll my own and with one hand."

He whistled. "I'll be damned! Excuse the language."

"I've heard much worse and have done a fair share of cussing myself."

He lit the cheroot from the rim of the kerosene lamp and handed it to her, then lit another for himself.

Tara refilled their coffee mugs, and they sat back in their chairs, relaxing after their most satisfying meal.

Sam watched her smoke the little cigar with a bemused expression. "Yes, ma'am, you are quite a woman, Tara Parker. I don't wonder that you intimidate some men."

"Do *you* find me intimidating, Sam?"

His eyes narrowed and the timbre of his voice, when he answered, was firm: "No, Tara, no woman will ever intimidate me; nor will any man."

She locked eyes with him. "I believe you. You're too much your own man to be pushed around by anybody."

There followed an exchange of smiles that were almost conspiratorial, an acknowledgment that they were kindred spirits.

"Now you tell me about yourself, Tara."

She related how she had quit school to go to work for the De Beers Mining and Development Corporation and how enthusiastic she was about her job. "I'm about to be made a special assistant to the president. He's my uncle, but no nepotism is involved, believe me. I can do the job better than anyone else on the payroll."

"I'll be damned! And I believe you, too. You're not the kind to solicit favors from anyone."

"Especially from relatives." She looked thoughtful. "Sam . . . have you ever considered entering private industry?"

He grimaced and massaged his beard with the heel of one hand. "Yeah . . . it's crossed my mind. Had a few offers from companies wanted me to chart terrain for them, plot likely places where there's gold, silver, oil. Just didn't hold enough appeal for me, that's all."

Tara squinted hard at him through the haze of cigar smoke hanging over the table. "Maybe De Beers can make you a more appealing offer. . . . What do you think?"

He leaned forward, bracing his elbows on the tabletop, regarding Tara thoughtfully. "For some reason, the idea seems more appealing already."

"Oh? Why is that?"

"Because none of them fellers who tendered me the offers were nearly as pretty as you. Might be nice to have you for a boss, Tara."

His crooked smile induced a warm, fluttery sensation low in Tara's belly. She squirmed restlessly in the chair. "I wouldn't be your boss; my Uncle Nils would. And there's the chief engineer in charge of product development."

"No matter. I'd get to see you whenever I wanted."

She cast him a haughty sidelong glance. "Whatever gives you that idea? You'd be working in the field, not in the Silver City offices. I daresay we'd seldom see each other."

"Hmmm . . . we'll see." He took a gold watch out of his pocket. "Would you believe it's after midnight? I'd better look outside and see how the horses are faring. Then we had better turn in. Tomorrow stands to be a hectic day. Why don't you fix the bunks? There are blankets in a box underneath the bottom bunk."

He put on his winter gear and opened the door. The force of the wind drove him back a step, and snow cascaded into the cabin.

"Jesus! It's worse than ever." He bent forward like a man dragging a heavy weight and plunged out into the white maelstrom.

Tara had to lean against the door to bolt it shut.

The little log cabin shuddered and creaked like a living thing under the onslaught of the elements. She got out the blankets and unrolled the mattresses on the two bunks.

Then we had better turn in—there was something intimate about the casual statement. How many times had she heard her grandfather say the same words to her grandmother? She had never slept in the same room with a man before; and this would be practically in the same bed. Her cheeks were flaming again, and she pressed her cool palms against them. An excitement she had never experienced before, except in dreams, was rising inside her. Tara had never been so aware of her body. Subtle physical alterations over which she had no control were taking place, and it was rather alarming. Her nipples were rigid and sensitive to the wool of her undershirt rubbing against them; her loins were hot and itchy, as if she had fallen victim to a rash.

Sam was pounding on the door, startling her out of her reveries.

"I'm coming." The moment she unbolted the door, the wind slammed it against her, almost bowling her over.

Sam came in quickly, and together they closed and bolted the door.

"I've roamed these mountains for many a year," he confessed, "and never have I seen a worse blizzard. No telling how long we'll be cooped up here."

Tara wasn't worried. She was a fatalist.

"Let's hit the sack," he said. "Upper or lower?"

"Lower."

He stoked the fire one last time while Tara got into bed and rolled herself up in two heavy blankets; then he walked to the bunk and vaulted onto the upper tier. He had extinguished the lamp, and now the sole illumination was the eerie flickering light of the fire. It had a mesmeric effect, and Tara quickly drifted off to sleep.

She woke up, shivering from the cold; her nose and cheeks were numb. It was pitch dark.

"Sam," she called out, "are you awake?"

"Have been a spell. It's like an icehouse in here. Must be twenty below out there, and this damned shack has more chinks than a picket fence. I'll get the fire started again, and then we'd better roll up in our blankets before the hearth. That way, when it goes out again, we'll still have the benefit of the hot firebricks."

He leaped to the floor and felt his way across the cabin to the fireplace. Within minutes he was able to revive the dying embers, and crackling flames were leaping and twisting up the chimney.

Tara got out of the bunk, swathed in her blankets, and sat down cross-legged before the hearth. Sam joined her.

"Don't you want to go back to sleep?"

"When I warm up. You know, I think I'd like some coffee."

"You've got it." He got up and put a pot of water atop a tripod grill that straddled the grate. When the water was boiling, he dropped a linen sack containing coffee into the pot. "Let it brew for a while and we're in business."

The two of them were unusually quiet as they drank the coffee. Tara could feel the tension in the air; it was as if an electrical current was flowing back and forth between them. The coffee finished, they lay down to rest again, close together for warmth. Even through the thick layers of blankets, she was sensitive to the firm pressure of his hip against hers.

"Feel as if we're an old married couple," he said unexpectedly, causing her heart to accelerate. She had been thinking the same thing! In an exaggerated mountain drawl, he continued: "Hey, thar, Maw, think I heerd the young 'un cryin'."

Tara doubled up with laughter. She shoved him playfully through the blankets, and he shoved her back. They were both gasping with mirth now as the shoving match intensified, becoming more of a wrestling match.

The blankets were displaced, and now there was direct body contact between them. Sam rolled over on his side and forced Tara flat on her back, pinning her shoulders with his powerful hands. And as extemporaneously as the laughter had begun, it subsided. He bent low over her until their faces were no more than six inches apart.

"God but you're beautiful!" he whispered fervently. "I think I'm falling in love with you."

Without a word, she put her hands behind his head and drew his mouth down upon hers. Tara had never really been kissed by a man; the meaningless chicken pecks she had accorded pimply-faced swains after school dances did not count. This, then, was her first kiss, and as Sam's tongue slipped between her wet lips, even in her romantic swoon she told herself, *This was worth waiting for.*

Totally uninitiated in the ways of sex, she responded instinctively to Sam's caresses. She helped him unbutton her wool shirt and raised her undershirt up above her heaving breasts, completely oblivious of the cold as his mouth adored her shoulders and neck. She cried out in joy as his tongue teased her nipples.

There was no holding back on her part, either. A subliminal image flashed across her mind, of that day in the school outhouse when Eddie Smythe had exposed his male sexuality to her. With mounting fervor, she sought out the site of Sam's manhood, her fingers deftly unbuckling his belt and opening the buttons of his trousers and then, softly, lovingly, encircling his turgid staff. He moaned with pleasure, and his lips moved downward, toward her belly. Quickly she lifted her hips so that he could slide her trousers and drawers down over her legs and off her feet. In a moment he was kneeling over her and she had her legs around him, her ankles clamped at the small of his back. With trembling fingers she grasped his erection and guided it to her lubricious flesh.

Sam, meeting resistance, abruptly drew back. "You're a virgin!" he said with wonder.

"Yes, I've never been naked with a man in my life. But don't be afraid of hurting me. It has to happen sometime." She hugged him hard. "Imagine, all of the years I've been waiting for you, Sam Pike. Now, push —*hard!*"

There was an anxious, painful moment when she felt as if her body was being split up the middle, and she gritted her teeth; but wave after wave of mounting pleasure soon submerged the discomfort, and then they were moving together in slick, smooth rhythm, as if they had been practicing the exercise for years.

The paroxysms began at the very core of her being and spread, like a flash fire, to every part of her body. Never in her most extravagant dreams had Tara imagined that making love with a man could engender such bliss.

After it was over, he gathered her into his arms and pulled the blankets around their bare bodies, tightly molded to each other.

Outside, the wind-whipped snow piled up against the walls of the cabin until the drifts covered the door and the single window.

Inside, there was warmth and love.

CHAPTER TEN

Samuel Pike and Tara De Beers Parker were married in June 1898. That same year, Sam joined the staff of the De Beers Mining and Development Corporation as assistant to the chief of new product development.

Six months later, Nils told his niece: "What a windfall for this family when you met Sam Pike. First he saved your life; then he married you and saved us the disgrace of having an old maid. And since he's been working for De Beers, company earnings have jumped ten percent as a result of new mineral deposits he discovered. I'm going to propose to the board that we appoint him to a vice-presidency."

"That's very nice for Sam," Tara said wryly. "Do you think when he's a vice-president he'll spend more time at home?"

Nils came around his desk and put an arm about her waist. "I realize it's been rough on you, Tara, having your new husband out in the field so much, but that's where he's invaluable. Not only is the man one of the best topographers in the United States, but he's got a divining rod built into his head, a nose for terrain rich in mineral deposits."

"Speaking of deposits, here's an unusual order we received today from France. It's from a husband and wife who are chemists—Pierre and Marie Curie."

"What's the order?"

"Their American representative is asking for a large quantity of carnotite."

"Isn't that what Sam uncovered in the plateau region last month?"

"That's it. The assay department's report describes it as a 'mineral containing a hydrous radioactive vanadate of potassium and uranium.' "

"Uranium—that's the radioactive element in pitchblende, isn't it? But it's absolutely worthless."

"Not to the Curies, apparently. It seems it's indispensable to an experiment they're working on. Exactly what is radioactivity?"

"The emission of energy by matter and its transfer through space, according to your husband. Sunlight is a basic example. . . . Well, Sam says uranium's as plentiful as dirt in the mountains, so don't overcharge the Curies."

The following year, Sam Pike made another important discovery—a rich lode of molybdenum in Lake County. Little valued by most prospecting companies, molybdenum proved to be the key element in the hardening of steel, and as a result of Sam's intuitive foresight, the De Beers corporation enjoyed still another bonanza.

But, in early winter of 1900, Samuel Pike made what he regarded as his most important discovery, when Tara informed him that he was about to become a father.

Peter De Beers Pike was born in April 1901. Just one year later, Sam and Tara were appointed co-executive vice-presidents of the corporation and put in charge of the firm's new New York office. Neither of them was enthusiastic about the appointment.

"I think I shall die of claustrophobia living in that immense city with all those monstrous tall buildings," Tara lamented. "I've heard that in many places the sunlight never reaches into the streets. It must be like living at the bottom of the Grand Canyon."

Sam laughed. "I doubt it's that bad. But it will be hard on me as well, darling, leaving my beloved Colorado. At least Nils has promised that we won't have to stay in New York longer than three years at the outside."

Nils's prediction turned out to be prophetic. But not in any way that he could have foreseen.

The years that Tara and Sam and little Peter spent in New York City were more pleasant than Tara had anticipated. They lived in an airy, roomy apartment overlooking Central Park.

"It's like a picture postcard," Tara observed on their first Christmas in the big city as she and Sam surveyed the yuletide panorama from their wide bay window.

The park was truly a winter wonderland blanketed in snow with the frozen lake shining like a mirror. The people, men and women and children, skating and sleighing resembled the miniature figures adorning the Christmas pageant underneath the Pikes' festive tree.

Sam put an arm around his wife's waist and they turned to admire their three-year-old son in his Doctor Denton pajamas playing with his toys under the tree. The smell of pine needles induced in Tara a pang of nostalgia for Colorado, and tears welled up in her eyes.

"All of this makes me homesick," she said. "Not that I'm complaining, Sam. As long as we have to live in New York, this is the ideal place to be. At least we have beautiful scenery to look at. But it's only a tease for the real thing."

He smiled. "I know, darling. Patience."

Tara *was* patient. Keeping busy helped. She made friendships she would value all her life, and her social life flourished. There were countless parties, and she became active in charities and social work.

Under Sam's expert management, the New York office became one of the corporation's most profitable enterprises.

Early in June 1904, Sam told Tara, "Well, two years down and one to go. I'm holding Nils to his promise."

"The time has gone by so fast, it's hard to believe we've been here that long."

"Maybe you'd like to spend another three years in New York?" he teased her.

"Not on your life! I can't wait to get back home, mount old Rascal, and ride and ride and ride, and see the aspens on the mountainsides with their leaves glittering in the breeze like golden tinsel."

"Hold on to that dream, darling; it won't be long now. . . . By the way, Carl Linden and his wife have invited us to a school picnic next week aboard an excursion boat. Mostly a German affair."

Carl Linden was the United States representative of a German steel plant that bought molybdenum in volume from the De Beers corporation.

"That sounds like fun. Can we bring Peter?"

"Of course. That's who picnics are for—children."

On the morning of June 15, 1904, the Pikes and the Lindens boarded the 250-foot steamer *General Slocum* at the Third Street pier. The *Slocum* was a resplendent sight, with her coat of fresh white paint and the colorful banners and flags fluttering in the crisp breeze from all three of her decks. As clouds of black smoke billowed into the air from her twin stacks, and a bell sounded, hundreds of screaming children raced up the gangplanks like skittish mice, bowling one another over in their excitement. The adults brought up the rear.

"It appears we are badly outnumbered, Carl," Sam observed good-humoredly.

"Of the fifteen hundred passengers, only about eighty of us are men," Carl informed him.

Tara and Greta Linden exchanged proud glances as their children waved to them from above. Both Peter and Oscar Linden, who was a year older, were dressed in blue sailor suits with white piping and blue caps. In keeping with the nautical motif of the affair, the ladies wore middy blouses, short pleated skirts, and navy stockings, while the men sported blue blazers and white flannel trousers.

Once aboard, Sam and Carl separated from their families in order to make a tour of the steamer.

"She looks to be in A-one condition," Sam said.

Linden, a former German naval officer with a keen, practical eye, did not share that view. "Don't be fooled by the paint, Sam." He kept rapping cabin walls, the rail, and other objects with his knuckles as they proceeded along the deck. "She's thirteen years old and the worse for wear, I'd say. Look at this." He stopped by a life preserver hanging on the inside rail and squeezed it; the indentations left by his fingers did not rebound. "Old and decomposing."

Sam laughed, but not with much levity. "Say, you sound like a harbinger of doom, old man. I'll bet you were a real martinet in the service."

"You're damned right I was. There is no room for error aboard a ship, even a tub like this one. It's sloppy and undisciplined. Just look at those open hatches! I'm going to complain to the captain."

"You're *what?* Carl, this is supposed to be a picnic,

not a shakedown cruise! I'm beginning to regret that we came along."

Carl threw up his hands and laughed. "*Ach du lieber!* You're right, Sam, I'm sorry. After all, we're only going to Throgs Neck."

But, although Linden remained silent as they completed their circuit of the *Slocum*'s three decks, he could not conceal from Sam his stern disapproval of unlocked lockers, open hatches, and the generally sloppy condition of the steamer. Her crew were seedy, surly fellows, unshaven, for the most part, and wearing dirty uniforms. They shouted at the unruly children, threatening them and their mothers with dire punishment if they didn't behave; and they talked back to their officers. After the captain, William Van Schaick, appeared on the upper deck at the bow without a tie or master's cap, Linden could no longer contain himself.

"Look at that *Schweinhund;* he's a disgrace to the maritime service! I wouldn't be surprised if he was drunk. Do you know, he's the most incompetent seaman ever to operate out of New York Harbor. Three years after the *Slocum* was launched, he piled her onto a sandbar, injuring scores of passengers. And he did it again three years ago. He should have his license revoked."

There were two loud, mournful blasts from the *Slocum*'s whistle, signaling that the steamer was ready to cast off. As she drew slowly away from the pier and moved out into the channel, the predominantly German congregation on board broke into song: "A Mighty Fortress Is Our God."

"Well, we're off, for better or worse," Sam said. "Let's find the ladies."

Tara and Greta and the children were at the stern, waving farewell to the crowd back on the dock. Peter and Oscar soon turned their attention to other vessels heading downriver—ferries, tugboats, other excursion boats—leaping up and down and waving their arms as they exchanged greetings with the children on those boats.

The *Slocum* cruised at a leisurely pace up the East River for about an hour. The weather was fine, the water calm, and the journey uneventful. Even Carl Linden appeared to be relaxing and enjoying himself.

He sniffed the air. "What is that marvelous aroma?"

"Chowder," Sam decided. "From the galley."

"What's chowder?" Peter demanded.

"Soup," his mother told him.

He made a face. "I don't like soup. I want frankfurters on rolls with lots of sauerkraut."

"And you shall have them." Sam swept his son off his feet and balanced him on one of his broad shoulders.

The steamer was abreast of 131st Street when suddenly a great hue and cry went up from amidships: *"Fire!"* The passengers at the stern were stunned.

"It can't be," said Greta, and hugged Oscar to her bosom.

"Somebody's idea of a bad joke," Tara said, but the dread building up inside her said differently.

Then, from the bow of the ship, a geyser of flame shot up into the air high above the third deck.

"Gott im Himmel!" Linden exclaimed, his face white as ashes. "This tinderbox will be *kaput* in no time."

It *was* a tinderbox, with its decaying wooden framework and fresh, flammable paint. Within minutes the front half of the steamer was an inferno, and, like stampeding cattle, the passengers up forward surged back to the stern.

"Get to the rail!" Sam shouted, and holding Peter

high over his head, he bulled his way through the crowd, Tara and the Lindens right behind him.

Then, to Linden's horror, the *Slocum* swerved sharply and headed into the high northwest winds, an act that accelerated the spread of the fire throughout the ship. "The captain is a madman!" he cried.

With the Manhattan coastline no more than five minutes away, Captain Van Schaick elected to set a course for North Brother Island!

The panicky passengers battled over life preservers like snarling animals—all in vain, for the preservers were so decayed that they fell apart when the people tried to put them on. The crew broke out a hose, but when the pumps were turned on, ninety percent of the flow squirted out of countless punctures in the rotting rubber. All around the doomed steamer, the other craft on the river were sounding their whistles and horns to summon fireboats to the scene.

As the *Slocum* limped toward the rocky shore of the island, there was a solid wall of human flesh jammed into the stern section, with no more room for the hundreds fighting to outdistance the ferocious flames. Helpless, they could only wait and watch in horror as the fire engulfed them. For the remainder of her life, many a night Tara would wake up in a cold sweat, the stench of burning flesh in her nostrils, the tortured screams of those men, women, and children ringing in her ears, a dirge from the depths of hell.

"As soon as she beaches, go over the rail!" Sam shouted above the pandemonium.

A death rattle issued from the *Slocum* as she ran aground.

"Now!" Sam cried. He cast Peter as far out from the ship as he could and dove after him.

Just before Tara leaped, she looked back and saw the steamer's upper decks collapse, burying hundreds in a tomb of fiery rubble. The lucky ones went over the side into thirty feet of water—lucky, that is, if it was more merciful to perish from drowning than from fire; few of the women and children knew how to swim. Scores were crushed in a tragic pileup of bodies.

Sam and Tara and the Lindens, along with the two boys, managed to swim beyond the tangled mass of dead and soon-to-be-dead bodies.

"Carl, let's get our families to shore and then see if we can help these poor wretches," Sam said.

Treading water, Tara removed her skirt and middy blouse. "Here, give Peter to me," she told Sam. "I'm a fine swimmer. You go on."

He handed the crying lad over to her with total confidence—Tara was more athletic than most men he knew—and swam back to the swarm of people around the stern. Carl stayed to help his wife and son ashore.

A wild-eyed woman shoved two small children at Sam as he moved among the survivors. "Save my babies! Oh, *please,* sir!"

He secured them by the necklines of their clothing and ordered the mother: "Hold onto my left leg. I can make it to shore; it's not far."

It was a herculean task, but, in his hypertense state, Sam was capable of it. It was the woman who failed; halfway to safety, she simply let go and slipped beneath the gentle waves.

Sam staggered ashore, to where Tara, Peter, Greta, and Oscar were waiting. He set the children down and hastily embraced Tara. "I've got to go back. Where's Carl?"

"He just went back to the ship to see if he can save anyone."

Sam bent, kissed her lips, and dove back into the river. Five times he made the trip from the *Slocum*'s stern to the beach, each time bringing a survivor with him. The last time he returned to the beach, he found Carl Linden stretched out supine on the rocks.

"I can't go out again," Carl gasped.

"Don't you, either, Sam. You're pale as a ghost and exhausted," Tara entreated. "You've already saved five lives."

"One more time," he wheezed.

"But surely the captain and crew can——"

Sam snorted. "Our brave captain jumped ship the moment she ran aground, and the crew, most of them, followed his example. No, I must go back. There's an infant in swaddling clothes floating out there." Staggering like a drunk, he went back into the water.

Tara pressed her knuckles to her mouth and watched him swim out with a strong premonition of doom. "Please, God, take care of my beloved!" She picked up Peter and hugged him tightly to her dripping body.

By now, a few police officers had appeared, and one handed Tara a blanket to throw over her soaking-wet undergarments. Gratefully she wrapped it around herself and Peter, momentarily distracted by a hysterical woman who was rushing about, calling to her missing child. When Tara's attention returned to the river, there was no sign of Sam.

"Sam? *Sam!*" Her voice went up an octave. "Sam, where are you? Oh, my God! Where is my Sam?" Casting off the blanket and setting Peter down, she ran into the water.

"Stop her!" Greta Linden screamed. "She doesn't know what she's doing! Carl, *do* something!"

Her exhausted husband got to his feet with great effort and staggered down to the water's edge. Two burly policemen caught him.

"Now, there, mister, where do you think you're going?" one asked in an Irish brogue.

"My friend, he's out there in the water. He saved so

many, but he shouldn't have gone back the last time. Please, help him."

"I know the one. He handed me two babies. Come on, Pat, he's a fellow deserves to live."

They peeled off their helmets, shirts, and undershirts and plunged into the East River, swimming out toward the stern of the *Slocum* with powerful strokes.

"Gor! This is hideous!" the older one exclaimed as he made his way with difficulty and mounting revulsion through a swarm of dead bodies floating face down.

Time and time again the two policemen dove down into the river, looking for Sam Pike. Their efforts were sorely hampered by thick clouds of bottom silt churned up by the beaching of the steamer. At last, having to concede defeat, they swam back to shore, where Carl and Greta were vainly trying to comfort Tara. She was weeping as if her heart would break.

"She's inconsolable," Greta said helplessly. "Maybe if—— Where is little Peter?"

"Back at the aid station with Oscar and the other children," Carl said.

"Go fetch him. Maybe the sight of her son will make her realize that her life is far from over."

He ran off, and Greta kneeled down and put her arm around Tara's quaking shoulders. "There, there, *Liebchen,* Carl is going to bring your baby to you. He will need you and all the love and attention you can provide, more than ever now that——" She caught herself.

"Say it, Greta," Tara sobbed: "Now that his father is lost to him forever."

"That is not true, Tara," the older woman reproached her. "Sam will be with you and his son through all eternity in spirit. He will watch over you and Peter and see him grow up to be a fine, handsome man."

Carl returned with Peter Pike, a fair-haired child with an angelic face and wide-set, luminous eyes like his mother's, red and swollen now from crying.

"Mommy, Mommy, where is Daddy?" He threw his pudgy arms around her neck and buried his face in the hollow of her throat.

Tara composed herself for his sake; it was no light chore. In a steady voice, she said, "Darling . . . Daddy was taken away from us by God. He was a very brave and noble man who saved many lives today. He will go on living in the spirit of those survivors who owe their lives to him. Now, you and I must be as brave as he was. We shall miss him terribly, and he can never be replaced. But it is our duty to go on living happy, fulfilled lives of our own. That is how Daddy would want it. Do you understand, love?"

Peter choked back his sobs and wiped his eyes with his clenched fists. "I think so, Mommy. I'll try."

"My little man. You *are* the man of the house now, you know." She hugged him against her and kissed his eyes and cheeks and hair.

Greta smiled at her husband. "I told you so. *Ganz gut,* Carl. *Alles ist gut wieder.*"

Unexpectedly, Tara got up, carrying her small son, and started walking along the beach.

"Where are you going?" Greta called after her.

Tara paid her no heed.

"Carl . . ." Alarm showed in Greta's eyes.

Carl rushed after Tara. When he reached her, he took her arm gently. "Come, Tara, we must take you back to your apartment so you and little Peter can get out of those wet clothes. You'll catch pneumonia. Also, we must notify your people in Colorado. Sam's next of kin."

She looked at him with vacuous eyes. "Sam's next of kin? Whatever are you talking about, Carl? Sam had to rush on ahead. He promised to meet us back at the apartment." She began to giggle then, a sound that made the hair on the nape of Carl's neck bristle. He was rooted to the spot as she continued on down the beach.

"Gott im Himmel!" he gasped, and crossed himself.

Greta was horrified. "Carl, what does it mean? Oh no, it can't be! Not like . . . not like . . ."

"Like her mother," he said grimly. "No, it can't be. It *mustn't* be. Merciful God, you could not inflict such an awful calamity on the same family twice in one generation!"

The two of them fell to their knees and commenced praying.

The Lindens' prayers were answered. Tara was taken back to her apartment by the police. The physician who was summoned diagnosed her condition as "temporary shock," prescribed a sedative, and put her to bed under the care of a practical nurse. She slept like the dead for fourteen hours, and when she awoke the following afternoon, she was thoroughly rational again and able to accept the cruel fact of Sam's tragic death.

Sam's body was discovered that same afternoon, along with more than a thousand other corpses, mostly women and children.

Small consolation to the grieving families of the dead, a year and a half later Captain William Van Schaick was convicted of manslaughter and sentenced to ten years in prison.

CHAPTER ELEVEN

Gilberta was awakened on Monday morning by the phone. She let it ring six times before reaching for it, and still she was too dazed to speak clearly:

"Mmm?"

"Gilberta?"

"Yes."

"You sound like a zombie."

"I am, Anita. What time is it?"

"Seven. Just time to shower and pack before the limo picks us up at eight."

Gilberta was silent.

"What is it, Gilly?"

"I'm not going back with you and Jeanette."

"You're not? But why? Gilly . . . something's wrong; I can hear it in your voice."

"Nothing's wrong . . . honestly." Gilberta tried to sound casual. "It's just that I didn't fall asleep until after three, and then I had hideous dreams."

Silence on the other end, then: "I don't believe you, and I'm staying on with you. Jeanette's a big girl; she can go back by herself."

"Don't be silly, Anita; I won't hear of your staying. Someone has to sit in on that meeting with the Tate stockholders. And there's my appointment with the SEC investigators at two-thirty—you know, Senator Drake's watchdogs. You'd think he'd give up chewing on that bare bone, that De Beers and Tate Industries have been violating the federal antitrust laws, but ever since Harmon refused to endorse his ticket last election, he's been out to get him through me. . . . No, you've got to fill in for me, Anita."

"I take it that's a direct order, boss?"

"You've got it, kiddo. Now, I'm going to try to catch a few winks."

"What flight will you be taking, then?"

"I'm not sure. I'll call you when I know."

"I *still* think you're not leveling with me, Gilly."

Gilberta hesitated. She was tempted to tell Anita about last night's conversation with Milos, but it was too lengthy and complex to go into over the phone. She compromised by telling Anita a white lie:

"The truth is, I heard from Milos Alansky. He wants to see me sometime today."

"Awww . . . I *thought* it was something like that. All right, that makes sense. I'll be anxious to hear what he has to say."

"He's meeting with Captain Laurentis this morning; that's all I know so far."

"All right, Gilly, I'd better hang up now and rouse your daughter or we'll miss our flight. Talk to you later."

Gilberta hung up the phone and lay back on the pillow. Why *was* she staying on? It had been an impulsive decision. Last night, Harmon told her he thought it would be a good idea for her to speak with Milos. Well, she already had. Of course, he was to be questioned by Laurentis this morning, and there was the possibility that something would come of that conversation that she should know about. At the thought of the attractive captain, she felt a flutter in her stomach. *Let's face it, Gilly; you've got a thing for the man!*

She sat up and lit a cigarette. Step by step she reviewed the grim dialog between Milos and herself last night. Even though the initial shock of learning about Jeanette and Julie's affair had worn off, she still found it hard to accept. No wonder her stepdaughter had broken into tears when she heard about his death; she was still carrying a torch for him!

Or—and Gilly involuntarily shivered, thinking it—were those tears merely a ploy, just as Gilberta's own display of shock had been when Laurentis informed *her* of Julie's death? Had Jeanette somehow found out about the apartment in the Towers? Had she come up to the penthouse that Fourth of July morning to confront them, and when Julie told her that Gilberta was showering, had she seized the opportunity to kill him?

No . . . it was pure fantasy. Jeanette didn't have the guts to commit such a reckless and dangerous act. And even if she had, she wouldn't have waited around in order to throw Julie's body over the terrace; she wouldn't have been physically able to. It had to be someone else—someone who was capable of lifting a heavy body; someone equally capable of——

You are in very real jeopardy. . . .

Gilberta snuffed out her cigarette and forced her mind to go blank. Agonizing over a problem or a threat contributed absolutely zilch to the outcome, positive or negative. On that note, she lay down, pulled the covers over her head, and went back to sleep.

It seemed only a matter of minutes before the phone rang again. It was Milos.

"I'm glad you decided not to take that flight," he said.

"Well . . . for one thing, after all that's happened in the past twenty-four hours, I'm emotionally and physically drained. I figured I'd stay here and sleep for as long as it takes to recharge my batteries." She glanced at her watch on the bedside table and was startled to discover that it was nearly noon.

"Sound idea. . . . Well, Captain Laurentis and I had our little chat."

"And?"

"We covered the same ground you and he went over. I supported your statement that Jules would never have committed suicide, and told him that he had a list of enemies a mile long. He asked me about Jules's women, and I said that that list was almost as long. He asked me to give him some names, but I said that since Jules and I made it a practice never to discuss our private affairs, I'd only be guessing."

"Did he buy that?"

"I think so . . . especially when I injected a red herring, said that Jules had served with the CIA for a number of years and was possibly still an agent at the time of his death. As a much-traveled businessman, I said, he had perfect cover wherever he went: Russia, China, England, Yugoslavia . . ."

"I don't think it's necessarily a red herring, Milos. It's occurred to me that Julie's CIA affiliations could have been a motive for his murder, directly or indirectly. That phone call he pretended was to Terry about a land deal . . ."

"Yes . . . Jules wouldn't have been so concerned over a simple land deal; he left the handling of those contracts to junior vice-presidents."

"Has Laurentis made any further progress on the case?"

"They found the truck. Your gamble paid off. It was stripped down to the very frame—wheels, engine, everything. Only the license plates enabled the police to trace it to me."

"And did he have any theories as to how it got where it did?"

"If he did, he didn't say so. But he asked me why a man as wealthy as I am would keep a pickup truck rather than a sporty foreign import. I told him that at various times in the past I've had expensive cars that have been ripped off. The truck presented a low profile. He bought that. . . . Say, as long as you decided to stay in town today, can you have lunch with me?"

"Sounds good. But I'm not dressed yet. It will take me about an hour."

"That's all right; don't rush. I have some business to take care of. I haven't contacted Jules's brothers as yet, but they've already been in touch with the police here. They heard about his death last night on the late news."

"What burial arrangements have you made?"

"Jules didn't want a big funeral, just a simple ceremony at St. Bartholomew's on Park Avenue and cremation, his ashes to be strewn over San Francisco Bay."

"And what time will it take place?"

"Eleven tomorrow morning. I'll fly his ashes out to the Coast in the afternoon."

"Seems silly to go home tonight, then. I might as well stay over."

"That's only sensible. . . . Will Harmon attend, do you think?"

"I'm sure he'll want to, but I can't say. He's really swamped with commitments right now. I'll phone him, though, the minute we hang up."

"All right; I'll make a luncheon reservation someplace and pick you up at one-thirty. All right with you?"

"Fine. I'll be waiting in the lobby."

She waited a moment after putting down the receiver, then phoned Harmon at the governor's mansion. He answered immediately:

"I've been hoping you'd call before I had to go out, darling. Have you seen Milos yet?"

"Yes; we had a long talk. He feels the way all of us do, that Jules would never take his own life. The police questioned him this morning."

"Any new developments on the case?"

"Only that they found a pickup truck belonging to Milos abandoned somewhere."

"A *pickup*——"

"Look, darling," she hurried on, "the funeral is to be held here in New York tomorrow. Can you fly in?"

"Damn! I've got two speaking engagements, a testimonial dinner——"

"Well . . . don't fret over it, Harmon. Jules detested rituals like this, and he'd be the first to applaud your absence."

"You'll come home straight after the funeral? I miss you."

"The earliest flight I can get. I miss you, too."

"Gilly, I've got to cut you short; Senator Jennings just walked in. I'll see you sometime tomorrow night, then."

"Yes. Good-by, dear."

After she'd hung up, she debated whether or not she should have told Harmon about the million-dollar bequests, finally deciding it was more prudent to have him hear about them through legal channels; that way, he needn't learn the real reason behind them.

It still seemed strange to Gilberta that Julie would name Jeanette in his will. *A man of conscience,* Milos had said. *Guilty* conscience was more like it! But why, out of all the women Julie had known, had he singled out this perfectly ordinary girl for reward? Well, there *were* other forms of reward, she reminded herself; perhaps the others were beneficiaries after all.

One thought continued to nag at her as she showered and dressed, the thought Milos had planted in her mind: that the killer was out to get *her* now. But that didn't make sense. What would he have to gain, if the police wrote Julie's death off as a suicide? Which, as things stood presently, they'd have to do. Unless . . .

Unless Milos was right, and the killer does *make that anonymous phone call!*

Milos had made a reservation at Lüchow's, his favorite restaurant.

Watching him devour huge portions of *sauerbraten,* red cabbage, and potato pancakes, Gilberta smiled. "I don't know where you put it all; you're so slender."

He glanced up, but only to look at her plate. "You're not eating."

"It's going to take time before I regain my appetite," she apologized.

He speared her *schnitzel* with his fork and transferred it to his plate. "I'll eat for the two of us."

Gilberta lit a cigarette and sat back, sipping her wine. "Milos . . . what will Julie's death mean to Marston, Limited?"

He shrugged. "Not a thing. We lost the best damned captain to be had, but the ship will sail on undaunted. Jules built his team through the years with just this end in mind: to make himself dispensable."

"And you, Milos—he groomed you to step into his shoes, and it's business as usual." She smiled thinly. "That's where he had it all over me as an executive. There are times I delude myself that I am *in*dispensable."

He only nodded and went on eating.

For years Milos Alansky's prodigious appetite had

been a target for affectionate jibes from his friends. Joking about it one night, Julie had told Gilberta, "He's the only skinny trencherman I've ever met." Now, watching him as he lustily consumed every morsel on his plate, and hers, she saw what Julie had meant. Only she would have phrased it differently: not "trencherman"; "glutton."

Suddenly her mind was playing word games:

Gluttony . . .

Greed . . .

Of course! Why hadn't she thought of it before? Milos Foreman probably had the most to gain by Julie's death. Milos—brilliant, ambitious, devoted to Julie, but for so many years only a satellite illuminated in the reflected light and glory of the Man Himself. As fiercely loyal to Marston, Limited, as Milos was, there had to be occasions when his subordinate position was a bone in his craw.

He was staring at her over the tops of his horn-rimmed spectacles. "What are you thinking about, Gilly?"

Her laughter was hollow. "Something Julie once said. He called you a 'skinny trencherman.' "

" 'Glutton' is more like it," he said, grinning.

You *said it, Milos, not me.*

"I'm sorry, Milos, I forgot what time you said the service would be."

"Eleven. We can go together, if you like, only it will have to be early. I've still got some last-minute arrangements to make."

"You'd better go on ahead, then. Waiting around a church is my idea of nothing to do. . . . You know, I just realized, I have nothing appropriate to wear. When we leave here, I think I'd better do some shopping."

"Can I drop you somewhere? I've got an appointment uptown."

"No thanks, Milos. I think I'll try to walk off this lunch. I'm not used to such heavy fare early in the day."

He winked at her. "You mean you got full just watching me."

Back at the suite, she hung up the purchases she'd made at a fashionable salon on East Fifty-third Street —a tailored navy-blue linen suit, white silk blouse, and pillbox hat—got out of her clothes and into a robe, and curled up on the couch with *Secret Sins,* a paperback she'd bought in the hotel gift shop. Once she interrupted her reading to phone the De Beers main office in Silver City, but was told by the receptionist that Anita was in a meeting and, if Gilberta didn't want her called out, would return the call as soon as it was over.

It was two hours later when Anita finally called. "I'm sorry to keep you waiting, Gilly, but it's been one full day."

"How did everything go?"

"The SEC matter went fine, thanks to Jason." (Jason Fielding was the company's chief counsel.) "Their gumshoes slunk out of here with their tails between their legs. As for the Tate stockholders' representatives, they were extremely pleased with our projected earnings for the quarter."

"Good girl."

"How are things on your end?"

Gilberta related only part of her conversation with Milos, carefully avoiding any reference to Jules's will, the pickup truck, or Jeanette, and told Anita she'd be staying over another night, since the services were to be held tomorrow.

"I feel guilty not attending the funeral," Anita said.

"Julie would forgive you . . . if he could."

"I know; he hated funerals."

"Did he?"

Now, how would Anita know that?

"You know, it's strange, our being such close friends, that we've never discussed Julie," Gilberta said.

"What's to discuss? He was a very private person. He kept people at a distance, even his friends."

There was a side to Jules that he never revealed to anyone. Not even you. . . .

Impulsively, guided by intuition, Gilly said bluntly, "Anita . . . did you ever have an affair with Julie?"

There was silence on the other end of the line.

"Anita . . . are you there?"

At last: "Yes, Gilly."

"Yes you're there or yes you and Julie had an affair?"

"Listen, Gilly, you're my best friend, but you have no right to ask me a personal question like that. You and I have always respected each other's privacy."

"I know, I know; I don't know what came over me. It's just that you and I have been like blood sisters since college. We've never had secrets from each other."

"Haven't we?" Anita was on the offensive now. "What about *your* relationship with Jules?"

"What are you talking about?"

"You know damned well what I'm talking about, Gilly. For the past year, you two had been having an affair."

"How do you know that?"

"I've known you a long time, my girl, and I think I know you better than anyone else, even Harmon. You've betrayed yourself in countless little ways, Gilly."

Gilberta, ever the pragmatist, dropped the charade. "I've been that obvious, eh?"

"To me, but I don't think to anyone else, except . . ." She let it hang.

"Except Jeanette."

Anita sounded surprised: "What makes you think *she* knows about you and Jules?"

"Isn't that who you meant?"

"Well, yes, but——"

"Then, what makes *you* think so?"

"I . . . I . . . Oh, hell, Gilly, no sense beating around the bush now. Jules was having an affair with Jeanette before he met you."

"She told you?"

"She didn't have to. . . . Listen, Gilly, did you ever get the feeling that Jules was cheating on you, playing around on the side?"

"Occasionally, but that's only normal possessive jealousy. Like acne, it goes away when you mature."

"No, I don't mean that; I mean really strong vibes. Your entire being senses that the guy's making it with someone."

"Only once. There was this P.R. gal who worked for Jimmy Carter. I'm sure Jules hopped into the sack with her, but it was nothing—a one-night stand."

"Okay, but what started those vibes ringing? I'll tell you. When a man and a woman have a sexual relationship of long standing, there's more than body chemistry involved; their minds get attuned. And when the man looks at another woman, no matter how blank his expression, his mate knows intuitively if he's got the hots for her."

"She tells herself: 'That's the way he looked at me the first time we met,' " Gilberta said quickly.

"Exactly."

"Exactly. . . . And now I've got the answer to the question I had no business asking you." Gilberta took a deep breath. "You and Jules—you *were* having an affair. That's how you knew about him and Jeanette."

Anita sighed. "Yes, Gilly. It was four years ago,

election time. I served with him on the committee to elect Harmon governor, remember?"

"Sure, but I scarcely knew Jules then. Anyway, he was engaged to that Denver oil heiress, what's her name, wasn't he?"

"She broke it off when she found out about us."

Gilberta let out a short laugh. "I'll be damned! I wonder if there was any woman in Colorado old Jules didn't bed down."

"Jules was highly selective."

Gilberta laughed. "Well, of course! . . . And now that we've complimented ourselves, let's drop the subject."

"As long as we're leveling with each other . . ."

Gilly tensed. "Yes?"

"I didn't buy that yarn about your spending Saturday up at the cabin. . . . I don't think Jeanette did, either."

"Look, Anita——"

"I tell you only to warn you. That Captain Laurentis didn't strike me as a fool."

Figuring that Anita would never let it go, but would bring it up again at some later date, Gilberta decided to make a clean breast of everything. Slowly, and without omitting a single detail, she told Anita the whole sordid story, adding that Milos thought she was in danger from the killer. "But," she ended, "I told Laurentis, before he questioned you, that I was at the cabin, and he bought it, so not to worry."

"But I *will* worry. My God, Gilly, it's all so frightening!"

"This little girl can take care of herself; you know that better than anyone else. Now, what do you say we continue this conversation when I get back to the office?"

"Sure, Gilly. And Gilly?"

"Yes?"

"Friends?"

"Friends," Gilberta assured her, and hung up.

Well, well, well—one surprise after another. So, Anita had had an affair with Julie, too. A couple of cool cats, those two, always so polite and formal with each other in Gilberta's presence. Just two nights ago, Jules had asked Gilberta if she thought that Anita was having an affair with Harmon—and he'd played it deadpan all the way, the bastard! Here he'd been screwing her best friend all that time, dumping her when he got bored, and for whom? A callow, unsophisticated, immature twit! How it must have burned Anita. She'd sounded so blasé when she spoke of it; but Gilberta knew better. Anita wasn't one to take rejection lightly, not with *her* family background.

Suddenly it hit Gilberta like a lightning bolt. Perhaps it wasn't Jeanette who had come up to the penthouse that Sunday morning. Perhaps it was the woman whose lover she'd stolen—the woman who, in the space of a few short years, had been displaced twice in Julie's affections, the second time by her closest friend! Yes, perhaps it was *Anita* who——

The phone rang, breaking into her thoughts. She picked it up on the third ring.

"Mrs. Killington?"

She recognized Laurentis's voice. "Oh, hello, George. And it's 'Gilly,' remember?"

"Right . . . Gilly." He cleared his throat.

"But how did you know I was still here?"

"Well, as you suggested, I spoke with Milos Alansky—this morning—and he said you might be staying over another day."

"Another *two* days, since the funeral is tomorrow morning."

"I understand you saw him last night."

"We had a drink. Poor Milos—he was devastated by the news. . . . I know you spoke with him, by the way. I met him for lunch. He mentioned something about your finding his pickup truck."

"Yes—abandoned way out in Riverside Heights, stripped right down to its frame."

"Stolen?"

"Must have been, though I can't figure why anyone would want to steal a beat-up old van."

"Milos really has the most rotten luck. This is the fourth car he's had stolen, and the reason he bought it in the first place was because he was sure no one would ever rip off such a monster. . . . About Jules—have you come up with any new clues?" she asked.

"No clues whatsoever, old or new. Unless we tune in to something very soon, it will go down as suicide on the books."

"But that's not the truth!" she protested, as another part of her cautioned: *You damn fool, let it alone! If it's suicide, there's no way you can be implicated.*

"It's not up to me. The commissioner is suddenly very anxious to close the case. I have hunch the CIA is exerting pressure on the department. You knew that Marston was an agent, didn't you?"

"Yes; but that was years ago."

"Don't you know that old CIA men never die? And they don't fade away like old soldiers, either. It's the same as being baptized a Catholic; you can never abdicate, not truly."

Julie's words sprang to her mind: *Nobody quits the agency. . . .*

"Are you saying that the CIA could have been involved in some way in Jules's death?"

"Your guess is as good as mine. . . . But to get to the reason for my calling: When Mr. Alansky told me that you might stay over today, I figured that since the funeral's tomorrow, you'd probably stay the night, too. I see I was right."

"Elementary, my dear Watson?"

He laughed. "And since I'll be attending the funeral service too, I was wondering if you'd like me to pick you up and we can go together."

"*You're* going?"

"Just to look over the mourners who come to pay their respects."

"Most of them won't be mourning."

"All the more reason to look them over, if you grasp my meaning."

"I do indeed."

"How about it? Shall I pick you up?"

"That's most considerate of you. Yes . . . I'd appreciate it."

"Ten-thirty?"

"I'll be ready. . . . Well, good night, George."

"Sweet dreams . . . Gilly."

She was smiling when she hung up the phone. She liked the shy way her name rolled off his tongue.

Sweet dreams . . . Oh, if only she could be assured of that! Just last night she'd been haunted by nightmares so vivid and real, she might have been aboard the *General Slocum* on that fateful June morning in 1904 when her great-grandfather died a hero's death in the deep waters alongside the stern of the burning steamer.

She phoned room service and ordered a light supper, and ate it at a table by the window, which overlooked the park. The glitter and greenery recalled tales her grandfather had regaled her with when she was a child—stories of his own childhood. His parents, Sam and Tara Pike, had lived briefly in New York, and his fondest memories of that period were of the park blanketed with dazzling white snow on Christmas morning; of the miniature figures skating on the pond; of the steam billowing out of the police horses' nostrils. But mainly New York City was a symbol of tragedy to Peter Pike, just as it now seemed to his granddaughter, Gilberta.

When she'd finished eating, Gilly fixed herself a tall scotch and water, climbed into bed, and settled down to read her paperback. When she discovered that she was reading the same sentence ten times, she tossed it aside, went into the bathroom and took a sleeping pill, and returned to bed. The last thing she remembered, before finally drifting into oblivion, was a line from *Macbeth:*

Sleep that knits up the ravell'd sleave of care. . . .

CHAPTER TWELVE

Tara De Beers Pike and her three-year-old son Peter accompanied Samuel Pike's body back to Colorado. In keeping with his wishes, he was buried on the mountain where he and Tara had first met in the infamous blizzard of 1898.

Tara moved into her grandparents' mansion outside Silver City. Lars De Beers, at seventy-six, was still chairman of the corporation, but full authority for the management of the mammoth industrial complex remained in his son Nils's hands. Mina De Beers, at seventy-two, shared excellent health with her husband, and the two of them traveled extensively. As for their daughter Karen, now forty-six, she was still a beauty and could have remarried a score of times but for the deterrent of her mental disorientation. Just as she had refused to accept Robert Parker's death, she now would not acknowledge Sam Pike's.

One night shortly after Tara's return to Colorado, Karen announced at supper: "I just received a letter from your father today, and you will never guess what happened. Imagine, in London he ran into Sam at a fashionable London club. What a fine time they had."

Little Peter stared at her wide-eyed. "Grandma, Papa's dead, in heaven."

Karen laughed and wagged a finger at the boy. "What a way for you to talk, Petey. Grandma should wash out your mouth with soap."

He started to protest, but Tara silenced him. "Finish your dinner and no more talk. You too, Mother."

Karen and Peter resumed eating, both wearing childish pouts.

After dinner, Tara and her uncle Nils retired to the library to talk over coffee and brandy.

"I know it's soon to be asking, Tara, but when do you plan to return to work?" he asked.

"I don't believe in extended mourning, Nils. I can be ready by Monday morning."

He gave her a broad smile. "That's the best news I've had in almost three years! Do you know, I've been slaving seven days a week ever since you and Sam went to New York. Once you're settled into the groove again, I thought I might take Marjorie and the children on a holiday abroad."

"You certainly deserve it. And being busy can only be good for me at this point." She stood up. "Well, it's settled, then. First thing tomorrow, I'll see to engaging a nurse for Peter."

Nils looked puzzled. "But why? Your mother and grandmother are perfectly capable of taking care of one small boy."

Tara grimaced. "I'm thinking of all those trips Grandpa and Grandma take. Petey would be alone with Mother, and the way she was speaking about my father and Sam tonight . . . It just isn't healthy for a growing, impressionable child to be subjected to too much of that sort of fantasizing; I know from my own experience. Do you know, there was a time I actually believed that the reason I never saw my father was that he was always traveling?" An expression of distress spread over her serene features. "A frightening thing happened to me on the day Sam died. When they told me he had drowned, I refused to believe it. I was determined *not* to accept it. I remember taking Petey and walking off down the beach, babbling that I was going to meet Sam a little later on. Let me tell you, Nils, it was a precarious moment. It required all of my inner strength to exorcise the demon that was trying to possess me."

Nils stood up then and put a hand on her shoulder, his face creased with concern. "My poor, dear Tara, what hell you've been through. Thank God for that inner strength, so tragically lacking in my sister."

"I love Mother, but I don't want her to bring up my child."

"I understand, and I agree completely. A nurse it will be."

In the year that followed, Tara immersed herself in the complex affairs of the De Beers Mining and Development Corporation. During the three months Nils and his family were in Europe, she assumed total control of the operation and made all the management decisions, a herculean responsibility.

"You can't go on like this indefinitely, Mrs. Pike," her private secretary warned her one morning. "Look at you, so wan and pale."

Tara smiled. "I feel perfectly fine, Doris. *Really.*"

The woman shook her head. "You have three secretaries, and all of us together can't keep up with you. You know what they say: All work and no play makes Jack a dull boy."

Tara laughed and went on signing the stack of letters and contracts in front of her on the desk. "I will never be a dull *boy,* dear."

"Oh, you know what I mean." Then, with sly casualness: "Is that handsome Professor Devine coming in this afternoon? I have him down on the calendar."

"I expect he will be in, then."

Donald Devine was a mining engineer who worked as a consultant for De Beers, among other firms. Tall and lean, with a shock of beautiful white hair, he was one of the state's most eligible and sought-after bachelors. For a time, he and Tara had been the object of excited office gossip. It was true that he had been making persistent romantic overtures to Tara ever since her return to Colorado, all of which she rejected politely but firmly. With Sam's demise, the fires of her normally passionate nature had been banked, and she intended to keep it that way for a while.

Not until Nils returned from Europe, and her work load was cut in half, did Tara begin to think about a social life again. And this time when Devine argued his case, she listened. It was Christmas Eve, 1905, during a small party at the De Beers home. Devine and Tara were warming themselves before the enormous fireplace in the parlor, sipping hot toddies and listening contentedly to the flames crackling and the wind whipping fine snow against the windowpanes. At last he broke the silence between them:

"I don't know why I torment and humiliate myself this way, but, like Pavlov's dogs, I have no control over my reflexes. So, once again, Mrs. Pike, I request the pleasure of your company at the big holiday cotillion at the Hotel de Paris in Georgetown."

Tara smiled at him over the rim of her cup. "Thank you, and I accept with pleasure, Professor Devine."

Devine's mouth flew open and the cup slipped out

of his hand, spilling the steaming brew down the front of his ruffled dress shirt and tuxedo trousers.

From that time on, Tara saw Don Devine on an average of twice a week—he escorted her to the theater and the opera and Denver's finest restaurants—but never on any occasion was he less than a perfect gentleman. At first, she was grateful that he didn't press himself upon her; but, as the months went by and he never kissed her other than a chaste peck on the cheek when he said good night, never laid a hand on her except to hold her elbow when they were walking, she began to ask herself, *Why doesn't he find me desirable?* After her lengthy period of celibacy, following her husband's death, she felt her woman's body coming alive, and yearned to be made love to once again. Could it be, she wondered in her frustration, that Donald Devine, despite his exterior aura of masculinity, was a homosexual?

And then in March 1906, Tara's hopes were lifted when Don invited her to travel to California with him the next month.

"They're holding a convention in San Francisco—mining engineers and geologists from all over the world," he told her. "A symposium on gold and silver will be the dominant attraction, and it occurred to me that you and your uncle might find it worthwhile to attend."

Tara's smile was flirtatious.

"I don't think the company can spare the two of us out of touch at the same time, but," she added quickly, "*I* would be delighted to go with you, Don."

"I say, that's good news. Have you ever been to San Francisco?"

"No."

"You'll love it. In my estimation, it's the most sophisticated city in the United States, New York included."

"I can't wait for you to take me on a guided tour!" She grasped his arm in an intimate gesture, and he flushed scarlet.

"I really must be going now. I didn't realize it was so late."

She accompanied him to the door, and in the dim foyer, she put her hands on his shoulders, stood on tiptoe, and kissed him tenderly on the lips. With a startled expression, he drew back, mumbled something unintelligible, and fled down the front steps.

Tara had mixed emotions as she watched him hurry along the graveled path to the circular drive, where his carriage awaited him. Things would improve once they got to San Francisco, she reassured herself. Don was basically a cautious, self-conscious man with a strong sense of propriety. He was bound to entertain reservations about her. After all, as an heiress to the vast De Beers empire and his employer into the bargain, she must seem to him a most formidable woman, perhaps—and she thought this likely, knowing the male ego—even threatening. Well, she was convinced that once they were in San Francisco, far away from the territorial imperative the De Beers were accorded in Colorado, his inhibitions would dissipate. "I can play the clinging vine as neatly as any woman, Don Devine, if the occasion demands it," she said aloud, and smiled.

They left Denver on April 10, traveling to Ogden, Utah—a key terminal in the cross-country train route from New York to California—where they boarded a Union Pacific luxury sleeping car. The accommodations, too restricted for Tara's taste, were nevertheless comfortable and quaint: adjoining suites with a connecting door between them.

Devine made a formal ritual of locking that door and presenting Tara with the key. She could not suppress her laughter.

"Don, I am a woman of the world, not a hothouse virgin. I know you to be a perfect gentleman, and I insist you unlock that door. I am confident you would never open it without an invitation from me. Now, if you'll excuse me, I'll change my clothes and wash up."

Without a word, he went into his own room and closed the door, hard.

Tara took a sponge bath at the washbasin, then powdered and cologned her body and put on a lacy camisole and matching panties of passionate pink. She inspected her image in the full-length mirror on the back of the bathroom door and smiled. Don would probably faint from embarrassment if he saw her dressed—or, rather, *not* dressed—like this! Rummaging through the little curtained closet where she'd hung her clothes, she pulled out a casual dress of lime-green crepe de chine, with semi-gigot sleeves, and slipped it over her head. Then, a quick run of the comb through her hair, a dab of lipstick, and she was ready. She knocked on the door connecting their rooms.

"Donald, are you decent?"

He opened the door. He had changed into a pair of white linen trousers and a polo shirt that gave him a rather roguish mien.

"Shall we have some lunch?"

"To be sure, but I had better change into a shirt and tie."

"Nonsense! We're out past the frontier now, roughing it. Time to put aside our drawing-room customs and manners. Personally, I feel quite abandoned."

He coughed and backed off from her.

Tara stood spraddle-legged, hands on hips, fixing

him with a disapproving stare. "Donald Devine, what is wrong with you? Or is it me? Are you afraid of me?"

"Of course not! Whatever gave you an idea like that?"

"Never mind; let's go to the dining car."

He compromised in the matter of proper dress by wearing a jacket over his polo shirt.

Lunch was light and tasty—cold poached salmon with hollandaise sauce, a salad, and rice pudding for dessert—and their conversation pleasant, centering on the panoramic view that greeted their eyes whenever they chanced to look out the window, which was often. When they'd had a second cup of tea, they retired to their compartments and spent the remainder of the afternoon reading and making conversation through the open door between the rooms.

About four o'clock, Tara yawned and put down her book. "I think I'll take a nap," she called to Devine.

"Right. I'll close the door."

"No need; you won't disturb me. See you at suppertime."

She dozed off quickly and did not awaken until the late-afternoon sun slanted through the window into her face. Through half-closed eyelids, she saw Donald standing in the doorway watching her. She smiled.

"What are you looking at?"

"I'm sorry; forgive me." He was badly flustered. "It's just that . . . that . . ."

"Please tell me." She sat up and regarded him inquisitively.

He was beet red. "I was admiring you in the same spirit that I admire this wonderful countryside. You are one of nature's rare beauties."

Tara was infused with a glowing warmth. "Why, Don, what a lovely thing to say."

"It's true." He started back into his own compartment.

"No, don't leave; stay and talk to me."

"It's really time we dressed for supper," he said, deftly declining the invitation. "I think the company in the dining car will be a little more formal than at lunch."

"I suppose so."

"See you when you're dressed." He backed out and closed the door.

Tara chose a pale-peach dinner gown with a bell skirt trimmed with lace ruffles. Reluctantly, she wore a small boned corselet to emphasize the wasp waist.

"You look gorgeous," he told her as they made their way to the dining car. He was wearing a formal dress suit, with a white starched shirt and black tie.

"Thank you, and you look very handsome."

"Thank *you.*" He took her hand, bowed low over it, and pressed his lips to the satiny flesh.

Tara was encouraged. With each passing hour on the train, he seemed to be less inhibited, more relaxed.

They both ordered the featured entree—veal in a rich Bordelaise sauce, garnished with truffles and capers—and, for dessert, an American favorite: deep-dish apple pie served with hard sauce.

"I am positively going to burst," Tara lamented on their way back through the coaches to the first-class section.

"I never should have eaten that second piece of pie," Devine commiserated.

When they arrived at their rooms, Tara suggested, "Let's change into something more comfortable, set up the table in one of our compartments, and play cards."

"I'd like that. What's your game? poker? pinochle? red dog?"

She winked. "Dealer's choice. I must warn you,

though, I am absolutely merciless when I play cards—a veritable predatory tigress."

Devine laughed. "I'll take my chances."

The connecting door was closed while they changed. Tara selected a silvery-blue velour peignoir ruffled at the sleeves and hem and edged in creamy medallion lace. She belted it loosely at the waist with a sash of the same material. Then, standing before the door mirror, she removed the two silver combs that held the French knot at the back of her head, and her hair tumbled down her back like a dark, gleaming waterfall. She brushed it out, then tied it back with a blue satin ribbon.

When Devine knocked tentatively at the door, she was sitting on the lounge facing him, her posture relaxed and languid.

"Come in, Don."

He had removed his jacket and shirt and wore a calf-length dressing gown over his trousers.

"Well, don't *we* look domesticated—a typical married couple preparing for bed."

He laughed uneasily. "Hardly. You, Mrs. Pike, are not exactly the stereotype of the average American housewife."

"Come in and set up the table, will you? I have the playing cards."

There was a table folded up against the wall underneath the windows. Devine bent over in the confined space between the lounges to unfasten the latch that held the table fast, and, in doing so, his left arm pressed down on the tops of her thighs. The feel of his hard bicep against her flesh sent vibrations coursing up her legs and into her loins, stirring emotions that had lain dormant too long. When he stood up and raised the hardwood table, propping it upright with a single fold-back leg, she saw that his face was inflamed and the veins were throbbing at his temples.

"Here, Don, sit next to me," she said, smiling sweetly.

"I think it better that I sit across from you." He slid into the opposite lounge.

"Why is that?"

"Well, if we're going to play cards, we shouldn't be able to look into each other's hands."

She feigned dismay. "Do you think I would cheat?"

His smile was wry. "No, but *I* would be tempted. You know what Cartier, the old whist master, said: 'A peek is worth two finesses.' "

"How droll. Is that what we're to play—whist?"

"My preference is poker."

"Good; so is mine. Five-card stud?"

"Suits me fine."

"What stakes?"

He was surprised. "Stakes? Do you play for money?"

"What other reason is there to play?"

"All right; you name the stakes."

"A dollar a card, and double on the last card."

Devine's eyebrows lifted. "That's a little rich for my blood. Remember, I'm not a De Beers."

There was a knock at the door, and a black porter poked his head inside. "What time you want me to fix up your berths, folks?"

"We'll let you know later. Not for some time. Oh, porter, would you please have the dining-room steward ice a bottle of champagne and bring it back when it's cold."

"Yes, ma'am."

"Champagne?" Devine said after the porter had gone. "After all that wine we drank at dinner?"

Tara winked. "*In vino veritas,* as the Romans used

to say before their orgies got under way. It breaks down the inhibitions."

Devine grunted. "Let's play cards. Fifty cents and a dollar last card is as high as I'm going."

"Agreed."

Tara won the first hand with a pair of aces. Devine captured the next two games, but Tara came back with three of a kind. She was dealing the next hand when the porter returned with a bottle of Mumms, embedded in a bucket of cracked ice, and two wineglasses. He set the tray on the table, uncorked the wine, and half filled the glasses.

"Will there be anything else?" he asked.

"No, thank you." Tara handed him a twenty-dollar bill, telling him to keep the change, and he departed, a huge smile on his broad face.

She lifted her glass: "To a wonderful vacation in San Francisco."

They clinked glasses and drank, Tara draining hers and reaching for the bottle.

"Easy there, my girl. We don't want to get drunk, do we?"

"We don't? Speak for yourself, Don." She refilled her glass. "Now, where were we?" She glanced at the three cards lying in front of her. "Yes, I get the next card." She dealt one to herself, one more to Devine, a last to herself.

"One dollar," said Devine.

"I'll see you and raise you two."

"Hey! The limit is one."

"Oh, don't be such a tightwad."

"All right; just this one time. I'll call you." He anted up the two bills.

Tara displayed her hand. "Pair of queens."

With a triumphant smile, he fanned his cards on the table. "Aces and eights."

Tara lay back on the cushion. "The dead man's hand. That was what Wild Bill Hickok was playing when he was gunned down."

Devine raked in his winnings. "Well, I am not about to be gunned down."

"Don't be too cocky," she said mischievously. "There are more ways than one to skin a cat."

He regarded her quizzically. "You say some of the most ambiguous things."

She gave him a lazy smile. "Pour us another, will you?"

The two of them were becoming giddy, and Devine spilled wine on the table.

"Oops! Oh well, never cry over spilt wine, they say."

"That's spilt *milk,* silly."

"No, this is distinctly wine." He mopped some up with his index finger. "Taste."

She took his hand and guided the upthrust finger to her mouth, inserting it all the way up to the knuckle. He tickled the roof of her mouth, and she felt a blush spread over her face and a tingling in her nipples. There was a rosy sheen suffusing Devine's face, too, and he withdrew the finger with the look of a man who has touched a hot stove.

Tara laughed. "Have no fear; I won't bite you, Don." She tilted her head to one side and contemplated him speculatively. "I think we've had enough cards for one night. What do you say we put up the table?"

He complied without speaking, setting the wine bucket on the floor, then settled back in his seat.

Tara picked up the bottle, and handing him his glass, she filled it to the brim, pouring what was left into her own. "I'd like to propose a toast, Don: To love."

"To love," he said self-consciously, and sipped from his glass.

"Have you ever been in love?"

"I never had the time."

Tara laughed. "Surely a strong, virile young man like you must have *made* time for women every now and then? I mean, to be perfectly frank, men have certain *needs*, just as women do."

"I say, isn't it going a bit too far, Tara, to inquire into my personal life? How would you feel if I delved into *your* private affairs?"

Tara hooted. "Delved into my private affairs? Now, that's a bona fide sexual innuendo if ever I've heard one. . . . All right, fire away. What would you like to know about my intimate life?"

He started to rise. "I think it's time we readied ourselves for bed. All this champagne had gone to our heads."

She put a hand on his chest and gently shoved him back onto the lounge. Placing her glass on the windowsill, she stood up. "No; you'll leave when we've finished this highly significant discussion. . . . My private affairs, yes. I was a virgin until I married Sam Pike. I've never been with any other man, not even since his death, and, quite frankly, this prolonged abstinence becomes increasingly frustrating. . . . Donald, don't you find me desirable?"

"I told you this afternoon. You are an exquisite beauty."

"No; I'm not speaking of distant admiration but of physical contact. Don't you feel any *physical* desire for me? Because I confess I think you are one of the most sexually stimulating men I have ever met."

Avoiding her demanding gaze, he stared into his wineglass, rolling the stem between his fingers. When at last he answered her, his speech was slow and halting: "Tara . . . you are *infinitely* desirable. It's just that . . . well, it's a long story and . . ."

She sat down. "And?"

"I'm not sure you want to hear it."

"Why don't you let *me* be the judge of that?"

He drained his glass in one gulp and reached for the bottle. Discovering that it was empty, he let out a long sigh and, turning to face her squarely, began:

"I was seventeen years old at the time, living on the family farm in Ohio. My brother Bob, twenty-three, had just married a girl named Marcia Davis—a bit of a tart, to hear the townspeople tell it—and brought her home to live with us. My folks didn't like her, but they kept quiet for Bob's sake. I didn't like her, either, though at first I didn't quite know why. I just sensed that she was somehow a threat to our household.

"At seventeen, as you must know, the male animal is particularly weak, vulnerable to temptations of the flesh. I was no exception, and Marcia exploited this weakness whenever she could. Every morning, just as I was about to go downstairs for an early breakfast with my father and brother, she'd confront me in the upper hallway. Her robe would be loosely belted, so that it revealed her flimsy nightgown; and she'd make certain that I had a good look at her cleavage.

"One morning she called me into her bedroom—Bob was already downstairs—and said that the window sash was stuck, would I fix it. Of course, there was nothing wrong with the sash; the window opened easily. She thanked me, and before I could leave, she stepped in front of the window, clad only in her nightgown. With the sun at her back, she might as well have been naked.

"Day after day she would stage these provocative acts, until I was literally mad with lust for her. It became an obsession with me. I couldn't get her out of my mind, night or day. Lurid fantasies infested my brain: Marcia and I performing every conceivable sexual act. There was bound to be a breaking point.

"It happened on a July morning. My father and Bob

were out mending fences, and I was assigned to clean out the barn. I was in the midst of my chores when Marcia came through the door.

" 'Do you know I've never been up in the hayloft?' she said. 'What's it like up there?'

" 'Nothing but hay,' I told her. 'You wouldn't be interested.'

" 'That's for me to decide,' she said, and walked to the ladder leading up to the loft. 'Here, give me a hand. This ladder is awfully rickety. Brace it for me.'

"She was dressed in a brazen fashion, as she usually was: a peasant blouse that showed off her ample bosom to best advantage and a skirt that was scandalously short. I went over and held the ladder, and she proceeded to climb the rungs. She gathered up her skirt around her thighs with one hand and——" Devine slumped forward and buried his face in his hands. "God, how I tried not to look up, but I was too weak. I . . . I *had* to. And it was my undoing. I saw what I had been envisioning in my tortured dreams. She didn't have a stitch on under her skirt.

"It was as though I was in a trance, the hapless fly plunging into the spider's web, the doomed rabbit hypnotized by the obsidian eyes of the snake. I climbed up the ladder after her. She was waiting for me, sprawled out on a mound of hay, her smile inviting. I was trembling like a leaf in a high wind; my head was spinning; my throat was parched.

" 'I've always heard that hay is best for rolling in,' she said, and began to take off her clothes. The sight of her naked . . ."

Devine raised his head, and Tara would never forget the haunted look in his eyes.

"What happened next was a nightmare straight out of a Hieronymus Bosch painting. We went at each other like two jungle animals, biting, scratching . . . And it went on and on, all afternoon. When I got back to the house, I thought I'd die of shame and remorse. But the very next day, I went to the loft hoping she'd come. She was already there, waiting.

"After that, we took to meeting in the fields, in the woodshed, even in her and Bob's bedroom. That's how crazed I had become—cuckolding my beloved brother in his own bed!

"And then one day the laws of chance caught up with us. My family was going to church, as we did every Sunday, only this time I feigned illness to be with Marcia. She was an atheist and never attended church. As soon as my brother and parents had left the house, I was in her bed.

"A short while later, I thought I heard a noise. Marcia must have heard it, too, because she struggled to sit up, and when I looked at her face, I was shocked to see the sudden transformation of her features. One minute she was smiling; the next, her mouth was agape and her eyes were wide with fear.

"I turned my head to follow the direction of her stricken gaze, and I couldn't believe my eyes. It had to be some crucl specter conjured up by my guilty conscience. There, standing in the doorway, was Bob. I'll never forget the look on his face as long as I live. Shock, disbelief, pain, revulsion, grief—it was all there, in his eyes.

"We lay there paralyzed, speechless, waiting for the ax to fall. But Bob only turned away and walked down the hall.

" 'He's gone to fetch a gun!' Marcia screamed. 'He's going to kill us!'

"I was hoping he would. Death, at that moment, would have been merciful for me. At least I would have been spared the ordeal of facing my brother.

"The next thing I knew, Marcia had thrown on her

clothes and was climbing out the window onto the porch roof. She was calling for me to follow her; but I couldn't move. I just sat there on the bed, numb, waiting for Bob to come back, and the next thing I knew, my father was standing in the doorway. My mother had forgotten her purse, he said, and they'd had to come back for it. Then, suddenly, he was shouting at me:

" 'What the hell are you doing in here, naked as a jaybird? Where's Marcia? Where's Bob?' His eyes were wild; and before I could answer, he had turned and run downstairs.

"I got up then and went to my room to dress. When I went downstairs, I found him sitting slumped over the kitchen table, weeping. I begged him to tell me what was wrong, but all he'd say was, 'The barn . . . the barn . . .'

"I ran out the back door and across the yard to the barn. Even before I reached the open door, I saw him. He was hanging by the neck from a rafter. I rushed in and cut him down, but it was too late. Bob was dead."

Devine, tears streaming down his cheeks, lifted his head and met Tara's horrified gaze.

"This white hair . . . I'm not as old as I appear. It turned white almost overnight. But it is not the only mark of Cain I bear." He turned his head away. "You see," he said, and his voice broke, "since that day, I have not been with a woman. I . . . I am totally impotent."

Tara clasped a hand to her cheek and gasped, "How . . . how *terrible* for you."

He stood and, without a word, hands hanging limply at his sides, walked like a zombie into his compartment and closed the door behind him.

A few minutes later, the porter came to make up

Tara's berth, and as soon as he'd gone, she climbed into bed, wishing for blessed sleep to dispel the frightful images that whirled in her brain: Bob Devine swaying from the rafter, his neck twisted by the cruel noose, his face bloated and near black from suffocation; Don writhing in lust atop his Jezebel sister-in-law, their bodies meshed in piston rhythm . . .

To her amazement, Tara found herself becoming aroused by her lurid fantasizing, and was ashamed, but consoled herself with the thought that the flesh was weak, and at the core of every human being, there was a primitive beast. She ran her hands up over her thighs and belly, imagining they were Don's hands; cupped her breasts and teased the nipples with her thumbs until they were taut pegs. Flames licked at her loins, and she moaned softly as her desire mounted.

Oh, Don, I want you so very desperately. I will *have you!*

For a man as virile as Don to be rendered impotent seemed to her an obscene irony—a tragedy as great as his brother's suicide. A woman of enormous determination, Tara made up her mind that, during her stay in San Francisco, business would be of secondary importance. Foremost was her vow that she, Tara De Beers Pike, was woman enough to resurrect Devine's dormant libido!

CHAPTER THIRTEEN

San Francisco was everything Donald Devine had told Tara it would be.

"And more," she said, as they surveyed the sprawling city from a promontory atop Nob Hill, sanctuary of the rich and famous. Chinatown; Fisherman's Wharf; the Golden Gate Bridge; the Barbary Coast; Portsmouth Square—so many little cities unto themselves.

"See how the setting sun fills the mouth of the harbor with dazzling fire," he said. "That's why they call it the Golden Gate. Tomorrow we'll take a trip on an excursion boat across the bay to Oakland."

"I can barely wait. Oh, Don, I'm enjoying myself so much!" She took his arm and squeezed it.

"So am I." To her delight, he put an arm around her waist and hugged her against him. "There's a magic about this city—I sensed it the first time I set foot in it—and never have I felt it more strongly than right now."

"I feel it, too," she said, smiling up at him.

"Magic," he repeated. "Magic and miracles . . . I wonder if . . ."

"You wonder if?"

"Never mind; we'd better get back to the hotel. We'll just have time to change and have a light supper before the opera."

"I can't believe we're going to see the great Caruso tonight, and in my very favorite—*Carmen.*"

"Come along, then."

They took a carriage back to the ornate Palace Hotel, where they were booked into adjoining suites on the sixth floor, and began to ready themselves for the evening's entertainment.

Tara allowed herself a half-hour's soak in a hot tub, to which she'd added French bath oil that whipped up into a froth of bubbles as big and soft as marshmallows. Then she dressed quickly, first slipping into a blue silk teddy and a *strâpontin*—a small waist cushion to support the heavy skirt of her ball gown, which was of ice-blue slipper satin and sported tiny bouffant sleeves and a plunging neckline. Her long hair she tucked up in a chignon snood made of platinum and gold threads and adorned with multicolored sequins. White satin slippers and silk stockings held up by frivolous black garters completed her ensemble. When she had finished dressing, she sat down on a divan near a window and looked out across the city, bathed now in soft twilight. There *was* a magic about it, as Don had said.

Not long after, he knocked on her door. "Are you ready?"

She rose and opened the door for him. His eyes devoured her.

"You're a veritable feast, Mrs. Pike."

She cocked a saucy eyebrow at him. "A feast? Do you mean to say that I make your mouth water?"

He reddened. "A figure of speech."

"And you, Donald, look very princely tonight."

Devine was wearing the formal male attire of the era: black tie and tails set off by a white ruffled shirt and a red cummerbund.

"I don't think we'll have time for supper before the opera. We're running late."

"That suits me fine. I much prefer a late intimate supper afterward."

"Then, shall we be off? We'll be early, of course, but it will afford you an opportunity to review the passing parade of San Francisco's First Ladies as they arrive."

"Splendid! I'll just fetch my opera glasses from the bedroom."

The spectacle of so many elegantly turned-out women and men milling around on the sidewalk under the theater marquee, while truly dazzling to Tara, was totally eclipsed by the stellar performance of the inimitable Caruso that night. Indeed, he was called out for so many curtain calls, Tara lost count. And as she and Don made their way to one of the line of carriages waiting at the curb, she felt heady with excitement.

Upon returning to the Palace, they went directly to the main dining room, where they ordered a sumptuous meal: *consommé à la princesse; poisson à la dauphine; pommes duchesse; salade de concombres;* and *fromage* and assorted fruits for dessert.

"The most delicious meal I ever ate," Tara said as they sipped cognac with their coffee.

It was after midnight when they went up to their rooms. "Do come in for a nightcap," she invited him. "This afternoon I had a bottle of Remy Martin brandy sent up."

There was no hesitation on his part in accepting—a good sign, she thought.

"Pour us a brandy while I change into something more comfortable," she told him, indicating the dark green bottle on a silver tray on the coffee table in the sitting room.

She went into the bedroom and undressed, then stood naked before the vanity table mirror. Abhorring false modesty, Tara acknowledged that she had a sexy body: long, well-shaped legs and curvaceous hips; a gentle swell to her belly; slim waist and high, firm, pear-shaped breasts. She stretched her arms above her head, admiring the thrust of her nipples.

Tara, you are irresistible tonight, she mused. *You* will *accomplish your purpose with Donald Devine. You* will *cure his impotence!*

With solid confidence, she donned a gossamer-light peignoir with wide butterfly sleeves and a long, floaty skirt belted at the waist with ribbon braid. She let down her hair and brushed it till it took on the texture of gleaming ravens' feathers. Shoulders thrust back, she marched into the sitting room to accomplish the conquest of Donald Devine.

He rose at her entrance. "You look lovely."

"Words, words, words," she teased him. "Haven't you heard that actions speak louder than words?" She went up to him and put her hands on his shoulders. "Donald, show me how lovely you think I am. Kiss me."

He tried to back off, but she entrapped him by wrapping her arms around his waist. "You'll have to hurt me to break away."

"I say, Tara, a joke is a joke, but don't carry it too far."

"I'm not joking, Don." She tilted her face up, her scarlet lips slightly parted. "Kiss me and I'll release you, I promise."

His face was a montage of conflicting emotions: uncertainty, apprehension, dismay, and—yes, she was sure—desire.

She stood up on tiptoe so that her mouth was only inches from his face. "Do it, Don."

"Damn!" he said softly. "You're an unconscionable vixen." With sudden determination, he pressed his mouth hard against hers.

It was as exciting as the first time she and Sam Pike had kissed, and she knew it signified a critical penetration of Don's psychological defenses. She forced his lips apart with her tongue and wriggled it about inside his mouth like a playful snake. His arms tightened about her, and he did not draw back when she thrust her pelvis hard against him.

Tara terminated the kiss, but, with her arms still locked around his back, she walked him to the couch and pushed him down. "Now, lie still and relax, darling," she whispered, shrugging out of the peignoir.

Don stared as though mesmerized. "You're . . . you're even more lovely than I could have imagined," he said with awe.

She laughed softly. "What do you mean, *could* have imagined? Haven't you ever thought about me this way, naked in your arms? Be truthful, Don." She grasped his hands and guided them to her breasts. Her nipples nestled into the palms, and she felt his hands tightening on the soft, pliant mounds.

He swallowed several times before he was able to reply. "Yes . . . I am not without my fantasies and yearnings, but they are futile indulgences. I told you, I am incapable of pleasing a woman."

"That's not so; I'll prove it to you." She unfastened the suspender clips from his trousers and unbuttoned his fly.

He recoiled and attempted to force away her hands. "My God! Tara, stop it this instant!"

"I will *not* stop. Now, take off your jacket and shirt; it will make things less awkward."

"I most certainly will not. You are either insane or intoxicated."

"Intoxicated, yes, but not from alcohol; from the notion of you and me lying naked in each other's arms, which we're about to be very soon."

Like a man in a trance, he obeyed her instructions and removed his swallowtail jacket and his shirt. "I must be insane, too," he muttered.

"Now your pants," she commanded.

When he complied, and was dressed only in his white union suit, she giggled. "Men wear the most unattractive underclothing," she said, and slipped her hand inside the drawers and grasped his flaccid penis.

"It's no use," he gasped.

"You're as tense as a board," she complained. "Lie back and let your body melt into the couch. Your bones are dissolving. You are no more than a lump of putty."

He did as she suggested; but, despite all of her tender ministrations, his member remained limp. "I *told* you."

Undeterred, Tara helped him out of his union suit, then began cooing to him the way a mother croons to an infant: "Remember how it was before your brother's death? You and Marcia, the lofty heights of your passion . . . Remember, remember, remember, and stop thinking about your brother. Robert is dead, and all your grief and self-flagellation can never change anything."

She kissed his lips and his eyes and his throat and his hard, muscular chest, nuzzling the thick, fair matting. Her lips coursed down his body. Her efforts were at last rewarded when she thrust her tongue into his navel. He shook as if afflicted with palsy, and an agonized moan escaped his lips.

The agony and the ecstasy, she thought—Siamese twins, inseparable.

She kissed the hard, flat belly, ridged with muscle, and then she confronted the last citadel. Taking his member gently in one hand, she bent her lips to it and coddled his hard testicles in her other hand. And she adored him with all her heart and soul as no other woman had ever worshiped the masculinity of a lover.

Unexpectedly, the spell was broken and he came to life in her hands and mouth. He was flaunting it now like a proud guidon. He sat up and put his arms around her and pressed her back on the cushions.

"It's a miracle!" he cried.

"You said this was a city of magic and miracles."

"I want you so desperately that my desire verges on madness."

"Then, take me, my love . . . *take* me."

She opened her thighs to him, and he mounted her with haste. In a moment, they were moving together with all the naturalness of experienced lovers.

Devine was a starving man. When he peaked the first time, Tara thought he had burst inside her, and even after his prolonged orgasm, there was no diminution of his erection. They spent themselves three times before he withdrew from her and lay on his back beside her.

"What a woman you are," he whispered.

She smiled and stroked his belly. "And what a man *you* are."

"Thanks to you. My darling, I have loved you from afar for so long and dared not express it to you, believing it would forever be a lost cause." He raised himself up on one elbow and looked into her eyes. "Now it can be said, what I've longed to say since the first day I met you: I love you, Tara, and want you to be my wife."

She took his face in her hands. "Dear, sweet Donald,

don't you think it would be wise to wait a few months to see if you still feel the same way? Right now you're grateful and——"

"That's not it at all," he said in exasperation. "I love you fiercely; I always have. Please . . . *please* say you'll be my wife."

Tara kissed him gently on the lips. "I promise I'll give you my answer soon, but not till we get back to Colorado and I have a chance to deliberate in my home surroundings. There's little Peter to think about."

"Darling, I love Peter as if he were my own flesh and blood. And the boy likes me."

"That's true. Still, I must think it through. I warn you, though, that if I do marry you, I will be a part-time wife. There are my responsibilities to De Beers, you know."

"Of course. I wouldn't dream of asking you to give up your career."

"You are a good man, Donald Devine. Any woman would be proud and honored to be your wife."

He bent down and kissed her, tenderly at first, then insistently, and Tara felt the hot flash of desire consume her once more. She reached down to encourage his passion, but discovered that he was ready to perform at her pleasure.

"This time you lie back," she said, "and let me do the work."

He laughed. "Work? That's the first time I've heard sex referred to as work. What a delightful occupation."

Devine did as Tara requested, and she straddled his hips and placed one hand on his chest. The other hand clasped his male member and positioned it as she shifted her buttocks and impaled herself on it. Moaning softly, she began to move up and down, slowly at first, teasingly, then faster, and still faster, till Don cried out:

"God—it's almost more than I can bear! I must be in heaven, because you are an angel."

Tara was amused, and afterward, when their passion was spent and they lay close together like two nestled spoons, she playfully slapped his buttocks. "That's a fine thing to say to a woman when she's fornicating. An angel, indeed! A depraved angel, at that."

They walked naked into her bedroom, arms around each other, and got into bed. Don lay on his side, cradling Tara's head against his chest.

"Good night, my darling," she whispered. "Sleep tight."

"I'm too exhilarated to sleep."

But sleep came quickly, to both of them—a deep, peaceful slumber, the product of complete happiness and fulfillment and love.

And while they slept without a care, the pale horse of the Apocalypse was galloping full speed toward San Francisco. . . .

It began more than 200 miles northwest of the city, far out to sea. The watch officer was standing on the open bridge of a freighter cruising through calm water. Moonbeams cut a shimmering, silvery swath across the Pacific all the way to the horizon. All was still, save for the gentle lapping of the water against the boat's hull. And then, suddenly, the officer gave a start as he heard it—a sound as of distant thunder at first, but growing louder by the second, erupting into a deafening roar like that of a speeding train. As he reached for the binoculars around his neck, he was thrown off balance and had to grab the guardrail to keep from falling. To his astonishment and horror, the ocean had begun to boil and froth and was shaking the freighter as a terrier might shake a rat.

Blanching, he staggered into the wheelhouse, where the helmsman was clinging for dear life to the wheel.

"What's going on, sir? I can't control her!"

"Maybe the end of the world; I don't know!" the officer cried.

"Sir—*look!*" With bulging eyes, the helmsman gaped at a solid wall of water, dead ahead, descending on the hapless ship at better than 100 miles an hour.

"Dear God!" the officer gasped, and crossed himself.

Then it was upon them, and ship and crew were buried under millions of tons of seawater that crushed the steel hull as if it were an eggshell.

Increasing in violence, the shock wave raged along the 300-mile San Andreas fault toward the unsuspecting city of San Francisco.

The mammoth quake reached land shortly after 5:00 A.M., demolishing coastal cliffs, uprooting thousand-year-old redwood trees, and reshaping the coastline for hundreds of miles.

Police Sergeant Jesse Cook, on night patrol, had stopped to chat with a friend, Al Levy, who was on his way home from an all-night poker game. "Ever seen a dawn like this before, Al?" he asked, pointing to the blood-red sky to the east.

Levy frowned. "I don't like it, Jesse. Something strange is in the air; you can feel it."

As if on cue, from all parts of the sleeping city, dogs began to bark, cats to caterwaul, and horses to whinny in a concert of fear.

"Jesus Christ!" Cook grabbed Levy's arm. "I must be seeing things!"

Far down Washington Street, through the misty gray dawn, the two men witnessed a terrifying sight. The pavement reared up like a giant wave and came rushing in their direction. Undulating in snakelike fashion, it hurled both men to the ground.

On the sixth floor of the Palace Hotel, Tara and Devine went flying out of bed as the building began to dance like a whirling dervish, and furniture caromed from wall to wall like billiard balls.

"It's an earthquake!" Devine shouted.

On hands and knees he crawled to the window and held fast to the sill. Tara followed him. She could not believe her eyes. As far as she could see, tall buildings were swaying from side to side, an urban forest assaulted by hurricane winds. One by one, they began to topple as the force of the shocks intensified.

"We've got to get out of here!" he said. "Throw on a robe; we don't have time to dress."

Tara put on her peignoir, and Devine his trousers, and cautiously they made their way through the suite to the door.

In the hall, pandemonium was rampant, a mob scene the like of which Tara could not have imagined in her maddest dreams. Men and women in various stages of undress—many of them stark naked—were battling to get through the exit doors.

"Let them go at it," Devine said. "We've got time. This is a sturdy structure."

They paused before the open door of 622, and Devine exclaimed, "I'll be damned!"

Standing in the middle of his parlor, clad in a bathrobe and slippers, was the rotund tenor Enrico Caruso. Clutched to his chest was an autographed photo of President Theodore Roosevelt. With plaster and glass tumbling down all around him, he broke into song.

Tara clapped her hands in sheer delight. "Who but an Italian would sing *Pagliacci* at a time like this? *Bravissimo!*"

His performance was rudely interrupted when a crystal chandelier crashed down from the ceiling, missing him by inches, after which his valet grabbed him by an arm and shoved him into the hall.

Caruso rolled his eyes at Tara and lamented: *"Mama mia!* To think I left Naples to escape from Vesuvius, only to walk into an earthquake!"

By now the milling crowd in the corridor had thinned out, and they were able to make their way down a staircase as a calm ensued. The initial shock had lasted forty-five seconds, though it seemed like an eternity. They were in the lobby when the second tremor struck, throwing everyone to the marble floor. It lasted twenty-five seconds before subsiding for good. Tara and Devine struggled to their feet and hobbled out into the street, their bodies bruised and battered.

Although the earthquake was over, the once-proud city was convulsing in its final death throes. Buildings were toppling over, one upon another, like dominoes. Gas and water mains exposed by huge fissures in the ground were erupting in geysers of flame and water, and the fires spread quickly. Bodies were strewn in all directions, heads, legs, and arms twisted and crushed, everything splattered with bright-red blood.

Caruso and his valet followed Tara and Devine out into the street, where the opera star collapsed on the ground. A policeman astride a horse came galloping toward them.

"No time for rest!" he shouted. "Ten minutes from now everyone still here will be trapped by the spreading fires! Get down to the Bay Area or go up Nob Hill!"

Caruso groaned and got to his feet with help from Devine and the valet. At that moment a handsome young man, wearing an evening cape and high silk hat, came striding along the sidewalk. He was twirling a cane and whistling as though he hadn't a care in the world.

Caruso spied him and slapped a hand to his forehead. "Who else but John Barrymore would *dress* for an earthquake?"

"Who is John Barrymore?" Devine asked.

"Only the world's greatest actor," Caruso told him, and, rushing forward, he embraced Barrymore in a gargantuan hug. "Jack, old fellow, what are you doing here?"

"Right now I'm looking for a place to buy a drink. Just came from a bachelor party, and the damned earthquake broke all the booze bottles. . . . Well, cheerio. See you around, Enrico." And he continued on down the block.

Tara, Devine, and Caruso and his valet joined the ranks of refugees who were heading for Nob Hill. Jefferson Square was so clogged with humanity that it was virtually impassable. They detoured around it and began the arduous trek up the Hill.

When they reached the top, they were greeted by a view tragically different from the one Tara and Devine had marveled at only the day before. The scene was unreal, a figment out of Dante's *Inferno*.

On the waterfront, men and women were battling like wild animals to clamber aboard the ferries that would carry them to safety in Oakland across San Francisco Bay. Behind them, office buildings, dwellings, and churches were engulfed in flames. Wooden structures went up like torches, while those with steel beams and girders writhed and twisted like living things as the intense heat caused the steel to melt and buckle. The pride of San Francisco, the stately city-hall building, which had taken twenty years to build at a cost of $6 million, was reduced to a mound of rubble.

The entire city was bathed in an eerie reddish glow from the reflection of the conflagration on the thick curtain of smoke that blanketed everything for miles around. And, while the holocaust raged on all sides, the human beings still inhabiting the area played out grisly and bizarre dramas: Looters—ghouls—robbed the dead and the dying, in many cases cutting off fingers to obtain valuable rings—a hazardous occupation, for patrols of soldiers and police shot them down without mercy on sight. One man was undressing a young girl with the intention of raping her. Three rescuers grabbed him, and two of them held him down while the third castrated him. Shopkeepers banded together to salvage what wares they could, and before it was over, scores of would-be thieves swayed from makeshift nooses suspended from the rafters of razed buildings.

Ultimately the fire was stopped at Van Ness Avenue when fire fighters successfully used dynamite to create backfires. But it was too little too late. When the final statistics were tabulated, it was learned that in three days the San Francisco earthquake and fire had devastated over 3,000 acres, or 550 city blocks, and 29,000 buildings; upward of 800 people were killed; and damages ranged well above $500 million.

It was dusk when the fire fighters extinguished the flames—or, more accurately, hosed down the smoking embers—along the waterfront. Then an orderly procession of survivors marched down from Nob, Telegraph, and Russian Hill and waited their turn to board the ferries that would take them to Oakland. Once there, the refugees, penniless and many of them without a shirt to cover their backs, were given refuge in the local armory and other public buildings.

Tara telegraphed the De Beers office in Silver City, requesting money for clothes and their train fare back to Colorado. Two days later, she and Devine were heading east on a sleeping car of the Southern Pacific Railroad.

"It was a harrowing experience," she said, snuggling against him on the lounge seat, "but if I had it to do over again and knew what lay in the future, I would still go to San Francisco, fire or no fire."

He laughed softly. "I know what you mean. If we hadn't gone, you and I would never have been brought together, and I'd still be an introverted, bitter shell of a man. My darling, I am forever in your debt."

"And you are forever in my heart, my love."

They embraced passionately, and when Tara had caught her breath, she said, "Do you think these berths are too small to make love in?"

He ran a hand underneath her skirt and squeezed her thigh. "I could make love to you on a picket fence."

"Then, what are we waiting for?"

CHAPTER FOURTEEN

Donald Devine and Tara De Beers Pike were married in the summer of 1907.

"I'm happy that you are a member of the family," Nils told Devine at the wedding reception. "Sam Pike's untimely death was more than a personal tragedy to the De Beerses. He was a staunch pillar of our economic community. . . . After all, I'm not getting any younger, and since Tara is next in line to succeed me, it's a great comfort to know that she has a strong man like you to depend on. I daresay you know almost as much about the corporation as she and I do."

Devine clasped Nils's hand firmly. "I appreciate your confidence in me. Rest assured I will do everything in my power to justify it."

The following year an epidemic of influenza struck Silver City, and within a span of three days both Lars and Mina De Beers died. Nils, who also contracted the disease, recovered, but was left with weak lungs. In 1910, he developed tuberculosis and was confined to a sanatorium just outside Denver. Over the strenuous protests of both Tara and Devine, he resigned as chairman and president of the multifaceted industrial empire and appointed Tara chairwoman of the board and Don president.

Peter Pike, now eight years old, was the image of his father: tall for his age, slim and supple as a poplar, with fair, curly hair and pale-blue eyes. Only his skin—a rich bronze—was evidence of his Indian heritage. Like his mother, he, too, was a born horseman, and at least twice a week together they would ride through the plains and mountains on their favorite mounts.

As the world entered the second decade of the new century, the clouds of war were gathering over Europe. Then, in June 1914, a Serbian nationalist assassinated Archduke Francis Ferdinand of Austria-Hungary at Sarajevo, and by summer's end the Allies—England, France, Russia, Belgium, Serbia, Montenegro, and Japan—were involved in a world war with the Central Powers—Germany, Austria-Hungary, and the Ottoman Empire.

War held a great fascination for Peter Pike, as it did for so many idealistic and naïve young men of that era of innocence. He spent at least two hours a day at the public library, poring over newspapers, journals, and maps, gleaning every scrap of information, every dispatch from the front, that he could uncover. And at the supper table at home, he'd report what he'd learned.

"You'll see; it won't be long before the United States joins the Allies," he predicted one night.

"Maybe so, but I'm thankful that if we do become involved, you are too young to be drafted," Tara declared. She found her son's enthusiasm frightening.

Peter, glum-faced, picked at his food in silence, then, unable to contain his anger, stormed away from the table.

"Why do you ruffle his feathers like that?" Don

asked Tara. "You know how he idolizes everything about the military."

"Yes," she replied, sighing, "and I pray this terrible war ends before he's old enough to act on his misguided emotions."

But, as the war in Europe ground down to a virtual stalemate that dragged on through the next three years, it appeared that Tara's worst fears could well be realized.

A brilliant student, Peter completed high school in two years and announced that he wanted to attend college in the East.

"What do you want to study?" Tara inquired.

"Law . . . or maybe engineering."

Don, trained as an engineer himself, was delighted, and suggested Peter apply to the Massachusetts Institute of Technology. Peter warmed to the suggestion and sent off his application and high-school transcripts that very week. Shortly thereafter he received an acceptance from the M.I.T. Board of Admissions.

His departure from Denver, the following September, was heart-wrenching for Tara. As she and Don saw him off at the train station, she tried, unsuccessfully, to hold back the tears.

"I miss you so terribly already and you haven't even gone."

"I'll miss you, too, Mother."

"It will be the first time we've ever been separated for a long period of time."

"There is a time for everything, it says in Ecclesiastes," Devine reminded her. "And this is the time for Peter to leave the nest."

"I know. . . . Promise you'll write us at least twice a week?"

Peter winked at his stepfather. "I promise." He shook hands with Devine. "Take good care of her."

"The best."

Up until this moment, Tara had looked upon her son as her "little boy." Now, regarding him standing alongside her husband, she was compelled to face the truth: At fifteen, nearly six feet tall, with broad shoulders and his father's craggy features, Peter Pike was every inch a man. . . .

In his first semester at M.I.T., Peter made the Dean's List by earning straight A's. By spring semester, however, his grades had fallen somewhat, owing to his preoccupation with the war in Europe. No American was less surprised or more elated when, on April 6, 1917, the United States declared war on the Central Powers.

Back in Silver City, Tara and Devine accepted the news with pessimism, despite the fact that, with America's intervention, the De Beers corporation stood to triple its profits.

"I hope Peter doesn't do anything foolish," Tara lamented.

"You forget; he's not even sixteen yet," Don reminded her.

Still she continued to worry, and when they didn't hear from Peter for the next five weeks, she became alarmed. "I'm going to phone the school. Maybe he's sick."

"We'd be the first to be notified if he was," Don assured her. "My guess is he's preoccupied with boning up for his final exams." When he saw the skeptical look on Tara's face, he added, "Listen, darling, if we don't get a letter by the end of the week, *then* we'll call."

Tara agreed; but for the next four days, a frown marred her lovely features.

On Friday morning when the couple came downstairs for breakfast, the maid was laying the mail on the dining-room table.

"There's a letter from Master Peter," she said.

"See? I told you." Don smiled at Tara, and then he saw the postmark and his heart sank. "It's from France," he informed her.

Tara swayed and put a hand to her throat. "Dear God, no!"

"Better sit down." He held out a chair for her and then stood behind it so they could read Peter's letter together:

Dear Mom and Don,

I realize what a shock it will be for you both when this letter arrives. I'm sorry about that, but, really, it's better this way. When the United States got into the war, I simply couldn't sit back and continue to lead the country-club life at M.I.T. I wanted to do my part, like every other American guy worth his salt. So I enlisted, and here I am at the Allied Expeditionary Force training center at Issoudun, where the 94th Aero Pursuit Squadron is being formed.

Our instructors are chiefly veterans of the Lafayette Escadrille, a group of American volunteer aviators, who, when the U.S. declared war on Germany, transferred to the Army Air Corps. They're invaluable, since they have a year's combat experience under their belts. Major Raoul Lufbery is our commander. He was one of the first Americans to sign up with the French right after the war broke out.

I've never met a finer bunch of guys than are in the 94th—Eddie Rickenbacker, James Norman Hall, John Huffer, and David Peterson, to name a few. Tomorrow morning I make my first solo flight. . . .

* * *

It was dark when the charge of quarters woke Lieutenant Peter Pike: "Rise and shine, Lieutenant. This is it."

After a quick breakfast, Peter and another newcomer to the 94th Squadron, Second Lieutenant Eddie Rickenbacker, reported to Major Lufbery on the airfield.

"You fellows are lucky." The commander ran his hand lovingly over the wing fabric of a fighter. "Brand-new Nieuports. Sweetest little fighter in the air. . . . Okay, climb aboard."

Peter frowned. "Where are the machine guns?"

Lufbery grinned. "Oh, yes, that was an oversight on my part. I should have told you. Our guns haven't arrived yet."

Rickenbacker snorted. "What do they expect us to do, throw rocks at Jerry?"

"It may surprise you to know that's how all of this got started. At the beginning of the war, the airplane wasn't considered a fighting machine. The sole function of the Army Air Corps was to do reconnaissance work. The Krauts, too. It was kind of a friendly rivalry. Our guys would wave to their guys when we passed and vice versa.

"One day a German Fokker almost rammed one of our planes, and the French pilot got so damned mad he threw a monkey wrench at it. The heinie pilot responded by drawing a pistol and pumping two shots into the Frenchy's fuselage. It was the beginning of a feud that got hotter every time both sides went up. Rifle and pistol fire was exchanged regularly. Then a British observer had an inspiration. He mounted a machine gun on a swivel base behind his rear cockpit, and first time he spotted a Fokker, he blasted it out of the sky. And that's how dogfighting was born.

"Okay, I'll be in the lead ship. Rickenbacker, you'll

be my wingman, and Pike, you cover Rickenbacker's wing." Lufbery pulled on his helmet and goggles and climbed onto the wing of the lead ship.

"Good luck, sonny boy," Rickenbacker said as he prepared to climb aboard.

"Stop calling me that," Peter complained. "I'm twenty years old."

The older man hooted. "In a pig's ass you are! I'll bet you never shaved until you signed up. Truthfully, how old are you, Pete?"

Peter colored and dropped his eyes. "Almost sixteen."

Rickenbacker laughed and clapped him on the back. "You fooled the recruiters. Good boy! You have guts, Pete, and I'll trust you as my wingman any day."

Both Rickenbacker and Peter Pike passed their solo flight with flying colors. But there was still much to be learned from the veteran flyers of the 94th: the importance of keeping the sun behind you when you dove on a foe; how to shake off an enemy on your tail by kicking the rudder hard and bringing up the nose sharply to throw the ship into a spin. Lufbery explained the maneuver: "Let her take one and a half revolutions in the spin with the engine stalled out, then cut on your engine again and *voilà!* you slide off in the opposite direction while Jerry is wondering what in hell happened to you."

Many of the American combat skills were borrowed from German aces like Max Immelmann and Baron von Richthofen. In the famous "Immelmann turn," the pilot made a half loop; at the top of the loop, he would abruptly roll the plane over so that he was flying upright again and headed in the opposite direction. In most cases the enemy pilot, caught off guard, would have to complete the loop in the customary manner, and the other pilot could execute a quick reversal. The original pursuer would suddenly find himself the pursued.

Baron Manfred von Richthofen's "flying circus" had taught the Americans the value of formation flying. The Red Baron had pioneered the flying wedge, which placed the fighters in a V like wild ducks, each plane covered by a wingman off to the side and behind him.

It was the Americans, however, who devised the method of forming a circle around crippled planes to shield them from enemy attack.

"Good old Yankee ingenuity," Lufbery told them, "straight out of the Wild West—you know, like when the Indians attacked a wagon train. . . . Another thing: if your ship catches fire, don't panic and jump for it. Chances are you can sideslip and keep the flames away from the cockpit long enough to land safely and get out in one piece."

By the time the 94th finally got its machine guns, Peter, like the other rookies, was confident he could hold his own with the German pilots, and was anxious to prove himself. His chance came early in May, when, as part of a three-fighter patrol that included Rickenbacker and the flight leader, Captain Peterson, he was assigned to his first combat mission.

Lufbery shook hands with the three of them before they boarded: "Good luck and good hunting."

It was a cold gray dawn when the three pilots began their patrol over Saint-Mihiel. Below them the uneven wooded terrain, covered with pockets of swirling mist, had a stark, prehistoric look. The enemy trenches were winding snakes that stretched from horizon to horizon, and when the Nieuports flew over, the long, ugly snouts of the German antiaircraft guns poked up into the air, and the space around the Americans was saturated with dark cotton puffs of smoke and fire.

No sooner had they passed Saint-Mihiel than they

were socked in by thick rain clouds, and the downpour lashed the tightly stretched fabric of the wings and fuselage with a vengeance. In such circumstances, it was near impossible to maintain contact, and the procedure was, every man for himself.

Peter kicked his rudder and nosed the fighter down in a long, sweeping glide, heading back for French territory. Descending to 1,000 feet, he spotted a hole in the thick overcast and dove through it, breaking out into clear air space and hedgehopping across the ravaged countryside until he spotted a familiar landmark. A half-hour later he touched down on the airstrip at Toul.

Lufbery, Chambers, and Campball ran out to greet him as he vaulted off the wing to the ground.

"Did Rick and Captain Peterson get back yet?" he asked.

Lufbery answered him in a concerned voice. "Pete got in just before you, but no sign of Rick so far." He frowned up at the sky, which was rapidly darkening as the storm swept in from Germany. "He damned well better shake his ass before it's ceiling zero."

There was the rumble of distant thunder, and the western sky flared up with sheet lightning.

"Hey, listen!" Campball yelled. "Do you hear it?"

Lufbery grinned in relief. "I know that sound the way a man knows his lover's voice."

At the sound of the distinctive *thrumming* of the Nieuport's engine, Peter tilted his head backward and peered into the mist. "Am I hearing things, or is there more than one plane approaching the field?" he asked anxiously.

The three men were silent, listening attentively. Suddenly Lufbery clapped a hand to his forehead: "You're damned right there's more than one plane heading this way, and if my ear doesn't deceive me, they're German Fokkers! They must be right on Rick's tail. Come on," he shouted, "let's get up there and help him!"

As Peter's fighter still had a quarter of a tank of gas and was all warmed up, he was the first to take off.

The German pilots, intent on stalking Rickenbacker, had not realized they were near an Allied airstrip until they were almost over it, and when they saw the American fighters lifting into the air, they turned and headed back for their own lines.

Peter, with his lighter, faster plane set at full throttle, was closing fast. In fact, he was still climbing when he caught up with the slower of the Fokkers. Realizing that escape was impossible, the German pilot accomplished a skillful reversement and met the Nieuport head on, guns spitting. Thanks to Lufbery's repetitive indoctrination in defense tactics, Peter anticipated the German's maneuver. He hit the rudder hard, slipped off to the left, then spiraled down on the Fokker's tail as it flew past.

When the Maltese cross on the German's tail was centered in his sights, Peter squeezed the trigger. Cross and tail assembly exploded, and shards of wood and fabric were sucked into the backwash of the Nieuport's prop. The Fokker flapped around dizzily like a wounded bird for a hundred yards or so; then, abruptly, it seemed to stop dead in midair and fell like a stone in a flat spin toward the ground. The flaming arc of its tail threw off sparks like a Fourth of July pinwheel.

Peter was overcome with excitement and exhilaration. To him had gone the honor of drawing first blood in the combat debut of the 94th Squadron! He banked and headed back for the field, just in time to see Lufbery destroy the second Fokker with a methodical barrage that raked the doomed plane from prop to tail. It exploded in a ball of fire, and when the smoke cleared, it had vanished; all that remained of it were particles that glinted in the mist as they drifted slowly earthward.

That night, at a banquet in honor of the victorious Americans, the mayor of Toul offered them the key to his city. "Anything and everything you want is yours," he promised.

"*Every*thing?" Lufbery inquired, looking round the festively decorated basement of the city hall and settling his gaze on a saucy wench whose luscious bosom threatened to spill out of her daring peasant blouse at any instant.

The plump Frenchman kissed his fingertips and blew the kiss into the air. "Everything. *Vive les Américains!*"

Lufbery returned the salutation: *"Vive l'amour!"*

The mayor put an arm around Peter's shoulders. "And you, my young friend . . . I understand it was you who made the squadron's first kill. Would you do me the honor of signing your autograph for my youngest daughter? Come, I will introduce you to her. Her name is Gilberta."

He led Peter around the banquet table and over to a corner where a young girl was chatting animatedly with two boys. She smiled as her father and Peter approached.

The instant their eyes met, Peter knew, without a shadow of a doubt, that he was in love. She was about his age, he judged. Enormous violet eyes dominated a fragile oval face with a flawless complexion. Her nose and mouth were delicately sensual—not overt, but provocatively promising. Her figure was slender and willowy, though with softly rounded breasts and hips.

"Gilberta, this is Peter Pike, the young American lieutenant who shot down those two Boche today."

"Only one of them," Peter amended self-consciously. "How do you do, Gilberta."

She curtsied. "It is an honor, Lieutenant Pike."

"Tonight you will be the official representative of this proud city, Gilberta," her father said. "You will be his companion and escort, and remember, his wish is your command."

The girl blushed crimson, and it was contagious; Peter's cheeks and ears burned.

"Now I must attend to my other guests." The mayor bowed to Peter and withdrew. So did Gilberta's two friends, whispering and casting covert looks back over their shoulders.

"Well, Lieutenant Pike, what is your wish?" Her smile was like a burst of sunlight.

"I am in your hands, and please call me Peter. 'Lieutenant' sounds so stuffy and formal."

She took his arm. "First I will take you to my father's wine cellar and you can select your beverage for supper . . . Peter."

He was glad to leave the crowded, noisy banquet hall and have Gilberta to himself. As they walked down the narrow stairs to the wine cellar, a level below the basement, their hips brushed, and her breast on that side pressed against him. A blaze of passion enveloped him, more intense than any ever aroused in him by a girl. To his profound dismay, he discovered that he had an erection, which he attempted to hide by surreptitiously thrusting a hand into his pocket. Fortunately it was very dim in the cellar, the only illumination provided by oil lamps set in wall sconces the length of the long, narrow room. One wall supported the wine racks, extending from floor to ceiling.

"Is your preference champagne?" she asked.

"Actually, I prefer Burgundy, if you have it."

She laughed. "My father has the best-stocked wine cellar in all of Toul." She placed a finger over her pursed lips. "Let me see, now . . . the Burgundy vineyards should be on the top shelf."

She fetched a high step stool from the opposite wall and carried it to a rack halfway the length of the cellar, then proceeded to climb to the platform on top. When she bent over to squint at the labels in the bad light, her bell skirt, with the starched petticoat underneath, flared up and out, affording Peter a tantalizing glimpse of her legs and thighs all the way up to her lace-edged panties. Exerting great willpower, he tore his eyes away from her and banished the lewd thoughts generated by the incident. He walked ten paces away and leaned back against the wall.

"What's wrong, Peter?" she called to him.

"Nothing. It's just that it's a bit warm down here." He slipped a finger inside the high, tight collar of his uniform jacket and pulled it away from his Adam's apple.

Gilberta stepped down off the stool, cradling a dusty green bottle in the crook of one arm. She held it out to him: "The best wine from the district."

"I can't wait to try it."

He followed her back up the steep stone steps to the main level, his eyes fixed on the backs of her legs. They were the most shapely he had ever seen.

There was feasting and drinking and dancing until the early hours of the morning. At 2:00 A.M. Lufbery told his men that it was time to return to barracks. Before Peter joined the others, he pulled Gilberta into a dark alcove at the back of the hall.

"Thank you for a most wonderful evening," he said, holding both of her hands in his.

"It was wonderful for me, too."

There was an awkward silence; then he blurted out, "I think you are a wonderful girl."

She smiled, and her violet eyes crinkled up at the corners. "And you are a wonderful boy—man, that is."

He laughed. "You're not all that far off."

She moved closer to him, so that her bosom was almost touching his chest, and tilted her face up to him. "Would you like to kiss me?"

"With all my heart and soul."

He put his arms around her, and she slipped her arms around his neck. Their mouths met eagerly, and for Peter, every cliché he'd heard about romance was suddenly appropriate and real. Rockets exploding in his head; cymbals crashing; the two of them afloat on a fleecy cloud . . . He attempted to keep a distance between their lower bodies so that she would not be offended by the surging evidence of his intense desire; but she thrust her hips and belly fast against his loins and undulated her pelvis.

Now he did push her away gently. "I can't endure being this close to you another second. I'll go mad with desire for you."

Her breath was hot and sweet against his cheek, and her eyes were heavy-lidded. "I, too, want you very badly, Peter. When will I see you again?"

"Tonight, tomorrow night, the night after that, as many nights as you will allow me to see you."

There were tears in her eyes now. "Every night for the rest of our lives, if only it were possible."

He shook his head in wonder at what was happening to them. Mere hours ago they had been total strangers, and now . . . "Gilberta, I know how insane this must sound, but I am desperately in love with you."

"No, no, *mon cher,* if it is madness, then I am mad as well . . . and I never want to be sane or reasonable again. I love you so much, my heart aches."

They were startled when a voice behind them—Rickenbacker's—said, "All right, you two lovebirds, break it up. Time to go back to camp and get our beauty sleep. We've got to look nice for the Krauts tomorrow, kiddo."

Peter gave her a last quick kiss on the cheek. "I'll be around this night after chow. Will you be here?"

"Waiting with bated breath."

Outside the city hall, the men of the 94th Squadron piled into waiting trucks, everyone talking boisterously at the same time. The unanimous topic was the quality of the wine and the French women:

"The best gams I've ever seen."

"Their boobs ain't bad, either."

"I, for one, am an *arse* man."

"For the first time, I know what a *real* French kiss is."

"How come they all speak such good English?"

"They were chosen especially for this shindig, the girls and women in Toul who could speak the best English."

"That little number who latched onto Peter, she's quite a dish."

And now Peter was barraged by jokes and barbs:

"I wouldn't mind a little piece of her at all."

"You think Pete got into her pants?"

"Naw; he doesn't want to lose his cherry to a Frog."

His temper flared, and he lunged across the truck at his tormentor. He managed to get his hands on the man's throat, but three other pilots dragged him off.

"Cool down, kiddo," Rickenbacker soothed him. "It's all in fun. You've got to hold on to a sense of humor to get through this war."

"I'm sorry." Peter sank back onto the hard wooden seat with his head bowed.

Rickenbacker tried to revive the jovial mood of the party, but somehow all of the buoyancy was missing.

It was a relief to everyone when they pulled through the gates of the field.

"Be it ever so humble, there's no place like home," someone said.

That night, Peter lay awake thinking of his beloved Gilberta. Every detail of her face and form was so vividly etched in his imagination that she might have been there at his side in the flesh. Her angel flesh. He reached out to touch her and the vision vanished. He thrashed about on his hard cot, tormented by desire so fierce that there was only one way to quench it. A feeble substitute for his love object, but it provided sufficient surcease so that he was able to drift off to sleep at last.

CHAPTER FIFTEEN

Nine days elapsed before Peter Pike saw action again. Heavy spring rains and a thick overcast grounded both the Allied and the German aircraft. On the tenth day, the clouds dissipated and the sun broke through.

Throughout the morning and early afternoon, the pilots of the 94th flew missions over the German lines. As soon as one group returned to gas up, another would take off. At 3:30 Peter was sitting on his cot, writing a letter to his mother, when Rickenbacker burst into the barracks:

"Come on, kid, a Pfalz fighter just crossed the front-line outposts and is headed this way!"

Minutes later they were airborne. They covered the distance to the trenches without seeing the Pfalz or any other enemy planes.

Peter and Rick were flying wing tip to wing tip, and the older pilot signaled with his hand that they should split up and patrol in opposite directions. Peter formed a circle with his thumb and forefinger, acknowledging the order, and hit his rudder, at the same time moving the joy stick to the right. The Nieuport peeled off from the sister ship and went into a long, sweeping sideslip to the northeast.

Peter flew all the way to Pont-à-Mousson, then turned back south again. He was approaching Toul when he spotted a dark speck on the horizon, moving on a collision course with his ship. He climbed sharply into the sun and began to circle in lazy spirals, waiting for the unknown plane to arrive. Soon the distinctive silhouette and the high black crosses on the wings and tail identified it as the sought-after Pfalz.

As it passed far below him, Peter dove after it. When he dropped out of the protective blinding glare of the sun, the German in the observer's seat saw him and shouted a warning to his pilot. Opening his throttle full, the German pilot began to climb in preparation for an Immelmann turn. At the same time, Peter became aware of Rickenbacker's Nieuport diving at the Pfalz from a ninety-degree angle. Deferring to his buddy, he let Rick have the first shot at the German and banked into a turn, ready to back him up if he missed. It was a provident move, for the Pfalz sideslipped Rick's attack, reversed, and headed back for the German lines.

Peter promptly got on his tail. The dogfight took place at 10,000 feet, and the German pilot, taking advantage of the altitude, nosed down in a steep glide to increase his airspeed. Peter stuck to him doggedly. It was risky, because he would present a fat target for the "Archie" batteries when the two fighters crossed the lines at between 2,000 and 3,000 feet. Because he was so close to the Pfalz, he counted on the antiaircraft gunners holding their fire to avoid hitting their own ship.

Closing on the Pfalz to a distance of about 200 feet, he opened up with the twin machine guns. The tracers cut a streak of living fire into the German's tail section. Lifting the Nieuport's nose, Peter fired another burst.

The tracers described an arc like water pouring out of a hose and scored a bull's-eye on both cockpits. Pilot and observer died instantly. Seconds later the Pfalz struck the ground and disintegrated in a ball of fire.

Peter pulled up in a steep climb, with shells bursting all around him, and, outdistancing the fire, headed back to the base. Rickenbacker, on his wing, waved his gloved fist in the air in a victory salute.

As soon as they landed, Rickenbacker leaped out of the cockpit and ran over to Peter's plane. When Peter vaulted to the ground, he hugged him and pummeled him affectionately. "Kid, you've finally arrived. Scratch that, no more 'kid'; you're a *man!* A man I'd have backing me up any time, no matter how tight the situation." He grinned. "Now we've got to get you laid."

That night when Peter visited Gilberta Boyer, the whole family—mother, father, sister, and two brothers—greeted him like a conquering hero. The mayor blew a kiss into the air, one of his favorite gestures when he was especially pleased, and lauded the young pilot.

"Already you are becoming a legend in Toul. All of the farmers were in their fields when you made your magnificent fight against the Boche plane. *Mon Dieu!* The Germans are no match for the Americans. Your pilots, as the French say, *jeter de la poudre aux yeux.* That is, you threw dust in their eyes."

Peter blushed and demurred modestly: "I was just lucky, sir."

"No, no, no, I will not have it!" He threw his arms around Peter and kissed him on both cheeks. "You are a bold warrior, and I predict that before this war is over, you will have been awarded your country's Medal of Honor."

Later, when the family tactfully withdrew to other portions of the house that adjoined the city hall, leaving the two young lovers alone in the parlor, Peter told

Gilberta, "I like your father, but, frankly, I prefer to get my kisses from you."

She laughed and moved closer to him on the settee. Tilting her head back, she said, "Then, kiss me, my love."

He glanced around nervously. He had visited Gilberta almost every night since their first meeting, and whenever they were left alone like this, he could not rid himself of the anxiety that one of the family members was spying on them. When he suggested it to her, she laughed.

"Why would they eavesdrop on us, Peter, when in their hearts they know exactly what we are doing and saying? After all, it is our national slogan: *Vive l'amour!*"

Peter cleared his throat. "Nevertheless, I think it is time to state my intentions to your parents—that I love you and want to marry you. Then I will feel better about what we are doing."

Her eyes widened in merriment. "What we are doing? What *are* we doing?"

"Well, you know: kissing and touching and——"

"These are only natural progressions of courtship," she said, running her hand up the inner side of his thigh. "But, up till now, we haven't done the thing that I have been aching to do since I met you. . . . Oh, Peter, we must find a place where we can be alone, *truly* alone, to do as we desire without inhibition."

He sighed. "Yes, yes; I can't stand being with you, so close to you, and yet not close enough."

"All right, I will find a way. On Friday night there is a special mass at the Catholic church for the war dead. The family will attend, but I will say I am not feeling well. Yes, on Friday night we *will* be alone at last." She took his hand and pressed it to her breast.

Every minute that passed from that night until their

rendezvous on Friday seemed endless to Peter. Even the customary excitement and elation he felt high in the sky in his Nieuport, anticipating the sight of an enemy fighter, was missing. Each mission was no more than a drab exercise. And then Friday morning finally arrived, and the ensuing hours seemed to drag more than any of all the preceding days. Love was definitely a form of madness, he decided. But, oh, what a marvelous malady!

At supper mess, he picked at his food.

"What's wrong, Pete?" Rickenbacker asked. "Off your feed?"

"He's not sick; he's just in love," Lufbery teased. "Are you seeing Gilberta again tonight?"

"We have vague plans," he muttered.

"Vague plans?" There was a loud hoot from someone at the end of the table. "Hell! If I had myself a succulent little wench like that Gilberta, I can assure you *my* plans would be anything but vague. One very purposeful plan: getting in her pants."

Peter got up and stalked out of the tent, fuming as their laughter trailed after him. What nettled him more than anything else was that the taunt had been right on target. *Getting in her pants* . . . He'd had no other thought for the past week.

He went back to the barracks, shaved for the second time that day, laved himself liberally with cologne, and adjusted his flight cap at a jaunty tilt, with the point centered over his right eyebrow. He waited for fifteen minutes before a truck rumbled up to the main gate and showed its cargo manifest to the MPs on duty.

One of them nodded to Peter. "Here's a ride to Toul, Lieutenant. Hop aboard."

It was after eight o'clock when he walked down the block to the Boyer homestead. Feeling like an arch criminal, he glanced furtively in all directions before slipping into the narrow alleyway that ran down one side. He stopped at the delivery door and knocked twice. Gilberta opened it immediately.

"My darling, I thought you'd never get here," she said breathlessly. "I've been pacing the floor for the past hour."

"I've been pacing impatiently all week."

She threw herself in his arms and they embraced, swaying back and forth on the small staircase landing. Her breath was hot on his face. "I simply can't wait an instant longer," she panted. "Come, quickly." She took his hand and led him up a short flight of stairs to the kitchen.

"Are we alone?"

She giggled. "Do you imagine I'd be taking you up to my bedroom if we weren't?"

They literally ran up the stairs to the second story and down the hall to the last room on the left. Once they were inside, she shut the door and locked it.

"My God!" he exclaimed. "You don't think anyone will interrupt us, do you?"

"No, silly; it's just a reflex." She clapped her hands. "Well . . . who's to go first?"

"Go first?"

"Yes; we can't make love with our clothes on."

"To be sure." He shifted uncomfortably from one foot to the other.

"If you're shy, then I'll begin." She unbuttoned her prim starched blouse and took it off.

The sight of her bare shoulders and the upper mounds of her breasts peeping over the top of her pink lace chemise made him feel as heady as if he'd swallowed a glass of wine in a single gulp. Automatically he unbuttoned his tunic, casting it and his undershirt on a chair, while Gilberta stepped out of her skirt. Next he removed his trousers, his eyes devouring her as she stood there in her chemise, smiling seductively. Only his khaki undershorts remained. He felt her gaze riveted on the front of his shorts, where his intense masculine lust was asserting itself unabashedly.

Coyly, Gilberta slipped one strap down over her shoulder, then the other, peeling the chemise down to her slender waist and unveiling her small, perfect breasts.

"They look as if they were carved out of alabaster," he said.

She smiled prettily and cupped her hands beneath the resilient mounds, lifting them. "Oh, no, alabaster is cold and hard. This is vibrant flesh, hot flesh, yearning flesh. Oh, my darling, all of my body yearns for you, for your touch, your kisses——" She broke off and wriggled the chemise down over her hips, letting it flutter to the floor. "Yearns for your flesh," she finished. "Oh, *do* let me see you," she implored, going to him, arms outstretched.

In a moment, she'd unfastened his undershorts and pulled them down, exposing his straining erection.

"Do you know, I've never seen a naked man before —not like this."

Peter gulped, and his face was flaming. "I . . . I . . . the truth is, I've never seen a naked girl before, either."

Her expression was one of total disbelief. "Oh, my dearest, you don't have to say that for my sake. I mean, you are a man and a soldier. I didn't expect you to be a virgin like me."

"You're a virgin." He stated it, and it was glorious to know that he would be her first man—the *only* man she would ever know, if he had his way.

Gingerly she reached out and clasped his tumescent member, and, to her amazement, he began to ejaculate. "Dear, sweet Peter," she whispered, and caressed him until the spasms subsided.

He was too humiliated to look her in the eye. "I'm sorry," he apologized, "but, you see, I was in earnest about what I told you. You are the first woman I . . . I've ever been with. It's the truth. I'm a virgin, too. I'm really not as old as I look. I'm only sixteen."

The revelation filled Gilberta with sheer wonder; gratitude; delight that he and she were entering into the mature world of love and sex together and in innocence. Gently she took him by the hand and led him to her bed.

Peter needed no more urging. When she lay back on the pillow and lifted her arms, he climbed in beside her and pulled her close. His lips found hers, lingered there, then moved down her throat; the pulse in the hollow beat fast and furiously. His mouth covered one of her nipples, and it hardened against his tongue.

It seemed to Gilberta that he was possessed of a hundred hands. She felt as if she was being touched and caressed and teased by a thousand fingers. He played on her raging nerve endings the way a violinist manipulates the sensitive strings of a cherished, precious instrument. The thrust of his aroused manhood against the soft, fluttering swell of her belly was an incomparable thrill. And now she was impatient to cross the last frontier, to emerge from maidenhood into womanhood, the way a butterfly breaks out of its confining cocoon.

"Now, darling—*now!*" she urged him.

Trembling the way he had the first time he held the joy stick of a Nieuport, Peter slipped between her thighs. Her legs clenched viselike around his waist as she guided him to the orifice. She was amply lubricious with desire, but he was unable to penetrate her. Being a novice, he was discouraged.

"It's not going to work. Either I'm too big or you're too small," he lamented.

Gilberta was made of sterner stuff. "Don't panic, Peter. It's difficult with any girl the first time. If we persevere, everything will work out fine."

And persevere they did. Peter was in a cold sweat, and there was an imminent threat of a second premature ejaculation. He was on the verge of giving up, when her membrane gave way and the full length of him entered her. But then, try as he might, he could not contain himself for more than three strokes. Fortunately, Gilberta had been a hairbreadth from climaxing for some minutes. And in a tidal wave of lusty delirium, they went over the crest together.

Like all young lovers who discover each other for the first time, in the aftermath of ecstasy, they believed the sex act had been conceived exclusively for their own private pleasure.

"It could never be the same with any other man," she said, her eyes misty.

"Nor with any other woman."

"Will it always be this good, darling?"

"Even better. They say practice makes perfect."

"It was perfect the first time."

"My dear, sweet wife. I say that because you *are* my wife in every respect but for the technicalities of a marriage license and a priest waving his hand over us."

They kissed, and she patted his cheek. "I think you had better leave now. Church should be almost over."

"Good God! I forgot we're in your home, in your virginal bedroom."

"Not any longer."

Peter leaped out of bed and began to dress in haste. Gilberta donned a flannel robe and took him downstairs, to the delivery entrance he'd used earlier. They embraced one final time, and Peter stepped out into the alleyway, now pitch black. Then he headed for the cargo depot on the outskirts of the city, where he could catch a ride back to the airfield.

For the next two weeks, Peter and Gilberta were in seventh heaven. The day after their blissful consummation, Peter approached Gilberta's father and requested his permission and blessing to marry his daughter. The mayor and his wife were overjoyed, as were Gilberta's sister and brothers. The happy couple decided on a September wedding.

During that favorable period, it seemed that nothing could go wrong for Peter Pike. The Hat in the Ring Squadron, as the cocky young flyers dubbed themselves, were fast becoming a legend among the Allied Armed Forces. To a man, they appeared to be invincible.

Regrettably, it was forgotten that Dame Fortune can be a fickle mistress.

When Peter was at breakfast one morning, Lufbery informed him that he was being awarded a four-day pass, commencing on the following Saturday.

"That's great news!" Peter exclaimed, grinning from ear to ear.

"Going to Paris on your leave?" Peterson teased affectionately, and exchanged a conspiratorial wink with Lufbery.

"Haven't made up my mind," Peter answered with a straight face. *Fat chance! Paris can go begging, for all I care. I'm going to rent a hotel room in an intimate part of Toul, and every spare minute that Gilberta can find, we're going to spend luxuriating in a soft featherbed.*

"By the way, Pete," Lufbery said, "would you mind taking over Jim Hall's tour this morning? Just a routine patrol."

"Sure thing. What time?"

"Soon as you finish breakfast."

After he left the mess hall Peter fetched his flight

jacket, helmet, and goggles from the barracks and went out on the field, where Lufbery and a group of other pilots were gathered around a new fighter fresh off the assembly line. It was a Nieuport, but larger and more sophisticated than the little ships they had been flying.

"The new Nieuport twenty-eight," Lufbery announced. "Over the next two weeks, we'll be training in her."

Peter left them and walked to his plane, waiting at the head of the strip. The mechanic threw him a salute:

"All gassed up and ready to purr, Lieutenant. Happy hunting."

As it turned out, the patrol was a dull excursion. An occasional burst of ack-ack was fired at him when he passed over German territory, none of it even close. There was no sign of a German fighter in the air, and after a half-hour, Peter headed back to the base.

He landed and was just walking off the field when the antiaircraft guns around the perimeter sounded off.

The mechanic shouted, "There it is at nine o'clock! Looks like an Albatross!"

Peter whirled and rushed back to his Nieuport.

"Hey, Lieutenant, you can't take her up again. You're clear out of gas, and it'll take fifteen minutes to refuel."

"Too long." His eye was attracted to the Nieuport 28, looking trim and capable on an adjoining strip. "Is that baby fueled?"

The mechanic's jaw dropped. "You've got to be kidding, sir! You've never flown one like that before."

"So what? It can't be all that different from our Nieuports. Come on; knock the chocks away from the wheels!"

Muttering disapprovingly, the mechanic reluctantly obeyed the order as Peter scrambled onto the wing and into the cockpit of the unfamiliar plane. He lowered his goggles and lifted an arm in the air:

"Contact!"

The mechanic flipped the prop, and the engine roared to life.

Peter checked the instrument panel, scanning switches and gauges. It would take some getting used to, he admitted to himself, but the basic flying controls and instruments were vintage Nieuport, and with a sense of anticipation, he ran his hands along the joy stick and throttle and tested the rudders. "Smooth as honey," he mused. He advanced the throttle, and the fighter streaked down the runway and leaped into the air like a falcon after its prey.

Peter's comrades, meanwhile, had poured out of the barracks and were cheering him on—all but Rickenbacker.

"Damned young fool!" he swore. "Never fly a ship you haven't checked out in at least once."

Peter caught up with the Albatross two miles from the field. He climbed above it, then dove to the attack, firing a burst that sent wood and fabric exploding from the German's left wing. He squeezed the trigger again, but when he squeezed a third time, the gun jammed.

"Damn!" he cursed, and tugged at the ammo belt, hoping to clear it, but without success.

What he didn't realize immediately was that when the machine gun jammed, it caused a malfunction in the interrupter gear that synchronized the machine gun with the propeller, and the second, abbreviated burst had shattered the Nieuport's prop. Now, to his horror, the engine began to spew long ropes of flaming gasoline, which festooned about the Nieuport's fuselage. Reflexively, Peter stalled the plane out and went into a steep sideslipping descent to fan the flames away from the cockpit. But the new 28 did not function with the precision and alacrity of his old Nieuport, and a whirlpool of fire engulfed the cockpit.

On the ground, his comrades watched, paralyzed with fear. Fire was an enemy that terrified airmen far more than any German ace.

"Stick with it, Pete," Rickenbacker prayed. "Dear God, let him make it."

At an altitude of about 200 feet, Peter knew that he could not endure the flames another minute. Even if he managed to land, he would be cremated; his flight clothing was already afire.

As the ship skimmed over a meadow, he saw a wide stream dead ahead. When it was directly beneath him, he kicked the rudder so as to keep the Nieuport going in the direction of the stream, then hurled himself out of the cockpit and hurtled earthward, a living torch. The last thing he was conscious of was a thunderous splash, and then he blacked out.

By the time Lufbery, Rickenbacker, and the other pilots careened onto the scene in a truck, they saw Peter stretched out on his back and two French farmers peeling off his steaming clothing.

Lufbery addressed them in French: "Is he alive?"

"I think so, sir," one of them replied, "but he is badly burned."

"Thank you, *messieurs*. If you had not dragged him out of the water, he most surely would have drowned. . . . All right, men, let's get him into the truck and take him to the nearest field hospital."

A half-hour later, Lufbery and Rickenbacker were pacing up and down in front of a tent that served as a field operating room. Rick stamped out his cigarette with the toe of his boot as the flight surgeon emerged from the front tent flap, peeling off his rubber gloves.

"How is he, Major?" Lufbery inquired with bated breath.

"I'd say he's got a fifty-fifty chance. He's got second- and third-degree burns all over his face, neck, arms, and lower legs, but the heavy flight jacket protected his torso. However, we've got to evacuate him back to Paris as quickly as possible."

"Is he conscious? Can we see him?"

"You can see him, but he can't speak to you. He's in a semicomatose state and in deep shock."

They followed the doctor into the tent. Another doctor and two nurses were preparing to transfer Peter from the operating table to a stretcher.

Bending over him, Lufbery said. "How's it going, Pete? This is Luf, and Rick's with me."

He stared at them with blank, sightless eyes.

"Can he hear us, Doc?"

"I can't say for sure."

They made several other overtures, but it seemed that as far as Peter was concerned, there was no one in the tent with him at all.

"Let's go, Rick," Lufbery said resignedly. "We can't get through to him." A final word to Peter: "You're going to be okay, buddy. Hell, you'll be back with the squadron in no time."

On the truck ride back to the airfield, the pilots were silent, and suddenly Peterson exclaimed, "Gilberta! Who's going to tell her?"

Lufbery looked grim. "I guess it's up to me to tell her"—he took a deep breath and let it out slowly—"she's going to have to cancel her wedding plans. Peter won't be walking down any church aisle for a long, long time."

That same afternoon Major Lufbery, wearing his dress uniform, climbed the stone steps of the mayor's home with dragging feet and knocked on the front door. It was Gilberta who opened it. The instant she recognized Lufbery, she turned pale and clutched at the door for support.

"What . . . what's happened to Peter?"

"He's alive, Gilberta, but . . ." The horror in her eyes was almost more than he could bear. "May we talk?"

Gilberta nodded and stood aside to admit Lufbery. Mrs. Boyer came out of the kitchen, drying her hands on her apron. "What is it, Gilberta?"

"Mother, this . . . this is Major Lufbery, Peter's commanding officer. Peter has been . . . injured."

"Mon Dieu!" The older woman began to cry.

Lufbery put an arm around each of them and led them into the parlor. Trying to keep the emotion out of his voice, he explained in concise detail what had happened, and assured them that Peter would receive the best of medical care.

"Which hospital are they taking him to?" Gilberta demanded. "I'll catch the next train to Paris. I must be with him."

"There's no rush, my dear," Lufbery said. "He may not recognize you for days."

"Nevertheless, I'll be there at his side, holding his hand, waiting."

"Well, I can see there's no stopping you. But at least wait a day or so until the shock of it all wears off."

"The major is right, dear," her mother agreed. "And when you go, I will go with you. You'll need someone to lean on in the days ahead."

Lufbery stood up and put on his cap. "I'm sorry to have been the harbinger of such unhappy news. When he comes out of it, Gilberta, tell Pete the whole squadron is rooting for him."

Within the week, Major Raoul Lufbery would die in an accident uncannily similar to Peter Pike's.

When Gilberta and her mother arrived in Paris two days later, they were met at the train station by a captain of the Army Air Corps.

"I'm Captain James Mellon," he said. "Major Lufbery phoned and asked me to meet you. I have a car outside, and after you've settled into your hotel, I'll drive you to the base hospital to see Lieutenant Pike."

Gilberta thanked him and inquired about Peter.

"I really can't say, ma'am; it's too soon to tell much right now."

He drove them to the Grand Hotel—Gilberta had wired ahead for a reservation—and helped them inside with their luggage. There was a scarcity of bellhops in Paris, just as there was a shortage of everything else in these bad times. At the door of their suite, he handed Gilberta a card:

"I can be reached at this number. Just let me know when you're ready to go to the hospital."

"How can we ever repay you, Captain?" she asked.

He smiled and tipped his cap in farewell. "Just looking at you is payment enough."

They visited Peter at seven o'clock that evening. The chief surgeon conferred with Gilberta before he escorted her into the ward that Peter's bed shared with eight others.

"I know you are Lieutenant Pike's fiancée, Mademoiselle Boyer, but you mustn't expect too much from him. He's still a very sick man and may not recognize you. He appears to have episodic bouts of amnesia, which we hope will clear up when his condition stabilizes. Incidentally—and you had better brace yourself for this—as soon as he is able to travel, we'll be shipping him back to the United States. The medical facilities there are far superior to what we have here at the army hospital. He'll be needing plastic surgery, for one thing."

Tears welled up in Gilberta's eyes and the lump in her throat ached so, she was unable to speak. She nodded her head and walked toward the doorway leading into the ward.

It was a great relief to be in her beloved's presence and to see that he was alive and conscious; but, at the same time, she was disheartened at his grotesque appearance. Swathed in yards of white bandage, he looked like an Egyptian mummy. Only his eyes, nose, and mouth were visible, and they were badly blistered.

Summoning every bit of strength she had, and forcing a smile to her lips, she said, "I can't kiss you or touch you, my darling, but my love is reaching out to you with such intensity that I know you can feel it, just as I can feel your love reaching out to me."

It was a blatant lie, that second part, for there was nothing in his eyes to show that he was even aware of her presence. Still she remained with him for a half-hour, sitting on a white metal chair alongside his bed with the screen around it, smiling and chatting away as if he could understand what she was saying.

"Of course, we will have to postpone the wedding until you are well again, but that is of small consequence. The important thing is for you to recover fully, and then we can make new plans."

Even as she said the words, they sounded flat, hollow, unconvincing in her ears, and deep inside her, there was a kernel of dread that, in the ensuing days and weeks, would grow so large as to threaten to suffocate her.

The metaphor contained a bitter irony. Inside her

womb, there was a seed of another sort growing—the seed that Peter Pike had planted. As yet, Gilberta suspected nothing of it, mercifully; for when the realization came later, she would remember all too well the despair that had struck her heart this day.

BOOK TWO

CHAPTER ONE

The convalescence of Peter Pike was slow and arduous. It required ten operations, performed by the world's foremost plastic surgeons over a period of five years, to repair the severe mutilation the fiery petrol had inflicted on his face, neck, arms, and legs. Still, his physical wounds were of less concern to Tara and Don than his mental anguish. Of the accident, he remembered nothing. The nearest thing to recollection came to him at night in his dreams—repetitious, agonizing dreams that left him drenched in sweat, trembling uncontrollably, and on the verge of hysteria.

His mother and stepfather spent a fortune on a succession of psychiatrists, none of whom could wend their way through the intricate labyrinth of the mind at the center of which Peter Pike had isolated himself from the real world. Dr. Anton Blücher, a star pupil of the renowned Viennese psychiatrist Sigmund Freud, achieved the most progress.

"Your son is afflicted with a form of hysterical dissociation," he told them. "His harrowing experiences in Europe during the war—the misery, the bloodshed, the legalized murder, his own painful, near-fatal accident—are intolerable for a man of his sensitivity and humanity to confront a second time. Let me cite an example: I had a patient whose wife and two small children were killed in a boating accident. His reaction was to rid himself of everything that might remind him of his bereavement—photographs, clothing, toys, what have you—and he refused to discuss the accident or his lost loved ones ever again.

"Your son is responding to his trauma in the same way. He has blocked out the past—at least those portions of it that cause him too much pain. It is only in his dreams, when his conscious resistance slackens, that they are able to slip over the threshold of his subconscious and torment him in the guise of nightmares. The pattern of these seldom varies:

"He is trapped within a circle of flame that keeps getting smaller and smaller and tightening around him until his body ignites like a piece of dry kindling. Then, suddenly, the fire vanishes and he's bobbing around in the middle of a vast ocean, like a cork. The waves crash over him, monstrous waves, pounding him down, deeper and deeper, like huge fists. Just when he feels that his lungs are bursting, he hears a woman's voice and the waves allow him to come to the surface. As if by sorcery, land appears, and he swims frantically toward it. Then he sees the girl—a beautiful girl with long black hair that hangs down to her waist. She is beckoning to him. He redoubles his efforts, but no matter how fast he swims, the land and the girl never get any closer. In fact, they begin receding; he is being sucked back into the cruel sea by a malevolent undertow, and soon they disappear altogether.

"Now, the significance of the fire and the water even a layman can grasp—the plane crash, the flames, the creek that saved his life—but the dark-haired woman is another matter. . . . Mr. and Mrs. Devine, do you have any inkling where she fits into the picture, who she might be? A girl friend, perhaps?"

Tara shook her head disconsolately. "No; Peter never mentioned a girl in his letters."

"He never mentioned much of anything," Devine reminded her. "They were short and to the point—just enough to let us know he was in good health and safe."

"What about the war department? They must have a dossier on your son."

"One of the first moves we made, Doctor," Devine said. "But you are familiar, I'm sure, with bureaucratic red tape, particularly in wartime. There were vague references to two women who visited him in the hospital in Paris after the accident, but they were merely marginal notes made by a surgeon."

"What about his comrades in the squadron? Did you speak with any of them after the war?"

"Yes. Several of them visited him in the hospital here at home right after the armistice: polite, shy young men, not especially communicative. Peter didn't recognize them, and it appeared to make them uncomfortable and self-conscious." A shadow passed over his face. "Once, though, as I was waiting in the hospital corridor, two of his buddies came out of his room looking extremely downcast, and I overheard one of them say, 'It's far better to let sleeping dogs lie, all things considered.' That statement bothered me, for some reason. Of course, they could have been referring to something that had nothing to do with Peter. . . ."

"To be sure," Dr. Blücher agreed quickly. But he, too, found the remark strangely disturbing.

The first seven years of the Roaring Twenties had no significance for Peter Pike. He traced the chronology of the era from newspaper headlines glimpsed while reclining in bed or propped up in a wheelchair at a succession of hospitals and sanatoriums. Sacco and Vanzetti; Prohibition; League of Nations; Adolf Hitler and the Munich "beer-hall putsch"; Flapper; the Charleston and the Black Bottom; Al Capone and bootlegging; Herbert Hoover; Al Smith—he might have been reading fiction, for all the meaning these historic names and events held for him. That all changed on a morning in the last week of May 1927, when Peter Pike achieved a monumental breakthrough that struck his physicians and therapists speechless.

He was breakfasting with his mother and stepfather on the patio of the palatial De Beers mansion outside Silver City when it happened.

Devine had his nose buried in the Denver *Tribune* as he sipped his coffee. "Have you two been following the exploits of this Captain Charles Lindbergh?" he asked.

"The first man to fly the Atlantic Ocean alone," Tara said, for Peter's benefit. But he made no response.

"Here, look at these photographs taken at Le Bourget Airport, Paris, just after he landed," Don said, handing her the newspaper.

She examined them and passed the paper along to Peter. "Dear, look at the picture at the bottom of the page. Captain Lindbergh bears a striking resemblance to you, don't you think?"

"Does he, Mother?" Peter said listlessly, glancing at the photo, which had been taken at a reception in honor of the aviator the day after his history-making flight. He was about to return the paper to Devine when, suddenly, a subliminal image flashed across his mind like a fork of lightning. He brought the paper close to his eyes and examined the photograph. Standing beside Lindbergh, smiling directly into the camera, was a stunning brunette wearing a form-fitting gown with a décolleté neckline.

She is smiling at me! The face; the hair; the nose; the ripe, sensual mouth; the eyes—most of all, the eyes . . .

"I know this woman," he said aloud.

Tara was startled. "What woman, dear?" She leaned toward her son.

"Right here at the bottom of the page." He extended the paper and tapped the photo with a finger.

Devine stood up and came around the table to peruse the picture, looking over his wife's shoulder. "Very pretty girl," he said.

"Indeed she is." Tara looked up at him anxiously and then back to Peter. "Where do you know her from, darling?"

His brow was corrugated from intense concentration. "Damn it, I don't know! But I am absolutely positive that she and I have met."

"In France, during the war? Is that where you met her?" Tara asked excitedly. She caught Don's eye. "Could it be . . ."

Devine went to Peter and rested a hand on his shoulder. "That's it, isn't it, my boy—the girl you keep seeing in your dreams?"

Peter did not respond immediately; his eyes were riveted on the photograph. "I . . . I don't know," he said at last. "It could be. Then again . . ."

Tara could feel her heart thumping wildly. She reached out and grasped her son's hands. *"Think,* Peter! You must exert every resource of your brain. *Think! Think!* They told us two women visited you in the hospital in Paris right after your accident. Could she have been one? Could——"

Peter stood up so suddenly, he knocked over his

chair. He wore the look of a man who has just seen a ghost.

"Darling, you're so pale! Are you all right?" Tara left her chair and ran to him.

"Yes . . . yes, I'm all right, Mother." He put his hands on her shoulders and gazed intently into her eyes. "It's Gilberta."

"Gilberta who?"

"Gilberta Boyer, the daughter of the mayor of Toul —at least he was when I was stationed there."

"And you knew her well?"

"We were in love. . . . We were to have been married the following September."

"Oh, my God! You poor boy. That poor girl." She pressed her face against his chest to hide the tears that were streaming down her cheeks. "Why didn't she get in touch with us after you were sent home?"

Devine emitted a short, dry laugh. "She may well have tried to find him, dear. Do you have any idea how many French girls were besieging the military authorities with requests for information about their American boyfriends and, yes, even husbands who went back to the States, leaving them behind? The army did its best to discourage such inquiries, on the theory that if its servicemen had been sincerely in love with the women, they would have made every effort to renew their relationships after their discharge."

Peter looked like a man slowly waking from a deep coma. Memories locked up for so many years flooded his mind like so many celluloid film clips in fast motion:

Gilberta's lovely face reflecting the ecstasy of their lovemaking on what he would always think of—that first glorious moment they were together, body and soul—as their wedding night. Her face and form in countless guises and postures, as vivid and real as the snapshots of their loved ones the other pilots carried in their wallets . . .

The black crosses on the tail section of the German Albatross in his sites . . . Squeezing the trigger . . .

His own body writhing in the inferno of the Nieuport's cockpit, then tumbling end over end through the air, his clothing ablaze, down, down . . . The shock of icy-cold water . . . Oblivion.

He shook his head to clear it, and as the thought came to him, his eyes lost their glassy look: "Maybe it isn't too late."

"What do you mean?" Tara asked.

"Gilberta . . . maybe she waited for me."

Devine regarded him with pained sympathy. "My boy, it's been ten years. There are limitations to hope and sacrifice. A woman as beautiful and desirable as this Gilberta, there's every chance she resigned herself that you were not coming back to her and that by now she has married."

"No, no, she wouldn't do that, not my dear Gilberta."

His mother laid a hand on his arm. "Peter, dear, listen to me. I loved your father as deeply as a woman can love a man. But when he was taken away from us, in time I came to realize that we, the living, must put the past behind us and go on living full, productive lives of self-fulfillment. I met Don and I love him very much, and together he and I have found enormous happiness with each other. Gilberta, if she is a reasonable, intelligent woman, must have come to similar conclusions after a period of time with no communication from you. Don is right, you know. It is logical to assume that she has long since found happiness with another man."

His shoulders heaved and he sighed. "Yes, you're probably right, and if she *has* found love and family life with another man, I can't blame her. But the thing is, I must find out for myself."

"How can you?" Tara asked.

"There's only one way: by going to France."

Don frowned. "After what you've been through, do you think you're up to such an ordeal?"

Peter smiled, the first honest smile that had illuminated his face for ten years. The beauty of it brought tears to his mother's eyes. "I feel fit enough to lick the world," he assured him. He rubbed his hands together with relish. "Hey, where is the maid? I'm famished."

Tara closed her eyes and placed her hands together in an attitude of prayer. "Thank you, Lord, for the blessing you have bestowed upon this family on this memorable day."

The stationmaster at Toul eyed the tall, slender young man who stepped off the train from Paris with no more than casual interest. Judging from his outfit—tweed jacket with matching knickers, heavy knee-length socks, hiking shoes, and plaid cap worn at a rakish angle, the peak tilted low over the left side of his forehead—an American, to be sure. The stationmaster straightened up from the mail sacks he was sorting out as the stranger approached him.

"Excuse me, sir, do you know a gentleman by the name of Anton Boyer? He was the mayor when I was stationed here during the war."

The red, beefy face was wreathed with a smile. "Anton Boyer? Indeed I do. He retired some years ago."

"Would you know the whereabouts of the family now?" He did not dare mention Gilberta for fear of what he might learn prematurely.

"Yes; they live on a small farm on the outskirts of the city."

"Can I engage transportation to take me out there?"

The stationmaster pointed to where a single cab was parked at the curb. "Right over there," he said.

The cabbie, much to Peter's relief, also knew the Boyers' address. "About a half-hour's drive, monsieur," he said.

Peter settled back, aware that his heart had begun to pound in anticipation.

The trip into the countryside actually took about forty-five minutes. At one point the cab turned off the main highway onto a dirt road that wound through a grove of trees. A quarter of a mile along it they stopped in front of a small, rustic farmhouse set back some 200 yards from the road.

"Do you wish me to wait, monsieur?"

"I'd be much obliged."

He got out and walked up a cobblestone path to the house. Beads of perspiration broke out on his forehead and the backs of his hands, and his throat felt dry, parched, as did his lips.

Steady, old man, steady.

He was halfway to the front porch when the door opened and a man came out of the house. He was heavier than he had been when he was the mayor, and his hair was white and sparse, but Peter recognized him immediately.

Anton Boyer came down the steps, squinting at the new arrival with myopic eyes. "Can I help you, monsieur?"

"I trust you can." Peter was grim. When they stood face to face, he folded his arms across his chest and said, "Don't you know me, Mayor Boyer?"

The stout man cocked his head from one side to the other, inspecting Peter from a variety of angles. "There is . . . something," he began falteringly, "but I . . . Yes, we have met before, I think, though I can't——" Recognition and shock illuminated the old Frenchman's face. "No! It can't be!" He crossed himself as if he were in the presence of a supernatural being. "You . . . you are . . . It's impossible!"

Despite his extreme tension, Peter had to smile. "But it is, sir. Mayor Boyer, I am Peter Pike. I think perhaps you had better sit down. Come along." He took Boyer's arm and led him gently back to the front steps. "Let's sit down here and I'll explain everything to you."

"Yes, do. So much to explain." He kept staring incredulously at Peter and shaking his head.

"I'll start at the beginning, with the accident . . ."

He spoke for almost an hour, describing in detail all that had occurred in the past ten years, and when he was done, Boyer began to sob, covering his face with his hands.

"The tragedy of it! My heart breaks for you, Peter . . . and for my darling Gilberta."

"How is she?" he asked tensely.

"She is well, and living in Paris."

With whom? Peter wanted to ask, but he could not utter the words that he knew, intuitively, would elicit a devastating response. "I was sure she was well. I saw her picture in an American newspaper several weeks ago, with Captain Charles Lindbergh. It was the shock of seeing her face that rescued me from the purgatory I'd been trapped in for so many years. Wasted years," he added bitterly. Now that he'd completed the narration, it had to be faced: "What is she doing in Paris?"

Tearfully her father told him: "Peter . . . Gilberta is married."

He'd been expecting it; still the confirmation rendered him numb.

"She . . . she has a child, a nine-year-old daughter, Linda."

Peter laughed callously. "Nine years old, is that a

fact! Obviously she didn't waste too much time grieving for me."

Boyer wiped his eyes on his sleeve and grasped Peter's arm tightly. "You don't understand. Gilberta grieved for you for almost five years before she married Pierre Landrau, a member of parliament."

"I find that difficult to believe—five years, indeed!" Belated understanding hit him with the force of a lightning bolt. "The child . . . You don't mean——"

"Yes, Peter, little Linda is *your* child. Gilberta was pregnant when you left her."

Peter felt as if all the pain and grief in the world had come tumbling down on him. Tears sprang to his eyes; unable to control them, he let them flow down his cheeks unchecked.

The old man moved closer and put an arm around his shoulders. "There, there, both you and Gilberta are the victims of pitiless destiny. What is done is done, and nothing can undo it."

"I must go to see her at once," Peter declared.

"If you do that, you will only compound the suffering you and she have endured already. . . . You see, Peter, her husband is a fine man. He married her with the full knowledge that her child was illegitimate. He loves Linda as if she were his own. Let me tell you, Gilberta has had more than her share of hard times. When she was only a few months pregnant, she moved to Lyons and stayed with her maiden aunt. If she had remained here, she would have been ostracized, and Linda would have worn the stigma of bastardy throughout her formative years. In Lyons she pretended that she was a war widow. God knows, there was a legion of them. She worked in a dress shop six days a week to bring up Linda properly. Then she met and married Pierre and——"

"Wait! Does Linda know about me?"

"No; she believed what the people of Lyons believed—that her father was killed in the war."

"Damn!" Peter pounded a fist into his palm.

"Peter, you can't turn the child's world upside down and tell her you are her father. At her tender age, she would find the truth incomprehensible. In her heart, she would always believe that you deserted her and her mother."

"I appreciate that, but consider my feelings, sir. I still love Gilberta with all my heart, and I love my daughter as well, even if I have never seen her. After all I've been through, do you think it's fair to deprive me of what has been missing from my life for the past ten years?"

"No, and that is the point. Life is not fair and never was. I can't force you to abandon Gilberta and the child if you are determined to reinstate yourself into their lives. I merely implore you to consider the consequences very carefully before you do anything rash. . . . Gilberta is happy; she has grown to love her husband very deeply. Linda loves him, too. He *is*, after all, the only father she has ever known. Do you really believe that you can give them a better life than the two of them have now? You are a good man, a fair man, Peter. Now, be honest with yourself. In your heart, you want to do the thing that is best for Gilberta and Linda. A truly loving man would willingly deprive himself for the betterment of his loved ones. He would give his very life."

Peter's shoulders sagged and he stared at the ground for a long time before answering. "You're right, of course. I was considering only my own selfish needs. Gilberta and our child, their happiness, their peace of mind—that above all else must come first."

Boyer gave Peter's arm an affectionate squeeze. "It requires a very special man to make the sacrifice you are making, Peter. But then, I knew you were very special the first time I met you, just as Gilberta did."

Peter and the old man stood up and embraced each other warmly.

"Do you think," Peter ventured, "it would be possible to see my daughter? From afar, that is. I wouldn't let her see me."

Boyer considered for a moment, his face creased in thought. Then he flashed Peter a broad smile. "The child attends the Sacred Heart Academy in Paris. Every afternoon at three, Gilberta waits for her outside the school. Directly across the street there is a small park. You could wait on one of the benches."

"Bless you, Mayor!" Peter exclaimed, clasping Boyer in a final bear hug. "Bless you!" And he turned and walked back down the path to the road and the waiting cab, never looking back.

Two days later, at 2:45, Peter was seated on a bench, screened by a lilac bush, in the small park across from the Sacred Heart Academy. The anticipation of seeing Gilberta again and the child he had fathered was more intoxicating than any high to be derived from spirits.

At five minutes before the hour, a chauffeured car drew up to the curb before the wide stone steps of the academy. Peter lifted his opera glasses from his coat pocket and, through a space in the branches, trained them on the woman in the car. It was Gilberta, even more beautiful than he had remembered her. The nubile fifteen-year-old had blossomed into a woman. Like a man starved, he feasted his eyes on the cameo-perfect profile, the elegantly upswept raven hair. God, how it pained him to be so close to her, yet bound not to betray his presence!

His heart accelerated as the front doors of the school opened and the students came milling out of the building and down the steps to the sidewalk, all jabbering like magpies. He moved the glasses back and forth, trying to pick out Linda. He found her easily: the image of her mother, a rare beauty, only she had inherited his fair skin and blond hair.

"My daughter," he said in a whisper.

She bounded into the waiting car and kissed her mother on the cheek, and in a moment they were whisked away, out of Peter's life. This time forever. . . .

For the next five years, in the family tradition, Peter immersed himself in the De Beers Mining and Development Corporation. Nils was dead of consumption. His son Karl was now executive vice-president, his authority second only to that of his Aunt Tara, the chairwoman of the board, and Donald Devine, the company president. Peter's title was Chief of New Product Development.

Expansion had been drastically curtailed by the Great Depression; but, like Standard Oil, Ford Motor Company, and other industrial giants, De Beers had the financial staying power to weather the terrible blight that had crippled the American economy ever since the Crash of 1929. With the election of Franklin Delano Roosevelt to the presidency of the United States, and the promise of the New Deal, the theme of the Depression, "Brother, Can You Spare a Dime?" was replaced in the public consciousness by "Happy Days Are Here Again."

The year 1932, aside from Roosevelt's landslide victory over the Republican incumbent Herbert Hoover, was memorable for Peter De Beers Pike in that two radical changes occurred in his personal life:

In June of that year, he was married to Constance Deal, an heiress to the Tate copper empire in Arizona, thereby merging by bloodline, if not by legal charter, two of the richest and most powerful industrial complexes in the world.

The second event came to pass on the morning after the election, when Peter went down to breakfast and found a letter beside his plate. His chest muscles contracted sharply when he observed the French stamp and postmark and the black border around the envelope. He opened it with trembling, clammy fingers and began to read:

Dear Peter,

This is as difficult for me to write as I have no doubt it will be for you to read. As you must have guessed when you saw the black mourning border around the envelope, what I have to tell you is grievous news. Two weeks ago, my beloved Gilberta and her husband were killed in a motor-car accident on the outskirts of Paris.

At present, your daughter is residing here in Toul with me and my wife. I don't remember if I mentioned this to you when last we spoke, but my wife is critically ill, permanently confined to bed. And I, though in fairly good health, am nearing my seventieth birthday. Surely this gloomy, illness-ridden household is not the proper environment for an active fourteen-year-old girl.

I think, Peter, that the time has come for you to claim the child you and Gilberta conceived in your deep love. I have taken the liberty to tell Linda the truth. She is a most precocious child, and, while it came as a shock to her initially, she has come to accept the circumstances with a maturity far beyond her years.

It is my wish—and I know it would be Gilberta's—that Linda take her rightful place with her natural father in the United States. Both Linda and I anxiously await your decision.

Devotedly
—Anton Boyer

So absorbed was Peter, he didn't notice that his wife had entered the room and was standing at his side.

Constance Pike was a tall, slender woman with china-doll features and flaxen hair that gleamed like a sheet of hammered gold in the sunlight. Her deep-blue eyes, normally sparkling, were filled with concern as she watched her husband slowly fold Boyer's letter. "Bad news, darling? It is; I can tell by your expression."

"Gilberta and her husband were killed in an auto accident." Peter had made no secret of his wartime affair with Gilberta Boyer, nor of the fact that he'd fathered her child.

Constance winced and put a hand to her cheek. "How shocking! What about the child?"

"Linda's fine. She's living with her grandparents. . . . Please sit down, Connie. What I have to say may come as an even greater shock to you."

She sat down at his side, looking at him expectantly.

He took her hand. "Connie . . . Linda's grandparents are old and ailing. They want her to come to the United States and live with us."

A look of astonishment came over her face.

"Of course, the final decision is up to you, my dear. What do you think of the idea?"

Constance stood up and walked behind his chair. Bending, she put her arms around his neck and pressed her cheek against his. "What do I think? To become a wife and the mother of a fourteen-year-old daughter all in the space of five months . . . Oh, darling, it's too marvelous!"

He turned his head and they kissed tenderly. "I never

doubted for an instant that you would approve. . . . Well, then, I must make travel plans. What would you say to a premature second honeymoon . . . in France?"

"I'd say that I'm the luckiest woman in the world."

Peter stood and took her in his arms. "That makes me the luckiest man. . . . Wait till Mother and Don hear that they're about to become grandparents."

"Much sooner than they expected." Her eyes sparkled mischievously. "Then again, not all that much sooner."

"What do you mean?"

"Darling, I think perhaps *you* had better sit down." She put her hands on his shoulders and pressed him down onto the chair, then sat on his lap, her arms about his neck. "The thing is, Peter, in a manner of speaking, our cup runneth over. Not only are we going to become the parents of a daughter; we're also about to become the parents of . . . well, we can't know the sex yet."

He gaped at her in disbelief. "Do you mean to say that you . . . you . . ."

"Yes, dear—I'm pregnant. Dr. Selby confirmed it on Friday." She took one of his hands and pressed it on the soft swell of her belly.

Peter wore the expression of a wondrous child on Christmas morning. "By God! Today I'm not going to motor out to the plant; I'm going to *fly* there!"

CHAPTER TWO

Gilberta awoke at dawn. Her disturbing dreams had put her into a cold sweat, and all her nerve endings were screaming. She took two aspirin and a Valium and then lay back, waiting for the pills to work. But she could not go back to sleep, for thinking of the ill fortune that dogged the members of the De Beers clan in matters of the heart. Great-great-grandmother Karen; great-grandmother Tara; grandfather Peter; Gilberta's mother, Linda—all had lost their lovers in tragic accidents. Perhaps the reason Gilberta had never fallen in love was that she was determined not to follow in the footsteps of her ancestors. Not that she wasn't fond of Harmon; she was. And Julie and her lovers before him—she had cared for them very deeply. But *love* them? No.

Gradually her limbs became relaxed, and she closed her eyes, but when sleep still did not come, she forced herself out of bed and padded to the bathroom, where she turned on the shower. While it was running, she phoned down to room service for a gin and orange juice and a light breakfast.

When the waiter arrived with her tray, a half-hour later, she greeted him at the door wrapped only in a bath towel. His embarrassment amused her.

"Just set it down right over there, please," she said, pointing to the coffee table.

He kept his back to her, and as soon as he'd poured the coffee, he fled.

Gilberta dropped the towel, and nibbling on a piece of toast, she began to dress. Her underthings were wisps of black lace. She smiled at herself in the vanity mirror as she applied her makeup. *Julie will appreciate the sentimental irony of it, wearing black undies to his funeral—wherever he is, heaven or hell!*

The navy-blue suit fit her as though it had been custom-made. When they were in college, Anita was always telling her with grudging admiration that she should become a dress model.

I still could, she told herself immodestly.

She took her time over breakfast, then picked up where she'd left off in her paperback, finishing it just minutes before ten o'clock. And when George Laurentis drove up in front of the Essex House precisely at 10:30, she was waiting outside under the awning.

"You are an exceedingly punctual policeman," she said, climbing in beside Laurentis.

"And you are an exceedingly punctual beautiful woman," he shot back.

Gilberta laughed. "Does the police academy have a charm school? Or is it a course in Irish blarney?"

"We cops of Italian descent don't need any course in charm or blarney; we have our own native brand. . . . Say, I like your outfit. Very chic, yet low profile—just right for church."

"I'm glad you think so. What about the hat?"

He cast a quizzical look at the small pillbox she was wearing. "Neat, pert, without being 'cute.' I like it."

"Gad! I had no idea policemen took such an interest in female attire."

"Can only speak for myself. The way I see it, if you like pretty women, you have to notice the packaging."

"Packaging? You make us sound like articles of merchandise. 'Would you like it gift-wrapped, sir?' " she mimicked.

Laurentis favored her with a smoldering stare. "Wrapped or unwrapped, it's the gift that counts."

She did not reply, but her gaze was as bold as his. *I think it would be great fun to have you "unwrap" me, Georgie.* "Is this your personal car, or is it an unmarked police car?" she asked.

"This, dear lady, is a nineteen seventy-six Thunderbird—not exactly the kind of transportation the city of New York provides for its minions of the law."

Laurentis slammed on the brakes as a woman crossed Fifty-ninth Street against the stop light directly in the path of his car.

"Damned fool!" he muttered. "Look at that cop on the corner! He simply ignored her when he should have been writing her out a ticket."

"For crossing the street against a light?" Gilberta exclaimed. "Captain Laurentis, you're beginning to sound like Captain Bligh!"

"It's no joke, Gilly," he said seriously. "Do you have any idea how many accidents are caused by minor infractions like that? No law is arbitrary; every one is devised for the protection of our collective society. We pay for that service by relinquishing a certain degree of individual freedom, sure, but it balances out. Freedom, in this system of ours, does not give one the right to go through a stop light, nor, as Oliver Wendell Holmes put it, to 'shout fire in a crowded theater.' Do you understand?"

"I do indeed," she said meekly. "I stand corrected. That woman *should* have gotten a ticket."

Halfway down the block, they drew up behind a pick-up truck that looked remarkably like the one Gilberta had abandoned uptown, and she tensed.

Grabbing the bull by the horns, she said, "You know, I've been thinking. That truck you found—Milos's—could the *murderer* have stolen it?"

"Possibly. But we haven't established that there *was* a murderer."

"Now, George——"

"All right, let's say there was. And let's say he had to make a quick exit and took the truck rather than some flashy number because he thought he wouldn't be spotted. What bothers me is, he didn't *have* to steal it. Hell, all he had to do was walk out of the building and hail a cab. Mind you, if he *did* steal it, he accomplished it at great risk. He had to take the elevator down to the basement garage, and there was every chance that someone—an apartment employee, a tenant—would see him get into the truck and drive off."

"You're right; it really doesn't make sense at all."

"No . . . unless he needed the truck to dispose of evidence that would incriminate him, tie him in with Marston."

"What kind of evidence?"

"Unfortunately, we'll never know. When we found the pickup, as I told you, it was completely stripped. If there *was* anything in the way of evidence, the vandals took it with them. In fact . . . the killer may have counted on just that happening. He—— But never mind; I'm talking shop again, just thinking out loud. It's an occupational hazard to be tolerated by policemen's wives and other captive audiences."

He turned right on Park Avenue, then left on Fiftieth Street, cruising till he found a parking space. Gilberta was about to open her door, but he put a hand on her arm:

"When will you be leaving New York?"

"Well, I had planned to go home right after the ceremony."

"Didn't you tell me you had to be back here Thursday on business?"

"Yes. Actually, I was going to fly in Wednesday night, since my first appointment is nine A.M."

"Since it's already Tuesday, wouldn't it make sense to stay over?"

She hedged. "I told my husband I'd be home tonight, and Anita expects me in the office bright and early tomorrow morning."

"The boss doesn't have to punch a time clock, does she?"

She laughed. "I must confess, it doesn't make much sense to fly back for just one day. . . . I'll call Silver City after the ceremony and explain. . . . Why are you smiling?"

"Because I have the rest of the day off, so we can move up our lunch date."

They walked back to Park and around the corner to St. Bartholomew's Church. Milos Alansky was standing in the foyer.

"Good, you're on time. . . . Captain Laurentis, this is an unexpected pleasure. Not that the occasion is a pleasurable one." He laughed nervously and extended his hand.

Laurentis shook it. "I'm on duty, so to speak, Mr. Alansky."

"Duty?" Alansky looked anxiously at Gilberta, then back at Laurentis.

"Just like in the movies, Milos," Gilberta said cheerfully. "All of us attending Julie's funeral are potential suspects."

"Present company excepted," Laurentis said with a smile.

"I demand my equal rights," she said playfully. "Women are just as capable as men of committing murder."

Still smiling, Laurentis replied, "In that case, since I wouldn't want you to think me a chauvinist, I assure you, Mrs. Killington, you will receive *equal* consideration as a suspect."

Obviously uncomfortable, Milos said quickly, "Enough banter, folks. Let's go inside. The services are about to begin."

Although she was not a religious woman, Gilberta was always imbued with a sense of serenity, of inner peace, when she entered a large cathedral. Here the harsh cacophony of New York City traffic was almost totally quelled by the thick stone walls of the structure; and she found the coolness of the air as natural as that of a mountain glade, refreshing like no tomblike air-conditioned air could ever be. As they walked down the nave to their seats, her eyes were drawn up to the vaulted ceiling, so high that in the dimness the fanning was scarcely discernible. Sunlight filtering through a breathtakingly beautiful stained-glass window spread a halo about the large crucifix in the apse.

Gilberta followed Alansky into a row near the front of the church and sat down on the austere wooden bench. Before he slid in beside her, Laurentis genuflected in the aisle. She made no comment; still he smiled self-consciously.

"Old habits are hard to break."

"They're unbreakable," she said.

Gilberta surveyed the assembly that had congregated here to pay their last respects to Jules Marston: business associates, stockbrokers, personal friends, wearing the same drab uniforms they wore to shareholders' meetings. She recognized a few politicians and Jules's two brothers and their families seated in the front row before the altar.

The bishop who conducted the service resembled a large black bird with a white satin breast in his voluminous vestments. Happily for Gilberta, his eulogy was short and not too saccharine.

After it was over, they stood in line to express condolences to the family in the antechamber by the front doors.

Walter Marston's wife, Sylvia, whom Gilberta had met twice, fixed her with a mirthless, vulpine smile. Gilly knew she suspected her and Jules of being lovers. Well, the self-righteous bitch was right!

"It was such a shock, Sylvia," she said, grasping the woman's gloved hand.

"Tragic. . . . When did you see Julie last?" Her tone was an accusation.

"Last month in Denver."

"It was good of you to come. Julie was so . . . fond of you."

"We were all very fond of him."

"To be sure." Her eyebrow arched ever so slightly. "Where were you when you heard the news?"

"At a reception here in city hall, following the Fourth of July ceremony."

"Oh, yes; I saw your speech on television. You were quite good."

"Thank you. . . . Now I really must be going."

"You're not coming to the crematorium?"

"I think not." She glanced at Laurentis furtively before she told the lie: "I have a plane to catch."

"I had expected to see *Governor* Killington here."

"He tried, but he just couldn't get away. These past few months have been extremely busy for him."

Sylvia's smile didn't conceal the thought, expressed in her eyes: *How convenient for you.*

Any other time, she would have stayed to fence with the harpy—in verbal combat she could cut Sylvia to ribbons—but George Laurentis's presence made her uneasy; those eyes and ears didn't miss a thing, she was sure.

"I can tell that you and Sylvia are bosom buddies," he said perceptively when they were leaving the church, confirming Gilly's intuition about him.

"You don't have to be Sherlock Holmes to deduce that," she said casually. "Speaking of whom, what did *your* deductive powers tell you about the mourners?"

"They're all rich and powerful."

"Is that all?"

He smiled enigmatically. "For the time being. I can't think on an empty stomach. How about it? Are you hungry?"

"Ravenous."

"Good. I've got just the place in mind."

A few minutes later, they were headed south on Lexington Avenue. When they reached Thirty-sixth Street, Gilberta said, "Where are we going? I don't recall any noteworthy restaurants in this area."

"Surprise."

She smiled. "I love surprises."

They went through the Midtown Tunnel and drove east on the Long Island Expressway until they reached Jericho, where, a short while later, they pulled into the parking lot of a large, sprawling rustic inn.

"The Milleridge Inn," he said. "Have you ever been here?"

"No, but I like it already."

The decor was Early American: beamed ceilings, pegged floorboards, pinewood tables and chairs with pitted surfaces. As soon as they were seated, in an intimate booth, the waitress, a pretty girl in a period costume, took their drink orders.

"Do you come here often?" Gilberta asked, taking a cigarette from her gold case and leaning toward him as he brought out a lighter.

"Pretty often. I have a place out here, in Huntington."

"A house?"

"It's on the way to becoming a house. I'm building it myself. It's been five years since I had the foundation put in—that's the only construction I couldn't do myself—but from the ground up, it's all my work."

Gilberta was impressed. "How marvelous. You are an extremely versatile and talented fellow, Captain Laurentis."

"Not at all; it's in the blood. I hail from an earthy family. My father was a bricklayer, my grandfather a mason, and it goes back for generations. I love the feel of wet cement and of a rough pine board. This house is a labor of love; every spare minute I can squeeze out of the job, I come out here to work on it. Mostly small things now—a garage, a workshop. The rest—dining room, living room, kitchen, den, and three bedrooms—is completed, even furnished."

"I'd love to see it."

He smiled. "Good; I love to show it off. We'll drive there when we've finished lunch." There was a subtle change in his demeanor. "But, unlike you, I *do* have phone service in my little retreat."

Her gaze and her voice were unwavering. "Well, then, it can hardly be called a retreat. Now, in our cabin, phones, radios, and televisions are taboo."

"Oneonta, you said, I believe?"

"Actually, near Oneonta, halfway to Cooperstown."

The waitress arrived with their drinks, and Laurentis took a sip of his martini. "That's one hell of a long way to drive to write a speech, isn't it?"

"Not to me. I love to drive; it relaxes me."

"Relaxes you? It's obvious you don't do much driving when you're here. Driving in New York is the thirteenth labor of Hercules. Do you keep a car here?"

Steady as it goes, girl. He's zeroing in on you now.

"No; I usually rent one if I need it."

"Then you rented one to go up to your cabin?"

"Yes." Then, forcing a smile: "I just told you I don't keep a car here."

Gilly could have kicked herself—it would be a simple routine matter for him to check her story out with the car-rental agencies in the city—but there always comes a time when one has to bite the bullet, and there was no evading his question. How could she have permitted him to ensnare her like this? More to the point, how could she have been so naïve—*stupid* was more accurate—as to believe that he'd accepted without question her alibi placing her upstate at the time of Jules's death?

He was smiling at her, and it took all her willpower not to show the anger she was feeling toward him at this moment. *His wife was right: he's nothing but a damned pig!* What on earth had ever possessed her to do such an adolescent thing as postpone her return to Denver and go gallivanting around Long Island with a man who could inflict so much harm on her? The answer came to her immediately: *You never* were *one to pass up an opportunity to be flirtatious with a good-looking man!*

Fortunately, he did not choose to pursue the subject. "Shall we order? I highly recommend the prime ribs."

She perused the menu the waitress had laid beside

her plate. "No," she said perversely, still angry with him and with herself, "I think I'll have the Cornish hen."

Conversation during the meal was casual and topical.

"Did you get a chance to see the Tall Ships at all?" he asked.

"Yes; we had a view from the plane as we were landing."

"It was quite a show, wasn't it?"

"Spectacular."

"How do things look from a Coloradan's point of view in the upcoming elections? Do you think Carter has a chance?"

"Out in our neck of the woods, we think he's a shoo-in. Don't underestimate rural America."

He chuckled. "That's right; Jimmy is a good old country boy. . . . Speaking of country boys, from what I read in the papers, your husband is developing quite a nationwide reputation."

"One day he'll be president," she said matter-of-factly.

Laurentis laughed. "I wish someone had that much confidence in me."

"Then, you must become a politician. Traditionally, their wives are the loyalest supporters in the party, Democrat or Republican."

"No way; I've got enough headaches as it is."

By the time they'd finished the meal and had a brandy, much of Gilberta's earlier anger had dissipated. She even responded warmly when he offered to show her his house.

Outside, it had become hot and sultry. As they walked to the car, Gilberta removed her jacket, and felt Laurentis's eyes on her breasts, thrusting tautly against the thin fabric. Again she was aware of his eyes on her

—this time on her legs—as she settled herself in the front seat. Her skirt was hiked up, exposing a six-inch expanse of thigh. She knew that her body aroused him, just as his aroused her. She wondered how many women he had made love to. Scores, without a doubt.

"Mind if I nap on the way?" she asked him.

"Not at all. These two-martini lunches do me in, too."

She closed her eyes. When next she opened them, the car was moving along a narrow, winding road beneath an archway of tall, majestic trees.

"Are we here?" she inquired, stretching and yawning.

"Practically."

Now the road ascended sharply, circumscribing a sizable hill.

"I found this spot by accident," he told her. "It's the highest point on the island, the real estate agent said."

"It's lovely. I have the feeling I'm back in the foothills of the Rockies."

"A refreshing illusion—no reminders that less than a half-mile away on all sides, the landscape is flat and drab for as far as the eye can see and crowded with cheap housing developments and shopping malls."

The road ended on top of the hill, where it joined with a graveled driveway that took them through a tunnel of pine trees. At the end of the drive, there was a grassy clearing in the middle of which sat a low ranch house. Laurentis turned off the ignition.

"You actually built this all by yourself?" Gilberta said wonderingly.

"Yep, with my own lily-white hands." He held them up for her scrutiny; they were large and square, with long, sinewy fingers. "Let's go," he said, hopping out of the car. She did the same on the other side, and kicked off her shoes.

"I have a thing about walking barefoot in the grass, especially thick, rich grass like this." She sat down on the ground and hiked up her skirt to unfasten her garters from her nylon stockings.

"Gentlemen don't peek, George," she said coyly, aware that he was watching her.

"Who said I was a gentleman? . . . Now, that's a novelty. I thought the garter belt went out with women's lib, blue jeans, and bra burning."

"There are times when I have a hankering to feel frilly and feminine."

"Good for you! Women in pantyhose remind me of stuffed rag dolls."

She laughed and stood up, smoothing down her skirt. "You have a point." She wriggled her toes in the damp, cool grass. "Ohhh, that feels so good!"

He took her arm. "Come along and I'll give you a Cook's tour."

He led her up a curving flagstone path to brick steps. On the left side of the house, there was a breezeway that attached to the unfinished two-story garage. Topside, there were naked rafters and studs on two sides. An aluminum ladder was braced against the garage.

"I'm coming down the home stretch at long last," he said.

"How will you occupy yourself once it's completed?"

His grin was wry. "Pay more attention to women, I guess."

"A commendable pastime."

He unlocked the front door and stood aside to let her pass. *"Entré."* He bowed and flourished with one hand.

There was a small foyer that opened into a large

sunken living room with shaggy wall-to-wall carpeting of a burnt-orange hue. The furniture was Colonial, predominantly heavy pine, and the walls were decorated with paintings and tapestries in the same motif: the American Revolution, Indians, scenes of northeastern locales of the era.

"I love it," she said, savoring the feel of the soft carpet on her bare soles almost as much as she had the grass.

The den was L-shaped; the short arm of the L served as a greenhouse and was solid glass on two sides.

"You have a green thumb, among your other varied talents," she observed.

"Like I said, the Laurentis tribe is of the earth."

"What is this?"

"Donkey's tail." He identified the others: "Schefflera, Boston fern, spider plant, Swedish ivy, African violet, philodendron."

The dining room was long, with a massive fireplace at one end and a bar at the other. As in the living room, the appointments were Colonial.

He took her back into the living room and down a hallway to a short flight of steps that led to the bedroom area.

"Not quite a split level," he said. "Splits have a clumsy look from the outside. This is a subtle compromise."

The three bedrooms flanked a small, square court that was more attractive than a conventional hall. They were all furnished in austere male fashion. In the master bedroom, a king-sized four-poster brass bed dominated the decor.

"Jel or water bed?" she asked.

"Neither—plain old Beautyrest with a bedboard underneath it."

"Figures," she said archly. "A big macho guy like you. You've done real well, George, but it could use a woman's touch."

"You want to apply for the job?"

"I wouldn't mind, but it would pose a conflict of interests, not to mention geography. I'm a dyed-in-the-wool Colorado gal, remember. I really don't dig New York, although this site is viable enough, I must admit."

He was standing in the doorway, leaning against the jamb, contemplating her with undisguised admiration and desire.

Gilberta planted herself in front of him, bare feet splayed, arms folded beneath her breasts. Her head was tilted. Her violet eyes were dark and mysterious. "Your libido is showing, George," she said in a low voice.

"Sorry; it's my Latin temperament. A woman like you ought to be required to wear a label, like with cigarette packs: 'Warning! This product could be injurious to your health!' *Mama mia!*"

Gilberta's laughter was throaty, and the pulses in her temples were prominent as the blood pumped faster in her veins. Suddenly the fires that she had kept banked throughout the afternoon flared up. She felt as if her entire body was blushing from head to toe. She wanted George Laurentis very badly.

He sensed her rising desire and walked to her and put his arms around her. "Warning labels never *have* put me off. What the hell! You only live once."

She smiled and moved against him, her arms encircling his neck. The hard length of his manhood nuzzled into the soft swell of her abdomen. She rotated her hips, teasing him to even more torrid heights of passion.

His mouth was strong and demanding, and his tongue darted between her parted lips. One of his hands moved down her back and caressed her buttocks. Pulling her skirt up over her hips, he slipped his fingers inside the waistband of her panties.

Gilberta shuddered and moaned at the electric touch of his hand on her bare flesh. Still holding her in tight embrace, he walked her over to the big bed and pushed her down. While he was removing her blouse and brassiere, she undid his belt and unzipped his pants. Now her hand worked down inside his Jockey shorts and caressed his hot, surging, turgid member.

Feverishly he finished undressing her—skirt, half-slip, panties—leaving only her stockings and garter belt. "You really turn me on like this," he said. He stood up, flung off his shirt, pants, and shorts, and lay down beside her.

Her eyes glistened with anticipation at the sight of his engorged penis. "Magnificent!" she whispered, spreading her arms and legs wide in wanton invitation.

He straddled her but made no effort to enter her. His lips brushed her eyes, her lips, then settled in the hollow of her throat. He could feel her pulse beat a frenzied tattoo against his mouth.

Gilberta gasped as his mouth covered her nipple and his tongue traced circles around her areola. She raked her fingers down his hard, muscular body; cradled his swollen testicles in both hands. He was, she decided, the most well-endowed man she had ever made love to.

His kisses traveled down her length, across her quivering belly, and he buried his face in her crisp, thick pubic hair. A convulsion wracked her body as his seeking tongue found its target, and she began to wail:

"No more; you're killing me! I won't be able to hold back, and I want you inside me when I come!"

He slipped between her quaking thighs, and she clutched his erection with greedy hands and rubbed it up and down inside her slippery labia. Then she positioned the torose tip at the orifice to her vagina.

For Laurentis, it was like entering the gateway to heaven. She was a strong woman, with a powerful sphincter that caressed him in ever-increasing rhythm. She ground her pelvis against his, timing the rotations to his strokes.

"Oh, Jesus!" A volcano in her loins erupted, and now arms, legs, body lost all coordination and she writhed around beneath him, a mass of fibrillating, ecstatic, singing flesh. She felt his climax commence, and it sent her own pleasure level soaring to unprecedented heights.

Afterward they lay side by side on the broad bed, totally spent, sunlight streaming through a window glistening on their sweat-soaked bodies with a sensual incandescence.

Gilberta fell into a deep sleep. She awoke in a state of disorientation, startled to find herself in unfamiliar surroundings. She sat up, bewildered and a little apprehensive.

What am I doing naked on a strange bed?

Abruptly she remembered. "George?" she called out. "Where are you, George?"

The house remained silent but for the humming of distant traffic, a barking dog, birds chattering in the trees.

She went into the adjoining bathroom, got into the shower, and turned it on full, luxuriating in the stinging spray and swirling steam. When she'd finished bathing, she wrapped an enormous bath towel around her body like a sarong and went in search of Laurentis. She discovered him on the patio, clad in his Jockey shorts, reclining on a chaise with a tall drink in his hand. A cigarette dangled from one corner of his mouth.

He grinned. "Hark! The sleeping beauty awakens!"

"No thanks to the handsome prince, whose role it is to wake her up with a kiss."

"Better late than never. Come here, wench."

She sashayed over to the chaise and sat down beside him, and he drew her close and kissed her on the lips.

"There you go, princess. Say, you look great in that outfit."

She glanced around curiously. "Is it safe to sit out here in the open almost naked?"

"Perfectly safe. I am king of this hill and nobody trespasses on my domain." He ran his hand up the inside of her thigh. "We could even fornicate out here with absolute impunity."

"Not this little ol' gal. I like my loving in luxury."

His fingers played in the moist nest of her womanhood. "Care for an encore before we go back to the city?"

"You're very persuasive, Captain. Is this how you interrogate *all* your female suspects?"

"Only the good-looking ones." He contemplated her with narrowed eyes. "Besides, who said you were suspected of anything?"

"Just a joke." She stroked his cheek affectionately. "You know, I can hardly believe this, all that's happened since you and I met as strangers at city hall last Sunday. Two days, that's all we've known each other, and look what we're doing." She giggled. "It's positively shocking."

He slapped her rump. "Come along, and let's see what other shocking endeavors we can dream up."

Their lovemaking this time was both more leisurely and more intense as they explored new avenues of delight: cunnilingus; fellatio; Gilberta assuming the top position; Laurentis mounting her from behind. And when at last they were spent, both were claimed by the sleep born of total exhaustion. Gilberta dreamed of her mother Linda.

Linda—the love child of a man and a woman who would never be husband and wife.

CHAPTER THREE

Peter and Constance Pike were jittery and uncertain as they got out of the taxicab and walked up the path to Anton Boyer's farmhouse on the outskirts of Toul.

"How do I look?" Constance inquired anxiously. "I feel like a wreck. I didn't sleep a wink all night."

"Nor I. But you look beautiful. What about me? I don't look too stern, do I? I do that when I'm nervous."

"You do look a trifle stiff, but hardly an ogre," she replied, smiling. "Well . . . this is it."

Before they'd even mounted the steps, the front door opened and Boyer greeted them: "Welcome to my humble abode. Please come in."

He and Peter embraced, and Peter introduced him to Constance. She pressed the old man's hand in both of hers:

"We share your grief for your daughter and her husband. It's a terrible tragedy. And that poor, dear child—what a horrible experience for her."

Peter was shocked by Boyer's appearance. Since last they had met, he had aged ten years, even more. He walked with a limp and appeared to be shrinking like an aging, withered piece of fruit.

"Come into the parlor and sit down," he invited them. "I'll call Linda. She's been preening and primping for this very special occasion for hours."

When they were seated on the ancient battered settee, he excused himself and went back into the hall. Peter could not sit still. He rose and began to pace back and forth for what seemed an eternity.

"Peter!" There was a catch in Constance's voice.

He whirled about and saw her standing in the doorway with her grandfather in the background.

She seemed taller and more developed now than when he'd watched her surreptitiously from the park across from her school. Her hair was a fan of cornsilk spreading across her back and down to her waist; her mother's beauty more pronounced now—the oval face and flawless complexion, the hint of burgeoning sensuality about her nose and mouth. She was a dream in a brown-and-gold plaid shirtwaist dress, a saucy lace petticoat showing beneath the hem of the full-shirred skirt.

She came into the parlor hesitantly, glancing from Peter to Constance. In a faint voice, with just a trace of a French accent, she said, "I am Linda. I am pleased to meet you"—the next words seemed awkward for her—"my father."

"Linda"—they were not easy words for Peter, as well—"my daughter." He held out his arms and she ran to him. "Linda, my own sweet Linda." He crushed her in his arms and kissed her cheeks and hair, their tears mingling.

Constance and Boyer were crying unashamedly, too. Finally Peter led her over to Constance:

"Linda, this is your new mother."

Constance drew the girl into her embrace. "I will do everything in my power to be a true mother to you."

"And I will be your daughter," Linda replied, kissing Constance on both cheeks.

Peter smiled and put his arms around the two of them. "I think we are going to be an extremely happy family."

In the years to follow, there was never any doubt in the minds and hearts of the three of them that Peter had been right. From the moment Linda arrived in Silver City, the entire family—Tara and Don and Nils's widow and her children Karl and Tess—embraced her as kin. Karen, now the matriarch of the De Beers clan at seventy-three, her self-delusions dimmed by time, was hardy and more mentally stable than she had been in years. And she doted on her new great-grandchild.

There was more joy for the De Beerses when Constance gave birth to a baby boy, whom they named Charles Deal De Beers Pike. From the day of his birth, Linda worshiped him. In fact, she was more like a second mother to him than a half sister.

"She spends more time with Chuck than I do," Constance complained with good humor. "She feeds him, changes his diapers, bathes him. I feel more like his aunt."

"She's practicing up for when she marries Jim Porter," teased Linda's cousin Jean, Karl's daughter, who attended school with Linda.

"Do you know what you are, Jean?" Linda stamped her foot. "You are a *provocateur!* I can't stand the boy!" But her rosy cheeks belied the denial.

James Porter was a senior at the Silver City High School, a four-letter varsity man, starring in football, baseball, basketball, and track. The idol of every starry-eyed girl in the school, he stood well over six feet and was ruggedly handsome, with dark, wavy hair and a smile that could melt even the coldest heart.

In her secret heart, Linda was hopelessly in love with him. And spurred on by the strain of De Beers determination that ran in her blood, she resolved that she could and *would* capture the heart of James Porter as he had captured hers.

Even at her tender age, Linda knew that the way to a man's heart was not through his stomach but through his special interests. And so, when she learned that, in addition to sports, Porter had a passion for mountain climbing, she signed up for mountain-climbing courses at the University of Denver, spending school holidays and the long summer perfecting her skill. And skilled she was—a "natural," her senior instructor called her.

Six months into the course, she was seated at a table in the school cafeteria one day with two girl friends when she noticed that Porter and several members of the school's Mountaineer Club were at a nearby table, engaged in animated discussion of their favorite pastime.

Porter was assessing climbing gear: "Crampons are essential to ice climbing, absolutely essential."

The girl next to Linda whispered, "What are crampons?"

"Downward-pointing metal claws that you strap to the soles of your climbing boots," Linda answered, in an unnecessarily loud voice.

Jim cut his eyes at her, but went on speaking: "Oscar Eckenstein invented the ten-point design, the most widely accepted kind."

"Personally, I prefer the crampon developed by Laurent Grivel," Linda said airily. "Grivel modified the design by adding two prongs pointing forward from the toe."

Porter turned on the bench and stared at her. "What do you know about Laurent Grivel?"

"Well, his crampon makes it possible for a climber to mount steep ice by driving the prongs into the ice with hard kicks and climbing the ice as he would climb stairs. It's known as the German method, and it's particularly suited for climbing the ice of the Alps."

"I'll be damned!" He got up from his table and sat down across from Linda. "Are you a climber?"

"Of course. This winter I intend to perfect the French technique."

"Say, you *are* a climber. The thing to be cautious of with the French technique is the use of the ice ax."

"I know—the *piolet-ancre* position. The ax must be placed perfectly or it comes loose."

He was beaming at her now. "Tell you what; if you'd like, I'll be happy to help you practice." And with a note of pride: "Last winter my father and I had a go at the Bossons Glacier in France."

"Did you climb it?"

"No; we were testing a variety of ice axes and crampons."

"Have you done any extreme climbing?"

"A fair amount. My big ambition is to make a first ascent. Next summer a buddy of mine and I are going to have a go at the North America Wall of El Capitan in Yosemite National Park."

"Is he from Denver?"

"California. Neat guy, Terry; you'd like him. Say, maybe you'd like to do some climbing with us in the summer?" Hastily he added, "Terry's parents would be along to chaperone."

"I'd love it."

They chattered away without pausing for breath, so engrossed in the subject of climbing that they were oblivious of the fact that, one by one, all of their friends departed, leaving them alone in the cafeteria. At last they were jolted back to reality by the appearance of the dean, who informed them their classes had begun fifteen minutes ago and, for their infraction, they'd both be required to stay after school and write a paper.

Linda accepted the punishment almost exuberantly. For those precious moments with Jim Porter, she would have stayed after school every day of the term.

It was the beginning of the happiest relationship Linda Pike had ever enjoyed up to that point in her young life. There was a natural progression of their romance that paralleled Linda's passage from adolescent girl to nubile woman: holding hands at the movies at first; shy, tight-lipped good-night kisses; long walks in the summer moonlight that instigated more passionate embraces. Linda was her mother's daughter, the mother who had lost her virginity to Linda's father in a steamy garret in Toul, France, when she was the same tender age. But the lesson of her mother, the ordeal she had gone through for years after the birth of her fatherless child, was indelibly etched on the girl's psyche. No matter how sweet and urgent the temptation, she was resolved to remain a virgin until her wedding night.

There was one night when her determination almost wavered. It was after a school dance, and she and Jim had driven out to High Point, a bluff where the young sophisticates of the community went to "neck." He parked in a secluded pine grove out of sight of the other inhabitants, and put his arm around Linda.

It was a night made for lovers: the scent of blossoms in the air; the sky a great glittering dome of stars; a full moon balanced like an immense orange on the crown of the distant forest. Linda closed her eyes and leaned back against his arm.

His ardent kisses on her lips and neck aroused her

as never before, and she offered no objection when he slipped a hand down the loose neckline of her dress and into her brassiere. It was sheer heaven to have him fondle her pliant, receptive flesh, and her nipple hardened against his gentle palm.

She stiffened as his other hand crept underneath her skirt and stroked the inner sides of her thighs; but the pleasurable sensations it kindled in her loins overcame the objection forming on her lips. And when he unzipped his pants and guided her hand to his tumescent flesh, she clasped it with tender, loving care. Not in her wildest imaginings had she envisioned the bliss she experienced now as she and Jim continued to explore and caress each other's body.

The tempo of their petting accelerated, each action and its reaction becoming more intense and inflammatory. Gently Jim pulled her down on the seat, then lay beside her and slipped his hand inside the elastic leg band of her panties. His searching fingers inflamed her to such a frenzy of desire that when he attempted to pull down her panties, she lifted her buttocks off the seat to help him.

Then, on the dark screen of her closed eyelids, there materialized a specter so vividly real that Linda cried out. It was her mother, Gilberta, and her voice rang through the corridors of the girl's mind like echoes from a tomb:

"No! You must control your desires! Restraint—haven't I always preached that to you in all phases of living? You will save yourself for your husband so that you will not have to endure my fate!"

Linda's eyes flew open and she reached down and stayed his hand. "I don't want to take them off. Please . . . can't we just keep on the way we were, stroking and touching? I can be satisfied with that."

"My God, look at me! I can't stand it any longer! Please, darling . . ."

"I want to so very badly, but it's wrong." She pulled up her panties and smoothed down her dress.

"Damn it, you can be infuriating!" he snapped. But, at sight of her startled expression, he changed his tone. "At least, make me come," he pleaded, bringing her hand back to his aching flesh.

She smiled and stroked him tenderly. "I'm going to make you very happy, Jim; you'll see." She removed her hand and bent over him.

"What are you doing?" he gasped, and jerked up on the seat as her lips closed over his glans and her tongue teased the inflamed nerve endings. "Oh, my God . . . oh, *wonderful!*" He placed his hands on the back of her head and held her there until he was completely spent.

They did not go to Yosemite that summer, because Jim's father suffered a heart attack in June, and his condition was unstable through July and August. However, Linda did get to meet Jim's buddy, Terrence Finch, who spent a month with the Porters as their houseguest.

"Isn't he adorable?" Jim's sister Carrie whispered to Linda when Terry first arrived. "He looks just like Douglas Fairbanks, Junior."

Linda shrugged. "He's nice-looking, but not as handsome as your brother."

"That's your opinion," Carrie sniffed. "Anyway, you're prejudiced because you've got a crush on Jim."

It was, of course, true. Nevertheless, there was a magnetism about the newcomer that intrigued Linda: the roguish smile, the naughty twinkle in his eye, the cowlick at the back of his head.

Carrie Porter's birthday was in late July, and the

Porters celebrated with a surprise party at the Seton Hotel, Silver City's most prestigious inn.

Linda wore a cocktail gown of peach georgette, a luxurious wrap dress defined at the waist with a satin sash and boasting a long, lavish ruffle from vee neck to mid-calf. She and Jim were on the dance floor when Terry approached them.

"Mind if I cut in, old boy?" he asked.

Jim grinned. "Be my guest. I want you two to be good friends before we tackle El Capitan next year."

Terry raised an impish eyebrow. "A *ménage à trois,* eh? That sounds jolly."

Jim gave him a playful rap on the arm. "I said *friends,* not lovers."

"You're blushing," Terry observed as he waltzed Linda around the perimeter of the ballroom.

"I am not," Linda objected. "It's very warm in here."

"Care to go out on the terrace?"

"No, thank you." There was an air of snobbery about him that annoyed her.

"So, you're really going mountain climbing with us next summer?"

"I am."

"Jim says you're an accomplished climber."

"I can handle myself on a mountain."

"I'll bet you can." He gave her a condescending smile. "You know, I don't believe you for a minute. You trumped up the whole mountain-climbing bit to ensnare my old buddy."

He was far too perceptive to suit Linda, and her crimson flush gave her away. "That's contemptible," she said bravely.

"But true, nevertheless. No mind; you'll be roped between the two experts."

"You're so modest."

"Just truthful. By the way, do you know why they call it the North America Wall?"

"Halfway up, there's a patch of black diorite on the wall that is shaped like the continent of North America."

"Bully! I must say you do your homework thoroughly."

"Has anyone ever told you what a phony you are, Terry?"

"Innumerable times."

"That effete British accent you affect, for instance."

"Of course. People are always telling me I look like Douglas Fairbanks, so I do my darnedest to fit the part."

"You're insufferable," she said, endeavoring not to laugh but failing.

He danced her off the floor, and they both erupted with hilarity. Jim went over to them.

"What's so funny?" he asked, taking Linda's arm.

"Your friend Terry, that's what," she joked.

Despite the fact that she considered Terrence Finch a clown and a conceited ass, Linda had to admit to herself that he was an irresistible charmer who was as ready to poke fun at himself as he was at others. And when he left Colorado to return home, she experienced a sense of loss, though she would never have admitted it, even to herself.

She and Jim continued to indulge in regular sessions of mutual masturbation throughout the winter, as she was adamant in her decision to be a virgin when she married. Meanwhile, her climbing skills continued to improve, under Jim's expert tutelage, and that spring they climbed Pike's Peak.

"Would you believe that old Zebulon Pike, when he discovered this mountain, predicted it would never be climbed?" Jim said, when they'd gained the top.

"Now even a duffer like you can climb it with one arm tied behind your back."

"I am *not* a duffer"—she smiled—"and I find it hard to believe that a relative of mine would say such a thing."

"Old Zeb a *relative* of yours?"

"Well . . . distant. He was my grandfather's grandfather."

"No kidding! In that case, I take it back. By the time we go to Yosemite, you'll be good enough to be a member of our team."

"Remember to tell that to Mr. Finch when you write to him. By the way, have you heard from him lately?"

"Last week. He's straining at the bit. Gad!"—he affected Terry's English expressions—"wouldn't it be something if we old chaps, pardon the expression, were the first to climb the North America Wall?"

Peter and Constance were opposed to Linda's forthcoming junket to California, but they would not forbid her to go.

"After all, she will be chaperoned by Terry's parents," Constance reminded her husband.

"But they'll be traveling alone on the train," he objected.

Linda giggled. "There is nothing one can do on the train that one cannot do in the back seat of a car."

"That's a point," her father agreed, with a sour grimace.

Linda swept her baby half brother up in her arms and gave him a resounding kiss. "I will miss dear Chuckie, though. I do wish I could smuggle him along in my knapsack."

On weekends, she and Jim would take inventory of their climbing gear: hardware—nuts, ropes, ice axes, crampons, pitons, carabiners; soft ware—climbing pants, shirts, sweaters, packs, boots. As the time for the trip drew near, they counted the hours, then the minutes. At last, on July 8, 1936, they boarded a train for San Francisco. Peter, Constance, Tara, and Don saw them off at the station.

"Don't take too many chances on the mountain!" Peter shouted, as Linda and Jim waved good-by from the rear observation platform.

"I'll send you a picture of me on top of El Capitan!" Linda called back.

And then, as the train pulled away from the station, it was enveloped in a cloud of smoke from a locomotive just arriving, and Linda and Jim retreated to the parlor car.

"Well, we're on our way at long last," Jim said, once they were comfortably seated.

"I'm so excited, and I can't wait to see"—she paused —"Yosemite National Park." She had almost said "to see Terry."

"Anything wrong?" he inquired.

"No; why should there be?"

"You look pensive suddenly."

She forced a smile. "Well, there is so much to think about."

The train trip was uneventful, even monotonous. The passengers occupied themselves by playing cards, checkers, or chess and eating and drinking, Jim and Linda included, and everyone seemed relieved when at last the train pulled into the San Francisco depot.

Terry was there to meet them, the familiar roguish smile fixed on his handsome face. He shook hands with Jim and gave Linda a brotherly peck on the cheek. "You both look marvelous, in fine fettle for our jaunt up the North America Wall. Have a good trip?"

"Fair enough, if you like sitting on your butt hour after hour," Jim said.

Terry laughed and winked at him. "I'm sure you two found intriguing ways to pass the time—unchaperoned and all that, eh, old cock?"

Jim grinned and gave him a playful cuff on the side of the head. "How dare you impugn the virtue of the woman who will one day become my bride."

For an instant Terry's eyes met Linda's, and a subliminal message was exchanged that caused her to flush and look away guiltily. He pressed down on his obstinate cowlick with one hand, a nervous habit, and said brusquely, "Well, let's round up your luggage and get out of here. We have a lot of work to complete before we tackle El Capitan."

They drove in the Finches' station wagon north to Santa Clara, where Terry's father operated a ranch.

"Beautiful country," Linda observed.

"Your first time in California?" Terry asked.

"Yes . . . but somehow I feel as if I know it. Maybe because my grandmother spent some time in San Francisco, during the big quake."

"Yes, she told me when I was there last year."

The three of them were seated abreast, Linda in the middle, her legs pinned between those of the two brawny young men. She was uncomfortably aware of the warmth of Terry's muscular thigh; much more sensitive to the pressure of his leg than to that of Bob's. It vaguely troubled her.

They received a hearty welcome from Ben and Dora Finch and Terry's twin sister, Laura. Linda was to share Laura's large, airy bedroom, while Jim bunked with Terry.

After a delicious supper of stuffed roast veal, baked potatoes, and platters of home-grown vegetables, topped off by strawberry shortcake, Mr. Finch and the boys retired to the den to make plans for the big climb, while Mrs. Finch and the girls cleared the table and washed the dishes.

When the ladies joined the men later on, they found the floor of the den covered with maps, charts, and photographs. Even diminished as it was in the photographs, the mountain looked awesomely formidable. Linda experienced a hollow sensation in her stomach as she scanned the multitude of pictures shot from a variety of angles. Mr. Finch and Terry had made notations on them.

"This will be our first bivouac site." Mr. Finch pointed to what appeared to be a narrow ledge on the largest photograph. "I estimate we'll spend nine days and nine nights on the wall before we reach the summit."

Linda was stunned. "Nine days and nights—I don't believe it!"

Jim put an arm around her shoulders. "Still want to go along?"

"She looks a trifle green around the gills," Terry said, smirking.

"Of course I want to go! I merely didn't expect it would take so long."

Mr. Finch continued: "Some of the layovers will be hanging bivouacs."

"Nights spent in hammocks suspended horizontally from the rock face," Terry added, "with only our goose-down jackets for warmth."

"And we've got to carry almost two hundred pounds of food and water along with us," Jim put in.

"Well, if that's the way it's to be," Mrs. Finch said, "you'd best get to bed right now, build up your strength."

Linda was glad; she was exhausted.

Later, as the girls were undressing for bed, Laura remarked, "You have perfect breasts. Mine are too pendulous."

Linda laughed self-consciously and quickly put on her pajama top. "Mine are far from perfect."

Laura gave her a lopsided grin. "Well, my *brother* thinks they are. In fact, he thinks you are perfect in every respect."

Linda turned crimson. "Your brother is quite a hand with the blarney," she said airily.

"No; he's really got a terrible crush on you. Of course, he would never admit it—Jim is his best friend—but take my word for it."

"That's extremely flattering, and I'd love to go on talking, but I really must get to sleep. I'm bushed."

It was easier said than done. She listened to the grandfather clock in the hall below strike one, then two, and then three as she turned and tossed restlessly, Laura's words ringing in her ears: *He's got a terrific crush on you. . . .*

And Jim is the man you're pledged to marry, Linda told herself.

But it was not enough to erase the image of Terry, with his crooked grin and his ridiculous cowlick and his teasing eyes.

CHAPTER FOUR

The next morning, Mr. Finch roused them out of bed at 5:00 A.M. Linda dressed in long woolen underwear, heavy work pants with leather patches on the knees and seat, flannel shirt, heavy ribbed socks, and sturdy leather climbing boots. She took with her two sweaters and a down jacket to wear at night and when they reached colder altitudes on the mountain. Before she went downstairs, she braided her hair and bundled it up underneath a knitted stocking cap.

They ate a hearty breakfast of bacon, eggs, flapjacks, toast, marmalade, and strong coffee.

"Stow it in, my hearties," Mr. Finch told them. "You won't taste grub the like of this again for some time."

"I've already loaded our gear and packs into the wagon," Terry informed them.

The plan was for Mrs. Finch and Laura to accompany them to Yosemite Park and check into a tourist hotel nearby.

"We'll watch you climb for a while, but once you get up real high, I get too queasy to look," Mrs. Finch said.

"Nonsense! Rock climbing is the safest sport in the world," Terry declared.

They piled into the station wagon at six-thirty and began the two-and-a-half-hour trip to El Capitan. It was a marvelous day for a climb, not a cloud in the sky and cool for July—cooler when they got into the mountains.

At nine o'clock Mr. Finch announced, "Okay, everybody, this is it," and they clambered out of the car and put on their knapsacks. Their down jackets and hammocks were tied down across the packs. Mr. Finch had them line up and inspected their equipment. He'd made an exceedingly thorough checklist:

"Take a few more pitons, Jim. Linda, let me see your chocks."

At last he was satisfied, and the four of them went to stand at the foot of the North America Wall.

Looking up, Linda was suddenly overcome by stage fright.

"Three thousand feet high and perfectly vertical," Terry said with a sly grin. "Sure you won't change your mind, dearie?"

She cast him a defiant look. "Not on your life, buster. Let's get moving."

They roped up, with Terry in the lead, Jim behind him, Linda third, and Mr. Finch last. The arrangement had been decided upon privately between Terry and his father.

"In case Linda gets into trouble, I'll be there to back her up," said the seasoned climber.

"But don't let her know that's the reason," Terry cautioned. "She's got an ego the size of El Capitan."

They made rapid progress during the first hour, and Linda was growing more confident with every step. It was evident that Terry was an expert climber. He drove his pitons into cracks in the wall with strong, accurate strokes, all at the same precise angle. If one climber fell, the force of his abrupt halt at the end of the rope would drive the piton down and inward, so that unless the rock broke, he would be comparatively safe.

From time to time they would pause to study the rock wall above them, looking for fissure systems that would direct the course they would follow. Once, Linda directed her gaze downward and saw that Mrs. Finch and Laura had departed in the wagon.

"Up there at nine o'clock," Mr. Finch shouted. "I think it's the crux pitch on this first leg of the climb."

About 100 feet up and to the left, there was a chimney crack, a wide slot into which the body could be wedged; and a slow ascent could be made by inching one's way up with snakelike motions.

By the time they had all reached the top of the chimney, the sun was on the verge of setting, and a cold wind was sweeping across the face of the rock wall. They made some additional progress, but, when they came to a fairly wide ledge, Terry announced that they would bivouac for the night.

They ate a cold supper of dried beef, biscuits, and pork and beans, finishing off with chocolate bars and cocoa from the large thermos bottles they had brought along. There was just room on the ledge for four hammocks laid out end to end and secured to the rock, so that no one would roll off while asleep.

Even bundled up in two sweaters, her down jacket, and wrapped in a blanket, Linda was chilled to the bone. She lay there, shivering, in the darkness, listening to Jim, Terry, and Mr. Finch discussing the next day's schedule.

"It looks like smooth sailing until we get to that overhang straight up," Jim said.

"I don't anticipate any real problem," Terry responded confidently. "I can do that overhang with ropes and *étriers* in a breeze."

In spite of the discomfiting cold, Linda dropped off to sleep quickly out of sheer exhaustion. And she slept until the glare of the sun against the clear-blue sky awakened her.

At eight o'clock, after a breakfast of high-energy foodstuffs—bread, peanut butter, and a vile concoction of canned eggs and bacon made up for climbers—they began the ascent again. They reached the overhang in two hours and stopped to reconnoiter. It was plain to all that Terry had been overly optimistic in his assessment of the task the previous night.

"There's no way to put up protection, hammer in a piton, because you've got to hold on for dear life with both hands," Jim told him.

"I might be able to put a couple of chocks in that crack." Terry pointed upward. "Then I can run a rope around it."

He untied himself from the other three and fixed a separate 100-foot line to a piton that he secured to himself. Cautiously he began the ascent of the overhang, while the others looked on with bated breath. He reached the fissure and, holding fast to a protuberance with one hand, managed to insert two chocks and run a rope around them. He kept on inching his way upward.

"Reminds me of a fly walking on the ceiling," Linda said. She was shivering, not so much from the cold as from fear for Terry's safety.

"He's almost there," Mr. Finch said in a hushed voice.

Terry was within arm's reach of the ledge. He crawled up one more foot, stretched out his right hand, and grasped the edge. When he got a secure grip, he brought his other hand up. Taking a deep breath in preparation for hauling himself up onto the ledge, like a man chinning himself on a bar, he raised his body carefully.

Then it happened!

He felt the rock crumbling under his fingers, and made one last desperate attempt to swing a leg over the top before it gave way. Too late.

Linda screamed as Terry's body hurtled past them, almost striking his father, twisting and turning all the way to the full length of the rope. With great presence of mind, Jim took his pick and braced it under the piton against the rock wall. When Terry reached the end of the rope, the impact caused the oversized steel nail to quiver, and the crack widened perceptibly, but it held. It was top-quality line, and Terry rebounded like a doll on the end of a rubber band. When he stopped bouncing, he hung there limply, swaying to and fro in the breeze.

"He's unconscious!" his father shouted.

"The rope's slipped up over his chest!" Jim called back. "I've got to get to him before he dies of suffocation!"

He secured another rope on a piton, wrapped it three quarters around his waist, and slid down it smoothly and slowly in one of the best demonstrations of rappelling that Linda had ever witnessed. When he reached Terry, he was relieved to see that they were suspended no more than six feet from a narrow ledge. Building up momentum like a child on a swing, he propelled himself over to the ledge and pulled his friend over to him. There he was able to relieve the tension on the rope that constricted Terry's chest. Almost immediately Terry began to stir and mumble. Within a minute he was conscious, but extremely unsteady.

"How do you feel?" Jim asked gravely. It was all he could do to maintain his own equilibrium in this precarious situation; he could not support the other boy as well.

"Okay, I guess. Bloody stupid of me," Terry replied.

Jim examined the wall on either side. To the left, there was a finger traverse that followed the ledge to a sharp corner and around it out of sight. He called up to Mr. Finch and Linda: "Can one of you work your way over about twenty feet or so and tell me what's around that corner?"

"I'll do it," Linda volunteered.

She untied herself from Mr. Finch and secured herself with a solitary rope, which Finch tied on to two pitons. He admired her agility as she worked her way across the wall to a flat half-moon shelf. To her surprise and delight, there was a series of flat descending shelves that had been obscured from her view by an outcrop of rock.

"There's a regular flight of steps leading down to a wide ledge just off the corner where you are!" she yelled down to Jim. "I'm coming down."

"No—stay where you are!"

"Balderdash!" She went down the steps carefully until she was on the same level as Terry and Jim. "If you can swing him over in this direction, I may be able to hook the line on my pick and pull him in."

"It's too dangerous," Terry objected. "My weight could pull her off the ledge. Look, I can manage on my own, make it along the wall to the corner. Go on, Jim, you lead the way."

Jim had no difficulty traversing the rock. At the corner, he paused and appraised his friend's progress, holding his breath. It was obvious that Terry was not his skilled, confident self—fear and agony distorted his face—but he was determined, and as he approached the corner, his performance gained.

More relaxed now, Jim went around the corner and joined Linda on the shelf. They embraced in silence, waiting for Terry to make the turn. He did, and Jim reached out to steady him, guiding him across a two-foot gap to the shelf.

The two boys shook hands. "I owe my life to you, old buddy," Terry said.

Jim grinned. "A piece of cake, old buddy. . . . Okay, let's see about making it back up to where your dad is. Let your rope go, Terry, and the three of us will tie up."

Terry and Jim roped themselves together, and Jim was in the act of handing the line to Linda, with his back to his friend, when, without warning, Terry suffered a momentary blackout, a delayed reaction to the punishment he had absorbed in his brutal fall.

Linda saw what had happened, and she lunged past Jim and clutched at Terry's arm as he started to topple backward off the ledge—an impulsive and dangerous action in such confined quarters. Inadvertently, she struck Jim with her hip and threw him off balance. He clawed for a handhold on the wall, but encountered only smooth stone. He fell away into space.

Linda pulled Terry face down on the ledge and threw herself across him in anticipation of the inevitable impact when Jim reached the end of the line. He and Terry were roped together some six feet apart, so the fall was a short one. The jolt rattled her teeth, and she and Terry slid a harrowing foot or so along the rock shelf, but they held.

"It's all right, Jim," she called down to him. "Climb back up the rope. Please hurry! I don't know how long I can hold on here. I've got my foot wedged in a niche up here, but my leg is beginning to quiver."

His voice was quiet but limned with terror. "Linda . . . I can't make it up the rope. I struck a sharp outcropping when I fell, and I think I broke my arm. It's useless."

Linda was panic-stricken. "Jim, I can't haul you up alone!" She screamed up to Terry's father: "Mr. Finch, hurry down here and help me!" Her braced knee was being inexorably bent as Jim's weight drained her strength. The rope gave way inch by inch.

"No time!" Jim shouted. "Only one thing you can do: cut the rope. There's a knife in Terry's belt."

"I can't! I can't!" she wailed. The tears were streaming down her face. "Oh, dear God! Help me, *please!*"

"God damn it! *Cut that rope before we all go!*"

She clutched at the unconscious boy's clothing and felt for his knife with her free hand.

What transpired next would be burned into Linda's mind for the rest of her days. There was the knife in her hand, the blade glittering in the sunlight. There was the razor edge touching the rope where it bent over the lip of the rock and then sawing back and forth across the hemp. There was the severed rope whipping away and down out of sight under the weight of Jim Porter. No more drag now. Linda lay there limp with the death dirge of the doomed climber shattering her eardrums, fading fast, diminishing in pitch until there was silence but for the weeping sound of the wind playing over the cold, hard stone.

She had no idea how long she lay there, crouched over Terry; nor, later, any clear recollection of how she and the Finches got down from the mountain. It was all a blur: the crowds milling around at the foot of the wall, faces upturned expectantly; the other climbers all around them, equipped with coils of rope, slings, and other rescue gear—professionals of the Yosemite ranger corps—handling her with the gentleness they would accord a child . . .

Then, miracle of miracles, she was on solid ground and being led to an ambulance, while policemen and rangers formed a cordon to hold off the cheering onlookers.

Peace at last on the stretcher; a white-jacketed attendant smiling as he slipped the needle into her vein . . .

Merciful blackness.

Linda was released the next morning. Learning that Terry had a mild concussion and was being held for observation, she went directly to his hospital room. He was sitting up in bed, gazing out the window, when she entered.

"Are you feeling better, Terry?" she asked softly.

The face he turned to her was pale; the eyes puffy, as though he'd been weeping. "I'll survive. What about you?"

"It was only a case of hysteria."

"No wonder. God! It's a miracle you're not in a straitjacket after what you had to do. Dad told me that you cut the rope to save my life."

"That's not quite accurate," she said defensively. "I had no alternative. Jim kept begging me to cut it. It was that or the *three* of us would be dead now. I couldn't hold on any longer."

"You could have saved yourself and let me go over with him. I mean, it's not fair that you should have to carry this burden for——" He bit his tongue.

She sat on the edge of his bed. "For the rest of my life—is that what you were going to say?"

He averted his gaze. "I don't know what I'm saying, or thinking. Forgive me, Linda."

"It's all right." She took a deep breath. "Terry . . .

I would have done exactly the same thing if your positions had been reversed. If it had been you on the other end of the rope, I would have cut it to save Jim. Choice never entered into my decision; I had none."

Their eyes locked, and each saw in the other's something that went beyond the mutual grief they felt over Jim's tragic demise. Guilt. Guilt that transcended the natural guilt all survivors of disasters invite upon themselves. And it would be a while before they were able to rid themselves of it.

Linda returned to Colorado, bearing her grief back to the family and friends who had loved Jim. For almost a year she was obsessed by a need to recount the grisly narrative over and over to anyone who would listen.

One day her father and stepmother confronted her with the suggestion that she seek psychiatric help.

Seeing the look of consternation on her stepdaughter's face, Constance hastened to add, "You can't seem to put what happened out of your mind. It's as though you have taken on a religious vow."

"You think I'm mad?" Linda asked.

"Not mad; a medical affliction—a wound of the mind and spirit," Peter said. "Look at yourself in the mirror and tell me that you don't look sick."

Linda glanced at her reflection in the looking glass, then quickly turned away. Her father was right. She was pale as a ghost, and there were deep circles under her eyes.

"There's a sanatorium right here in Colorado, outside Denver," Peter said, and paused. Odd how the circle had come full swing. His grandmother Karen had required psychiatric treatment when she was about Linda's age. He frowned. And there was himself. Mental disorder had stolen ten years out of his life after the war. And now Linda . . . "I'll make the necessary arrangements tomorrow . . . if you agree."

Linda sighed. "All right. If you think it will do me any good, I'll go to your Bedlam."

She spent the next six months in the Waverly psychiatric home, a luxurious establishment that catered to the wealthy. Linda was repelled by most of her fellow inmates, idle society matrons with the time to indulge their neuroses. The doctors professed that she was making progress, "slowly but surely," but their clichés did not impress Linda.

The first significant breakthrough in her condition was effected by a visit from Terry Finch the summer after the ill-fated expedition at El Capitan.

Linda took him for a walk in the sanatorium's vast arboretum. The most impressive display in the garden was a maze constructed out of privet hedges, very thick and impeccably manicured.

"They say it took ten years to grow like this," she told him. "It's really quite elaborate. Let's see if you can locate the center."

"I'll give it a go."

She followed him into the labyrinth, and for almost an hour Terry wended his way through its twisting corridors, frustrated by blind alleys and paths that doubled back on themselves. Eventually he did reach the center, a small, quaint garden in the center of which was a marble fountain. They sat beside it, on a small stone bench, and chatted—trivial, "make-talk" words. As the conversation ground to a boring halt, Linda took the initiative:

"Why are we playing childish games, Terry? We keep avoiding the subject, pretending it never happened, when we both know Jim's death is the thing that is foremost in our minds right now."

"Agreed." He slapped his hands down on his knees. "Do you dwell on it as much as I do?"

"I imagine so. . . . Sometimes I manage to contain it in a small cage at the back of my mind, but not for very long."

"Me, too." He took her hand. "Linda, you know that I've been in love with you since the first time I laid eyes on you. No, don't interrupt; please let me finish." He exhaled loudly. "The one person who dominates my thoughts even more than Jim does is you. I love you, Linda, love you very deeply, and I want you to marry me."

"Terry, it's out of the question."

"Why? Don't tell me you don't care for me. I know differently; I always knew. It's the key to why the two of us are plagued with so much guilt. In our secret hearts we know that if he had lived, you two would never have been married. The truth is that you were falling in love with me, or perhaps you were falling out of love with him. It doesn't matter; either way, your relationship with him could not have lasted."

Linda buried her face in her hands and began to weep. He moved closer and cradled her in his arms.

"Oh, yes, my darling, let it all come out. 'The truth shall make you free.' That's it, Linda; we must both acknowledge the truth, that we love each other, for only then will we be free from the bondage of Jim Porter's ghost."

"I'm glad we came here," she said, smiling up at him. "This maze—that's what we've been trapped in for almost a year, a maze of self-deceits, self-delusions, and blind alleyways of memory."

He helped Linda to her feet and put an arm around her shoulders. "It's time we found our way out."

The following year, Terrence Finch and Linda De Beers Pike were married in a quiet ceremony attended by only family and a few intimate friends. That year they would conceive a daughter, Gilberta, and five years later a son, Terrence, Jr.

CHAPTER FIVE

Gilberta stirred and opened her eyes. She patted the bed next to her. The indentation made by Laurentis's body was still warm. She heard him singing above the splatter of the shower—an Italian aria that was vaguely familiar to her. She looked at her watch on the night table: 5:30.

She was smoking a cigarette when Laurentis came out of the bathroom, toweling himself briskly and whistling through his teeth.

"Hi, beautiful. Enjoy your nap?"

"Too much so. God! I feel as though I've spent the entire day screwing and sleeping."

"What's wrong with that?"

She snubbed out the half-smoked cigarette in an ashtray. "Listen, George, after I grab a quick shower, I want to go back to town. I can still catch a flight back to Denver."

He frowned. "Come on, Gilly, I thought you were kicking over the traces for this one day. There's still plenty we can do before it's over."

She lifted an eyebrow. "You've got to be kidding. *What* haven't we done?"

He laughed. "I wasn't thinking of sex; just partying in general."

"No, I've made up my mind. I've been behaving irresponsibly enough without adding insult to injury. Anita is competent, but I know there are certain matters she won't touch without consulting me."

"I keep forgetting you're a tycoon. Okay, you call the shots."

She stood up, went to him, and kissed him lightly on the lips, running her fingers through the thick black hair on his chest. "My own little King Kong." She grabbed a handful and tugged.

"Ouch! That hurts." He reached around her and gave her backside a resounding slap. "I ought to turn you over my knee and paddle you."

She wrinkled up her nose. "If you do that, I certainly won't make a plane tonight." She slipped out of his grasp and ran into the bathroom. "See you in five minutes."

"*No* woman takes a shower in five minutes," he said, laughing.

He didn't know Gilberta De Beers Killington. When she set her mind to doing something, she did it.

Five minutes later, when she came out of the bathroom, she was surprised to see him still in his Jockey shorts, hunched over on the edge of the bed, one elbow braced on his knee, his chin resting on his clenched fist.

"Hey, you look like a Rodin."

"Yeah—*The Thinker,*" he said abstractedly.

"Heavy thinking at that. What is it?"

He looked up at her, and she didn't care for the calculating glint in his eyes. He was wearing his policeman's hat; she could sense it.

She stepped into her lace panties. "So don't tell me; see if I care," she said lightly.

"Fact is, there's nothing to tell—nothing concrete." He got up and began to dress. "That's the most frustrating business about this job. We're always clutching at beads of quicksilver. You know it's there right in front of you, but it keeps slipping away. No matter. Shake your tail and we'll head back to New York."

He was quiet during the drive back, responding to her conversation, but only desultorily. It was clear to Gilberta that something was on his mind.

He dropped her off in front of the Essex House at seven o'clock. She kissed him on the cheek and opened the car door.

"I'm not absolutely sure I *will* be back in New York tomorrow night—depends on what's come up in my absence—but I'll call and let you know. . . . Thanks for a glorious day."

He smiled. "The pleasure was all mine."

She grabbed his thigh. "Not quite, dear boy—not all *your* pleasure, by any means. *Ciao.*"

She stood on the sidewalk a moment and watched Laurentis drive away, then hurried into the hotel and up to her suite to pack.

Unable to make an earlier reservation, Gilberta had booked a seat on the red-eye special. At that hour, the plane was only half filled and she had no seat mate, for which she was grateful; she was in no mood for small talk. She ordered a scotch and soda to wash down her Valium, and adjusted the seat to the reclining position. She lay back, staring at the ceiling and thinking about George Laurentis. There was no way a keen, deductive mind such as his would buy her claim that she had rented a car to drive up to the cabin; she was sure of that now. His casual question about it over lunch hadn't fooled her one bit. Before the next day was over, he would know that she had lied. And it would no doubt occur to him that if she had lied about the car, she could have lied about being at the cabin. And if she *wasn't* there at the time of Jules's death, where was she? Perhaps at the Towers penthouse? Before the murder? During? As a witness? As the killer?

It took some effort, but Gilberta forced her mind to go blank and closed her eyes. In moments she was fast asleep. And, with one exception—when the stewardess came round with sandwiches—she did not wake up till the 747 touched down.

She claimed her suitcase and then hailed a taxi. The cabbie, recognizing her, gave her the VIP treatment:

"Hi, Mrs. Killington. Welcome home. I saw you on the TV Sunday. You really knocked them dead."

"Thank you"—she looked at his ID card on the meter—"Mr. Jensen. It's good to be home."

"Say, isn't that terrible about that Marston feller? They're saying now he could have been murdered."

Gilberta bolted upright. "Murdered?"

"Yeah. On the ten o'clock news. . . . He was a friend of the governor's, they said."

"An extremely good friend. A great loss to Colorado and to the whole country. I attended his funeral this morning."

"My wife thinks it was a broad—excuse me, ma'am, a *woman*—who did it. Myself, I figure it was some . . . woman's husband. They say this Marston was quite a guy with the ladies."

"No more so than any other good-looking man, I would imagine. But someone in the public eye, like Caesar's wife, must be above reproach."

"Caesar's wife? Is she in show business?"

Gilberta stifled the urge to laugh. "She was, in a way. Poor thing is dead now."

"Rough deal. You read the papers, it seems like everybody's dying."

"How true. Yes, there are people dying today who never died before," she said, and this time it was harder to contain her mirth.

"It's the bad ecology, Mrs. Killington. All the big companies, they're poisoning the air and the water and the food."

"You should be in New York, Mr. Jensen. Colorado is a garden of paradise by comparison."

He shut off the meter as they drove up the circular drive of the governor's mansion.

"That'll be three-fifty, ma'am."

She gave him a five-dollar bill and told him to keep the change. He got out and held the door for her and carried her suitcase up the steps to the front door.

"Thank you, Mr. Jensen, and have a good night."

"Thank *you*, Mrs. Killington." He tipped his cap and left.

Gilberta let herself in quietly. There were night lights burning in the hall and on the staircase landing. She removed her shoes and carried them in one hand and the suitcase in the other and ascended the stairs. The long upper hallway was dimly illuminated by wall-sconce lamps. The door to the master bedroom was shut, and she walked past it to the adjoining guest room. She and Harmon respected each other's need for privacy on certain occasions.

She undressed and climbed into bed without even brushing her teeth or removing her makeup. Her husband was a light sleeper and would certainly wake up at the sound of running water. During the past few days, her desire for sleep had been insatiable—a common experience when she was under great stress—and she fell asleep immediately.

When she awoke, the sun was streaming through the east window. She rose, took a shower and brushed her teeth, then put on a red velour robe and pompon slippers and went downstairs.

Bentley, the butler, greeted her in the lower hallway: "What a pleasant surprise, Mrs. Killington. When did you arrive back?"

"In the wee hours, Bentley."

"You should have wakened me. I could have prepared you a snack."

"Thank you, Bentley, but my only hunger was for a good night's sleep."

"The governor is working in his office. Since he didn't mention it at breakfast, I assume he does not know you are here?"

"No; I didn't want to disturb him. Bentlcy, would you be a dear and bring me a tray into the governor's office. Is he alone?"

"Yes, madam. I will attend to it. Cook's serving waffles and sausage, or perhaps you'd prefer eggs?"

"Yes; the waffles sound too fattening. Have Sally whip me up a Spanish omelette and light toast . . . plenty of coffee. Better bring an extra cup for the governor."

She walked down the long hall to the far end, where Harmon had converted his predecessor's leisure den into a work area. She knocked. His resonant voice carried loud and clear through the heavy oak paneling:

"Come in."

She opened the door. "Trick or treat."

His face lit up when she entered. "Gilly . . . what the devil! When did you sneak in?" He got up and came around the desk to embrace her. She offered her cheek for his kiss.

"Middle of the night, darling. I didn't want to wake you."

"Well, you should have." He walked her over to the desk with an arm about her waist. "It sure is good to have you back, Gilly. Here—sit in my chair." A wry smile twisted his mouth. "You probably deserve it more than I do, in any case."

She smiled and sat down. Harmon posted himself on a corner of his desk, swinging one foot to and fro. He was a nice-looking man but with rather nondescript features, except for his shock of thick silver hair: tall, slightly portly, with the carriage of an army officer. He reminded Gilberta of any of a number of film actors who portray bank presidents, generals, board chairmen, or politicians and who forever remain nameless in the public mind.

"You look wonderful, Gilly, considering all you've been through since you got to New York."

"It wasn't a strain on me, Harmon," she lied. "All sympathy goes to poor Julie."

His eyes clouded over. "God, yes! I still can't accept that he's gone. And now they're saying he might have been murdered. Well, at least they're finally on the right track, the police."

"Up till last night, they were still calling it suicide. I only learned about this new theory coming home in the cab last night. The cabbie said he heard it on the ten o'clock news."

"What do you think, Gilly? I mean, we both know he had scores of enemies, but do you recall his ever mentioning one in particular?"

"The police asked me much the same question, but I couldn't come up with any names." She stood up and walked to the bay window; gazed out across the rolling lawn. "You know, Harmon," she said slowly, "Jules tried to reach me Saturday, too. Anita said he left a message for me to call him at Milos's apartment. I did, Sunday, shortly before my speech, but there was no answer. . . . I know it's foolish, but I can't help feeling guilty. Perhaps if I hadn't gone to the cabin . . ."

Bentley appeared in the doorway, bearing a tray with a covered dish, a coffee urn, and two cups and saucers. "Shall I serve you there, on the table by the window, madam?"

"That will be fine, Bentley." She stood aside while the butler set down the tray and poured the coffee. When he'd gone, she said, "Join me, Harmon?"

"Yes; I could do with another cup of coffee."

Gilberta attacked her omelette with gusto. "I'm famished. I haven't had a solid meal since yesterday noon."

Harmon lit a cigarette. "How did the funeral go?"

"Well enough, I guess. Jules's brothers were there with their wives. I spoke to that harpy Sylvia."

He snorted. "Shedding crocodile tears, no doubt."

"No; she didn't even pretend. She looked like a cat simpering over a bowl of cream."

"She shouldn't count her chickens so soon. From what I've heard, he left the bulk of his estate to the Marston Foundation." He observed her cryptic smile. "What amuses you?"

"Nothing . . . nothing at all. I was merely visualizing the knock-down court battle the Marston brothers are going to instigate when they find out that Jules all but cut them out of his will." The true source of her wry amusement was the contemplation of Harmon's reaction when he learned that he and his daughter were Jules's beneficiaries to the tune of $1 million apiece.

"Is Jeanette home?" she asked.

"Yes; she went riding with the Middleton lad."

"You think it's serious?"

He shrugged. "I doubt it. Jeanette has always favored older men."

Indeed she has!

Gilberta put down her fork and stood up. "I've got to shake my can. Poor Anita is no doubt going mad at the office."

"I've spoken to her twice. She's holding her own. Good girl, that Anita."

"I couldn't do without her. Now, if you'll excuse me, darling . . ." She bent to kiss him. "See you at supper."

"I don't know about that. Manning wants me to meet with Senator Gerritson and Congressman Levy regarding the shale-oil-development bill."

Gilberta clinched her lower lip between her teeth, a sign that she was vexed. "I'd steer clear of any involvement in that bill, Harmon. Don't forget, the De Beers Corporation has millions invested in research on developing a profitable method for reclaiming oil from shale. If you take sides on the issue, the opposition may—not may; positively will—accuse you of using your position for the benefit of your wife's company."

His expression soured. "Jesus! I never thought of that. You think I should beg off on that meeting?"

"Not at all. I think you should attend, but as a nonpartisan onlooker. The executive branch must maintain neutrality. The bill is strictly for the senate and the legislature to decide."

He rubbed his prominent jaw. "You're quite right, my dear." He smiled. "Of course, you always are."

"Have a good day, darling." She strode out of the den with long, brisk steps and went upstairs to dress.

A short while later, wearing a tailored linen-weave dress and low-heeled pumps, she left the house through the back door and walked to the garage. Ted Lansing, the government-house handyman, was polishing the chrome on her Volkswagen in the drive. When Harmon was elected governor, Gilberta had impressed on him the importance of setting an example for his constituency in their personal living style: "If the voters see the first family driving around in expensive gas guzzlers, you can't very well ask them to save fuel and tighten their belt buckles."

"Looks sharp, Ted," she said.

He touched the peak of his cap. "Thank you, ma'am. Glad to have you back."

"Glad to *be* back." She slipped behind the wheel, and Ted closed the door for her.

"Drive carefully, ma'am."

It was a thirty-mile drive to the new offices of the De Beers Mining and Development Corporation on the outskirts of Silver City—a low, rambling building that conformed in style to the rugged landscape around it. Gilberta parked in her space in the parking lot behind the structure and entered through the rear door.

"Good afternoon, Mrs. Killington," the blonde receptionist greeted her.

"Am I that late?" Gilberta exclaimed. "Well . . . did you have a pleasant Fourth of July, Ginger?"

"Fabulous! How about you?" She clamped a hand over her mouth. "Oops. I'm sorry, Mrs. Killington. I clear forgot about poor Mr. Marston. You have my condolences."

It was said in wide-eyed innocence; yet something in the girl's tone irritated Gilberta. Coldly she replied, "Condolences? I'm not related to the Marston family."

"No, but you and he were very good friends. I'd sure hate to lose a good friend that way."

"To be sure. I assume Miss Thatcher is in her office?"

"Yes, ma'am. She's been the first one in for the past two mornings."

Gilberta walked through the general offices on her way to her office, exchanging nods and smiles with various employees. Unlike so many indifferent companies, where the office workers are jammed together like cattle in a vast barnlike work area with their desks almost touching, De Beers provided each employee with his or her own glass-partitioned cubicle.

She entered the executive quarters, a complex of large, well-appointed private offices, and then the Presidential Suite, as it was called, which consisted of a large anteroom where two secretaries worked at adjacent desks, Anita Thatcher's office, and, at the end of the long carpeted corridor, Gilberta's, the largest and most luxurious.

The secretaries looked up from their typewriters when she approached.

"Good morning, Mrs. Killington," they said in unison.

"Cecile . . . Margie," she said mechanically. "Is Miss Thatcher free?"

"Yes; she just got off the phone. A call from California," Margie added.

Gilberta walked to the door of Anita's office and knocked.

"Come in."

Anita's round face lit up like the sun when she saw Gilberta. "Gilly . . . thank God! One more day of holding down the fort and I would be climbing the walls."

She got up and came around the desk. They hugged briefly and touched cheeks.

"Nonsense! You handled the SEC and the stockholders' meeting every bit as well as I could have. . . . Margie said you were talking to California. Anyone I know?" She sat down in a leather chair in front of Anita's desk and lit a cigarette.

"Your brother. Says he's been trying to reach you since yesterday morning at the Essex House. Didn't you get his messages?"

"No. My instinct tells me he didn't leave any; they're

very punctilious about relaying messages at that hotel. What is he doing in California and what does he want?"

"Negative to both questions. He was very guarded, almost mysterious."

"Typical Terry. Well, if it's important, he'll call back. What's on the agenda for the rest of the day?"

Anita sat down at her desk and consulted her memo calendar. "Let's see . . . Jason wants to confer with you as soon as possible about the SEC matter. . . . Oh, and there's a Frank Weller has a tentative appointment with you at three o'clock. He's from the State Department. I told him we'd check with you and verify before noon."

Gilberta frowned. "Frank Weller? The State Department? I don't get it."

Anita's eyes met Gilberta's. "It has something to do with Jules. He said it was a highly personal matter."

Gilberta felt a tightening in her gut. "State Department, my ass! Ten to one this Weller is with the CIA."

"You're probably right, but what on earth does he want with you?"

"I can't even begin to guess." She refused to ponder over it; when one practices too diligently at hiding a secret, one is almost certain to give it away.

"How was the funeral?"

"Funereal. You know—you've seen one, you've seen 'em all."

"I thought you were coming back directly after the services."

Anita's gaze was calculating and inquisitive. *I can read you like a book,* she'd once told Gilberta.

"I'd planned to, but Captain Laurentis was there—to check out the mourners, as he put it—and asked if we could talk when it was over. We had lunch." She wanted to let it go at that, but Anita was like a dog hot on the scent.

"Must have been a long lunch," she said. "Terry tried to get you at the hotel until after six last night. He finally called here."

"It was the captain's day off, and he asked me to go to the Guggenheim with him. Frankly, Anita, the past few days have been so traumatic, I leaped at the invitation; thought it would take my mind off things for a while."

"A cop who's a museum freak?"

"I was surprised, too. But Laurentis is educated. Told me he was a Rhodes scholar, in fact."

"Well, how about that! Will you be seeing him again?"

"I don't know. If he wants to ask me more questions, I imagine." Gilberta decided it was time to take the offensive. "Anita . . . I've been thinking about our conversation yesterday—Julie's various affairs, namely with you and Jeanette and me." She leaned across the desk and snuffed out her cigarette in an onyx dish. "What I'm about to say is highly confidential; at least right now it is. When Julie's will is probated, it will be public record, but until then, mum's the word."

"Check. Shoot."

Gilberta crossed her hands on the desk and rotated her thumbs, a habit of hers when she was shooting from the hip. "Milos confided in me that both Harmon and Jeanette are included in Julie's will—a million dollars apiece."

Anita's mouth dropped. "I'll be damned! A million dollars? But why on earth——"

"Milos says Julie thought Harmon would stand a better chance of succeeding in politics if he was financially independent. Also, he had a strong sense of obligation toward people he cared about, Milos says, and he felt he owed Harmon a debt."

Anita nodded. "I can guess why, so spare yourself."

"I'm thick-skinned, kiddo; you know that. Yes . . . he owed Harmon a debt because of me."

"And Jeanette? Strike that. If you're Harmon's wife, *she's* his flesh-and-blood *daughter.*"

"What puzzles me, Anita, is why Julie didn't leave anything to you, and Milos would have told me if you were mentioned in his will. I mean, wouldn't he feel the same sense of obligation toward a woman he'd had an affair with and then thrown over for her employer, not to mention her best friend?"

In the epitome of the cliché, Anita "never batted an eye." "That doesn't speak well for my performance as a mistress, does it. You must think I didn't score many points with old Julie, God rest his soul."

"I don't believe that for a minute. Julie thought the world of you, Anita. He spoke highly of you, as both a woman and a human being, on many occasions . . . when I hadn't the slightest notion that you two had been lovers."

"Why, then, do *you* think he left little Anita out in the cold?"

"I don't know, but there must be a reason."

Anita shrugged. "Well, Gilberta, let's not belabor the point. If you must know, Julie set me up with a trust fund when he dumped me for Jeanette. I'll survive. Listen, can we continue this conversation over lunch? I'm starved, and it's almost that time."

"You go on. I'd better clear some of the paperwork off my desk before the CIA shows up. We can talk later."

"Okay. If you need any help, holler."

It did not take Gilberta as long as she'd expected to attend to the pile of memos and correspondence that had accumulated in her absence, and when she'd dictated her last letter, she put in a call to her mother in Thousand Oaks, California, where her parents were spending the summer on their newly acquired cattle ranch.

Linda Finch sounded relieved to hear her daughter's voice: "Oh, Gilly, we've been so concerned about you! Harmon called to tell us about poor Mr. Marston and to let us know that you'd be staying over in New York for the funeral. You *are* back in Colorado now, aren't you?"

"Yes; I'm at the plant."

"What a dreadful shock it must have been. I know you were all very close friends. . . . Harmon said that Mr. Marston was murdered. Is that true, Gilly?"

"Well, the police seem to think so—now. At first they thought it was suicide. But Anita and I told them that Jules would never do that; it wasn't in his nature."

"They questioned you, then?"

"Yes, shortly after I gave my speech. There was a small reception at——"

"Oh, your speech . . . yes! Dad and I saw you on the late news. You were marvelous, darling."

"You're prejudiced."

"Damned right I am, and I have every right to be. Your father and I are very proud of you. Without you, we couldn't afford to take a whole summer off. I was saying just the other night how guilty I felt, leaving the total burden of management on your shoulders, and Dad said that what worried him was that the board of directors would find out just how dispensable he and I are."

"Not true. Let me tell you, I'm going to feel a lot better when you two return and take up some of the slack."

"We're planning to return at the end of August."

"Good. . . . Mother, I'm going to cut this short. I'm still playing catch-up and I've got an appointment in fifteen minutes. I just wanted to let you know that the prodigal has come home."

"It was considerate. I won't keep you."

"Say hello to Dad and give him a kiss for me."

No sooner had she hung up than her phone rang. "There's a Captain Laurentis phoning long distance from New York, Mrs. Killington," Margie informed her.

Gilberta froze. This call could mean only one thing: Laurentis had discovered that she'd not rented a car on the day before Julie's death! Taking a deep breath, she said, "I'll speak to him, Margie."

"Hi there, Gilly. Glad you got back safely. Got your nose to the old grindstone again?"

"You bet," she said lightly. "When I'm away, the work never goes away; it just compounds. . . . To what do I owe this unexpected pleasure, George?"

His voice fell an octave, as if he did not want to be overheard by eavesdroppers. "No special reason; I just felt like speaking to you. I'll never forget yesterday, not ever. You are one helluva woman, Gilly. I think I'm in love for the first time in my life."

"I won't forget it, either, George," she said softly, but not because she was afraid of the girls listening in. At the De Beers company, eavesdropping on private phone conversations merited an automatic dismissal. She decided to take the plunge: "Any new developments on the case? I hear the department's changed its tune."

"Yes, but we're still batting zero."

They chatted for a few more minutes and then she cut it short. "I'm sorry, darling, but I really must go; I have an appointment."

"Okay. Listen, don't forget to let me know when you'll be back in New York. We can drive out to my place again."

"That's very tempting . . . if I can make the time."

"You'll make it."

There was a click, and Gilberta hung up.

Greatly disconcerted, she got up from her chair and began to pace. She had been certain that Laurentis was phoning to notify her that she was being charged as a material witness in the murder of Jules Marston, and here he had invited her to a love tryst!

I think I'm in love for the first time in my life.

Men did so exaggerate when they had the hots for a woman. Still . . . there could be a germ of truth in what he'd said, in which case there might be an implied message in his call: *Don't worry about the lie you told me about renting a car and driving up to your cabin near Oneonta. I'm not submitting it as evidence.*

Not yet, anyway!

CHAPTER SIX

Frank Weller was one of those "gray men" who blend into whatever surroundings they happen to be in at any given moment—bank, business office, department store. A chameleon. His smile, when he greeted Gilberta, was strained. "Mrs. Killington, it's a distinct pleasure to meet you. And my humble apologies for taking up your valuable time."

She returned the smile and shook his hand. "Please sit down, Mr. Weller. . . . Now, what can I do for you?" It was her observation that people who openly professed humility possessed little or none at all.

He took a small black wallet from inside his jacket and opened it. "My ID, Mrs. Killington."

"Central Intelligence Agency," she said. "I figured that business of being with the State Department was a ruse."

"We prefer to keep a low profile. I'm sure you can appreciate that." He glanced around furtively. "I must caution you that what is said between us in this office is strictly confidential."

"I understand."

"The CIA is conducting its own independent investigation of the murder of Jules Marston. You knew, of course, that he was one of our agents?"

"Past tense. Jules told me he had retired shortly after John Kennedy was assassinated."

His smug, narrow smile reminded her of something Laurentis had said: *Old CIA men never die. . . .*

"Well, let us say he was semiretired. Jules Marston was a credit to the agency—a gentleman, a true patriot, a representative of the American ideal—and he will be sorely missed."

Gilberta crossed her legs, took a cigarette from her case, and tapped it on the back of her hand. Weller leaped up and flicked a handsome lighter under the cigarette as she put it between her lips.

"Thank you. . . . Now, Mr. Weller, will you please come to the point? Of what service can I be to you and the CIA?"

His pale-blue, watery eyes blinked several times before he answered: "It is not what you can do for us, Mrs. Killington; it is what the CIA can do for *you*."

"Do for me?" She was baffled and somewhat apprehensive. She had a premonition that the "wolf" was about to cast off his "lamb's" clothing.

"Mrs. Killington, there is no gentle way to put this. The CIA is aware that you and Jules Marston were having an affair; that in fact at the time of his death, you and he were rendezvousing in the Towers apartment complex in New York. The penthouse apartment there is leased by one Milos Alansky, Jules Marston's business associate, but that was a cover-up. It was occupied by you and Mr. Marston."

Gilberta was badly shaken by the casual, impassive disclosure of this most intimate episode of her carefully guarded private life. This totally nondescript-looking stranger had it in his power to destroy her marriage, to destroy Harmon's political career, and, more terrifying than anything else to Gilberta, to destroy her highest hopes and ambitions for the future.

"How did you find all this out about me?" she inquired meekly, thoroughly intimidated by this monster who was toying with her and, she was certain, enjoying every second of it.

He looked amused. Pompously he replied, "Why, Mrs. Killington, everyone knows the CIA's reputation for meticulous investigation work. We dig and we probe tirelessly; we leave no stone unturned to find that for which we are looking."

"Invasion of privacy, some of us call it."

"Let's just say there are no secrets kept from us—damned few, anyway. In this age of the hydrogen bomb and the ICBM, when the world is teetering on the edge of Armageddon, individual privacy and self-interest must be sacrificed for the collective security of the human race."

"Your rhetoric leaves me cold, Mr. Weller. Are you threatening me with this knowledge of my relations with Jules Marston?"

"Not at all, Mrs. Killington," he said affably. "The CIA has no intention of embarrassing you or"—very pointedly—"Governor Killington."

"Then, what *is* your intention?" She waited for him to drop the other shoe.

He didn't oblige her. "Mrs. Killington, if you are honest and cooperative with me, I have the authority to make a solemn vow to you that this . . . this . . ."

"Is *sordid* the word you're looking for?"

He smiled. "I give you my word that your relationship with Jules Marston will never leave the files of the CIA."

How ominous—forever more to be a possession of the Central Intelligence Agency!

"What do you want to know?"

"I want you to reconstruct, to the best of your memory, all that took place from the moment you arrived at the Towers on Saturday until the instant of Marston's death—every detail you can recall."

"Enlighten me, Mr. Weller. If Jules and I were under such close surveillance by the CIA, how is it that you don't *know* what happened?"

"Mrs. Killington, we like to keep tabs on our people, but we were not staking out Marston's residence; there were no watchdogs on his tail. He had top-security clearance within the agency. It was enough to know that he would be there with you over the Fourth of July weekend. And, of course, we had no inkling that someone was out to kill him. Now, then, would you please 'enlighten,' to use your word, me."

"One thing, Mr. Weller: You say that if I go along with you, you'll bury the dossier in the CIA files. What about the police? Will you tell them anything?"

"I gave you my word. No one will ever learn about you and Marston from us. However, should any new evidence come to our attention that points to *you* as Marston's killer . . . well, our agreement is contingent on your innocence. And unless it is proven to the contrary, our belief that you are innocent will prevail."

"Thanks for small favors. At least, at the moment, you believe I *am* innocent. . . . All right: I arrived at the apartment . . ."

She left nothing out—not the sexual encounters; not the intimate conversations with Julie; not the alleged phone call to her brother. She described how they'd watched the Tall Ships commence their majestic sail up the Hudson River, how she had left Julie watching the procession through binoculars and gone back to her bedroom to take a shower. Beads of sweat glistened on her forehead, and her hands trembled, as she relived that traumatic moment when, returning to the terrace, she found his dead body sprawled out behind the flowering shrubs.

She slumped in the chair and covered her eyes with her hands. "I'm sorry. It's so vivid in my mind, as if it was happening here and now."

"I understand. . . . That was a very thorough recapitulation. How much time elapsed, would you say, from the moment you left the terrace to shower until you returned and found the body?"

"Twenty minutes at the outside."

He clasped his hands together in his lap and lapsed into intense introspection. "That's incredible! You said there was no sign of a break-in—the police verified that—which means one of two things: either Marston let the killer into the apartment willingly, since he was someone he knew and trusted, or the killer let himself in. Who else besides the two of you had a key to the apartment?"

She hesitated, not wanting to incriminate Milos.

"The super, for one," he said, answering his own question. "And probably"—he looked up at Gilberta—"Milos Alansky."

"Yes, as a matter of fact. Milos used it sometimes when we weren't there and he was in town on business. But he wasn't even in New York at the time of the murder; the police verified that, too."

"True." He was silent for a while; then, shaking his head, he said, "The part that gets me is that the murderer waited around, hidden in the apartment somewhere, all that time you were packing and carrying your baggage down to the garage in the basement, for the moment when he—or she—could throw Marston's body over the wall. There's only one possible explanation: he hadn't counted on your being there and *had* to wait, for his plan to succeed—to make Marston's death appear a suicide. And, as things stand now, unless you come forward with your story, or the police come up with some evidence, that's how it will go down in the books: suicide."

Milos had said much the same thing.

"One question, Mr. Weller: Isn't it possible that Jules was murdered because of his affiliations with the CIA? It's not all that uncommon, is it?"

"We're exploring that very possibility at the moment. I can tell you now: Marston was last assigned to a case critical to the national security."

"Then, it seems obvious to me that you have established the motive for the murder."

"Obvious but not conclusive. . . . That phone call he said he made to your brother—are you certain he didn't mention *something* about it, something you might have thought was insignificant at the time?"

"He refused to discuss it; but, as I told you, he seemed bothered by it."

"I have a gut feeling that that call was to the killer." He stood up. "Well, I guess that about covers it. I won't take up any more of your valuable time, Mrs. Killington. . . . You won't believe this—I can't blame you—but this has not been a pleasant experience for me, either. I don't like to play the voyeur, but I had no choice. The agency had to find out whether or not you could supply us with any vital information beyond what you disclosed to the police. They may close the case as a suicide," he said grimly, "but we are determined to nail Marston's killer. And when we do"—his voice lowered to a whisper, and there was a glint in his eyes—"that, too, will be listed in the record as a suicide."

Gilberta got up and walked to the door with him. "If anything else pops up out of my subconscious, I'll let you know."

"I'd appreciate that, Mrs. Killington." He took a

card from his wallet and gave it to her. "I can be reached here, or contacted, twenty-four hours a day. Good-by and thank you again."

She closed the door and leaned back against it for support. Her legs were rubbery, and there was a throbbing in her temples. Mustering every bit of inner strength she had, she straightened up and walked unsteadily to the recessed serving bar on one wall of the office. She half filled a water tumbler with Chivas Regal and sipped it slowly until her jitters subsided. A soft knocking on the office door caused her to stiffen. She turned around.

"Come in."

It was Anita.

Observing that her tapered black skirt had a slenderizing effect on her figure, Gilberta was reminded of what Julie had said about Anita being thick through the leg and thigh.

Anita came in and shut the door. "My God, you look ghastly! I take it your session with Mr. Weller was not exactly exhilarating."

"*Enervating* is more like it. . . . Anita, the CIA knows about me and Julie. I had to tell Weller all the gory details, everything that was said and done that weekend up till the instant Julie was killed. Weller's implication was clear: if I didn't level with him, Harmon would learn of our affair."

"The dirty bastard! Say, I can use a drink myself."

"Help yourself." Gilberta went back to the desk and sat down. She lit a cigarette with shaking fingers.

Anita came over and sat down in the chair that Weller had occupied. "What a bunch of sadists they must be."

"They've got ice water in their veins, but I really can't fault them in this instance. Julie was one of their own, and the agency is out for blood. If they do find the killer, I feel sorry for him."

"Or her."

Gilberta laughed without humor. "Yes . . . why do all of us do that consistently—assume that the murderer is a man? Chauvinism in reverse, I suppose. We're convinced that only the brute male is capable of committing violent acts."

"We have a tendency to forget the law of the jungle: the female is deadlier than the male. So what happens now?"

"Nothing, hopefully. I was a good little girl and told all."

"All?" Anita raised an eyebrow. "Wow—*that* must have curled Weller's hair!"

"I spared nothing, believe me. The CIA stands a better chance of catching the killer than the police do. They're not hampered by the courts and the ACLU; they're a law unto themselves."

"Happy hunting to them, I say. The s.o.b who murdered Julie should be strung up to the nearest tree. Did you tell Weller about the mysterious phone call Julie made Saturday night?"

"Yes, and he thinks that it was to the killer. He said that Julie was involved in a case involving national security, but that was as much as he'd tell me."

Anita put down her glass to light a cigarette. "Do you know what strikes me as odd? If it *was* the killer Julie was speaking with that night, how could he be sure that Julie wouldn't tell you who he was phoning? In which case it would have been necessary to kill you, too; yet he let you go scot free."

"It's a point; but if the killer knew that Julie was a gung-ho government agent, he'd probably figure that he would never confide in his bed partner—certainly not a matter involving national security."

"How could he be so sure? Unless . . ."

"Unless he was a fellow agent. I've considered that myself. Well, one thing's for sure: with the CIA involved, we'll never know the whole truth."

Anita stood up. "I'd better get back to work. Thanks for the drink."

Long after Anita had left, Gilberta sat in her chair, sipping a second scotch and chain-smoking. Despite Weller's assurances that she would not be bothered again, there would always be a dark cloud of doubt in her mind. Her dossier in the CIA secret files was a club that at some future propitious time could be wielded most effectively at one of the word's richest and most powerful women.

She started when the phone rang. *God damn it, don't go to pieces,* she chided herself. She lifted the receiver.

"It's Mr. Finch, Junior, calling long distance, Mrs. Killington."

"Hello, Terry."

"Gilberta! For God's sake, where have you been hiding? I tried to reach you all day yesterday at the Essex House."

"Sorry about that, little brother. What's so important? You sound as though you're wound up like a clock spring."

"I'm half out of my mind. Julie's death leaves me out on a long limb. I was going to use my influence with Senator Paxton to help Julie close a big deal. In return, he was going to finance a business deal I've got on the burner."

"Inconsiderate of him to die," she said with cold sarcasm. If it was possible, her brother was even more self-centered now than he had been as a child. "Maybe it's for the best, Terry. Now you can devote your time to the campaign."

"Shit, Gilly, I can beat Prescott with one hand tied behind my back. . . . I can't afford to lose this deal; it's too big."

"So what are you going to do about it?"

"I want the De Beers Corporation to finance it. It's only ten million."

"Only ten million! Talk about *chutzpah,* you've got enough for the whole family. You may not have learned much about corporate fiscal policy working here, but you should at least know that I do not have the unilateral authority to authorize a loan of that size; nor do Mother and Father. That kind of financing requires the approval of the full board of directors."

"What about the family personal fortune? You could tap that. It would only be for a few months, and you'd get the whole amount back with interest."

"That would mean liquidating assets. Even the De Beers estate doesn't have that kind of cash flow. Mother and Father would never agree to that. I'm sorry, Terry, you're going to have to tap another source."

"Go to hell, you bitch!" He slammed down the phone.

Gilberta sighed and put the phone back in its cradle. *Terry, you haven't changed an iota over the years; you're still the spoiled, headstrong, tantrum-throwing brat today that you were at five.*

She got up wearily and walked over to the bar to fix still a third drink. It was unlike Gilberta to drink in the afternoon, but today was one of those days when Murphy's law was especially applicable: Anything that can go wrong will go wrong.

She stood at the picture window behind the desk, gazing out across the crowded parking lot at far horizons beyond the crown of the forest, beyond the mountain peaks shrouded in mist, across the barrier of time.

Had there ever been a time when she had been carefree and innocent?

She closed her eyes, and an image of Loon Lake flashed across her mind.

CHAPTER SEVEN

The summer of 1953 was particularly memorable for Gilberta. She was twelve years old, and Terry, Jr., was seven. As had been their custom every summer for years, the Finches permitted the children to select one friend each to accompany them on their vacation at the family's hunting lodge high in the Rocky Mountains. It was an ideal place for youngsters to exercise the high spirits and exuberance that infected them at the end of the endless, monotonous school year.

This year Terry brought along little Brian, a redhead with freckles and enormous blue eyes, and Gilberta her best friend, Elizabeth Cooley, a pretty girl of fourteen whose nubile physical attributes were the envy of all her schoolmates. Not that Gilberta was sexless. At twelve, the promise of the future beauty she would become was very evident; but so was her innocence.

The only unpleasant note to these summer idylls was the constant friction between Gilberta and her brother. To his friends and family, he was an angel; indeed, he had an angelic quality about him, with his fair, soft, curly hair, smiling blue eyes, and the dimple in his chin.

It seemed to Gilberta that she was the only one with clear vision to penetrate his façade.

"He's an absolute monster," she confided to Liz before they embarked for Loon Lake.

But Liz, like everyone else, found him to be a charmer. "He's never been anything but sweet to me," she said.

Gilberta sniffed disdainfully. "You know why he's always hanging around you? He likes to brush against your behind and your boobs. The other night I caught him out in the shrubbery, peeking in your window while you were undressing."

Liz passed it off with a laugh. "Oh, Gilly, you know how boys are—though I must admit, Terry is somewhat precocious for his age."

Gilberta's ledger of insults, embarrassments, and affronts that Terry inflicted on her grew daily, and with it, her resentment and frustration. But she was not the only one he tormented; just the only one who bore him a grudge. A natural leader, and the biggest boy in his class, he would bully his friends, but they never took offense. All he had to do was flash the smile, throw an arm around his victim's shoulders, say "Aw, come on, I was only kidding," and all would be forgiven. He could recite the most blatant falsehoods and none doubted his word. What griped Gilberta most—and she admitted it to herself sometime—he was the apple of his mother's eye.

Like all bullies, there was a streak of cowardice in Terry's nature that he successfully concealed behind a façade of bravado. One of his fears was water. But, whenever the four of them went down to the lake on hot, sultry afternoons, he would pretend to find swimming boring, and demand that Brian play some game or other with him on the beach.

This particular day, Gilberta and Liz were sunbathing on the little dock by the boathouse, lying on their stomachs on the hot wooden planks, luxuriating in the feel of the sun beating down on their backs and lazily watching the boys cavorting in the shallow water that lapped gently at the white, sandy beach. Suddenly Liz lifted her head as, abruptly, the timbre of their raucous voices became louder and louder:

"You sonovabitch, you do that again, I'll deck you!" Terry shouted.

"Says who?" Brian screamed.

"Says me!" And Terry punched his friend on the side of his head.

Gilberta seemed totally oblivious. Liz grabbed her arm:

"Hey, Gilly, they're fighting."

Gilberta yawned. "I couldn't care less if they kill each other."

"Well, I'm going to stop it." Liz leaped to her feet and hopped off the dock onto the beach. The boys were wrestling on the sand, arms and legs kicking and flailing.

"Hey, you two, break it up!" she shouted. "They'll hear you clear up to the house, and then you'll be in for it." She stood spraddle-legged over the combatants, then wrapped her arms around Terry's neck and dragged him off Brian.

"Hey, you, leggo!" He struggled furiously at first, but Liz held onto him for dear life, crushing him against her body, and suddenly he went limp in her arms.

Brian, still sprawled on the ground, looked up at him in surprise. "What's so funny? What are you smiling at?"

"Nothing that would interest you." Terry pressed back against Liz now, rubbing his hard, tight buttocks across her thighs and leaning back against her breasts.

Brian got up and brushed himself off. "I'm going back to the house. You coming?"

"I'll be up a little later." He turned to face Liz as she released him. The crafty smile was pasted on his face.

She placed her hands on her hips and demanded, "Now, what was the fight about?"

He looked sullen. "The fink tried to drag me out over my head."

"Oh, Brian wouldn't do that. He knows you're afraid of water."

"I am *not* afraid of water," he said, stamping his foot. "I just don't think swimming is any fun. If I wanted to, I'd learn how."

"You really should learn for your own good. I mean, you're always out in the boat. Suppose you fell overboard."

He hung his head silently.

"Say, how would you like me to give you a swimming lesson?"

He regarded her quizzically, with his head cocked to one side. "You mean it?"

"Yes, I do. I'm a good teacher. I have a certificate from the Red Cross."

"Okay—sure," he said, and there was a mischievous twinkle in his blue eyes. "What do I do first?"

He looked her up and down boldly. Liz was wearing a skimpy bikini: the top was no more than a narrow bandanna; the bottom, two wisps of cloth front and back that left little to the imagination. On their way to the water, he fell behind so that he could watch the saucy flexing of her buttocks.

They waded out until the water was waist deep.

"The first thing to learn is the dead-man's float." She stretched out face down in the lake with her arms extended in front of her and her legs churning the water like scissor blades. About ten feet out, she stood up. "Now it's your turn."

"I'll sink like a rock."

"Come on; don't be a sissy. Here, I'll support you until you get the hang of it." She came back to him and spread out her hands, palms up. "Now, you lie down across my hands. Stretch your arms out ahead of you like I did and move your legs back and forth, kicking with your feet."

He followed her instructions. His kick was awkward, and water splashed all over Liz, but he made progress.

"Very good," she said, and kept walking along with him.

They were in the shadow of the dock when Terry came up for air. He grinned and blew a stream of water at Liz. "Boy, was that ever fun!"

"I *told* you swimming was fun."

"I wasn't talking about swimming."

The sly innuendo was clear, but Liz pretended she didn't understand. "Now we'll try floating." She lay on her back with her arms spread out to the side and her legs apart. "The important thing to remember in floating is to keep your head tilted back in the water."

Terry snickered. "Your boobs float like two rubber balls."

She stood up and scowled. "Terrence Finch, you should have your mouth washed out with soap! You're a naughty boy!"

He moved back underneath the dock and beckoned for her to follow. "Now watch *me* float," he said.

When he lay back in the water, Liz was shocked to observe that he had removed his trunks.

"Come on, Lizzie, you've got to support me. Here, hold me up by this." He wiggled his stiff penis at her.

Liz was mesmerized, beset by conflicting emotions: disgust for him and for herself for staring at him; curiosity. She knew all about sex between men and women, but she had never gone further with a boy than kissing and nervous touching. Once she had let a boy slide his hand halfway up her thigh before pushing him away, and the pleasurable sensation was still vivid in her mind hours later. The female animal within her took erotic satisfaction that she had the power to sexually arouse this male, young as he was.

Trancelike, she walked underneath the dock and stretched out her hand. Her fingers clasped him.

"Rub it! Rub it!" he gasped. His hands fastened on her halter and pulled it down, exposing her breasts.

Above them on the dock, Gilberta was dozing in the warm wash of the sunshine. Some remote sound awakened her, and she raised herself up on her elbows and looked around the beach and the lake. There was no sign of Liz or Terry. Then she realized that the sound she had heard was splashing under the dock.

Now, what are those two up to? she mused. She got up on her hands and knees and crawled to the side of the dock. Grasping the edge with both hands, she craned her neck down so that she could see what was happening below.

She could not believe her eyes. Her best friend and her little brother in obscene embrace! He was kissing one of her bare breasts and had one hand down inside her bikini briefs. She was fondling his—— Gilberta's mind rejected any further extension of the scene. She stood up quietly and walked off the dock and up the hill to the house.

Later, when Liz and Terry returned to the house, Gilberta acted as if the repulsive episode had never happened; but inside she was seething with rage and maniacal hatred directed toward both of them. She came to two momentous decisions: She and Liz could never be friends again. It brought an aching lump to her throat; she had loved Liz like a sister for so many years. She would be civil toward her until the vacation was over, but once they were home, she would make a clean break, maybe even tell her the reason. As for Terry, this time she was determined to wreak terrible vengeance upon him!

A few days later, Terry announced at breakfast that he was going fishing. "Want to go along, Dad?"

"Not today, I'm afraid. I have an appointment in town."

"And I won't hear of your going alone," his mother said.

Terry flew into one of his tantrums, but it was to no avail; Linda was adamant. "If you could swim, it would be different. The answer is *no!*"

Gilberta put down her napkin and said, "That's all right; I'll go with him."

Terry looked at her, surprise written all over his face. "*You* go fishing? I don't believe it."

"I just feel like going out in the boat."

"Gee, sis, you're a good kid after all."

She smiled at him sweetly. "When do you want to start?"

"Right now. I'll go upstairs and put on my trunks."

"I'd like to go with you, Gilly," Liz said, "but I simply must wash this filthy hair of mine."

"That's okay, Liz. I'll take some magazines to pass the time while the monster is fishing."

Linda frowned. "Don't speak like that about your brother, Gilly."

Gilberta smiled. "I was only kidding, Mom."

Terry came bounding down the stairs, wearing his trunks and carrying a towel over his arm. He tossed it to Gilberta. "Here, carry this. I've got to get my gear out of the shed."

"I'll meet you down at the dock."

Gilberta walked down the hill to the boathouse and unlocked the door. Inside was the Finches' sleek sixteen-foot powerboat. She went to the front of the shed and pulled up the wide folding door.

When Terry arrived, she was sitting in the driver's seat, gunning the twin engines. "Hop aboard, Terry."

He scowled at her. "Who said you could drive?"

She shrugged and slid over into the passenger seat, and Terry settled himself behind the wheel and eased the throttle forward. The powerful engines roared, and the boat moved out of the boathouse into the lake.

"Good day for fishing," he said. "They ought to be biting over at the cove." He steered for a spit of land a mile off at the east side of Loon Lake.

Gilberta thumbed idly through a copy of *Cosmopolitan* magazine.

When they were abreast of the little peninsula, Terry took the boat into shore on the other side of it. They glided into a lagoon where the water was like a mirror.

"Heave the anchor overboard, Gilly."

"Yes, *sir.*" She climbed back over the seat into the stern, picked up the heavy steel hook, and dropped it over the gunwale as Terry cut the engines.

While Terry was baiting his line, Gilberta put up the canopy over the stern seats.

He sneered at her. "What's the matter—afraid your lily-white skin will burn?"

"It's not like bathing on the dock," she explained.

"Out here you have the reflection of both the water and the sky." She settled back on the nylon cushions that doubled as life preservers and began to read.

Terry felt a strike on his line within minutes. "How about that?" he whooped. "Tonight we're going to have a real fish fry."

Gilberta wrinkled up her nose. "I hate fish."

One hour later he had eight lake bass in his creel. "One more and we can go back." He cast the line far out, and the hook fell close to the bank.

Gilberta compressed her lips and put down the magazine. She stood up, clenching and unclenching her fists. The expression on her face was unadulterated malice. She took a deep breath and lifted her arms, hands facing her brother; then she rushed at him. Her hands struck him on both shoulder blades and he went flying out of the boat into the deep water.

He came to the surface, sputtering and screaming like a banshee. Gilberta shuddered. Never had she seen a look of such abject terror on a human face.

"Gilberta, *save me!*" he wailed, arms and legs thrashing wildly.

"You filthy little bastard!" she shouted. "From the time you could walk and talk, you've been the bane of my existence!" She doubled over and pounded her fists on the gunwale. "But what you did with Liz the other day, for *that* you're going to die!"

He was hysterical, and his outcries were growing weaker and hoarser, as was his stamina. He went under, only to bob up to the surface, then went under again. The last time he went down, his head did not reappear; just a hand—a hand clutching at heaven for life.

Terry's final pathetic gesture restored Gilberta's sanity. It was as though an alien being had captured her mind and her body, and now she was overwhelmed with horror at the deed this other creature had committed.

She dove out of the boat and swam toward the spot where Terry had submerged. A powerful swimmer, she closed the distance swiftly and then jackknifed deep into the water—clear and green, with the sun's rays slanting at angles like so many luminous spokes.

A bass glided past her, the bubbles from its gills tickling her nose. She could see clear to the bottom, an eerie surrealistic world, unrelated to the world of fresh air and blue sky above.

There he was, motionless, knees drawn up, head turned down—a curled fetus floating in the earth's womb. Gilberta reached him in two strokes, hooked both hands underneath his armpits, and propelled him to the surface like a torpedo. His eyes were closed, and his skin had the ashen look of a corpse. No time to feel for a pulse, to see whether or not he was breathing. Gilberta rolled him over onto his back, cradled his chin in the crook of her left arm, so that his nose and mouth were out of the water, and swam toward the boat with one arm.

It required a herculean effort to lift him over the gunwale, but adrenaline had given Gilberta extraordinary strength. She climbed in after him and stretched him out supine on his back, then bent over him and pressed her ear to his mouth. If he was alive, his breathing was too shallow to discern. There was a thready flutter in his wrist, so erratic it might have been a twitching muscle.

She rolled him over, tilting his head to one side, so that his cheek rested on the back of his left hand, straddled his hips, and pressed her palms against his back just below the rib cage. She bore down, released the pressure, bore down, again and again, to the cadence of her own breathing.

Some water was expelled from his trachea, but he remained inert, unconscious. Before long, Gilberta was reaching the limit of her endurance. Sweat ran in torrents down her face and her body, dropping like rain onto his tanned, still back. Still no response.

"Don't die, Terry! You mustn't die! Please, dear God, help me!" In desperation, she rolled him over onto his back. "I'll bring you back to life, Terry! I'll breathe my life into you!"

She held his nose, put her mouth over his open mouth, and forced warm air into his lungs. His chest rose, then fell as she withdrew to inhale. She put her mouth over his again and exhaled. Many times she did this; it seemed an eternity.

Hope flared within her breast as his pallid eyelids flickered; was nurtured when his limbs spasmed. Awe replaced hope as the blue lips moved.

"Gilly . . ." Barely audible.

Miracle of miracles! Terry's eyelids fluttered open slowly, and his blue eyes—pools of terror—bored into hers.

"It's all right, little brother." She stroked his cheek tenderly. "You're going to be fine." She kneeled beside him and lifted him gently, cradling him in her arms, pressing her cheek to his cold cheek, sobbing as if her heart was breaking. "Terry, I'm so sorry. I don't know what came over me. Can you ever forgive me?"

He sat up and looked at her in puzzlement. "Gilly . . . you're crying. Don't . . . it's all right. . . . Gilly, you saved my life." He reached out and wiped tears from her face with the back of his hand. "You're the best sister in the world. I love you, Gilly, I truly do, even if I don't show it." He put his arms around her and drew her head onto his shoulder.

She hugged him fiercely. "I love you, too, Terry—even if I chose a very drastic way to prove it."

When they got back to the house, their mother was sitting on the front porch with Liz.

"How did you get so wet?" Linda asked with concern. "And you, Gilly, in your new shorts and blouse." Her voice rose to a higher register. "You didn't fall overboard, did you? Oh dear, what *happened?"*

Gilberta opened her mouth to speak, but Terry interceded. "It's all my fault. I pushed Gilly overboard, and she splashed me back."

"You pushed your sister overboard?" Linda was aghast. "What a terrible thing to do! She could have hit her head and drowned."

Terry hung his head in silence.

Gilberta had never seen her mother so angry at Terry. She went to him and slapped him across the face. "This is the limit, Terry! Now, you march upstairs, young man, and stay in your room for the rest of the day."

"Yes, Mother." Before he went into the house, he looked at Gilberta. "I'm sorry about what happened, sis."

And his expression was inscrutable.

CHAPTER EIGHT

Gilberta turned from the window and sat down at her desk again. The incident at Loon Lake had been a turning point in her life. From that day forward, neither she nor Terry ever mentioned the incident, and he did not torment her anymore. If anything, after his near brush with death at her hands, he was as wary and afraid of Gilberta as she had once been of him. It was a complete reversal of roles.

She picked up the phone. "Margie, notify all department heads that there will be a meeting in the boardroom at five-thirty this afternoon. Thank you."

There was one infallible cure for worry and anxiety, she reflected: work. And work she did for the next ten days, to the exclusion of all else, rising at 7:00 sharp, immersing herself in the complex machinations of the De Beers Mining and Development Corporation from 9:00 until 7:00, grabbing a light supper at home, a quick shower, and falling straight into bed.

"You're going to drive yourself into a nervous breakdown if you don't let up, Gilly," Harmon warned her. "Do you realize we've been celibate since your return from New York?"

Her smile was strained. "You're right: I've been neglecting you, sweet. Like the song says, Harmon, 'tonight we love.' Satisfied?"

"It's not the sex that bothers me; it's your health."

"Fiddlesticks! I'm as healthy as a horse, and my mind is made of cast iron; no loose bolts rattling around in there."

He did not comment, but there was a subversive aspect to the way he was contemplating her that made Gilberta uncomfortable.

"What are you thinking, Harmon?"

He shook his head vigorously. "No, no, nothing at all. Nothing to do with you, at least."

"Liar." She looked down at her plate, the scrambled eggs and crisp bacon suddenly unpalatable.

Gilberta knew damned well what Harmon was thinking about: her mother's breakdown after the nightmare on El Capitan Mountain; her grandfather's amnesia after his plane crashed; her great-great-grandmother's refusal to accept her lover's horrible death, and pretense, till she was in her seventies, that he was simply "traveling." Her great-grandmother Tara alone, of all the women descendants of Lars and Mina De Beers, had managed to keep a clear head in the face of an overwhelming tragedy, though it took every bit of willpower. Decidedly, there was in the De Beers family tree a strain of what Gilberta chose to call "mental eccentricity."

Irritable with herself for such unprofitable woolgathering, she stood up and threw down her napkin. "I'm really not hungry." She stopped at his chair and bent to kiss him. "Remember, we have a date for tonight."

On Thursday morning of the following week, Gilberta booked a late-afternoon flight to New York. The De

Beers Corporation was at a crucial stage of negotiations with a West German leasing company, and her presence was demanded at a meeting to be held at the Plaza, where the head of the company and some of his staff were staying, Friday morning. Before she boarded the plane in Denver, she made a long-distance call to Laurentis at his office, telling him she'd be in New York sometime that night.

As soon as she arrived at the Essex House, the desk clerk said, "Mrs. Killington, there's a gentleman who's been phoning you since seven o'clock. Here are the messages he left."

She took the chits and scanned them in the elevator. They were all the same: "Gilly, phone me when you get in, no matter what time. George. UN 5-6200."

As soon as the bellhop had deposited her bag in the suite and departed, she kicked off her shoes, made herself a strong scotch and water, lit a cigarette, and, getting comfortable on the couch, dialed Laurentis's number.

"Hello . . . Laurentis here."

She laughed and mimicked his deep, stern tone: "Hello . . . Killington here."

Warmth crept into his voice. "Gilly! I've been counting the hours. I thought you'd be here a week ago."

"Couldn't get away."

"All work and no play makes Gil a dull girl."

"Do you think I'm dull?"

"Love is blind. . . . Look, can I come over there?"

"You mean now? God, George, I'm bushed, and I wouldn't be very good in bed. I'll take a rain check, though."

"Gilly . . . I'm not pushing because I'm horny. There's been a new development in the Marston case, and I'd like to discuss it with you as soon as possible."

Adrenaline pumped into her blood, and instantly her fatigue vanished. She became wide awake and alert. "That's different. By all means come over."

She hung up and finished her drink and cigarette. Her mind was racing like a rat on a treadmill, going nowhere. The moment of truth was at hand; she sensed it. A "new development," he'd said. Well, she would know soon enough.

She undressed and took a quick shower and brushed her teeth. Back in the bedroom, she put on the new peignoir she'd bought for this trip to New York—a lacy violet concoction that matched her eyes—brushed her black hair till it shone, and applied just a touch of rouge and lipstick.

Inspecting herself in the mirror, she grinned. "For a gal who's too bushed to have sex, you certainly are taking a lot of trouble to make yourself seductive," she said aloud. She felt positively wicked. Would George Laurentis treat her the same way Bogie treated Mary Astor in *The Maltese Falcon*? Screw her good and then pack her off to the pokey?

She was dabbing perfume behind her ears and in her cleavage when the door chimes sounded. She checked herself one last time in the mirror, then went to the door.

"Every time I see you, you get more beautiful." He shut the door behind him and took her in his arms, kissing her lips and then the side of her throat.

"How ardent we are tonight, Captain." She took his hand and led him into the living room. "Sit down and I'll get you a drink."

While her back was to him at the server, he talked to her: "You sure don't *look* like you're bushed. You're radiant."

"You have an exhilarating effect on me, love. I now have my second wind." She brought him the drink and confronted him, arms folded beneath her breasts. "But you didn't come over here at this hour to tell me how radiant I am." She tried to sound casual when she said it: "Now, what is this new development you mentioned?"

"Sit down." He patted the cushion beside him.

She sat down on the couch facing him, with one arm draped over the backrest and her legs tucked in against her haunches.

He rolled the highball glass between his palms. His forehead was puckered in concern. "Night before last, there was a murder, a shooting over on Park Avenue. The victim was a private investigator name of Nick Vasile. Not just an ordinary gumshoe; you had to be recommended before he'd take you on as a client. He was hired by a lot of movie stars, socialites, politicians" —he faltered there, she observed tensely—"a lot of VIPs. From all indications, someone took out a contract on him. It was a very professional job. His jewelry and wallet were all on him. . . . Anyway, when we shook down his office, we had to get a locksmith to open his safe. Among the other valuables we found was a confidential ledger listing all of his past clients, dates he was in their employ, and the fees he charged them."

His eyes edged away from her intent gaze. "Brace yourself for this, Gilly: one of the names on that list was Governor Harmon Killington, of the state of Colorado."

She recoiled as if he had slapped her across the face. No, a slap, a blow of any sort, would not have packed as much of a wallop. "Harmon? I don't believe you." She bridled defensively. "What is this, some kind of cheap police tactic?"

"No, it's not, Gilly." His voice was soft, calm. "I'm not that kind of cop. I detest subterfuge. Believe me, your husband is one of Vasile's clients—or was, at any rate. He'd been paying Vasile five hundred dollars a day for two weeks, and his file was still open when Vasile was gunned down."

Gilberta clapped her hands to the sides of her head. "It . . . it's incredible, wild! It doesn't make any sense. Why would Harmon engage a private detective, one based in New York, no less?"

Laurentis lit two cigarettes and gave one to Gilberta. "We intend to question him about that. We'll question *all* of Vasile's clients." His eyes narrowed against the cigarette smoke curling up one cheek. "I can hazard a guess, Gilly. How about you?"

"I wouldn't have the remotest idea. Well, tell me, why do *you* think Harmon hired him?"

He laid a hand on her knee. "The only logical answer is that your husband wanted to keep tabs on you."

"Oh, no! That's absurd."

"Is it? Can you be that sure? I mean, women who are cheating tend to underestimate the acumen of their husbands and overestimate their own cunning. Let's face it, Gilly; you're an extremely sensual woman." He grinned. "I don't flatter myself that I was the first or only man to take you down the primrose path. My guess is that the governor has been on to you for some time."

Gilberta's shoulders slumped. "Damn! How could I have been so blind, so smug, so naïve? You're right, of course; Harmon's no fool. A fool doesn't make it to the governor's mansion. Well . . . what happens now?"

"My partner and I will fly out to Colorado and have a little chat with the governor. He may be able to provide us with information that will give us a lead to Vasile's killer. And, with any luck, the domino theory will prevail. If we can put the finger on Vasile's killer, we may come up with Marston's, too."

Gilberta said nothing for a time. Her mind was racing. She massaged her throat with one hand.

Laurentis was studying her face intently. Then, softly: "Is there something you have to say to me, Gilly? I don't think I have to explain to you that in revealing classified information to you, I've broken a cardinal commandment of the department. I could be suspended, put on trial. It was an act of faith on my part, Gilly. I trust you; I believe in you. What about you? Do you trust me?"

She looked down at his big brown hand resting on her knee, and sighed. "You know, don't you—that I didn't rent a car to drive up to my cottage. Why didn't you confront me with it when you first found out?"

"I wanted you to level with me."

"All right; I'll do just that. . . . I never went upstate at all. I never left New York." She paused and looked at him, but he merely nodded. "George . . . Jules Marston and I were lovers. I was in the apartment with him when he was murdered. . . ." She gave him a detailed report of everything that had transpired in the penthouse that weekend, just as she had narrated it to Milos, to Anita, to Frank Weller. "You've got to believe me, George: I did not murder Jules Marston. And I did not throw his body into the street."

"I *do* believe you, Gilly. . . . Well, we've scaled one mountain, which gives us a solid foothold on the next. There has to be a connection between Marston's murder and Vasile's; I feel it in my gut." He moved closer and took both of her hands in his. "Don't you see? Vasile was the top man in his field. It's almost a certainty that he knew all about you and Marston and your love nest in the Towers. Which means that your husband knows."

"Oh, my God! You don't think Harmon hired a . . . a——"

"Killer? No; I can't see an ambitious politician like your husband sticking his neck in a noose."

She thought for a moment. "Nor can I," she agreed. "But if he knew all along about me and Jules, why didn't he come out with it?"

"I don't know. Maybe he would have eventually if Marston hadn't been murdered. At any rate, we'll be questioning him tomorrow. . . . You know, I think it would be a good idea if you were present when we confront him."

"Oh, George, must I? It's bound to be nasty."

"Think of it this way, Gilly: 'The truth shall set you free'—both of you."

She sighed. "Very well. I should be able to wrap up my business affairs around five. . . . All right, George, you make the flight arrangements." She shook her head. "Poor Harmon—I've really screwed things up for him."

"Well, let's put it to bed for tonight." His hand found the slit in her peignoir and stroked her bare thigh. "And speaking of bed . . ." His soulful eyes questioned her.

Gilberta shivered with pleasure at his touch. "We really shouldn't . . . but . . . I could use the relaxation." As his fingers probed the warm nest between her thighs, she moaned softly. "Anyway, I couldn't say no now if I wanted to."

He lifted her off the couch and carried her into the bedroom, setting her gently on the bed. She removed the peignoir and watched him with shining eyes as he undressed. The nude male form never failed to arouse her, no matter what her mood. But then, she was always in the mood for George Laurentis.

Her heartbeat accelerated as he got into bed beside her and took her in his arms. Heat flashed through her body as his hard, urgent manhood left its searing imprint on her soft belly like a branding iron. His mouth and hands adored her—lips, ears, throat, breasts, belly, thighs, buttocks; his tongue teased the citadel of her womanhood. She cried out in ecstasy:

"Hurry, darling; I can't endure it an instant longer!" She welcomed him into the bower of her arms and legs, enfolding him with a fierce hunger.

Then his flesh filled her, engorged her to full measure. It was an even more savage consummation than on their previous matings. When sweet fulfillment came at last after three orgasms, Gilberta was at peace with the world. Her hip bones and pelvis were tender from his pounding, and she savored every twinge and ache.

"I love you, Gilly."

"And I love you, George." For the first time in her life, Gilberta meant it. "But it's a dead-end for us; you know that as well as I do."

"Damn it! I won't accept that! I don't want you on a one-night-stand basis. I want you forever, Gilly."

She reached up and caressed his cheek. "Dear, sweet, wonderful George, I adore you. . . . Remember what you told me that first day we met? Something about wives and police work mixing like oil and water."

"That was before I got to know you, Gilly." He took her hand and pressed his lips to the soft pink palm.

"Darling, if you can separate reality from romance, you'll realize that a permanent relationship between you and me would never work. You're too much of a man to be satisfied with half a loaf; and I have responsibilities that can't be shirked, familial obligations . . ."

He looked sullen and reached for the pack of cigarettes on the nightstand. "Yeah, I keep forgetting, you're a tycoon. I wouldn't fit into your world."

She threw up her hands and laughed. "Hey, don't look as if the world is coming to an end. We have a perfectly wonderful relationship the way things stand.

That can continue for as long as you want it to, darling."

"Can it?" he said skeptically. "What about when you become the First Lady?"

Her smile faded. "That's a pretty dim prospect right now, wouldn't you say, George?"

"We'll soon know," he replied grimly.

CHAPTER NINE

The meeting with the representatives of Weber and Müller, Limited, was terminated at four o'clock that afternoon. Gilberta was more than satisfied with the agreements both sides had reached.

"You drive a hard bargain, Mrs. Killington," Mr. Weber declared as they shook hands before parting, "but I cannot think of anyone I'd rather be bested by."

"You make us sound like adversaries, Mr. Weber. In truth we are allies, partners. This arrangement is going to be profitable for both parties."

"Well stated, dear lady. And now *auf wiedersehen.*"

After he left, Gilberta put through a call to the governor's mansion in Denver. Harmon was in his office.

"Darling, I've decided to return to Denver tonight," she told him.

"Tonight? Why, I thought you had planned to stay over until Monday and do some shopping."

"I know, but I've changed my mind. Something has come up."

"Oh? Did the West German deal fall through?"

"No; in fact, I got them to agree to everything I asked for. This is something that can't be discussed over the phone."

Silence, then: "I see. . . . Well, I wish you hadn't mentioned it, then. Now I'll be sitting here chewing my fingernails until you get here."

"I'm sorry, darling. Look, I've got to rush or I'll miss the flight. See you soon."

As traffic was heavy, she didn't get back to the Essex House until 5:45, which gave her only fifteen minutes in which to pack and check out. Laurentis had left a message saying that he and Cavelli would pick her up at 6:00 sharp.

When she walked out of the hotel at 6:05, Laurentis's Thunderbird was parked at the curb. Cavelli got out and held the door open for her while George put her luggage in the trunk.

"Sorry I'm late," she said, as the car pulled into the mainstream of traffic.

"No sweat," Laurentis assured her. "We'll make it with time to spare. . . . Did you notify the governor that you're coming back?"

"Yes; he was surprised. . . . Don't worry; I didn't say anything about my police escort."

He was not amused. "Nobody's escorting you, Gilly. I merely suggested that you return with us for your own comfort and peace of mind."

"Sorry again. I'm wound up like a clock spring."

"Sure."

"George . . . I'd like to ask a favor of you."

"Fire away."

"Before you question Harmon, can I have a few moments alone with him?"

"I don't see anything wrong in that; do you, Bill?"

"Not at all."

"Thanks." She reached across the seat and put a hand on his shoulder.

* * *

Gilberta slept for most of the flight to Denver. Laurentis didn't wake her until the 747 was about to make its final descent.

"Fasten your seat belt, Gilly," he said. "We're here."

She sat up and smoothed out her dress. "So soon? But it feels as though I dozed off for just a few minutes."

He grinned. "You've been sleeping like the dead ever since this bird took off."

"Self-protective, I guess. I'm not looking forward to this."

"Believe me, I'm not, either," he said, suddenly grim.

Governor Harmon Killington, dressed in robe and slippers, was having a nightcap in the study while he watched the late news. When it was over, he snapped off the television with the remote control and lay back in his reclining leather chair with his eyes closed. He was dead tired, but he couldn't go to bed until Gilberta returned. Something was very wrong; of that he had no doubt. Her voice had betrayed her anxiety. What could have happened in such a short time to compel her to come home? The deal had gone through, she'd said, and——

"Harmon . . ."

The ghostly whisper startled him upright in the chair. When he turned, he saw Gilberta standing in the doorway.

"Gilly . . . you're here, finally." He stood up and rubbed his eyes. "Now, what is this all about?"

She entered the study and closed the door, leaning back against it. "It's about Nick Vasile." She watched him closely for a reaction, but he only stared at her blankly. "He's dead—murdered, just like Jules Marston."

"Nick Vasile?" he said, looking puzzled; but his

ruddy complexion faded to pasty gray, and his voice was tremulous. "Who the hell is Nick Vasile?"

"It won't work, Harmon. You may make campaign promises sound convincing, but the lie is written all over you right now. You hired Vasile to spy on me and Julie. Don't deny it. The New York police have Vasile's records, and your name is right there on his list of clients."

"The police? Jesus!" He walked to his desk on unsteady legs and, with trembling hands, half filled a glass from his water carafe. He used it to wash down two red capsules he removed from the drawer.

Gilberta approached the desk. "What are you taking—hemlock?"

"Very funny, my dear. My ulcer has been acting up."

"The police are here now, Harmon, waiting in the living room. They were generous enough to let me prepare you before they interrogate you."

He sat hipshot on the desk, head slumped forward on his chest, the fingers of one hand clasping the bridge of his nose—the picture of abject resignation.

"Harmon, did you have Jules killed?"

"Don't be ridiculous! I didn't give a damn about you and Julie. I've known about you two for months."

"Then, why did you hire Vasile to watch me?"

He looked up at her. His mouth was twisted in a grotesque smile. "*Watch* you is exactly what I hired him to do—for your own good, and mine. In the past, you've conducted your sexual dalliances on a discreet level. But there was no way your affair with Jules could have gone undetected; his public profile was too strong. You didn't realize it, obviously, but wherever you went, the two of you stood out like the proverbial sore thumb. Leasing that penthouse in New York—how naïve can one be? With every passing day, the threat increased."

"A threat to whom?"

"Not 'whom'; *what*. A threat to my political career and, indirectly, to your own. How could a bright woman like you, who hoped to become First Lady one day, be so blind to the risks you were taking?"

"But with Julie dead, the threat would disappear. . . . Why don't you admit it, Harmon? You paid Vasile to spy on me, yes—and to have Julie killed!"

He shook his head. The expression on his face discomfited Gilberta. It seemed to convey pity, despair, even a certain empathy toward her. He affirmed it:

"Poor Gilly . . . poor, dear Gilly. The family curse came home to roost again in this generation."

"What in God's name are you talking about? What family curse?"

As if she didn't know what he was alluding to. And, suddenly, she was consumed by dread.

He addressed her gently, like a father trying to reason with a recalcitrant child: "The taint in the blood of the De Beers lineage. Karen . . . Peter . . . Linda . . . and now you. Only Tara escaped unscathed."

She walked over to him and grabbed his shoulders. Her face was ghastly, her voice on the brink of hysteria: "Harmon, what are you saying? Tell me, Harmon! Don't torture me with your damned circumlocution! Say it!"

"It was you, Gilly," he said tonelessly. "*You* murdered Jules Marston. Then the notorious self-protective family syndrome took over. You blacked out the unthinkable deed."

She wrung his shoulders, snapping his head back and forth. He accepted it listlessly.

"You're lying, Harmon! You're trying to drive me mad, like that poor woman in *Gaslight*! You're a diabolical fiend! Liar! Liar! *Liar!*" She closed her eyes, and her grip on his shoulders relaxed. In slow motion, her body slid down the length of him, slumping to the floor.

Laurentis and Cavelli burst into the study. They froze at the sight of Gilberta on the floor.

"What happened? What did you do to your wife, you——" Laurentis checked himself. "Governor . . ."

Killington's face was a death mask. "I told her the truth, sir. I told her that she murdered Jules Marston."

Gilberta was not unconscious; she could hear what they were saying with exceptional clarity. She felt as though she was a disembodied spirit hovering above her inert flesh-and-blood form on the carpet.

Harmon explained his role in the Marston affair to Laurentis while Cavelli phoned for an ambulance: "Vasile was in the corridor outside the penthouse posing as an electrician. It was his intention to pick the door lock and let himself into the apartment after Jules and my wife left for the ceremonies at city hall. I wanted to find out just how careless Gilberta was becoming. Did she leave incriminating evidence around the rooms, advertising her presence as a tenant? After all, Milos Alansky used the place when he was in New York, entertained friends there. There was the chance that one of his bitches would find out about Jules and my wife and blow the whistle to the media.

"Vasile was hiding in a stairwell when he saw Gilberta come out of the apartment, carrying two valises, and get into the elevator. He said she looked very strange. After a while, she came back up in the elevator, still carrying the two suitcases; but they appeared to be lighter than when she had gone down. His vague suspicions were confirmed when she came out of the apartment with the suitcases and took the elevator down again.

"He went to the door and knocked. When he got no response, he let himself in and made a quick tour of the penthouse. He found Jules dead on the terrace. He knew it had to be Gilberta who'd killed him, because an hour earlier Jules had come out into the hall to put garbage down the chute, and in that time, no one else had entered the penthouse.

"He had to move quickly: she might come back. He was right. No sooner had he concealed himself in a kitchen cupboard than he heard her enter the apartment. He waited until she'd cleared all of her possessions out of the place and departed for good. Then he placed a collect phone call to me here on my private line.

"Needless to say, I was horrified by what he told me, lost control. But Vasile was cool and pragmatic. He suggested that if Marston's broken body was found in the street below, the police would believe it had been a suicide. Even if they were suspicious, it would be almost impossible to prove otherwise without any witnesses. And the sole witness, the murderer—my wife, Gilberta—would hardly come forward to testify against herself.

"Sole witness?" Laurentis lit a cigarette. "What about Vasile?"

Killington's smile was thin-lipped, weary. "Ah, yes, Vasile. Obviously the potential threat that he posed was intolerable. I mean, a man like that in a position to blackmail the governor of Colorado. . . . To blackmail the potential president of the United States." He shook his head and covered his face with his hands.

"So you put a contract on Vasile?"

"It had to be done. I have friends. Ironically, it was Jules Marston himself who had made me aware of these . . . these *people*. In the course of his career, Jules sometimes found it expedient to eliminate certain dangerous enemies. Yes, I had Vasile 'hit.' I believe that is the term."

He turned and looked at his wife. "It never entered my mind that she would block the traumatic experience out of her consciousness; that was an unexpected gift."

It was then that the floodgates damming up that dark and secretive portion of Gilberta's mind gave way. She viewed it like the replay of an old movie:

One foot poised to step into the shower when the phone rang. In an atypical impulse, picking up the bathroom extension. Julie's voice. And another familiar voice:

"Hello, Julie?"

"Your timing is great."

"Can you talk?"

"Yes. She's in the shower."

An obscene laugh: "Just finished screwing her, eh?"

Julie's reply was even more obscene: "She can't get enough of it. Tell me, are all the women in your family as horny as Gilly?"

"Like all thoroughbred mares, allowance must be made for their hypersensitivity and idiosyncrasies. Well . . . how'd your little talk with Ahmad go last night?"

"He says they're going to go for the deal. I don't trust that Arab, but there's no profit in it for them to screw us. The ball is in your court now."

"No sweat. I have Dwayne Hacket in my hip pocket. He's got a piece of the action on this deal. You won't back down on me, will you?"

"I promised you the ten million if you could swing the uranium caper, and I'll keep my word."

"It's a shoo-in, but you'll have to sit tight until after the November elections, when Hacket deposes my brother-in-law from the governorship."

"I don't know . . . Dwayne Hacket is not my idea of a strong dark-horse candidate. He's an unknown."

"Ahhh, but he *won't* be unknown after he exposes

your affair with the incumbent's wife on the senate floor."

"I'm not happy about setting up Gilly this way. She meant a lot to me for a long time."

Her brother's cackling: "But greener pastures beckon, eh, old buddy? I hear a certain supreme court justice's daughter is slated to be the newest addition to Sheik Marston's harem. That can't hurt your position in the future."

"Well, I still regret having to hurt Gilly. She's a fine woman."

The venomous retort: "She's a heartless bitch!"

"I never knew you felt that way about your sister."

"I've been kissing the royal arse for years. Gilberta is a very powerful and very dangerous woman. Did I ever tell you she tried to kill me when we were kids?"

"Come on, now, laddy, aren't we being unusually paranoid?"

"It's true, but irrelevant. . . . Anyway, Harmon Killington playing the role of cuckold will not heighten his image with the righteous voters of Colorado. Nobody likes a patsy and a loser in love or anything else. Pity breeds contempt."

Gilberta sinking down on her knees in a posture of supplication, tears streaming down her cheeks: *Please, dear God, don't do this to me! It can't be happening. It's* not *happening. I'm dreaming it all.*

Julie asking: "You're positive you can get title to that uranium land?"

"Thousands of acres in Lake County. Do you know, when my great-grandfather discovered molybdenum there back at the turn of the century, it was considered worthless?"

"World War Two and Los Alamos certainly proved how wrong they were. . . . Well, it looks as if everybody is going to get what they want. The Arabs get their black-market uranium, you get your ten-million-dollar loan, and Marston, Limited, gets an exclusive fifty-year lease to do business with the OPEC nations."

"That's right, partner, everybody gets what they want."

Except me.

Gilberta placing the phone back on the hook without a sound, turning to look at herself in the mirror above the sink—at the face of a stranger, a face white as snow; eyes, two hot coals burning into the snow.

Gradually the pain and the self-pity diminished, and then there was no feeling at all. Briefly. Relentlessly the pendulum of her feelings swung in a diametric direction, anger building slowly but steadily till it became an all-consuming rage—rage directed at her brother but most of all at Jules Marston for laughing at her, making a dupe of her, selling her out. A flash of white light blinded her, and she felt as if her brain was exploding.

She stumbled out of the bathroom, the pain behind her eyes excruciating now, and into the living room, pausing to pick up the heavy iron poker.

He was back at his post by the parapet, peering through his binoculars at the procession of Tall Ships. The air was filled with the sounds of bands blaring, firecrackers exploding, planes buzzing the fleet overhead. He did not hear her as she came up behind him on bare feet.

Gilberta raised the poker slowly, straight up, over her head. She took dead aim on an imaginary vertical line bisecting his head and swung the poker downward with all her might; walked to the parapet, peered over the edge, and dropped the poker. It landed in the flower box of an apartment two stories below and was swallowed up by heavy foliage. In a zombie state, she went back to the dead man and, grasping his ankles, dragged his body over behind the corner shrubs.

The pain in her head totally gone now, she returned to the bathroom and took a shower.

She toweled herself briskly, went back into the bedroom, and climbed into a pair of black silk lounging pajamas, not bothering to put on underwear. They'd be coming off again in any case before noon, she was confident. She slipped her feet into black satin slippers and headed for the kitchen to turn on the oven in preparation for the soufflé. Then, whistling "America the Beautiful," she went to join Julie on the terrace.